NINE YEARS
Earlier

Rafe

T HE FLAME OF THE Zippo comes to life, warming the underside of my chin as I light another cigarette. I only smoke when I'm procrastinating.

This is my third in five minutes.

I inhale, blackening my lungs with chemicals I can't pronounce. As I exhale, I drop my head back against the wall and watch the haze melt into the night's sky.

Fuck it.

We're all going to die anyway.

On the other side of the street, the wagon creaks, then the door flies open, casting an orange glow over the cobbled stones. My eyes slide up to it and meet the gaze of a pissed-off fortune teller.

"Are you going to stand there all night?" She crosses her arms and leans against the door frame. "You're scaring off customers."

The last thing I should do today is smile. You don't smile on the day you bury both your parents, because there's nothing funny about watching dirt being shoveled on top of your mama.

But I can't stop amusement from curling my lips.

"I'd bet my entire investment portfolio that my mother has been your only customer since the Great Depression." Scowling, she opens her mouth to snap back, but then she pauses and does a sweep of the empty street. "Where is your mother, anyway?"

My amusement turns into a bitter laugh, fueled by irony. I drop my cigarette and grind it into the cobbles with the heel of my shoe. "Does your crystal ball need a polish? She's six-feet-under, darling."

I push off the wall and close the gap between us, taking the rickety steps up to her wagon two-at-a-time and stopping just inches from her. She wraps her shawl tighter around herself, her wary gaze jumping up to meet mine.

"You've been drinking."

"Yeah? Perhaps I was wrong about you being a hack."

"You don't need to be psychic to tell," she snaps, taking a step back into the wagon and giving a small shake of her head. "I can smell it on your breath. If you're here for a reading, well, I don't read for the intoxicated. Liquor makes it hard to see fortunes."

I tug out my money clip, snap a few bills off the roll, and drop them at her feet.

"You see money though, surely?"

Her eyes narrow. I take advantage of her silence and push past her. I hitch up my suit pants and sink onto the low stool in front of the table.

Another laugh escapes me, this one tasting even more bitter than the last. Of all the places I should be tonight, a fortune teller's wagon in the scummy part of Vegas isn't one of them. I sneer at the string lights and the candles because they do nothing to hide how pathetic it is in here. Raggedy throws and cushions in faded prints, stacks of dog-eared cards collecting dust.

Behind me, I hear long fingernails scraping the floorboard as the fortune teller picks up my money. She lowers herself onto the bench opposite me, her old bones cracking.

"I'm sorry to hear about your mother." She picks up a deck of cards and splits it in two. "But I'm a cartomancer, not a medium."

"I don't speak con-artist."

Her nostrils flare. "It means I tell fortunes with playing cards. I don't make contact with the dead."

"Good thing I'm not here to make small talk with my mother's ghost then."

Her eyes flick to mine, first with surprise, then they darken to a shade more sinister. "So you *are* here for a reading. When you came here with your mother three weeks ago, I offered you a reading and in return, you threatened to burn down my wagon, along with me inside of it." She tilts her head, casting a suspicious gaze over my features. "But now you've changed your mind."

I guess I have.

Mama was obsessed with fate. Lived her whole life by the turn of a tarot card or the shake of an eight-ball. It consumed her. She couldn't even go to Starbucks without trying to make sense of the dregs at the bottom of her paper cup.

Me; I'm a clean-cut skeptic, which is ironic, considering I own a casino. But any sensible businessman in any sector knows that relying on luck to be successful is like closing your eyes, leaning into the wind, and hoping it'll blow you in the right direction.

There's skill, and there are odds. That's it. Luck isn't for the optimistic; it's for the lazy and the desperate.

My mama was an exception; she didn't fall into either of those categories. She had hope in her heart and money in her pocket, which made her a walking, talking payday for quacks like this one.

Fortune tellers, psychics, mediums: they are all cheats. And there's nothing I hate more in this world than a cheat.

And yet...

I swallow the rock in my throat and rub at the scruff on my jaw.

And yet, this old lady in front of me—she knew my mama was going to die.

"You knew."

She slowly sweeps up the fanned cards and places them in a neat pile. "Your mother drew the death duo."

That fucking phrase. The first time I'd heard it, I had laughed in disbelief. Now, I don't find it so funny.

Less than a month ago, Mama had turned up at my penthouse suite, loaded with an overnight bag and a spark in her eyes. She gifted me a watch to celebrate me opening my first casino, Lucky Cat. But it soon became clear that supporting my struggling business venture wasn't her only reason for her visit to Sin City.

"There's someone I'd like to see," she'd said coyly, sitting at my dingy casino bar and white-knuckling a lemon drop martini. "A fortune-teller just off Fremont Street."

I'd rolled my eyes, but she'd insisted. *She's the best. Nobody in the Pacific Northwest reads playing cards. Come on Rafey, when in Vegas...*

I'd darkened the doorway of the wagon during the entire reading, fists in pockets, making sure she didn't get ripped off any more than she'd agreed to.

First, she drew the Seven of Hearts. A betrayal by a loved one.

Then, the Jack of Diamonds. The bearer of bad news.

Lastly, the fortune teller had flipped over the Ace of Spades.

The wagon had fallen silent. Eventually, my mama dragged her palms over her skirt and said, "Well, then."

Now, I grip the edge of the table and shoot the woman a blistering glare. "The Death Duo," I repeat. "You seriously telling me everyone who draws the Jack of Diamonds, followed by the Ace of Spades, keels over and dies?"

She hitches a shoulder. "It's a rare combination."

"Not that rare. The odds of drawing both cards consecutively from a single deck without replacing them is one in two thousand, six hundred and fifty-two."

"You've done your homework."

"No, I've done the math." I slip my hand in my pocket and brush my fingers over my dice. "It's statistics. The law of probability."

"Not everything in this world can be explained away with reason or logic." There's a smugness to her tone; one that makes me want to choke the life out of her. "But you're beginning to see that, aren't you? Otherwise, you wouldn't be here."

I run my tongue over my teeth. Drag my eyes to the dusty beams propping up the roof of the wagon. The odds of my mama drawing the supposed Death Duo were slim, but the series of events that happened in the month after are near-impossible to put a statistical probability on.

Mama died from a heart attack, despite having a clean bill of health. Then, less than a week later, my father died from a sudden bleed on the brain.

I huff out a laugh of disbelief. A week. Seven fucking days; that's all it took to wipe out half my immediate family. Seven days for the rug to be pulled from under my feet.

Today, it was Angelo who tugged the last square inch of said rug with his sudden announcement.

I'm not coming back to Devil's Dip.

We were standing on the edge of the cliff, three feet from our parents' freshly buried bodies when he told us. It wasn't so much of a bombshell but a venomous whisper; he'd muttered the words so quietly I thought the wind was playing tricks on my ears.

But with one look into his dark eyes, I saw turbulence and an iron-clad resolve.

I guess I'm a liar. I do believe in fate in some way. Like every made man, my life path has been mapped out for me since the day I was born. My father was the capo of Devil's Dip, and it was a given that once he died, the title would be passed to Angelo, my oldest brother. It was also a given I'd become his underboss, and Gabe, our youngest brother, his *consigliere*.

I've learned a hard lesson in seven days. Because now Angelo is halfway across the Atlantic, Gabe is fuck-knows-where, and I'm left standing at the end of my so-called path, *alone*, wondering where the road went.

The Cosa Nostra is my life, and I've spent most of my twenty-five years preparing for that underboss role.

Internships at Goldman Sachs and JP Morgan. A master's degree from Harvard Business School. Hell, the only reason I bought a casino in Vegas was to learn the ropes before I built my legacy back home.

Home. Fuck. I've always thought home is where my family is, but now I'm not so sure. I know I could always go back to the Coast. Uncle Alberto would take me on as a *Caporegime* for the Devil's Cove outfit, or if I wanted to keep my hands clean, he would give me a position on the board at his whiskey company in Devil's Hollow.

But being a lackey isn't in my blood. I'm born to build an empire, not lay the bricks for someone else's.

"Deal the cards."

My voice sounds more certain than I feel. The fortune teller's gaze lingers on mine, then she picks up the deck, shuffles through it, and lays two familiar cards on the table between us.

Last time, she'd made my mama cry and I'd been out for blood. I'd told her to wait outside, then kicked the door shut with the heel of my wingtip. Just as the flame of my Zippo came to life, the fortune teller held up her hands and said, "Wait. Your cards keep screaming at me."

I'd snarled something about her being a hack and that she wouldn't get away with conning two Viscontis, especially not on the same fucking day.

But today is different. Now, I'm sitting on the same stool my mama sat on less than a month ago, unease bubbling under my skin. My hand isn't clutching a lighter but my dice, and I'm squeezing them so hard they're about to become one with my palm.

"As I was *trying* to say last time, your card hasn't been dealt yet. Your fate hasn't been sealed." She breathes heavily and rubs her temples. "Yes, they are definitely your cards. They are screaming at me even louder than they were last time. I can barely hear myself think."

A sarcastic retort brews on my tongue, but I bite it down. Instead, I stare at the two picture cards in front of me.

The King of Diamonds and the King of Hearts.

"Explain it in a way that doesn't make me want to put my fist through a wall," I say, as calmly as I can muster. As she starts to speak, I hold up my hand to silence her. "And just because I'm listening doesn't mean I believe the shit coming from your mouth."

She straightens her spine. "In my preferred form of cartoman-cy," she says carefully, "we believe each soul is assigned a card long before it is brought onto this earth. It's called 'Card Calling.' The cards are often vague, with each suit and value representing the broader meaning or purpose of one's life. For example..." She reaches for the deck, peels off the top card and flashes it to me. It's the Ten of Clubs. "If a soul is called to the Ten of Clubs, they're usually drawn to travel. Perhaps they are destined to work abroad, or will find love in a far corner of the world." She places the card back on the deck and gives me a tight-lipped smile. "See, vague. But picture cards," she makes a sweeping motion toward the two cards between us before she continues, "are a lot more specific. They are a direct reflection of who a person will become."

Impatience bites at my edges. I may have skipped my parents' wake to be here, but I'm far from a convert. "Why do I have two cards?"

"Because fate couldn't decide what card to deal you. It's very rare."

"As rare as my mother drawing the Death Duo?"

"Much rarer, " she deadpans. Either she didn't pick up on my sarcasm, or she chose to ignore it. "I've never seen it in my lifetime."

"Mm," I grunt, rubbing my mouth. "So, I get to choose my fate." My gaze darts up to hers. "If you believe in that shit, of course."

She nods. "Of course."

"And if I don't choose?"

She shrugs, but the spark behind her eyes belies her nonchalance. "Fate will choose for you in due time." She leans in, urging breathlessly, "But wouldn't you rather know? Wouldn't you rather be in control of your own destiny?"

I *do* like being in control. My life is regimented; I'm a man of routine. I have a suit for each day of the week and my calendar is blocked out by the minute.

My jaw ticks. It's hot in this fucking wagon. The wooden walls groan against a gust of wind, and the engine of a super car roars from the direction of the faraway strip.

I'm sobering up, fast.

"King of Diamonds, or King of Hearts. I'm destined to become a businessman or a lover."

"So you *were* listening last time," she says with a smirk. One blistering glare from me wipes it off her withered lips in a second. "But yes. Power and money, or love and a family. It's that simple."

I curl my fingers around the dice in my pocket again. "But never both."

"*Never* both."

I swallow. "And all I have to do..."

"Is touch a card to seal your fate, yes."

I withdraw my hand from my pocket and the lady sucks in a lungful of air, a noise that grates down my spine like sandpaper. Last time I was here, my forefinger had been a millimeter away from touching the King of Diamonds. The idea I could guarantee my success as a businessman was obviously horseshit, but I'd considered it for the same reason atheists say a prayer moments before death.

Just in case.

But at the last second, I'd stopped myself. Something had stirred under my rib cage and I didn't like it. Truth is, I'd suddenly thought of my parents and what they had.

True love. Unrelenting, galvanized love. The type that puts you off your fucking lunch. In the Cosa Nostra, true love is rarer than any supposed Death Duo or whatever. In fact, my parents were the only people I knew who even came close to it. There's an old adage that a made man only marries for three reasons: business, politics, or to prevent a war. Just like I knew I was fated to be an underboss, I knew I'd marry a woman for pragmatic reasons.

But as I'd stared down at the two cards last time, there'd been a niggling voice in the back of my mind. *It'd be nice, wouldn't it? To look at a woman in the same way my father looked at my mama?*

But that was then; this is now. Now, there's another voice that's louder, one that's screaming *fuck true love*. Now, my parents are six feet under and have nothing to show for their love apart from a cheesy quote etched onto a joint headstone.

Now, my future isn't so certain, and everything I thought I'd have is slipping out of reach, thanks to my idiot brother.

I'm losing control.

I clear my throat, feeling the fortune teller's gaze bore into me. *Screw it.* I'm the first to admit I'm getting desperate, and giving into this hippy dippy shit, just once, won't hurt. I stretch out my fingers, steel my jaw, and touch the King of Diamonds.

The ground doesn't shake. Fireworks don't explode in the sky above us. Nothing happens except the flicker of candles and a groan of the wagon.

I smooth down my tie. "Is that all? Or do I need to offer a blood sacrifice too?"

She stares at me, wide-eyed. "That's all."

Grinding out a laugh, I rise to my feet, stretching to my full height and casting a shadow over the fortune teller.

"You're bad news, darling. You know that?" I drawl, fishing out a few more bills and dropping them on the table. "I hope you get what's coming to you."

It's her turn to laugh. "You'll be thanking me when you have the whole of Las Vegas at your feet."

My dingy casino, with its leaking roof and cockroach problem, comes to mind. "If I ever have Vegas at my feet, you'll be exterminated along with the rest of the rats." I turn toward the door.

"Wait," she says. I clench my jaw, my hand hovering over the door handle. "There's something else."

My shoulders form a tight line, and I can't stop my hands from curling into fists. It's not in my nature to hit a woman, but Christ, this one makes it tempting. "I'm not interested."

"You're not interested in knowing what your doom card is?"

I let out a hiss of air through my nostrils. "You quacks sure know how to upsell, don't you?"

"Just like every action has a reaction, every fate card has a doom card. Are you familiar with—"

"Stop. Talking." My throat is dry and my chest is itchy. Nothing but a cold, hard drink will scratch it. "Just tell me the card."

A beat passes. Then, behind me, there's a dull *thwack* that makes the hairs on the back of my neck stand up. I've owned a casino for almost a year now, and I'd recognize the sound of a playing card hitting a table in my sleep.

Silence hangs hot and heavy within the four cramped walls of the wagon. With a sneer, I roll my neck over my shoulders and glance at the table behind me. There's a lone card sitting in the middle of it, the flickering candles casting an unsteady glow over its glossy surface.

It's the Queen of Hearts.

"The red-haired lady," the woman says softly. "Lucky for most, unlucky for a select few. And for you?" She lets out a low whistle. "The Queen of Hearts is detrimental. You could have all the success in the world, but she'll bring you to your knees."

I grind my molars together, but say nothing. Without another word, I heave open the door and kick it shut behind me. I stand on the rickety steps and suck in a lungful of mild October air.

Now what?

A smoke will do, for a start. Then I'll find a seedy bar on a seedy street where nobody knows the name Visconti and I'll pour one out for my parents. I slip my hand into my pocket and curl my fingers around my lighter.

Suddenly, something crackles and pops in my chest. It bubbles out from under my ribs and fizzes gently under my skin.

I drag a knuckle over my jaw and shake my head, amused at my own venomous thoughts.

No. That's not me.

When I'd vowed to burn down the fortune teller's wagon last month, it was an empty threat.

Still, with the snap of my wrist, the Zippo's flame dances against the darkness, taunting me with possibility. Explosive revenge is Angelo's bag, and Gabe, well, he's proof it's often the quiet ones who are the most psychopathic. Either of them would burn down this wagon without giving it a second thought, but Mama always used to say I was the gentleman out of the three of us. *Your brothers have iron fists, Rafey, but you have the silver tongue and the voice of reason.*

As I slide the lighter back into my pocket, my fingertips graze over my dice, and another dark thought seeps into my brain.

Since the old witch has so much to say about fate, I'll let my dice decide hers. I draw them from my pocket, give them a good shake, and drop them at my feet.

They roll less than half a meter, then come to a lazy stop. I peer over and laugh.

Lucky number seven.

"So be it," I mutter to myself, loosening the tie around my neck. I slip it off and slide it through the door handles, forming a tight knot.

I bring my Zippo to the tip of it and set it alight.

I've never liked wearing ties, anyway.

CHAPTER
One

Penny

T HE BUS DROPS ME off at the end of Devil's Cove, and I stare down the length of its glitzy strip with everything I own slumped at my feet. The promenade curves gently to the left, hugging a white beach, and on the right, a row of hotels, bars, and casinos stretches out for as far as the eye can see.

Even under a blanket of Christmas decorations, I can tell it's barely changed in the three years I've been gone. Palm trees. Marble sidewalks. Rich suckers practically *begging* me to lift their wallets from the back pockets of their tailored pants.

Gritting my teeth, I throw my head back and glare at the lights flashing against the starless sky. They remind me of the winning symbols on a slot machine: *Ding, ding, ding! Jackpot!*

It may have been three years since I stepped foot in this town, but it hasn't lost its hold on me. I can feel its strong, icy hands reaching into my chest and curling around my soul, trying to bring out the grubby little thief that lives within. You'd think after such a long time, plus the scare I just had, its siren call would be easier to ignore. But the temptation makes my blood itch more than ever.

Alas, I finally learned what the word 'consequence' truly means, so as the skyline of Atlantic City, New Jersey, melted behind me in a smoky haze of my own doing, I made a vow to myself.

I, Penny Price, am finally going straight.

But that won't be possible in Devil's Cove.

I turn my back to the Pacific Northwest's answer to Las Vegas, and squint at the timetable pasted to the back wall of the bus shelter. Despite there being a wad of gum covering the 'Devil' in 'Devil's Dip', I can see enough to confirm there's not a bus heading to my hometown for another hour.

Well, isn't that just swell. I suppose rich people aren't exactly reliant on regular public transport.

Slumping against the bench, a tired groan leaves my lips in a puff of condensation. Running from your sins is exhausting. My neck aches from both obsessively looking over my shoulder and spending over sixty hours curled up in the backs of buses. All I want to do is get to my apartment in Devil's Dip, wash my hair, change my panties, and crawl into bed with *Excel for Dummies*.

I glare out to the inky Pacific, but to my right, the warm glow of Devil's Cove draws me in. My gaze slides unwillingly to the groups drifting in and out of glossy establishments.

I strum my fingers against the plastic bench. Chew on the inside of my cheek.

Well, I do have a bit of a dilemma. I took three Greyhounds and hitched a ride with a trucker, who kept one eye on the road and the other on my thighs, to get here. The whole journey cost me $174.83, which was exactly, to the decimal point, all the money I'd managed to snatch from underneath the loose floorboard in my apartment before I fled Atlantic City.

A bitter laugh brews in my throat. Of *course* it was. I'm the luckiest girl in the world, right?

My fingers gingerly brush against the four-leaf clover pendant resting against my collarbone. I used to say that with such conviction, but now...

Now, I'm not so sure.

The wind gnaws on the shells of my ears, and I stuff my hands into my pockets. My frozen fingertips brush over the silky lining, reminding me they are empty. Empty pockets, empty bank account, empty stomach. I'm not broke; I'm *destitute*. Seriously, there aren't even any forgotten coppers rattling around in the bottom of my purse among the library books I'll never get to return.

It suddenly dawns on me: I'm waiting for a bus I can't even afford to get on.

Well, then. I'm on my feet and sliding my suitcase across the road before I can stop myself. One last grift and then, seriously, I'll go straight.

I wish I could say the thought of conning one more man out of his hard-earned cash felt like a chore. That the thought didn't make my heart race a little faster or make my mouth salivate for a reason other than being hungry.

But I'd be lying, and, well, I'm trying not to do that anymore.

As I head along the promenade, bitter nostalgia nips at the heels of my boots. I peer into windows and gawp into the familiar-yet-foreign worlds on the other sides of them. Bespoke suits and thousand-dollar bottles of champagne propped up in ice buckets. Dining tables with more silverware than I know the use for. Christ, I'd forgotten. This town doesn't just scream money; it bellows it from the rooftops.

Slowing to a halt, I take in a group of women sitting in a corner booth of a bar. I can practically smell the Chanel No.5 from this side of the glass, and for a few seconds, I watch with jealousy as they laugh and joke in a way that only people who've never had a red debt letter posted through their door can. My own shabby reflection comes into focus and another realization hits me.

I'm *way* too under-dressed to be in Cove.

My faux-fur jacket won't fool anybody. Underneath, I'm wearing ripped mom jeans, a sweater, and Doc Martens. I've had the same pair of panties on for two days straight, and my hair is so knotty it no longer needs a hair tie to stay in its bun.

Looking like this, I won't get past any of the sour-faced security guards keeping the peasants out of the bars, and begging for spare change on the sidewalk doesn't really sound appealing, especially in the Early-December freeze.

Groaning into the collar of my coat, I know I'll have to commit just a *little* more theft to look the part. The opportunity practically falls into my lap when I pass a glossy boutique a few doors down, and by a stroke of luck, the girl behind the register isn't one I went to school with.

It's the type of boutique that has four dresses on each rack and definitely doesn't stock sizes in the double-digits, but maybe I'll squeeze into something. If it's elasticated.

As I step inside, the bored-looking girl behind the desk runs a judgmental gaze from my top-knot to my boots, and punctuates it with a plastic smile.

"If you need any help, just let me know," she drawls, before going back to scrolling on her phone.

I brush my fingers over velvet and silk. Scowl at price tags. After a quick dip into the changing room, I head toward the door wearing a green satin dress under my coat, my jeans and sweater stuffed into my purse.

Somewhere between the doorway and the sidewalk, an alarm starts screaming.

"Hey!" comes a voice behind me.

Shit.

I tighten my grip on my suitcase and break into an awkward run. I'm used to running—from store security guards, from my problems, whatever—but it's a hell of a lot harder when you're wearing a dress two sizes too small and are weighed down by your worldly possessions.

I steal a glance over my shoulder. The sales girl is wobbling after me in impossibly high heels, her cell to her ear. As she pulls it away to glance at the screen, I seize the opportunity to shove my body against the nearest door and fall through it.

A few moments later, she gallops past on the other side of the glass, a furious expression cut into her face.

I slide a few inches down the wall and let out a huff of hot air. It melts into a laugh of disbelief.

Shit, that was close. Despite the twisted victory humming under my skin, I know that was stupid. I shouldn't be stealing at the best of times, but right now, I need to keep a low profile more than ever.

"Are you coming in, or are you going to stand there all day?"

A gruff voice steels my spine. When I spin around to locate its owner, I'm met with cold eyes that fill with thinly veiled disgust as they roll over me. They belong to a man with a sharp suit and a face I'd happily put my fist through—you know, if I weren't five-foot-two and trying to be a better person.

Coming in? I shift my gaze around the small, dark room, and realize it's an entryway. He's guarding the top of a staircase, and next to him, there's a vacant desk with a neon blue sign behind it.

Blue's Den.

Odd. I'm not saying I'm an expert on every bar in town, but I can say I know them all by name, at least.

It must be new. I straighten up and smooth down the front of my coat. "This is a bar?"

"Does a bear shit in the woods?"

I stare at him for a few beats, letting my retort ripple through me like a silent wave. Only when it's left my system do I grab my bags and squeeze past him.

"A yes would have sufficed, asshole," I mutter.

Couldn't resist.

I don't take too kindly to men with attitude problems—never have. I guess it's hereditary, because my mother was the same. I grew up underneath the poker tables of the Visconti Grand Casino, where both my parents worked. My mother as a dealer and my father as security. If a patron gave my mother even the tiniest dash of sass from across a velvet table, they were out on their ass, sans their chips, long before they could grab their jacket from the coat room.

Our hatred of men was the only thing my mother and I had in common. Even in the looks department, we only mildly looked related if you closed one eye, squinted the other, and tilted your head to the side. She and my father were tall and slender. I'm short and kind of dumpy. They were tan and dark-haired, but I'm on a different Pantone color chart entirely. In the winter months, I'm borderline translucent, and in the summer, I'm a constant shade of pale pink. My hair is copper, which, according to my mother's stupid logic, is because she ate too many tomatoes while pregnant with me.

My father used to joke that I was the milkman's daughter. That joke turned into a bitter belief once he and my mother graduated from wine coolers and craft beers to hard liquor. By the time they were killed, I was wishing I was *anyone's* daughter but theirs.

Stepping off the bottom step feels like stepping into silk. Soft jazz and low lighting caress my cold skin, and the scents of tobacco and aftershave unlock nostalgic memories I didn't know I had.

Unlike the street above, this bar doesn't scream *money*; it whispers *wealth*.

I make a beeline for a seat in the corner that has a great view of the bar. As I slide between tables, my eyes shift from left to right, right to left, raking over the clientele.

My brain rattles through my well-worn checklist.

Wearing suits midweek? Check.

Drinking hard liquor instead of beer? Check.

Sitting alone? Check.

A zap of excitement shoots down my spine, and the scar on my hip *burns*. It always does when I've hit the jackpot. There are a dozen men in here, and all of them tick the boxes of a good mark.

Where to start? The bar, of course. After three years of fishing for marks in Atlantic City, I've noticed men who sit by the bar are more likely to take my bait. Maybe it's because the short distance between them and the bartender means they're more likely to get drunk and stupid.

My gaze slides to the bar and the lone figure leaning against it. The soft lighting evades him; everything but the broad planes of his shoulders and the sharp lines of his suit is concealed. But the moment I see a flash of amber in his glass and a glint of silver on his wrist, I know it doesn't matter what he looks like.

I kick my suitcase under the table and stride toward the bar, attempting a sexy strut, which is pretty hard in Doc Martens.

Reaching the bar feels like stepping on stage. I'm an actress, and while the leading man is always different, this role is *mine*. Has been since I turned eighteen and realized that, as a high-school drop-out, the alternative to putting my swindling skills to use was flipping burgers while a man barked orders over my shoulder, all for the privilege of seven-twenty-five an hour.

Despite feeling that familiar buzz of excitement just before the curtain goes up, there's a sadness biting at my edges, because I know this will be my last ever performance.

I'm going to make it my best.

Act One: Engage the mark in conversation.

I come to a stop two seats from where my freshly-appointed mark is leaning. Without so much as a glance in his direction, I slide off my coat and let it slip slowly down my shoulders to my hips, before draping it over the back of the stool. Before I started using the *For Dummies* books to aid my Grand Quest, my mission to find a career path outside of robbing stupid men, I worked at a strip joint for a while. It was all going well until a john poked at my belly and asked if I'd lied about my weight on my application form. I didn't quit because of his remark—I got fired because I sank my teeth into the hand he prodded me with.

It was then I decided I probably didn't have enough self-control to shake my ass for ungrateful men, but the whole experience wasn't a complete waste of time. Not only did I have actual female friends for a while, but I also learned this coat trick.

Immediately, I know it worked, because it suddenly feels like I'm standing in front of an open flame.

His gaze is warm, just like the satisfaction pooling in my lower stomach. It heats my cheek before sliding down my side and stopping at the high slit in my dress. As always, I pretend I haven't even noticed his presence, let alone felt his stare.

I slide my thighs across the butter-soft leather seat and smile at the bartender. Dark hair, soft features, and a grin made for customer service. It takes a few moments of rusty recognition until I realize it's Dan. We were in the same school year at Devil's Dip High, and I used to copy his science homework. It takes him a few seconds to recognize me too, and when his mouth drops open to strike up a conversation, I give a small shake of my head.

Thankfully, he closes his mouth, cuts a look to the man beside me, then plasters that polite smile back on. "Hey, there. What can I get you?"

Phew. I glance down to my left, at the large, suited forearm resting against the bar. Something stirs inside of me and it is too far south to feel appropriate. I want to believe it's because of the *very* expensive Breitling on his wrist, one with a clasp I could unbuckle in my sleep, and not because his olive-skinned hand is so large it makes the whiskey glass he's holding look like a fucking thimble.

Christ. I almost forget my next line.

"I'll have whatever he's having."

Silence. The type so dense that if you heard it on the other end of a phone call, you'd glance at your cell, frown, and say, "Hello?"

It feels like forever until Dan stops staring at me. He clears his throat and turns to the wall of liquor to fix my drink.

Glass clinks. Louis Armstrong seeps through the speakers, and unease drips into my bloodstream. This is the moment the mark is meant to speak up. The moment he says something chauvinistic, like, *Oh, I thought girls didn't drink whiskey?* To which I'd toss my hair over my shoulder, bat my lashes and reply with something equally as cliché. *Well, I'm not like other girls.*

But...nothing. My little fish hasn't even shown interest in my bait, let alone taken a bite. I hold my nerve for as long as it takes for Dan to slide over a low-ball glass and a napkin, and then I turn to face my mark.

Holy shit.

You're not meant to look like that.

Our gazes clash, and immediately, I know I'm not the first woman to lock eyes with this man and lose their heartbeat.

He's not just handsome; he's beautiful, and in a way that isn't up for debate, regardless of personal preference.

Tanned skin, black hair faded to perfection, and cheekbones you could chip ice off of.

His stare is just as likely to give me frostbite, too.

"I'm not interested."

I blink. "I'm sorry?"

"Apology accepted."

He turns his attention back to his cell, picking it up off the bar and unlocking it with a quick swipe of his thumb.

Wait, what?

For a few awkward beats, my eyes dart between the email he's tapping out on his phone and the indifferent set of his strong jaw. Realizing this man was younger, taller, and *hotter* than my average mark sent my thoughts scattering like marbles, and now, I'm clambering to pick them up and put them back in the right order.

I open my mouth and close it again. Confusion soon gives way to warm embarrassment, which then hardens into annoyance.

How fucking rude.

I mean, I'm not a fan of men at the best of times, let alone when they're being arrogant assholes. Growing up in a casino, and then spending my teens learning how to con the men who frequent them, I realized way younger than I should have that men have two settings: dismissive or predatory.

As much as I'd have preferred a man to dismiss me than prey on me, as my boobs grew and my swindling skills sharpened, I realized I could use their predatory behavior to hit their pockets.

And when I'm trying to hit their pockets, I don't like being dismissed.

Especially not in Act One.

I set my palms on either side of my glass and glare at the mirrored wall behind the bar.

"I'm not hitting on you."

"Sure."

The word trickles from his mouth, easy and final.

"Seriously," I mutter, cheeks growing hot. "I'd rather shit in my hands and clap."

The typing stops. Slowly, he lifts his head and meets my gaze in the mirror. Deep-green and intense. The hairs on the back of my neck prickle, and it feels like self-preservation to look away. But as always, stubbornness has me in a choke hold, and I grip the edge of the bar to force myself to maintain eye contact.

"I'm sorry?"

"Apology accepted," I bite back.

Triumph. It crackles and sparks in the pit of my stomach. But the moment my mark's phone goes dark and he places it on the table, his heavy gaze extinguishes my smugness like water on a flame.

He slides his forearm off the bar and slips his hand in his pocket. "Say that again."

For some reason, his tone makes the words *oh* and *shit* flash behind my eyelids. It's buttery and nonchalant. Almost *polite.* So why do I feel the need to steel my spine when I turn to face him?

Now, I have all of his attention and I don't like the way it feels against my skin. His green eyes glitter as they roll lazily over my features, and when they meet mine again, a small smile settles on the curve of his lips.

He waits.

"I said, I'd rather shit in my hands and clap than hit on you."

"Is that right?"

"Uh-huh."

"I see."

And with that, he takes a sip of whiskey and turns back to his email. As his fingers fly over the on-screen keyboard, it's as if we never had the exchange at all.

From the corner of the bar, Dan clears his throat. Blood thumps in my temples.

Now what?

Act One has gone up in flames. I forgot my lines and my mark is a bad actor. I need to start the show from the top but with a different cast. Oh, and *definitely* a different script, because I don't think the toilet talk works.

Trying to act natural, I turn away from the bar and prop my elbows up on its surface behind me. I subtly glance around the room, sizing up all the other men I *could* have chosen over this asshole. Absent-mindedly, my fingertips brush over the four-leaf clover hanging around my neck.

It's fine. Everything's fine. I'm still lucky, I just need a reset. I haven't grifted in Devil's Cove in years. Maybe the unspoken rules are different around here, and it's actually the men sitting in the shadows that make better marks. Looking right, I lock eyes with an older, *less athletic*, man in the corner.

He reaches up to scratch his nose and his wedding ring glints. *That's more like it.*

I flash him a smile and arch my back to reach behind me for my whiskey glass. As I bring my drink to my lips, the typing beside me stops.

"That whiskey is a hundred bucks."

My eyes slide to my discarded mark. He's still staring at his cell, and if it wasn't for the way his deep drawl drizzled down my spine, I'd have sworn I imagined him talking.

"A hundred bucks?"

"Not including VAT."

"I—wait, a *bottle*?"

His gaze finally comes to me, irritation and amusement fighting for space in its shadows.

"A glass."

I stare at the amber liquid in disbelief. In response, it calls me poor in four different languages. Perhaps it was a little...*forthcoming* of me to assume my first mark would play ball, and that he'd pay for my drink. It usually works. But then again, I'm not in Atlantic City anymore.

The worst part is; I hate whiskey with a passion. I glance at Dan, who's busying himself with wiping down the other side of the bar, but by the tight line of his shoulders, it's obvious he's listening. I wonder if he'll tip it back into the bottle for me and give me something more in my budget?

Like water.

From the tap.

I can feel hard, green eyes taunting me, and the quiet enjoyment that simmers behind them grates against my pride. I'm impulsive to a fault, stubborn like it's a disease, and before I can latch onto any common sense, I plaster on a sweet smile and clink my glass against his.

"Cheers to not being interested."

His smirk is the last thing I see before I toss my head back and slam the whiskey in one.

Fuck. My nostrils burn, my eyes water, and, as the empty tumbler clatters against the bar, I suddenly remember why I hate whiskey so much.

It was the last thing my parents ever drank. Not because they finally got sober, but because they got their heads blown off with a revolver before they could pour out another glass.

The hundred-dollar acid fizzes in my pipes and claws at my box of memories, trying to pry open the lock and bring me back to that day. When I squeeze my eyes shut to stop them from watering, I can hear my father's gargled pleas and feel my mother's warm, wet blood on the backs of my thighs from where I slipped in a puddle of it.

You know how lucky you are, kid? You're one in a million.

"Don't choke."

Gasping for air that doesn't taste like bleach, I pop an eyelid and glare at the man. His expression is as impassive as his tone, and it's clear he couldn't care less if I turned blue and keeled over beside him. If I did, at least I wouldn't have to worry about how I'm going to afford the poison that killed me.

I wipe my mouth with the back of my hand. "Why do you care? Thought you weren't interested."

He lazily checks the time on his expensive wristwatch. "I'm not. It's just what you say to someone who's choking."

He lifts his own glass to his lips and sinks the remaining liquid in one, without so much as a flinch. I hate how my eyes are drawn to the thick trunk of his throat as it bobs. He slides the empty tumbler across the bar with a sharp flick of his wrist, and a few moments later, Dan comes over with another whiskey and a glass of water. He places the water in front of me, and I gratefully gulp from it.

I hope to God it's free.

For a few minutes, we sit in blistering silence, but there's no doubt I'm the only one to feel its heat. From my sporadic glances at his reflection in the mirrored wall, I can tell he has already forgotten I'm here. He answers texts and emails on his cell, stopping only to sip whiskey and rub his jaw with the palm of his large hand, as if it helps him think.

My heart drops lethargically to my stomach, like a balloon leaking helium. If I wasn't such a stubborn idiot, I'd have left a long time ago, but now it's too late. I'm chained to this joint by a hundred-dollar tab—*not including* VAT—and trying my luck with one of the other patrons in here would just be embarrassing. They've all just witnessed me choke on two ounces of liquid, for God's sake.

Behind us, soft lighting floods the stairway. Shiny shoes appear, and seconds later, the suited man they belong to comes into view. He has a stack of files tucked under his arm and makes a beeline for the arrogant asshole beside me. I watch in the bar mirror as he mutters something in his ear, slides the folders in front of him, and waits. A curt nod from my former mark seems to be his permission to leave.

So, he's a businessman. An important one at that, judging by the amount of paperwork piled up in front of him on a Thursday evening, and the fact that he's spent at least two-hundred dollars on liquor. He opens the first file, scans the document, and draws a pen from his breast pocket.

For some reason, the way he drags his thumb over the tip of his tongue before turning the page makes my blood half a degree hotter.

Christ. My heart may be stone cold, but I'm still a woman, I guess. I clear my throat in an attempt to regain semblance and notice his shoulders tighten.

He meets my eyes in the mirrored wall, as if he knew exactly where to find them.

"How much?"

"I—what?"

"How much?" he repeats calmly. My blank stare makes a muscle clench in his jawline. "For you to go away. How much do I have to pay you?"

There's that annoyance again, gnawing at my chest. This time, I'm not just pissed at his dismissal, but at myself, too. Grifting is the only thing I'm good at.

I'm a little bit of talent and a whole lot of luck. Hell, I used to say I could swindle a man blindfolded. Probably handcuffed, too. And yet...

And yet, since the moment I stepped up to this bar, I've been out-of-sorts. Maybe I'm still shook-up from what happened in Atlantic City. Or maybe it's because my mark is good-looking and reeks of indifference.

But so what? I've dealt with worse. This is my last ever grift, and I'll be damned if I go out with a choke and a whimper.

With a quiet sigh, the man tugs out a money clip, snaps off a few bills, and tosses them between us on the bar.

"That'll cover the drink you choked on." He goes back to his document. I watch his pen scrawl a long, complicated signature with perfect precision.

"Plus VAT?"

He pauses, fighting the smile tugging at the corners of his mouth. Maybe it's the shadows and lack of sleep playing tricks on me, but I swear I see a pair of dimples. Without looking up, he tugs out another hundred and tosses it onto the pile.

I stare down at Franklin's judgmental gaze and swallow. "Plus tip?"

This time, the man's jaw clenches, but he says nothing. Instead, he pulls out another bill and slams it against the bar. The dull thud is louder than I was expecting, and it echoes behind my rib cage.

Silence. It's peppered with sultry jazz and the sound of a pen scratching paper.

"You're still here," he eventually muses. "Why is that?" He casts one folder aside and opens another. There's that thumb lick again, and I have no idea why it makes my vision jolt like that.

I swallow the lump wedged in my windpipe, slide off the stool, and close the distance between us, coming to a stop in the tiny gap between him and the bar. The cold surface kisses my bare back as I press against it, a stark contrast to the heat radiating off his body.

He stills. Nostrils flaring, he reluctantly matches my stare with one of his own. Any trace of humor is long gone. Now, it's a calm green sea, and I can't shake the uneasy feeling there's a strong, dangerous current running underneath its surface.

I wonder how many women he's tricked into diving in.

"I don't want your money," I say, trying—and failing—to match his indifference. His narrowed gaze drops to my hand, following it as I slide it across the bar's surface toward his wrist. "I want your watch."

My fingertip brushes over the leather strap, and a spark of excitement ignites in my lower stomach.

Against all odds, we've reached Act Two: The Proposition.

"You want my watch," he repeats sardonically, as if saying my own words back to me will make me realize how stupid they sound. But I don't relent. Sure, I could take the few hundred-dollar bills on the bar, pay off my tab and run, but where is the fun in that? I set my eyes on that Breitling before I saw who it belonged to, and I'm not leaving without it.

Time to double down.

As I turn to face his left hand resting on the bar, the fabric of his jacket grazes against my bare shoulder, making my skin crackle like static. I force myself to ignore it, honing in on his watch.

Jesus. Heat creeps up my neck and floods my face. His hand looks even bigger up close. Wide wrist, smooth, tan skin, and a sprinkle of dark hair poking out from underneath the watch strap. Thick fingers grip his pen so tightly that, briefly, I wonder if his cool, unbothered demeanor is an act, and he's actually planning on sticking that Mont Blanc in my neck.

I curl my fingers into a fist and inch it away.

"The Mulliner. Part of Breitling's collaboration with Bentley, I believe. It has an automatic flying tourbillon which beats more than twenty-eight thousand times an hour."

His lips twitch. They are plump and pink, with a deep cupid's bow that, annoyingly, makes my mouth water. "Impressive. Maybe you could get a job at Breitling, then you'll be able to pay for your own drinks."

I lean back against the bar, partly because I suddenly got a waft of his scent—a cocktail of expensive cologne and mint, and it's making me far drunker than I am—but also partly because I'm hoping his gaze will drop to my cleavage.

It doesn't.

"I don't want a job. I want your watch."

He cocks a brow. "Well since you asked so nicely." He turns back to his paperwork.

I slam my hand against his file, sending his pen mark flying across the page. Dark annoyance threads through his features, but only for half a second, before that bored expression is back.

"You're incredibly annoying," he says quietly.

"So I've been told."

"And at this point, I'd give you the shirt off my back to get you to leave."

I glance down at his shirt. Like every other part of him, it looks *expensive.* Crisp, white, molded to his body like second skin. He's forgone a tie in favor of a collar pin with two gold dice punctuating each collar point. A thin chain connects them. Begrudgingly, I like it.

"Your shirt, but not your watch."

"Not my watch."

"What if I win it?"

I look up at his face just in time to witness it shift. A spark of something, intrigue perhaps, dances within the walls of his irises. Now, the full weight of his attention presses heavily against my body.

His pen slips from his hand and lands on the files with a dull thud. "Win it? You want to make a bet?"

Out of the corner of my eye, Dan stills. I should take it as a warning sign, I know. But before I can process it, my mark smiles.

Holy shit. It's like looking at the sun. Not because his perfect teeth are blinding, but because it feels dangerous. Like if I stare too long, the handful of morals I have left will go up in a puff of smoke. Faint lines frame his eyes, making me realize despite his annoyance with me, he probably smiles quite often.

And he *does* have dimples.

"What bet?" He pins me with a sudden velvet charm that steals my breath from my lungs. I bet it secures multi-million-dollar deals and makes women drop their panties without a second thought. Hell, if I didn't have a hundred problems, I could see myself being one of them.

"A game of my choosing."

"Hmm." He runs a palm over his jaw, and a diamond dice cufflink winks at me. "What are the odds of winning?"

"Ten-to-one."

"You just made that up."

I hitch a shoulder and bat my lashes. "Maybe."

His gaze crackles and glimmers with amusement, lingering on mine a beat too long. I'm almost thankful when a buzzing sound slices through the air. His attention shifts to his cell next to me. I glance down and see the name Angelo flash on the screen.

"Excuse me for a moment," he says softly. He brings his cell to his ear, slides his other hand in his pocket, and saunters into the shadows.

With distance between us, I realize how fast my heartbeat is. It's fueled by adrenaline and something a little more...*fuzzy* around the edges. I turn to grab my glass of water and come face-to-face with Dan.

That customer-service smile is nowhere to be seen. He says something, but I don't catch it, because his mouth barely moves.

"What?"

His eyes sweep the room behind me, wary and wild. When he speaks again, it's only a fraction louder.

"I *said*, have you been in a mental institution for the last three years?"

I blink. "Er, no? Why?"

He glances in the direction my mark went. "Because only a crazy person would have the nerve to pull a con on Raphael Visconti."

Visconti.

Raphael Visconti.

Well, shit.

CHAPTER
Two

Penny

T HERE'S AN UNSPOKEN RULE on the Devil's Coast. It's etched into every craggy cliff and it pollutes every gloomy shadow.

Don't fuck with the Viscontis.

It's common sense, really. Not pissing off the mafia—specifically, the Cosa Nostra—is a law as old as time.

The Viscontis dominate the coastline. In fact, I'd bet my left kidney I could twist my head around three-hundred-and-sixty degrees like a fucking owl, and everything my eyes touched would be Visconti-owned. Every bar, hotel, casino, and restaurant in Cove, Hollow, and Dip, plus all the sorry souls within them.

I of all people should be able to spot a Visconti. It's not like I stumbled off a Greyhound bus and into parts unknown. I grew up, quite literally, under their roof at the Visconti Grand Hotel and Casino. I learned to crawl among their Brioni loafers underneath the poker tables; started my period in one of their gilded toilet cubicles. Had my first taste of liquor in one of their bars. Hell, one of them even taught me everything I know about advantage gambling and swindling.

Gripping the edge of the bar, I cast a wayward glance to the shadowy figure in the corner. The screen of his cell lights a path along his jawline as he holds it to his ear, and as he turns in a lazy circle, his eyes flash green under a soft spotlight.

Against all odds, I've made it to twenty-one and I credit that achievement to both luck and always listening to my instincts, even if they only whisper. Right now, my instincts aren't whispering; they are screaming at the top of their lungs.

Run.

Dan has moved on to collecting glasses from the tables. I snatch up the bills on the bar and leave one to pay for my drink. Unfortunately, I'll have to be a lousy tipper tonight, but as a fellow Devil's Coast resident, I'm sure Dan will understand. Sliding away from the bar, I slip on my coat and head toward the table I kicked my suitcase under.

Slow and steady. Cool and calm. Despite the awful sense of dread pressing down on my shoulders, my movements are relaxed and natural; anything else will draw unwanted attention.

I'm just a girl leaving a bar after choking on an overpriced drink. No big deal.

At the bottom step, I've bent down to pick up my suitcase when a voice slices through the air like a hot knife in a block of butter.

"Off so soon?"

Shit.

"Yeah," I say, as breezily as I can muster. "Got a train to catch."

"There are no trains on the Devil's Coast."

Double shit. "In the morning, I mean. From a different town. Gotta be up early to get there, so I should probably..."

Three slow footsteps, each one closer than the last. The weight behind them makes my excuse trail off into nothingness.

Balling my hands into fists, I glance up the stairs to the small sliver of light at the top of them. If I sacrifice my belongings, will I be able to get out the door before he catches me?

Blood thumps in my ears. Another two footsteps reverberate off the low ceiling, then heat brushes against the nape of my neck. Only a stuttered heartbeat later does the scent of warm whiskey and cool mint drift under my nose.

Christ, he's close. Goosebumps prickle down the lengths of my arms, and my knees threaten to buckle underneath me.

His thick, tranquil voice floats over the planes of my shoulders.

"Let's play your game."

It's a command masquerading as a suggestion, delivered with the sharp zap of a cattle prod.

It should scare me, but it just pisses me off. I've never taken too kindly to being told what to do, especially by a *man*, even if said man is a Visconti.

Raphael Visconti. Jesus. Despite my annoyance, I can't believe I had the gall to call *Raphael Visconti* a mark, even in my own head. He's the middle one of the Devil's Dip brothers, and unlike the Cove and the Hollow families, they haven't had a presence on the Coast for years, not since their parents died when I was around eleven years old. My memories of him in particular are hazy, probably because he's a lot older than me. He exists in flashes of sharp tailoring and charming smiles. I never got more than a brief glimpse of him before he disappeared behind a sea of suits or a locked door.

Everything I know about Raphael Visconti isn't from my child-hood memories, but from hearsay around blackjack tables in At-lantic City. His name was always uttered in a breathless whisper, often with a rumor attached to it. Invite-only poker games and parties that rivaled Jay Gatsby's: that kind of thing. It's hard to know what was true and what wasn't.

There are only two things I know to be fact.

The first is that Raphael owns the majority of the big-name casinos in Vegas.

The second is that I'd be stupid to swindle a man who owns the majority of the big-name casinos in Vegas.

I need to get out of this mess, and fast. With a false confidence, I spin around with a get-out clause on my tongue. He's standing closer than I'd thought and it takes me off-guard. I stumble backward, heels hitting the bottom step, but before I land on my ass, a strong hand reaches out and wraps itself around my forearm.

My defiance flickers like a candle in the wind. He's tall. Really tall, and now that I know who he is, he's also really fucking *big*. My eye line barely reaches the third button on his shirt.

Being in his shadow makes me uncomfortable, so I mount the bottom step and fold my arms in an attempt to level the playing field.

He smirks.

"You sure are persistent for a man that isn't interested."

His gaze drops to my mouth. "Oh, I'm interested."

Sudden heat flares against my stomach lining, and I let out a little involuntary puff of air. Something about the intensity of his gaze and the silkiness of his tone feels…*inappropriate.* I don't doubt he has women skipping to his bedroom with a lot less effort.

I fake a yawn. "Sorry. Gotta go."

Although his stillness is magnetic, I manage to tear myself away long enough to reach down, grab my belongings, and turn toward the entryway at the top of the stairs.

One step. Then another. My boot is hovering over the third when darkness shrouds me. I pause to squint up into the dim light and see a security guard, the one with the punchable face and rhetorical questions. He's looming at the top of the stairs, blocking the exit.

Fuck.

As if he'll give me answers, I glance back at Raphael. He's standing in the same spot, with the same tight smile tugging at his lips, hands resting easy in the pockets of his slacks.

My attention shifts over his shoulder, and that's when my confusion settles into something denser. The other men in the bar are now on their feet, all glaring at me. One steps into the path of a spotlight and turns his head.

I catch sight of his earpiece, and realization slaps me across the face.

Wearing suits mid-week. Sitting alone. Things I usually see as green checks, are in this case, massive red flags. It wasn't a coincidence that they were all sitting separately, because they're all bodyguards. They are *working.* And all for…

My eyes drop back to the Visconti. His dimples deepen. Cashmere charm and a razor-sharp smile.

"I'm afraid I have to insist."

Ice-cold dread trickles into my bloodstream. *Fuck.* Less than ten minutes ago, I thought this dude was a little fish that wouldn't nibble on my bait, and how wrong I was.

He's a great white shark about to swallow me whole.

My pulse strums in my throat, and my hands grow clammy. *Two fuck-ups in one week.* That's awful odds for a girl as lucky as me.

With defeat heavy in my stomach, I drop my bags on the step and smooth down the satin of my stolen dress. Outwardly, I'm calm, but internally, all of my organs are rattling with a new plan. My original game isn't going to cut it anymore—I need something less seedy. Something less likely to get me tossed off the Cove Pier in a body bag.

Guess I'm heading into Act Three.

"Well, since you *insist*," I snap in a tone that doesn't mirror the panic creeping up my throat. Raphael's amusement blisters my cheek as I make my way back to the bar and take a seat.

Dan catches my eye and gives a small, sorrowful shake of his head, conveying what I've already figured out: I'm well and truly fucked.

Raphael's large hands grip the stool next to me, then he pulls it away from the bar like it weighs nothing. He hitches up his slacks and perches on the edge of it. With a small, expressionless nod to Dan, he rests his forearms on his knees, steeples his fingers, and bathes me in his attention.

"Tell me more about this game."

My eyes slide unwillingly to him. His own gleam with quiet enjoyment, and, suddenly, I remember the time I picked up *Marine Biology for Dummies* at the library. There was this whole section about Great Whites, and how they can detect heartbeats in the water. He can hear mine thumping in fear and he *relishes* it.

Despite finding myself in the bottom of a pit without a ladder, my pride flares up like a nasty rash. I steel my jaw and rise to my feet. Without breaking eye contact, I slip off my coat again, and this time, I actually *see* his gaze warm the length of my body. It rolls from the skinny straps on my shoulders to the dip of my hip, down the length of my exposed right leg, and comes to a stop at my Doc Marten boot. Every inch he absorbs lays another brick of confidence in my core. And a fluttering feeling in my stomach, but I'm trying to ignore that.

He's just a man, for Christ's sake. Sure, a man with an infamous last name and surrounded by bodyguards who might chop me up and stuff me into my own suitcase, but, nevertheless, a man. And under the surface, they are all the fucking same.

I lean against the bar and run my necklace up and down its chain. *Game. Right.* I'm going for my least seedy tactic and hoping for the best.

"It's less of a game, and more of a...*quiz*."

Dan lays two drinks on the table. One's a whiskey, the other is bright yellow and in a cocktail glass. I glare at the glazed cherry and pink curly straw. "Changed your drink?"

"Changed yours. Lemon drop martinis are less of a choking hazard."

"Delightful," I retort dryly. I couldn't care less about the drink. Besides, I have a rightful suspicion that if I take so much as a sip, there's a good chance I'll wake up chained to a radiator somewhere dark and damp.

"A quiz. Tell me more."

"Five questions. If you answer any of them wrong, I get your watch."

He cocks a brow. Smirks in a way I've already grown to hate. "And if I get them right?"

"You won't."

A gruff little laugh escapes his lips, and as he rubs his large hands together, his diamond dice cufflinks taunt me. *How did I not realize who he was before?* "You're a confident little thing."

Little thing. A shiver of displeasure ripples down my spine. *Little thing* falls into the same category as *sweetheart* and *darling.* Patronizing expressions used by men to knock women down a few pegs.

It makes me want to hit his pockets as hard as I can.

"Let's begin." He is, of course, confident.

"You don't want to hear the catch?"

"There's a catch?"

"There's always a catch," I say smoothly, ignoring the way his voice darkens a shade. "None of my five questions are trick questions. In fact, the answer to each is very simple. However, the catch is that you must answer each question *wrong.* If you answer correctly, you lose, and I get that lovely timepiece on your wrist." I slide my hand out into the gap between us. "It'd look nice on me; don't you think?"

He regards my arm with mild disinterest, then glances up at me. Impatience flickers like flames in his irises. "Fine."

"Have you played this game before?"

His drink is halfway to his lips when he stills. "It wouldn't be smart of you to take me for a fool, darling."

A shiver rolls through me. "We haven't started yet. You can answer truthfully."

He thinks for a moment. His sip turns into a gulp, then he sets his glass on the bar. "Then no, I haven't."

A heady rush coasts over my skin, a blend of excitement and danger.

"Question one. Where are we right now?"

He hesitates. "The moon."

"Question two. What color is my hair?"

His gaze skims up to my messy top-knot. His throat bobs and he mutters something that barely leaves his lips. *What?* But before I can put weight to it, he bites out an answer. "Blue."

"And the color of *your* hair?"

"Blond."

"Fuck, you're good at this," I mutter, tucking a stray hair behind my ear.

"I'm good at most things."

The husky insinuation in his tone makes my pulse stop for a second. Something warm grazes my knee, and when I look down, I realize it's his own. *Was he sitting this close a minute ago?*

Ignoring the heat rising in my face, I continue. "Okay, how many questions have I asked you?"

He strums a thick finger against the bar at a rate three times slower than my heartbeat. He cuts a knuckle along the length of his cheekbone before saying with finality, "Twelve."

I exhale so hard the stray hairs framing my face flutter. "Shit," I mutter under my breath, scanning the room.

Raphael regards me with quiet glee. He picks up his tumbler, swirls the liquid around with a slow roll of his wrist. "Feeling the heat?"

"Yeah, because you're a fucking cheat," I snap back.

The swirling stops. "I'm sorry?"

By the chill threading through his words, I know replying with *apology accepted* wouldn't be the smartest decision. "You heard. You're a cheat."

He sets the glass down. "Say it again," he says softly, yet his gaze is anything but soft.

I fight the urge to apologize, even if it's just to relieve the tension building up under my rib cage, but this only works if I double down. "I *said*, you're a cheat. A liar, too."

His jaw muscle spasms. "A liar."

"Uh-huh. You told me you haven't played this game before, but you have, haven't you?"

"I already told you I haven't."

A beat passes. It turns into two. We stare at each other as thick and sticky realization trickles into the small gap between us.

That was my fifth question.

I wonder if he can hear the pulse thumping against my temples, or the ragged edge to my breathing. If he does, the hard planes of his face don't show it.

I *love* winning. The feeling of getting one over on a mark is as addictive as any drug. But tonight, my high is snatched away by the feeling of the walls closing in. When I look up, I realize with mounting horror that it's not the walls but Raphael's security team forming a slow, moving circle around us.

Oh, shit.

But then Raphael raises his hand. It's such a subtle move, I wouldn't have noticed it if it weren't for the glint of his citrine ring, but it brings his entire team to an immediate stop.

"You tricked me," he says simply.

"I didn't. I asked you before we started if you'd played the game before, and you said—"

"No," he finishes thoughtfully.

His silence screams. My triumph *whispers*.

I regard his inscrutable expression with caution as he drains his drink and rubs his thumb over his bottom lip. He rests his forearm on the bar.

For the shortest of seconds, I think maybe, *just maybe*, I might have gotten away with it. But then—

"Dan, pass me the hammer."

He says it so impassively. Like he's merely asked for the time, not because he has anywhere to be, but simply for the sake of making conversation.

My blood flash-freezes. "What? Why?"

He ignores me. Dan offers me a look halfway between an apology and an *I-told-you-so*, then bends behind the bar and comes back with a small hammer, the type that smashes up ice.

Or kneecaps.

I don't wait to find out.

Fueled by self-preservation and adrenaline, I combine the two tasks of pulling on my coat and walking backward toward the stairs. The room is a haze of amber, heat, and fear; everything blurry apart from the hammer and the large hand curled around its handle.

My heels hit the bottom step, but this time, no strong hand shoots out from the darkness to stop me from falling. When I land on my backside, the impact reverberates up my spine, sheer terror chasing after it.

Your sins will catch up with you eventually, Little P. They always do.

Raphael's cousin's parting words to me ring in my ears as black warmth ghosts over my chest. It's a shadow, from which a steel claw, glossy watch face, and a citrine ring glint.

"Please," I whisper into the darkness. The last time I said *please* with such desperation was when I was ten, in the alleyway behind the Visconti Grand Casino. It didn't stop the hands coming down on me then, and it doesn't now.

A rough palm with a soft touch comes down on my thigh. The silky fabric of my dress falls away at the deep split, and instantly, my stomach drops to my boots.

Has anyone ever touched what's under that pretty little dress of yours?

Fear runs into fury, blazing hot and dangerous.

No.

But it all happens so fast. I grit my teeth, squeeze my eyes shut, and grip the four-leaf clover around my neck as the hammer comes down to the left of me.

Crack.

No pain. No broken bones. I pop a lid and look down at my side slit, and white-hot embarrassment immediately floods my bloodstream.

A black security tag. It lies in smashed, plastic shards next to my quivering thigh. I didn't realize this dress had one, but of course it did. That's why the fucking alarm went off as I left the store.

It takes me three long seconds to remember to breathe. I draw in a lungful of air, and when I slide my eyes up to meet Raphael's, I let it out in an angry exhale.

Humor sparkles behind his gaze, like he's just heard a joke and he's looking right at the punchline. "You got lucky."

"Yeah?" I snap back.

"Mm. Sometimes they put ink in those things."

I glare at him. He's a cool drink of water to my burning inferno. A calm, green sea to my shaking storm.

I fucking *hate* him.

Before I have the semblance to bite back, he sticks out a hand and hauls me to my feet. My legs are trembling from leftover adrenaline. Without breaking eye contact, he hands the hammer to the nearest guard and unbuckles his watch in one, swift motion.

He leans forward, just close enough to reach into the pocket of my coat, and slips the Breitling inside of it. It falls like a dead weight to the bottom.

"Look after it." Something beautifully melancholic passes through his gaze, and despite my wanting to grab that hammer from his guard and crack him over the head with it, his expression echoes in the hollow chambers of my chest.

It's gone in the bat of a dark eyelash, replaced by that ever-present amusement.

A sassy remark is out of my mouth before I can stop it. Despite having scored one of the highest paydays of my life, I hate feeling like a man has got one over on me. It must be a knee-jerk reaction to level the playing field.

"Want to play again?" I ask with all the nonchalance I can muster. "I kind of like the look of that ring on your finger."

He smiles tightly. "I'd rather shit in my hands and clap."

I'd laugh at his reference to my earlier crude remark, if I weren't halfway to a heart attack. Yeah, I think I've pushed my luck to the limit tonight. A heavy beat passes, then he jerks his chin to the stairs behind me. "Go."

A soft, simple command, and one I'm more than happy to submit to. I snatch up my belongings and jog up the stairs, trying to ignore the gaze burning the nape of my neck.

It feels like a lifetime ago that I stood in this entryway, hiding from a pissed-off store clerk. It's crazy that I'd thought it'd be the most drama I'd encounter tonight.

The sour-faced guard watches me until I reach the door, then his gruff voice coasts over my shoulders. "You have no idea how lucky you are."

I pause with my hand on the doorknob. Suddenly, the four-leaf clover around my neck weighs more than the six-figure timepiece in my pocket.

I huff out a bitter laugh.

"Trust me, it's *you* who has no idea."

CHAPTER
Three

Penny

I T'S PAST MIDNIGHT BY the time I'm dragging my suitcase over the cobbles of Devil's Dip main street. Although just a forty-minute bus ride along a winding coastal road, it couldn't be more different from Devil's Cove. The sky is black and the streets silent, save for the harsh, salty wind cracking against my cheeks like a whip.

Dip is like Cove's scruffy cousin. The one that got disinherited from the will and no longer gets invited to family reunions. It's dirtier, darker. Even the glow around the Christmas lights is murkier. There's no money in its bars and restaurants, just old, tired men slumped over their beers and greasy chicken dinners after a long day of slinging cargo at the port.

Like moths to a flame, most residents gravitate to the bright lights of Cove for employment, just like my parents did. They take the six-one-eight bus from opposite the old church at the top of the cliff, work a twelve-hour shift waiting on the rich and the rude, then retreat back to the slums with an apron full of tips and aching feet.

I won't be joining them now that I'm going *straight*. In Cove, temptation and danger live in the light, making it near-impossible to miss. In Dip, the only things that can hurt me are the memories locked away in the Victorian townhouse five streets away.

I haven't been back there since the murder, and I don't plan on changing that.

I come to a stop outside a flaking green door. It's sandwiched between a bike shop and a funeral home, and if it weren't for the flickering glow of a nearby streetlamp, most mailmen would miss entirely the number eight carved into its wood.

It groans open with a little nudge from my boot. When the realtor handed me the keys a week after my eighteenth birthday, he mentioned the main door was busted, but the building owner was going to fix it "right away."

I guess we have different interpretations of what "right away" means.

I climb the narrow staircase to the second floor, dump my suitcase and purse on the lino tiles, and stride over to 8A's door. I hammer my fist against it and glare down at the door mat in disbelief.

Hi, I'm Mat.

Muffled footsteps, the turn of a lock, then a tall, blond guy darkens the doorway. He's wearing basketball shorts and an annoyed scowl. It softens into a lop-sided grin when he looks down at me.

"Well, well, well. Look what fly decided to return to the dump."

I ignore him. "Did you lose a bet?"

He frowns. "No?"

"So you bought this welcome mat voluntarily?"

We both glance back down at the floor and Matt chuckles. "You don't think it's funny?"

"I think it makes you deserving of being burgled."

"But it's a pun on my name. Jeez." He runs a hand over his floppy hair. "You, Penny Price, wouldn't know a good joke if it slapped you around the face."

Irritation slithers up my spine. "I've got a good joke."

"Yeah?"

"Uh-huh. Knock knock."

His eyes thin. "All right. Who's there?"

"Your favorite neighbor, and she's about to set fire to your welcome mat if she doesn't get the key to her apartment in the next five seconds."

Matt frowns, then breaks into an easy grin. "Still an asshole, huh?"

"Unfortunately."

With a small shake of his head, he walks down the hallway and invites me in with a lazy swoop of his hand. "Come in and make yourself comfortable. Finding this key might take me a while."

"Why? Have you become messy?" But as I come to a stop in the small, familiar living room, I know that he hasn't. It's as nice and neat as I remember, filled with gray and cream furnishings.

"No, Penny, but you gave me your key—what, almost three years ago now? Well, you didn't *give* it to me. You left it on my doorstep under a crate of beer and then vanished without a trace." He disappears into the kitchen, and metallic-punctuated rummaging ensues. "You're lucky I still have it. It's in *that* kitchen drawer. You know, the one you toss everything that doesn't have a home in?" More clanking. "Fucking hell," he grunts. "I've got phone chargers, sim cards, screws for god-knows-what." The noise stops. "Whoa, I've just found a Walkman. Remember them?"

"No, because I'm twenty-one."

"Hey! I'm only a couple years older than you, girl."

I bite back a smile and drop to the sofa. Bad idea. Soft cushions and warm nostalgia engulf my aching muscles like a hug, and for a brief moment, my lids flutter shut. After three years of living in a shitty studio apartment that shares a wall with a crack den, I can now appreciate how good I had it having Matt as a neighbor for the few months I lived here. The night I got the keys for my place, he knocked on my door armed with beer and a boatload of stories about the toxic couple who lived upstairs. As far as men go, he's great. Easy to talk to, doesn't have a wandering eye, and is stoned into tranquility most weekends. He teaches Physical Education and ice hockey at the posh academy in Devil's Hollow, and if I bet a stranger a million dollars if they could guess his profession in three tries, I'd be in a hell of a lot of debt. He has surfer-dude hair, likes his clothes baggy and NHL-branded, and he says annoying things like, "Just chill, man."

In an attempt to stay awake, I force my eyes open and focus on the television screen in the corner of the room. There's a news reporter talking at me, both expression and tone sinister. My gaze catches on the scene she's standing in front of. On the burning building and the thick tendrils of smoke melting into the dark sky above it.

Immediately, my throat tightens.

Matt appears in the doorway, a set of keys dangling from his forefinger. He glances at the screen. "Fire at a casino in Atlantic City. Think someone spent too much on the slot machines and wanted revenge?"

My fingers claw at the doughy seat on either side of me. *It's made national news? Shit.* "Mm. Maybe."

"The police seem to agree with me."

"What?"

"Earlier, they were saying they suspect it's arson, not like, sketchy wiring or anything."

My palms may be sweaty, but my blood runs ice-cold. "Arson."

"I don't know, but I'm sure we'll find out soon enough." His gruff laugh floats across the living room and touches my clammy skin. His mouth is still moving but I'm not listening, because now, I'm suddenly too aware of my stench—a cocktail of smoke and sin. Because now, all I can hear are those stupid words again.

Your sins will catch up with you eventually, Little P. They always do.

No. I'm safe here. Dip is quiet, and nobody saw me leave, let alone where I went.

"Hey, you okay?"

I manage a nod, mutter something about being tired, and rise to my feet.

"Here, let me grab your stuff," he says, snatching up my suitcase.

I follow him across the hall, half-listening as he says something about the lock being stiff, and then we're standing in the entryway to my old apartment.

Matt fist bumps a light switch, flooding the space with a stale yellow glow. I take it all in through one cautious eye, bracing myself for the worst. It's been untouched for three years, so I'm half-expecting the ceiling to have sunken in, or for rats to have taken over the bedroom.

Instead, it's frozen in time underneath a thin layer of dust. Nothing's changed. The hallway is still the size of a prison cell and as haphazardly painted. It leads to the living room which isn't much bigger. The two-seater sofa I bought off Craigslist has held up well. It faces a television set so old it has a dial on the front of it. I drop my gaze to the stained gray carpet, and make a vow to give it a good vacuum before I walk on it barefoot.

"It's just as I left it," I announce, warm relief flaring up inside my rib cage.

"It is? Jesus Christ," Matt mutters. I turn to see him leaning against the doorframe, bewilderment smeared on his face. "You could have told me squatters took over the place and I'd have believed you. I'd forgotten how...*shitty* it was in here."

I laugh and shake my head. When alcoholism took hold of my parents, our town house began to rot. The floral wallpaper wilted, and the granite kitchen counters lost their sheen, no matter how often I went at them with soapy water. I did what I could with stolen cleaning products and a bit of elbow grease, but there's only so many times you can scrub your mother's sick from the living room carpet before it leaves a lingering smell. There were only so many times I could force myself to care, too.

After they were shot, I bounced between foster homes for the next five years, staying in sterile rooms made for the occasional house guest, not orphaned teens. The day I turned eighteen, I got a call from a lawyer. Between the vodka shots and the incoherent arguments, my parents hadn't had time to write a will, but apparently, they'd had enough smarts to put money in an off-shore bank account for when I became of legal age. It was a bullshit story but I didn't care to dig deeper, because there was just enough money in there for me to buy this place. I only stayed for a few months before I packed up my shit and took a Greyhound to pastures new. I followed the bright lights from one coast to another and ended up in Atlantic City. My studio apartment there had the kind of mold that makes your lungs burn in the morning, so I'm kind of happy to be home.

Matt's gaze follows me as I cross the room and run my hand over the glass dining table pushed up against the far wall. I inch back the curtain and peer down at the cobbled street below. There's the bakery opposite, and if I push my nose up against the glass and look right, I can make out the red, plastic booths of the diner.

That's the thing about Devil's Dip. Nothing ever changes.

"What brought you back to town, anyway?"

The muscles in my back tense. Truth is, when I scooped my life into a suitcase and left Atlantic City, returning to the Coast was the last thing on my mind. I didn't consider it until I hopped off the bus that took me as far as Portland. Shivering under a bus shelter and at a loss as to where to go next, I typed in *quietest towns on the West Coast* into Google. Devil's Dip was number three on Wendy Wanderlust's travel blog. Coincidentally, there was a bus leaving for Devil's Cove in less than thirty minutes, and the price of the ticket amounted to the exact change I had in my pockets.

That's the type of luck that has summed up my life.

"Missed the amazing weather," I reply dryly.

He chuckles. "Yeah? You got a job yet?"

That's my next hurdle: finding a job in Devil's Dip. It's going to be near-impossible, because in a small town, there's only one of everything. One grocery store, one diner, one pizza place. It seems like the people who work in these establishments cling onto their jobs for dear life, and the only time there's ever a vacancy is when someone dies or retires.

"Nope, but if you hear of any going, will you let me know?"

"Ah, I'm sure there's a million bars and restaurants in Cove that'll have—"

I cut him off, firm and fast. "I want to stay local, so I'm only looking in Devil's Dip."

No Cove, no Hollow. It would be too tempting to stick my hands in deep pockets, and I'm trying not to do that anymore.

I turn around just in time to see suspicion thread through Matt's gaze. He opens his mouth, no doubt with a barrage of questions on his tongue, but I get there before he can. "Thanks for helping me with my stuff. Perhaps we'll catch up this weekend, if you're around?"

A hint that even an idiot couldn't miss. He pushes himself off the door frame and takes two steps back into the shadows of the hallway. "Sure thing, I'll leave you to it." He pauses at the front door. "You got any plans tomorrow?"

"Depends on what you're about to propose."

"A wedding. Free food, free liquor, and a good time. What'd you say?"

I frown. "Who's getting married?"

"Remember Rory Carter?"

I groan. Not because I don't like Rory—quite the opposite, in fact. She's one of the nicest girls on the Coast. She went to the only other school in Devil's Dip and also worked the night shift at the diner at the end of the street. Every time I went in, she gave me an extra portion of fries or a hot chocolate on the house, and I kept her company while she cleaned tables and did stock-checks.

She was probably only nice to me because my parents were killed, but still, she was the closest thing I had to a female friend.

No. I groaned because Rory is the same age as me, which means I'm at the age where people have their shit figured out.

I, on the other hand, am very far from having my shit figured out.

"Who is she marrying? Anyone I know?"

Matt cocks his head in thought. "No, don't think you'd know him. So, what do you say? You want to be my date?"

I chew on the inside of my cheek and mull it over. I guess it'd be nice to see some old faces, and I probably have a suitable dress gathering dust in my closet. Besides, maybe I'll meet someone who's hiring.

"I'm down, as long as you don't call me your date."

"No, you're not my date, you're my wing-woman. This girl I like is going."

"So, what? You want me to sing your praises to her in the bathroom?"

"No; I want you to look at me like you're in love with me and pretend to laugh at my jokes. Then, when she realizes how hot I look in a tux, I need you to make yourself scarce."

I stare at him in disbelief. "Has that ever worked for you before?"

He flashes me a wink. "Dunno, never tried it. I'll pick you up at two pm."

He breezes out of my apartment, leaving me with nothing but my thoughts and the noisy whir of the heating unit.

Shower. After almost three days in the back of stinky buses, smelling like a walking, talking ashtray, the thought of a shower is my idea of heaven, even if it'll be cold, because I haven't turned on the water heater yet. I drop my coat on the floor and peel myself out of this too-tight dress. Even though it's more expensive than all of my other clothes combined, I can't wait to throw it out. The rest of me may smell like smoke and sweat, but this dress *reeks* of whiskey and close-calls, and I never want to see it again. Plus, it's part of my past. Tomorrow, I'm going to wake up, and I'm going to be *good*.

The icy water streams down my body, dampening my hair and biting at the tension between my shoulder blades. In spite of it, I feel more relaxed because the promise of a new life is on the horizon. Coming back to Devil's Dip has given me a second chance and somewhere to start over. Somewhere Martin O'Hare will never find me.

I'm going straight.

I'm going to find a job and hold it down for longer than a week.

And I'm going to *finally* figure out what interests me in this world, other than taking men's money.

By the time I've dried off and detangled my hair, a tiny smile of contentment tugs at my lips. I pull on fluffy socks and pad down the hall toward the bedroom, where a single bed with a naked bulb swinging from the ceiling above it greets me. Sighing, I drop my bundle of clothes at the bottom of it, and something falls out of my coat pocket and onto the floorboards.

Raphael Visconti's watch. I sit on the edge of the bed and scoop it up. I run a thumb over the smooth crystal face and down the length of its leather straps.

Strangely, it's still warm, like he slipped it off his thick wrist and into my pocket just moments ago. Maybe it's the extreme fatigue, or maybe I'm just a certified psychopath now, but for some reason, I lift it to my nose and breathe in its scent. The tangy cocktail of leather and lingering aftershave sparks a small, flickering flame in the pit of my stomach, and for a dark, dangerous moment, I'm back in the bar. Surrounded by slow swirls of amber, flashes of silver, and glittering green.

I reflexively clench my thighs together.

Christ, I must be tired, because fuck him. I don't care who he is or how many bodyguards he has, he came at me with a *hammer*. The worst part? It seemed to be some sort of *joke* to him.

I fall back on the bed and let out a little laugh. I can't help it, because, despite being petrified at the time, I'm still heady from the adrenaline rush of it all. Big wins only come from big risks, and, well, I definitely risked it all tonight.

My amusement settles on my skin like dust and gives way to a dull ache behind my breast. To be honest, I'll miss my grifting ways. I'm not giving up the game because I'm bored with it, but because it's the right thing to do.

I've always known it was wrong, which is why I've spent the last three years trying to find a career that's *right*. When I arrived in Atlantic City, the first thing I did was scope out the casinos, and the second was sign up for a library card. Every Monday, I'd stand in front of the *For Dummies* section, close my eyes and brush my pointer finger along the spines. Whatever book I landed on I had to read, no matter how boring the topic. My logic was that maybe, just *maybe*, I'd find something within the pages that shone light on the darkness inside of me. Something that came close to the thrill of card counting or edge sorting or lifting a wallet out of a man's slacks while he was distracted by my tits.

But so far, no dice. German Grammar. Real Estate. Trainspotting. Every book I've picked up has bored me to tears.

I get up off the bed and walk over to my suitcase to put the watch in its front pocket for safekeeping. I'll figure out how I'll sell it tomorrow.

As I scoop up a pile of clothes from the bed, something lying underneath it catches my eye.

A card.

I pick it up and flip it over.

Sinners Anonymous. The letters are embossed in gold, and underneath, there's a number printed in silky black digits. I stare at it for a few heavy seconds, and then without thinking I snatch up the burner phone I bought at a truck stop somewhere in the Midwest and punch in the number.

The line rings three times, then it clicks into the voicemail service.

"You have reached Sinners Anonymous," a woman's robotic voice says. "Please leave your sin after the tone."

There's a long beep, followed by a static silence.

I sink onto the bed. Close my eyes and draw in a deep breath.

"Hello, old friend. It's been a while."

CHAPTER
Four

Penny

S OFT FAIRY LIGHTS, SILVER serving trays, and champagne flutes
wink against the pearl-gray sky. Around the edge of the
frosted lake, weeping willows shiver in the wind, and in the
middle of it, a mini orchestra plucks strings and practices rifts
on a floating platform.

The heart of the Devil's Preserve has been transformed into
the epilogue of a Gothic Romance novel, a picture-perfect Hap-
py-Ever-After. But no amount of romanticism can take away from
the fact that it's *freezing*.

Matt presses a champagne flute into my hand. "You know; I
think I'll get married on the French Riviera."

I drag my gaze from the rows of empty white chairs and regard my neighbor. He's leaning against the trunk of an oak tree,
drinking in the view over the rim of a beer bottle. The ceremony
doesn't start for another fifteen minutes, and he's already loosened his bow tie.

"You can't even spell French Riviera, idiot."

He flashes me a sideways grin. "You gonna be this pissy all
night? I already told you I'm sorry."

"Sorry isn't going to stop my nipples from getting frostbite."

Matt failed to tell me the wedding was *al fresco* when he invited
me last night. Didn't think to mention it when he saw me step out

into our shared hallway in a backless blue dress, with my coat slung over my arm, either. Now, despite being hot and bothered himself, he won't give me his jacket in case the girl he's here for gets the wrong idea.

"You can have my socks?" he offered after I'd subjected him to a blistering glare. "They aren't cashmere, but they sure feel like it."

I passed on his charming offer, instead settling for burying my chin in the collar of my faux fur coat and dancing a constant two-step.

"And what about you?"

"Huh?"

"Where do you want to get married?"

"I *don't* want to get married," I grunt. My response is an involuntary reflex. A decision so steadfast it's practically woven into my DNA.

"At all?"

"Nope."

"What if you fall in love?"

I swig the remains of my champagne, put the empty glass on a passing tray, and pick up a fresh one. "I won't."

"You can't possibly know that."

"Women don't fall in love, Matt. They fall into traps. They are lured in by sweet lies and smooth promises. Then years, maybe *decades*, down the line, they realize they're tethered to a stranger, their chains made heavier by things like babies and mortgages and mothers-in-law with unhealthy obsessions with their sons. Some get divorced; some decide it's easier just to stay shackled."

Heavy silence whistles in the wind. I turn to Matt and smirk at his expression. "What? Too much?"

"Fuck, Pen. Who hurt you?"

I laugh this time, ignoring how my necklace tingles at the question. My theory doesn't just stem from the man who hurt me, but also from my experience of swindling. I'd say eighty-percent of the men who have approached me at bars or casinos have been married. With every ring-clad hand that made its way to my thigh, another jaded scar formed on my heart. Sure, it made it easier to hit their pockets, but it also made me feel hollow inside. Because behind every married man is a woman who doesn't realize he's an asshole.

A lethargic symphony drifts from the lake and seeps through the gathering crowd like low-hanging fog. While Matt's eyes work like rovers, scanning arriving guests for any sign of his crush, I lazily drink in our surroundings. The women at the bar sipping martinis and cooing over one of their designer bags like it's a newborn baby. Men sipping whiskey in tight groups of three, muttering in a language I don't understand.

A language I don't understand.

My flute is halfway to my lips when icy unease freezes me to the spot. Gaze sharpening over the bubbles fizzing in my glass, I look back to the women at the bar and squint. The bag they're passing around isn't just designer, it's a fucking Birkin. The one with a six-year waiting list.

I swallow and give a slight shake of my head. *No. Surely not.* I turn my attention back to the men closest to us and run a frantic eye over their attire. They are all wearing tuxedos punctuated with silk pocket squares. Standard for a wedding. But then I hone in one man in particular, picking apart his details. The gold chain disappearing underneath a shirt collar. The large cross tattoo on the back of a tanned hand and the Rolex Daytona that sits above it.

Then something shifts in my peripheral vision, and my heightened state makes my head snap up to catch it. Between two oak trees on the other side of the clearing, a man lurks in the shadows. He's only detectable from his broad silhouette and flash of his eyes as they sweep the crowd. To the left, another shadow, another concentrated stare.

An iron-clad ring of security. And there's only one family on this coastline that would need that.

"Matt," I say steadily. "Who did you say Rory was marrying again?" I'm met by silence. "Matt?"

I tear my eyes from the shadows to look at him, but he's fixated on something else. With a rigid spine, he's watching a dark-haired woman in a red dress slip through the crowd and join a group conversing behind the seating area.

"Pen, get us some more drinks," he mutters, not taking his eyes off her.

"But your beer is full and so is my—"

He grabs the flute from my hand and pours both our drinks into a muddy puddle by his feet.

My mouth opens on instinct to snap back at him, but my brain decides against it. Judging by his witless stare, I'd get more information from the thick trunk he's leaning against, anyway.

I head to the bar, skin buzzing with awareness, ears straining to catch snippets of every conversation I pass. Rory Carter can't be marrying a Visconti. There's no fucking way. Her soon-to-be-husband must be one of their favored employees, maybe a manager at one of the clubs or restaurants in Cove or something. Because growing up, I'm pretty sure she was never one of *those* Devil's Dip girls, the ones who craned their necks when a blacked-out car rolled over the cobbles of Main Street. I can't imagine she wrote Dante Visconti's name inside a heart on her textbooks, or tried to get into one of Tor Visconti's clubs with a fake ID, hoping to catch sight of the man himself behind a velvet rope.

I reach the bar and wait patiently while the girl behind it figures out how to pop open a bottle of champagne. I'm fidgeting, my gaze wandering with both caution and intrigue, and not just because I'm surrounded by men with more blood on their hands than the entire population of Washington State Penitentiary combined. No, it's because there are two Viscontis I'm keeping an eye out for. One I only met last night, and the other I've known for years.

As if he knew I was thinking about him, a deep, soft voice touches my back.

"Last time I saw that coat, you shook me down for a grand."

I grip the edge of the bar, and my lids flutter shut. I don't turn around, not yet. Partly because the emotion creeping up my throat is too thick to hide, and partly because I don't want to be confronted by how fast time passes.

Nico Visconti was never a liar, but he's lying about this coat. The last time he saw it was when he dropped me off at the Devil's Cove bus depot at two a.m., a few weeks after my eighteenth birthday.

That's the problem with the Coast. My past hides in all of its shadows, threatening to jump out and choke me when I least expect it.

The warmth of his body orbits mine, coming to a stop beside me. I roll my neck to the right and meet storm-gray eyes underlined by a lazy smile. My heart cracks in two and I look away again, pretending to study the whiskey bottles lining the bar.

"Long time no see, Little P."

His nickname for me lights a match in the darkness beneath my rib cage. I hated it growing up. It felt condescending—made worse by the fact he's barely older than me. Only a couple years' difference in age, but we were always destined to be worlds apart.

I'd known Nico for as long as I could remember, but only by sight. He was the quiet, gangly kid that sat in the corner of the Visconti Grand Casino with a Diet Coke and a notepad. I'd learned from my mother that he was Alberto Visconti's nephew, and his father was the owner of the whiskey company in Devil's Hollow.

We first spoke in the coat room. I was ten, still growing used to the weight of the new four-leaf clover pendant around my neck. I'd started eating dinner between the racks of expensive coats, because I'd just learned the hard way that the men playing poker in the other room weren't really my friends.

Nico had crawled in beside me and stared at my reheated lasagna for what felt like minutes. Then he'd asked a quiet question. "Why have you started charging men a dollar to blow on their dice?"

I'd swallowed the real reason and told him what I desperately wanted to believe. "Because I'm lucky."

He'd held up the notepad that was always glued to his hand and tapped it with a thin finger. "Stupid people rely on chance; smart people know luck can be optimized by skill."

And then he opened his book and introduced me to the world of advantage gambling. "It's not cheating the house," he'd whispered. "It's using statistical probability and calculated observations to swing the odds of winning in your favor." He'd glanced toward the door as he spoke, and then leaned a little closer. "But still, you gotta promise not to tell anyone."

I didn't. For the next four years, we'd meet in the cloak room three times a week and practice card counting, edge sorting, and shuffle tracking, and I never told a soul.

Our routine was interrupted by the murder of my parents. Once the dust had settled and the police backed off, I grew restless with nights spent staring at the ceilings of guest bedrooms in foster homes, and started sneaking out to the casino. The first night I turned up, Nico asked me another simple question.

"Do you want to talk about it, or do you want to be distracted?"

I chose distraction, and that's when he taught me how to pick pockets. We graduated to bar tricks and distraction scams, and by the time I turned eighteen, the student was better than the master.

I breathe in a lungful of icy air and finally find the balls to look at Nico properly. Jesus. I knew he would look different, but not *this* different. His lanky frame has bulked and hardened into an imposing silhouette, and his childish grin has morphed into a handsome smile. He's transformed from a geek obsessed with numbers to a tattooed warning sign. Everything from his huge stature to the dragon breathing fire up his neck screams *danger, danger.*

It wasn't the three years at Stanford that did that to him, that's for sure.

"It's good to see you, Nico," I say with a small smile.

He nods, and then we wait in comfortable silence for the bartender. She looks up and lets the champagne bottle clatter to the counter top. "I'm so sorry, Mr. Visconti. What can I get you?"

"A Smugglers Club and a vodka with lemonade." He turns to me, brow cocked. "Unless you're more civilized these days?" I shake my head and he smiles. "Vodka and lemonade it is."

With a slight tremble, the bartender pours out a whiskey and fixes my vodka. She drops a wedge of lime in for good measure, and it reminds me of my mother, because that's what she'd do in the earlier days—add a wedge of lemon or lime or a sugar rim to her drinks to make her alcoholism look more sophisticated. She dropped the pretense pretty fast; by the end, she was slamming liquor straight from the bottle. I try not to think about my parents when I drink. If I changed my habits as a precaution, I'd have to admit I'm like them. And I am *nothing* like them.

"So." Nico slides my glass across the bar then leans his forearm against it. "What are you doing back here?"

My mouth opens to deliver the same bullshit excuse I gave to Matt. But Nico was like an older brother to me; I owe him more than that.

"Because you were right." His tight jaw disappears behind the rim of my glass as I take a big gulp.

When I turned eighteen and realized it was impossible to hold down a job without quitting or getting fired within training week, I decided to put everything I'd learned into practice and hit the tables in Cove. Blackjack was my game of choice, and card counting was always what I was best at. Of course, I avoided the Visconti Grand like the plague, but it took Nico no time at all to figure out what I was doing anyway. He was *livid*. Because although card counting isn't illegal, it's highly frowned upon in casinos. And in a Visconti casino? You might as well get on your knees and beg them to put a bullet in your head.

He was leaving town to study math at Stanford, and told me if I wanted to continue my antics, then I should do the same. He drove me to the bus station, handed me a brick of notes, and left me with a parting message.

"Remember, no matter how lucky you think you are, your sins will catch up with you eventually, Little P. They always do."

Now, Nico takes in the sea of guests over the top of my head. "Are you on the run?" he murmurs, just loud enough for me to hear.

"No." *Maybe.*

"Is anyone looking for you?"

"No." *Hope not.*

"Are you planning on hitting Cove now that you're back?"

This is the only 'no' I can say with confidence. "I'm going straight."

His eyes drop back to mine, a smirk playing on his lips. "Yeah?"

I nod. "I'm back at my apartment in Devil's Dip, and I'm looking for a regular job."

"Good idea. Cove's not safe right now, anyway. So do me a favor and avoid it all together, yeah?"

"Why?"

His attention drifts to behind my head again. This time, I follow his gaze and find Tor Visconti sitting on the back row of chairs, cell phone to his ear.

"Family drama."

I gulp my drink to squash the shiver rolling down my spine. Yeah, I don't want to know, not even just to be nosy. I've had enough drama in the last week to last me a lifetime.

We converse for a few more minutes, peeling back the layers of the last three years, when a sudden unease rolls through my body like a slow-moving tide. The anecdote I'm telling Nico trickles off. I'm all too aware, too *distracted*, by the cold shadow brushing the nape of my neck.

The moment I realized this wedding was polluted by the Viscontis, I knew it was only a matter of time before I had the misfortune to meet Raphael again. It's obviously the reason he's visiting the Coast. But still, even knowing it was inevitable, I'm not prepared for the way his voice drapes over my shoulders like a silk blanket.

"Nico, the ceremony is about to start, so I'm afraid I'll have to steal you away from your lady-friend here."

I swallow as the coldness shifts and then he's in my peripheral view. A hazy vision of navy, white, and gold. A satin-wrapped statue I don't have the balls to look at. Instead, I ignore both the thumping in my temples and the gaze blistering my cheek in favor of staring at my open-toed stilettos slowly sinking into the mud.

"But of course, it'd be rude of you not to introduce us first."

Introduce us? Annoyance creeps up my neck, itchy and hot. How does he not remember the girl who took a six-figure time-piece off his wrist less than twenty-four hours ago? The girl he chased with a *hammer?* Not only am I irritated, I realize I'm also partly offended. Stupid, really. But I thought about him all night, and yet, he clearly didn't think about me at all.

"Penny, Rafe. Rafe, Penny," Nico says lazily, swiping a limp hand between the two of us. He's leaning against the bar, once again distracted by something behind me.

I want to tell him we've already met, but then he'll ask how, and I don't think he'll take too kindly to finding out I swindled his cousin last night. Especially not *this* cousin. It doesn't pair well with me just telling him I've gone straight.

Unable to put it off any longer, I clench my molars together for courage and drag my attention upward. My eyes start at the shiniest pair of brown leather wingtips I've ever seen. They trail up the razor-sharp front fold of navy suit pants, climb the gold buttons of a waistcoat, and land on a gaze so intense it steals my next breath.

Holy fuck. Maybe it's because his edges are no longer softened by the liquor and mood-lighting, but his presence is even more imposing than I remember. Towering over me, he's a network of clean, straight lines, from the cut of his suit to the angle of his cheekbones and jaw. Every crease in his outfit is intentional; every jet-black hair on his head in its place.

Raphael Visconti is a picture of polished perfection. And something about that...well, it makes me feel out-of-sorts.

He smirks and an electric thrill crackles down my spine.

He remembers exactly who I am.

"It's a pleasure to meet you, *Penelope.*"

My cheeks grow hot at the sound of my full name. He's just been told my name is Penny, and yet he's assumed it's short for something. *Arrogant ass.* I refuse to correct him, because it feels like he'd be winning something if I did. Instead, I hold his stare and attempt to match his silky tone.

"The pleasure is all mine, *Raphael.*"

Triumph. It flickers in my chest as a slither of annoyance precedes his polite smile. It was fleeting, and if I'd have blinked, I'd have missed it.

I'm glad I didn't blink.

My high slips away the longer he holds my gaze. His stare is easy and unwavering, and yet the heat of it leaves me feeling like I'm running my hand under a warm tap. It grows hotter and hotter until I can't bear the burn and have to look away.

I turn my attention to Nico, partly to cool off and partly in the hope he'll save me.

"I've got to go," he grunts, swiping the whiskey glass off the bar. "Benny's about to catch a sexual harassment charge if he backs that server any farther into that corner." He stops beside me and squeezes my shoulder. "Let's catch up after the ceremony, Little P."

"Wait—"

But it's too late. I turn to watch as he slides through the crowd toward his older brother, and my stomach sinks like a deflating balloon. With that unrelenting stare still on my back, I know I have no choice but to grow a pair of lady-balls and turn around.

Raphael winks.

I scowl.

Then he pushes himself off the bar and takes a step forward. Before I can take one back, he slides his hand out of his pocket and reaches for the opening of my coat.

I hold my breath as he slowly sweeps one side of my coat open, revealing more of my blue dress underneath. His knuckles lightly graze against my rib cage through my thin dress, creating a crackle of electricity that contrasts with the blistering December chill now coasting over my hip.

I bite down a shiver and turn my attention back to his face, just in time to watch his gaze fall down the length of my body. His expression is indifferent, observant, like he's shopping for clothes and only stopped to look at me because I'm on sale, not because I'm his style.

Although, I'd bet every meager dime I have this man has never shopped the clearance rack in his life.

His eyes move back to mine, soft humor behind them. "Nice dress. Did you steal this one too?"

I blink. Then, coming back to my senses, I rip my coat from his hand and take a step back. "Yes," I snap. I mean, probably.

His dimples deepen, as if he's pleased with my answer. "Ah."

Burning with the desire to insult him back, I open my fat mouth before I can consider the implications of what's about to come out of it.

I nod to the Omega Seamaster on his wrist. "Nice watch. Would you like to lose that one too?"

"What? Sold my other one for crack, already?"

I—*what?*

His comeback is fast and unexpected, at odds with his buttery tone. Bewildered, I look around to see if any other wedding guests overheard, as if someone catching my eye and raising their eyebrows will confirm I didn't imagine his rude retort. But there's nothing but curious glances and whispers over crystal tumblers.

Before I have the semblance to think of a comeback, he turns toward the bar and rests his forearms against it. I don't know why I do it—perhaps I'm a glutton for punishment, or perhaps I like role playing as a kicked puppy—but I slip in beside him.

"Amanda, allow me."

I tear my gaze from his profile long enough to realize the bar girl is *still* struggling with the champagne bottle. She freezes, turns scarlet, and reluctantly hands it to Rafe.

"First of all, you need to remove the foil." To my surprise, he brings the lip of the bottle to his mouth and *rips the foil off with his teeth.* Christ. Something hot and primal flares between my thighs. I will every inch of my face not to show it. "Grip the top"—he wraps a large hand around the neck of the bottle, and places the other halfway down— "and the *trick,* Amanda, is to twist the body, not the cork."

A tendon in his large, tanned hand flexes. The *pop* is as sophisticated as he is.

A little hiss of air escapes my lips as he gently runs the cork around the brim, settling the gas fizzing out of it. He hands the bottle back to the bartender, who mutters something incoherent.

"Amanda?"

She looks up, her near-pained expression silently conveying, *haven't you tortured me enough?*

With a roll of his wrist, Rafe presents the cork between his middle and forefinger. "Always open it away from your face. These things can take an eye out." He cocks his head. "And with eyes like yours, that'd be a travesty, wouldn't it?"

He tosses the cork in the air, catches it, then slips it into his pocket.

Jesus Christ. This man is smoother than a freshly waxed floor.

He takes a lazy sip of whiskey and checks his watch over the rim. Then, as if he can hear my pulse thumping and he wonders where the noise is coming from, his eyes come my way. They run over my hair and down the parting of my coat, before stopping at my open-toed stilettos.

His lips tilt in amusement, because even this asshole knows it's stupid to wear open-toed heels this close to Christmas. As his gaze comes back up to mine, he rakes his teeth over his bottom lip.

"It was a pleasure, *Penelope.*"

A little lightheaded from the *pop*, and pissed off with myself for suddenly having a spine made of jelly, I swipe my drink off the bar and harden my glare. "Sure, let's do this again sometime."

He smiles tightly at my sarcasm and runs a large hand down the front of his waistcoat as his gaze coasts over my head and to the wedding guests around us. With a subtle glance back at Amanda, who's now pouring champagne into flutes with shaky hands, he curls his forefinger toward his chest.

I stare at it in disbelief.

Surely not. Surely, he's not *beckoning* me?

Anger flares up inside me like a nasty rash. I'm not one of his fucking maids, nor one of the suit-clad minions he summons with a flick of his wrist.

I open my mouth to tell him so, but when our eyes clash, my protest evaporates. His sea-green gaze flickers with something dark and alluring. Something that appeals to the weak-willed space between my thighs. My brain is too foggy from alcohol and velvet-clad insults to put a name to his expression, but I know, without a doubt, it's tailor-made for me.

Despite the feminist urge to kick him in the groin, I find I'm taking a step forward, and I give in to his gravitational pull. Once in his orbit, his warmth and soft scent of soap, cologne, and mint wash over me, sweeping away my next breath. Heart colliding with my rib cage, I squeeze my hands into fists and focus on the gold-tipped bow tie around the thick trunk of his throat. Which is perfectly shaved, of course. I'm not brave enough to look up, because I'm far too close to survive eye contact that intense. I stiffen as he stoops, and when his hard jaw grazes mine, it makes me headier than any liquor could. Then his deep voice vibrates gently against my earlobe.

"I'd rather shut my dick in a car door than do this again some time, *Penelope*."

A cool rush of air caresses my neck as he returns to his full height.

What?

Stupefied and shaken, all I can do is watch as his imposing silhouette slips through the crowd without so much as a glance back.

I stand there for a few minutes, trying to regain control of my pulse. As semblance returns to me, it brings a wicked thrill. It feels like I've just uncovered a deep, dark secret.

Raphael Visconti may look like a gentleman, may talk like a gentleman.

But he is anything *but* a gentleman.

CHAPTER
Five

Penny

M ARRIAGE IS A CRAZY gamble when you think about it. You're betting half of everything you own that you'll stay with that person for the rest of your life. How can anyone be so sure?

Rory looks sure.

Sitting a few rows from the back with Matt by my side, I watch Rory work through her vows, partly in disbelief she's marrying the eldest Devil's Dip brother, and partly in awe, because she looks so beautiful. She's a vision in white, although not dressed like a typical bride. Her dress is sleek and simple, most of it hidden by a huge puffer jacket. And when she tip-toes to brush a strand of hair from her soon-to-be husband's face, I swear I catch a glimpse of a Nike sneaker.

The moment I realized it was Angelo Visconti standing at the top of the aisle, my heart grew heavy with dread. It turns out Rory isn't marrying just any Visconti, but the one with the most ominous nickname: Vicious.

Oddly enough, Angelo is at the epicenter of one of my most visceral childhood memories. To this day I still don't know why, but I remember my father dragging me to Alonso and Maria Visconti's joint funeral when I was eleven. He woke me up before the sun, tugged a pink jumper over my head, and drove us up to the church on the cliff. He gave me a Thermos of hot cocoa and swigged something stronger himself. And then, along with other locals in bright clothes, we watched from the bus shelter across the road as the Devil's Dip brothers buried their parents.

At some point, Angelo Visconti looked our way, and he clearly didn't like the drunken, shit-eating smirk on my father's face.

So he pulled out a gun.

A shiver racks my body at the memory.

"The offer of socks still stands," Matt whispers in my ear.

"I bet you have the smelliest feet on the planet," I mutter back. I smirk at his chuckle and turn my attention back to the front.

Until the bride walked down the aisle, I'd been ninety-nine percent certain this marriage wasn't consensual. But then Angelo slipped his hands around Rory's waist and murmured something against her forehead, and the way she laughed was so sweet it gave me a toothache. Now, as Angelo repeats his vows, another part of my body aches.

He speaks low and soft, as if he doesn't give a flying fuck that nobody aside from Rory can hear his oath. The way he looks at her confirms this. It's like she's the only person in the Reserve, in the *world*, and if this were the case for the rest of his life, then he'd be perfectly content with that.

I bring my hand to my chest, reminding my heart of the jaded monologue I spewed to Matt earlier. *Love is a trap.* I can't help but wonder, though; would a few years of ignorant bliss really be worse than never feeling bliss at all?

"And for the moment we've all been waiting for, ladies and gentleman." The officiant looks up from his iPad and pauses for dramatic effect. "You may now kiss the bride."

In a sea of cheers and hollers, Angelo's hand finds the nape of Rory's neck and his smirk melts against her lips. Their kiss is so intense, so *hot*, that I feel like I'm watching it through a hidden webcam in their bedroom. With discomfort prickling my cheeks, I shift in my seat and cut my gaze to the right.

To the side of the arbor, I find a pair of eyes already on me, full of green enchantment that makes the noise around me fade as if it's coming from a neighbor's house. I'm pulled in for less than half a second before I glance away, weakened by the silk venom he'd injected into my ear earlier. Catching myself, I look back almost immediately, but it's too late. He swipes a thumb over his triumphant smirk and turns to mutter something in Nico's ear.

Why does it feel like I've just lost a game I didn't know we were playing?

Why did I step toward him when he beckoned me?

Squeezing my hands into fists, I rise and push against the tide rushing toward the newlyweds. As much as I'd love to congratulate Rory on her marriage right now, heading toward the arbor would mean heading toward Raphael Visconti, and I'd rather not be within a five-meter radius of his orbit.

Because at the bar, I clearly had trouble resisting its gravitational pull.

Despite smiling and laughing in all the right places during the ceremony, I spent a lot of time rifling through the darkest depths of my brain in an attempt to locate Raphael in my childhood memories.

I don't understand how I barely remember him. Not even from his parents' funeral. He's not exactly...*unmemorable.* Of course, I was young, and he would have been in his mid-twenties—even older than I am now. I remember Angelo because nobody forgets a face behind a gun, and I remember Gabe, their youngest brother, because who the fuck could say they don't remember Gabe?

As tuxedos and satin brush past my shoulders, I steal a glance back at Gabe and immediately wish I hadn't. Christ, he truly is something from a nightmare. He's even taller and broader than his brothers, and ink spills out unapologetically from underneath every hem, collar, and cuff of his suit. He doesn't smile, not even at his brother's wedding. I guess I wouldn't smile either if I had a scar running from my eyebrow to my chin.

I shudder and step out into the aisle. I'll head to the bar, grab Matt and me a drink, and wait until the crowd thins to extend my—

"Penny!" The wind carries a feminine trill to my ears, and I turn around to see Rory squeezing through bodies to get to me. We lock eyes and she breaks into a huge grin. "I thought it was you. I'd recognize that red hair anywhere."

I bring her in for a warm hug, breathing in her sweet scent. "You look so beautiful! Congratulations on your wedding."

"Yeah, yeah, thank you." She's breathless and the lazy swipe of her hand suggests she's had this conversation a million times today. "Anyway, I had no idea you were back on the Coast. I'd have invited you if I did!" She peers around curiously. "Who are you here with, anyway?"

"Matt Collins." Rory knows Matt from school, and he also used to help her father around the Preserve with odd jobs, like litter picking and refilling bird feeders. When a devilish smile spreads across her lips, I roll my eyes. "He's my neighbor, don't get the wrong idea."

"Matt's super nice, so maybe it's the *right* idea."

I laugh, not bothered to burden her with the fact I'm here as a stand-in until Matt's crush finally notices him. "How about you focus on your own love story today? You can worry about someone else's tomorrow."

Her eyes sparkle as they shift over my shoulder. I follow her gaze and find Angelo Visconti staring at her adoringly. "Not tomorrow," she murmurs, flashing him a shy grin. "Tomorrow, we'll be on our way to Fiji for our honeymoon." She drags her attention back to me. "I'll be back in two weeks. Will you still be here?"

It depends on whether I can find a job here. On whether my sins stay in Atlantic City, or seep across state lines. Of course, I don't burden the bride with this. "Sure," I say brightly.

"Then we must catch up properly when I'm back. I'm really excited to hear what you're up to these days." She looks up at me through thick, false lashes, and the hollow of my chest fills up with warmth. Rory's always been so nice, and she truly deserves all the happiness in the world.

I just hope a Visconti can give it to her.

"Aurora!" a voice shoots out from the crowds. Rory's lids flutter shut, then she gives an apologetic smile. "I better make the rounds. Hopefully I'll catch you on the dance floor later?"

She kisses my cheek and then floats away.

Before she can get out of arm's reach, I quickly reach out and grab her upper arm. "What does it feel like?"

She blinks. "What?"

"To be in love?"

I barely believe in it, so I have no idea why I feel compelled to ask the question. Morbid curiosity, perhaps. Like a man asking a woman what it feels like to give birth; it's an insight to something he'll never experience.

Surprisingly, Rory doesn't give me a one-word answer. She drags her eyes up to the darkening sky and chews on her bottom lip.

"It feels like your heart is walking outside of your body." Her gaze finds Angelo's again, and I watch in fascination as a pink flush creeps from underneath her necklace. "My heart now wears Armani and has a Glock for every day of the week."

My fingers slide off her puffer jacket and she slips away.

CHAPTER
Six

Penny

"WE'RE FRIENDS, RIGHT?"
I SHOVE the chocolate lava cake out of my fork's reach and cradle my stomach. It's the final dish of an eight-course dinner, and if I eat another mouthful, the zipper on my dress is going to give up trying.

"Sure." Matt says it in a dull tone that suggests he hasn't heard a word I've said. He's too busy staring at his crush, who I now know to be called Anna. She's sitting three tables down with a group of friends, and none of them have touched a single course. "Okay, how about this. When she goes to the bathroom, you go too. And then pretend to be on the phone and talk about how big my cock is or something."

I give him a few seconds to smile or laugh, *anything* that shows he's joking. It doesn't come.

"Do you think that'll get you the girl?"

His gaze slants. "Girls like big dicks, right?"

"Jesus Christ, Matt." I tug the cake toward me again. Just one more bite. "Why don't you just go and talk to her?"

"Have you smacked your head? She'll think I'm a weirdo."

I choose another mouthful of gooey goodness over pointing out the obvious. Chocolate tastes better than the truth. Hell, sometimes rat poison tastes better than the truth.

Darkness arrived somewhere between the scallops and the lamb: now tiki torches, red heat lamps, and the warmth of a love story cast a hazy glow over the clearing. The low, easy beat of the mini orchestra has picked up tempo and introduced a saxophone. As shiny stilettos move onto the dance floor and reluctant leather loafers follow, the night crackles with a good time.

A server refills my champagne. I turn to thank him, but my eyes are drawn to a dark figure over his shoulder. Raphael Visconti is leaning against the bar, yet *another* woman buzzing around him like a fly on shit. They've been coming and going all evening—different dresses, different hairstyles, but the same bone-cringing behavior.

Like all the women before her, her gestures are large and her laugh is loud. In contrast, Raphael is still and suave. He cocks his head to listen to her monologue; runs a thumb over a well-mannered smile.

Raphael Visconti is the perfect gentleman.

He's also the perfect liar.

The word *liar* buzzes on the tip of my tongue like sour candy. Call it instinct, or call it common sense; my gut knows that gentlemanly act is nothing but smoke and mirrors.

As if he can suddenly feel the venom in my thoughts, Raphael's gaze lifts up from the floor and locks onto mine. It flashes with dark amusement, and the way he says *Penelope*, by stretching out all four vowels in a cashmere drawl, whispers in the wind.

Heart racing, I spin around in my chair in an attempt to save face. I've *really* got to stop looking at him, because he'll start to think I'm jealous, or something. And I'm *definitely* not jealous.

I focus on a couple doing a drunk waltz on the dance floor. "Hey"—I kick Matt under the table to get his attention—"tell me what you know about Raphael Visconti. Asshole, right?"

He frowns, then glances over my shoulder. I know he sees a handsome man talking to a woman under a romantic glow, because his face melts into a shit-eating grin. "You gonna try your luck?"

"No." I pop the top button of my coat and Matt's gaze drops to the opening.

"Thought you were cold?"

I swat him with my purse. "Answer the question. Tell me what you know about Raphael Visconti, or else I'll tell Anna you've got crabs."

My threat doesn't dent his glee, because he parrots my earlier advice in a squeaky voice, which I assume is meant to mimic mine. "Why don't you just go and talk to him?"

I don't know why I didn't tell Matt about Rafe's rudeness earlier. I guess it's for the same reason I didn't tell Nico about us having met before; I'd then have to explain the whole swindling thing. Matt doesn't know anything about that, and as my only friend on the Coast, I'm going to keep it that way.

Besides, for some odd reason, I like being the only one to know Raphael's secret.

Before I can tell my friend I'd rather jump off the top of Devil's Dip cliff when the tide is out, the scrape of a chair makes his head snap to a ninety-degree angle. Both our eyes trail Anna as she gets to her feet, smooths down her dress, and totters in heeled boots over the dance floor toward the bar.

I can't explain why my throat gets tighter with every sultry sway of her hip.

Matt's tone drops the humor and picks up panic. "No, seriously. Go talk to him."

As if timed to precision, Anna slips into the gap beside Raphael, half a second after the other girl vacates it.

My hand curls into a fist around a chocolate-stained napkin. "Why? Worried he'll steal your girl?"

"Of course I'm worried, fucking *look* at him." Reluctantly, I do, and at the most unfortunate time. Something Anna said was funny, apparently, because he tilts his head up to the twinkling veranda and *laughs*. Not just a polite laugh either, but the type that comes from deep within the hard walls of his stomach. The type that's hard to fake.

I suppose he's a better liar than I thought, because for a crazy second, I almost believe it.

Jesus, I must be drunk.

"You didn't answer my question. He's an asshole, right?"

Matt looks surprised. "Rafe? An asshole? Hell no. As much as I'd like to say he's a dickhead, because a man *that* good-looking needs some flaws, he's not. His scholarship program pays for a hundred disadvantaged kids to get a full ride to Devil's Coast Academy every year. He funds the hospital's Make a Wish foundation, and remember when that weird blizzard blew through Dip four years ago?" Reluctantly, I nod. "He paid for all of the repairs and damages out of pocket. Must have cost him *millions*. He's a good guy, unlike some of the other Viscontis..."

I follow his pointed gaze to the other end of the bar, where Benny is attempting to impress a blond by pouring butane fluid from his Zippo into the palm of his hand. He makes a fist, holds the lighter underneath it, and then he *blows*.

Matt barks out a curse word as a fireball lights up the night sky, its vicious flames dancing way too close to the girl's eyebrows for comfort.

"What about that? Does arson get girls?" he mutters, tone laced with sarcasm.

A sharp gust of wind brings over a loud laugh, wiping the humor clean off my lips. Matt leans closer, nudging me with his thigh, and like two heads of the same snake, we glare as Anna giggles and coos over something Raphael says. The laugh shakes her lithe silhouette so violently that she staggers backward, and when Raphael's arm slides around her waist to steady her, we both hiss like snakes, too.

I bury mine under another mouthful of chocolate cake.

"I'm actually *begging* you now. Please go break them up."

"Not a chance."

"Just ask him for a dance—"

"There's no way in hell—"

"I'll give you a hundred bucks."

The offer gives me pause. I mean, I'm very fucking broke right now. *Eating ramen that's been sitting in my cupboard for over three years* kind of broke.

Last night, as I inhaled the tangy leather strap of Raphael's watch, I was high off the dollar signs. But now I've come back to earth and realized I'll probably have to leave the Coast to sell a Visconti watch, because the chances of a pawnbroker risking their life to accept it here is next-to-none. And who knows when I'll land a job?

"Make it two hundred."

"Aw, come on. I'm a teacher."

"Boo-hoo," I snap back. "You teach in a school with a forty-grand a year attendance fee. You're not exactly scraping pennies together to buy your own Crayolas, are you?"

Matt pauses. "Fine. One-seven-five."

"One-seven-five and you get rid of your welcome mat."

"Dammit. Two hundred and I keep it."

"Deal."

We seal it with a handshake, but the *triumph* skating down my spine is followed by thick, sticky dread. Typical. I was too blinded by the money to see the task at hand, and now I have to go over to Raphael Visconti, *voluntarily*, and strike up a conversation with him. The man who specifically told me he'd rather slam his cock into the door of an automobile before he talks to me again.

Matt's loafer nudges my ankle. "*Move.*"

"Shut up, I'm going," I hiss. I empty my champagne flute in three gulps, partly to drown out the butterflies that have no business loitering in my stomach, and partly to give me an excuse to head to the bar.

The table breathes as I rise to my feet. Fuck, I've drunk too much too quickly and I don't know why. It's not like I need liquid courage, because I have *luck*.

Luck. Right. I'd forgotten about my luck.

Rolling my shoulders back, I touch the four-leaf clover around my neck and shake off the nervous energy. He's just a man, for God's sake. And this is just a paid gig.

With a fresh wave of confidence, I stroll toward the bar, my eyes trained on my target. Maybe he can hear the determined stomp of my heels heading his way, or maybe he's developed a sixth-sense for trouble overnight, but his eyes slide up from his glass as I approach. Even back-lit by the bright lights of the bar, I can see his gaze roll over my black heels, up the parting of my coat, and come to mine. Something within it flickers to life, and strangely, I feel it in my own pulse.

Anna's anecdote dissolves on my arrival, and her lust-filled expression hardens into something that would scald me if it were tangible. She's unnervingly beautiful. Midnight-black hair, feline features, and a body I'm sure makes anyone with eyes do a double-take.

"So sorry, babe. Do you mind?"

She stares at me. "Mind what?"

"If I steal Raphael for a few minutes."

She shows no signs of moving, until Raphael's silky tone slices through the tension.

"It was great to catch up, Anna."

A heady thrill zaps through my body like an electric current. Even an idiot could take the hint, and Anna stalks off. I've definitely made a new enemy on the Coast, which is a shame, because

I'd like to have made friends first, but I'll worry about that later. Right now, I'm too focused on trying to pretend I can't feel the crackle of Rafe's presence as I order a drink.

"You know; I'm starting to think you have a crush on me."

My jaw tightens, and I keep my eyes trained on the bartender's swooshing ponytail as she fixes my vodka and lemonade. "What on earth would give you that idea?"

"Because you can't seem to leave me alone."

Irritation, embarrassment, and something more *vibrant*, tingle in my face like pins and needles. It's ridiculous, I know, but knowing there's no way he talks to other women like this makes a thrill buzz under my skin.

Pathetic. Because of course he talks like this to me—I stole his fucking watch.

"Or maybe I just want to see you shut your dick in a car door."

"Or maybe you just want to see my dick."

I freeze, then snap my head around to glare at him. When I allow a beat of stunned silence to pass, Raphael's lips tilt before disappearing behind a lazy sip of whiskey. He thinks he's *won*. My cheeks grow hotter than the heat lamp above my head, and I let out a sardonic laugh.

"Odd. Everyone seems to think you're quite the gentleman, but talking about your dick so much isn't exactly a gentlemanly habit."

The only thing that moves is the muscle flexing against his jaw. And then with the same reluctance one has when getting out of bed in the morning he drags his gaze to mine.

"And you? What do you think?"

"I think I'm not so easily fooled."

His eyes fall to my lips, a slow, devilish smirk spreading across his own. Although his smile is cold, it creates a warmth in my core, which drifts like a summer breeze between my legs.

"And you, Penelope? Are you a lady?"

I don't like the mocking edge to his tone. The silk marred with sarcasm gets my back up. I tilt my chin and harden my stare. "Yes."

He runs a hand across his face, wiping off a hint of amusement. "Ah."

"Ah *what*?"

"I'm not so easily fooled, either."

His tone is low and soft, as if designed for my ears only. A nervous energy rolls over the planes of my shoulders, and I press my palms onto the bar to bear the brunt of it. Of course he doesn't think I'm a lady. I'm *not*. No lady wears dresses with the security tags still on, nor do they make a living by tricking men out of watches on a Thursday night.

I let out a shaky huff of breath and Raphael's gaze narrows on the puff of condensation floating between us. "What was it you wanted, again? To play another of your tacky games?"

"If you're brave enough."

I don't know why I say it—I've gone straight—but it's out of my mouth before I can stop it. A knee-jerk reaction to an insult, I suppose, embedded deep within me like the rest of my flaws.

"No."

Raphael's tone is clipped and punctuated with a sip of whiskey. He turns his attention to the space above my head, as if looking for someone else, *anyone else*, to talk to.

He's given me an easy out, but I'm too proud to take it. "Scared you'll lose again?"

"What makes you so certain you'll win?" he drawls, amusement softening his edges again.

"Because I'm lucky."

His smile holds its shape, but I don't miss the ripple of displeasure that passes through his gaze like an undercurrent. Three heavy beats of silence pass. He scratches his throat and glances up to the starless sky as he sinks the last of his whiskey. With a sharp flick of his wrist, he slides the empty tumbler across the bar and basks me in the warmth of his attention.

"Do you have a game in mind?"

"Yes." *Nope.* But if three years of doing this dance have taught me anything, it's that you have to be the one in control. If I allow him to choose a game, my odds of losing increase a hundredfold.

I take a slow sip of my drink, buying the time to rake through my mental list of bar games. It takes longer than usual, because it's hard to concentrate over the voice screaming at me to walk away. Just like the quiz, it needs to be something safe, rather than flat-out cheating. I select one from my roster and place my glass on the bar with a satisfactory thud.

"Ready?"

Raphael holds up a palm. "We haven't settled on a wager."

"If I win, I get that watch, too." I nod to the Seamaster on his wrist. The thought of conning *Raphael Visconti* out of *two* of his timepieces makes my mouth water.

"And if I win?"

The sudden thickness to his tone raises the hairs on the back of my neck. I glance up from his wrist to his face and immediately wish I hadn't. I wasn't prepared for the danger that dances between the walls of his irises.

I swallow the lump in my throat, suddenly all too aware of my nipples tightening under the thin fabric of my bra. *He's only a man. He's only a man. He's only a man.*

"Well, what do you want?" I whisper.

He holds my eye for a beat too long. He licks his lips, and the tiniest glimmer of something *very* ungentlemanly passes through his green gaze. Just when I feel like the tension might suffocate me, he gives a small shake of his head. "For you to leave."

I blink. "What?"

He smirks at my surprise. "I'd like to enjoy my brother's wedding in peace, without you nipping at my heels." His eyes land on something behind me, and he lets out a wry breath. "Somehow, I don't think your date will mind."

I follow his eye line to Matt. Within the last five minutes, he's somehow managed to grow a pair of balls and move to Anna's table. He sits opposite her, sandwiched between two friends, and is staring at her with the intensity of a serial killer. I glance back at our own table and see four empty shot glasses neatly lined up on his place setting.

Figures.

"Deal," I say breezily. Fuck it, I'm not going to see him after tonight. He'll hop back on his private jet and return to Vegas, then maybe make an appearance around Easter, or something. I'll be long gone by then—hopefully.

One more swindle. Just one...and then I'll go straight like I said I would.

I order two large glasses of water, then look up at Raphael from under my false lashes. "What's your favorite drink?"

"Whiskey, of course," he says, amused.

I nod to the bartender. "Three shots of Sambuca, please."

My cheek warms under his soft chuckle. It's delicious and easy and I suddenly understand why women laugh so loudly around him.

"Okay." I line the two waters in front of me, then place the three Sambuca shots in front of him. "I bet you I can drink these two huge glasses of water before you can drink those three shots."

Raphael palms his jaw, his narrowed gaze sizing up my water and his shots. "There's no way you can do that. What's the catch?"

"All I ask is for a head start. It's a hell of a lot of liquid, isn't it?"

Suspicion sparks in his eyes. "How much of a head start?"

"Um, let's say, one glass?"

He considers it for a few seconds, then shrugs. "Seems fair. Rules?"

"Just one: no touching each other's glasses—you know, knocking them over or removing them. Ready for me to start?"

Watching me carefully, he nods.

I gulp my first glass of water in quick, easy chugs. I love this game for two reasons. The first is that slamming all this water is a great way to dodge a hangover. The second is that it's such a simple trick, yet nobody ever figures it out.

The head-start frees up one of my glasses, and the second Raphael starts drinking, I'll put the glass upside down on one of his shots. He won't be allowed to move my glass as per the no-touching rule, and I'll happily sip the second glass of water with a smug smirk on my lips and a new six-figure timepiece on my wrist.

Wiping my hand over the back of my mouth, I set down the empty glass and turn to Raphael. "Thanks for the head start," I say sweetly.

"Anytime."

"Ready?"

His gaze sparks. Staring at my wet bottom lip, he nods slowly.

But what he does next is much faster. It's so smooth and efficient that my liquor-fueled brain takes a while to catch up. He pushes all three of his shot glasses together, so their combined circumference is bigger than the rim of my empty glass. Before I can reach for my water in a last-ditch attempt to win this game fairly—impossible, of course—there's a flash of metal, a clunk and a *plop*, and then I'm staring at a gun submerged in water.

My water. His gun.

My pulse leaps in my throat and I stagger backward. As I stare at the weapon, with its barrel bobbing among the ice cubes and its grip resting on the rim I was about to put my lips on, everything in my peripheral dims.

I've been this close to a gun twice in my life. The first time, it was lifting up the hem of my dress in a dark alleyway, and the second, it was pressed against my temple.

Hiss. Click.

Do you know how lucky you are, kid? You're one in a million.

The jaunty sound of the orchestra fades and my heart grows louder. Its beat resonates in the hollow of my chest under a cloak of numbness.

I couldn't move if I tried.

The gun moves in a flash of citrine and silk. I regain enough composure to follow the weapon as Raphael pulls it out of the glass and wipes it down with his pocket square. His suit jacket swishes open, and, just like that, the threat is gone, disappearing behind the velvet-clad curtain.

He rests a forearm against the bar and diverts his attention to something on the horizon.

When he speaks, there's a calmness in his voice that does little to thaw the ice in my blood.

"You see the issue with luck, Penelope, is that it has an awful habit of disappearing when you lean on it." His dice cufflink winks at me as he sinks a shot. "You should consider relying on something a little sturdier." Another shot, another thud. "Like intelligence, or knowledge." His gaze drops to my lips. "Or, if you don't have either of those, perhaps that beautiful face of yours." He slams the last shot glass onto the bar and wipes his smirk away with the back of his hand, before sauntering forward until he's shoulder-to-shoulder with me.

I try to ignore how the heat of his arm burns through my coat, or how the fiery licorice scent of his breath taunts my loss. Instead, I focus on the liquor wall behind the bar, trying to control my breathing.

He stoops low, his sharp, cold cheek caressing mine. "The exit is to your right." Then he slides a large hand around my wrist. It's hot and dominant and, I *swear*, I can practically hear my skin sizzle where he grips me.

I swap trying to control my breathing in favor of not breathing at all.

"Be careful in the woods, Penelope." His grip slips from my wrist, and his fingertips burn a slow trail down the length of my palm, before releasing me. "Bad things hide where you can't see them."

And then he's gone, camouflaging himself among the sea of suits.

I don't hang around. Although struggling to remain calm, autopilot takes control of my body, and I spin on my heels and snatch my purse up from the table. I can't bring myself to look at Matt, and I hope he doesn't notice me leaving, either.

Breaking into a half-run, I disappear between the trees and into the shadows. The security thins and the brush thickens, until the darkness is all-consuming. The lively timbre of the orchestra finally melts away, and the silence is an eerie reminder I'm all alone.

My groan slices through it, painting the night gray.

I've been lucky since the night that lady stepped out into the alleyway and gave me her necklace. Lucky to the point where it's practically my only personality trait. I was worried it had left me when I got caught in Atlantic City, but I chalked it up to being a stroke of misfortune. After all, I was lucky enough to make it back to the Coast with all the money I had left, and then secure a six-figure watch on the same night.

But maybe that was another stroke of misfortune too, because it led me to Raphael Visconti.

I've picked up pace without even realizing it. My lungs burn and my eyes prickle with tears I'm too stubborn to shed. As I brush my fingers over the rough bark of one tree and reach out for another, my foot catches on a root, rolling my ankle underneath me.

"Fuck," I hiss out into the darkness.

How terribly unlucky of me.

Ankle screaming in agony, I hobble on. I don't stop, not until the trees thin and a hazy orange glow cuts through the clearing. A few seconds later, a lone street lamp comes into view, and the ground hardens underneath my muddy stilettos. Now that I can see what I'm walking on, I pop off my heels and start a shaky descent down the steep hill, staying close to the edge of the winding road that leads back to the main town. When my feet get sore, I put my heels back on, which is a dubious improvement.

As the adrenaline coursing through my veins drops from a buzz to a quiet hum, it makes room for another feeling: unease.

Your sins will catch up with you eventually, Little P. They always do.

Nico's words whisper at the back of my brain like a memory I'm trying to suppress. Maybe they had a deeper meaning, one even he wasn't aware of. Maybe sinners don't get to be lucky. Maybe, good luck happens to good people, and bad luck to bad people.

I haven't been good since I was ten. Why *should* I be lucky? What have I done to receive good luck in this life, aside from swindle people and cheat them out of their money?

I'm so lost in the swamp of my own thoughts that I don't realize I've missed the turn onto Main Street until a gust of salty air slaps me around the face.

I'm at the port. My teeth chatter as I sweep my gaze over the sudden clearing. Despite the time, it's a hubbub of activity. In the foreground, trucks beep and reflective jackets wink in their headlights, and behind them, cargo ships bob and jerk over the rough waves of the Pacific.

My gaze drops to my shoes. They're caked in slushy mud and I can't feel my toes. The thought of trotting back up the cliff to my apartment makes me groan aloud, so I decide to rest against a stocky admin building for a few minutes.

I drop my head against the brickwork, emotion choking my throat as I watch men work. I'm not typically an emotional person, but I *do* tend to get a little teary when I'm tired.

I need someone to talk to.

I need a friend.

Fishing my burner from my purse, with frozen fingertips I dial the only number I know off the top of my head.

The line rings three times, then the voicemail clicks in.

"You have reached Sinners Anonymous, please leave your sin after the tone."

I inhale a lungful of air; exhale it against the starless sky.

"Hey, me again. I know, I know. Two calls in less than twenty-four hours. Crazy, considering you haven't heard from me in three years, right?"

I sniffle to nothing but static, blinking back tears. I open my mouth but close it again, realizing I don't want my oldest and only friend to think I'm an idiot. Yeah, even if it's only an automated hotline. Sighing, I stab *End* and drop my cell back in my purse.

"If this is karma for what I did to the Hurricane casino, then just give me a sign," I mutter to the universe.

A sudden bright light passes over my face. I squint and cup a hand over my eyes, studying a large truck approaching the transit shed, its headlights on full-beam.

A beer-bellied trucker hops out of the cab and a port worker emerges from the transit shed, radio in one hand, clipboard in the other. Their conversation is peppered with confused glances at clipboards and lazy sips from insulated mugs.

Eventually, the worker claps the trucker on the shoulder and turns in my direction. The truck's headlights glow like an aura behind him.

That's the last thing I remember before the scalding heat and the deafening boom. The last thing I see before the night's sky lights up orange, and then my world bleeds to black.

There's my sign, I suppose.

CHAPTER
Seven

Rafe

W HISKEY UNDER THE ROCKS, Devil's Hollow.
Tension drips off the craggy ceiling, and underneath it, made men plot revenge against one of their own.

Voices are low and expressions are somber. Leaning against the bar gives me a view of the club through a wide-angle lens, and I drink it all in over the rim of my low-ball glass.

"What do you call a nightclub full of quiet Viscontis?"

My gaze skims left, where Castiel, my oldest cousin and soon-to-be capo of Devil's Hollow—if Uncle Alonso ever fucking checks out—is pouring out two fingers of whiskey.

I cock my head and consider the punchline. "No idea."

"Me either. Never seen it before."

He smirks and I huff out a sardonic laugh. I down the rest of my whiskey in one, but before I slam the glass against the bar, he grabs it from my hand.

"Easy there, *cugino*," he drawls. "This bar top is African Black-wood. Just had it fitted last week."

My eyes fall to his ring-clad hand caressing the wood grain. "If you touched your woman like that, she might not be sitting in the corner swiping right on every man on Tinder."

We both look up at Alyona. She's the long-legged heiress to Russia's largest vodka distillery and Cas's unwilling fiancée. By the way he's glaring at her, I don't doubt the feeling is mutual. She sits crossed-legged in a velvet booth with a face like a spanked ass, eyes glued to her cell. Sure enough, her thumb is working overtime.

Cas grunts and refills my glass with Smugglers Club whiskey. Sometimes, I wonder if being the CEO of the company means he ever gets sick of drinking it. He gently slides a napkin across the bar and places my glass on top of it, before bringing his to his own lips. "I wish Dante would have given me a heads up he was going to blow up the port tonight," he mutters into the amber liquid. "I'd have dropped her slap-bang in the middle of it."

"Such a hopeless romantic."

"I'll leave that title to Vicious." His cell vibrates in his pocket. After pulling it out, he glances at the screen and strides away with it to his ear.

I swipe my fresh drink and regard my brother Angelo and his new wife with the same level of interest one has when watching a David Attenborough documentary. They're standing in the center of the room, oblivious to the tense conversations being had around them. Angelo's hands are cupped tightly around Rory's jaw as he murmurs something for her ears only. His dinner jacket is slung over her shoulders, concealing most of her wedding dress.

Mild amusement prickles at my skin. Angelo's nickname isn't Vicious for nothing. He's forcing a calm exterior for his wife's sake, but the vein thumping in his left temple tells me he's going to slip away to an empty room at the first opportunity and rip apart everything in sight.

His temper is, and always has been, like a gas leak. Bring a small flame near him and he explodes, seemingly out of nowhere.

Sometimes, I wonder if he really did go straight for nine years, or if it was a long fever dream on my part.

I'd like to say he returned to the Cosa Nostra and finally claimed his rightful role as the capo of Devil's Dip because he came to his senses, but it was actually because he lost his fucking mind.

Long story short, he wanted Uncle Alberto's twenty-one-year-old fiancée, and when he didn't immediately hand her over on a silver platter, he popped a bullet in the old man's head and started a war with his eldest son and successor, Dante.

I knew Dante was a cunt the moment he cheated at one of my poker nights, but I didn't realize he was lobotomized, too. He blew up the Devil's Dip port, which all three Visconti outfits, including his own, run their businesses out of.

Angelo and Rory break into a game of tongue tennis, and I'd rather pop my eyeballs out than watch the match. So, I shift my gaze to Gabe, our youngest brother and newly appointed *consigliere* of the Devil's Dip outfit. He's sitting at a poker table with three of his most-trusted *soldati*. Like Angelo, he's calm in appearance, but his gaze is lit like a live wire.

My brother is a mystery, and despite being as thick as thieves growing up, all I know about him now is that he has a constant hard-on for violence and a hatred for sharp tailoring. I've probably seen him in a suit twice in my life: today at Angelo's wedding, and nine years ago at our parents' funeral. As he grunts orders at his men, he twists his bow tie around his fists, like he's weighing up who he should strangle with it.

He suddenly stabs the map on the table with a thick finger, and a figure flinches in the booth behind him.

It's the lady my cousin Benny picked up at the wedding. My eyes skim over her then move an inch to the right, to the idiot himself. He meets my gaze with a smug smirk, then raises his glass to me. *Cheers.*

I wipe my hand across my mouth in a poor attempt to hide my amusement. Seems like only minutes ago Nico and I were watching him shoot his shot with her on the dance floor, taking bets on how long it would be until she kicked him in the nuts.

"You owe me twenty grand."

Speaking of Nico. He saddles up beside me at the bar and pours out two shots of Don Julio '42. He slides one across to me with a flick of his wrist, giving zero shits about the African Blackwood.

"Read the room, *cugino*. Now's not the time to be settling trivial bets."

Nico laughs. "Double or nothing says he fucks her."

A pulse flickers in my jaw. "Deal."

Like everyone else in the family, Nico knows I don't, *can't*, turn down the opportunity to play a game or make a bet, even if it's guaranteed I'll lose. My self-control is iron-clad and galvanized, and yet, the *click-clack* of a dice or the *thawp* of a roulette wheel spinning is like crack to me.

My whole life is a game, but it's a predictable one. I own half the hotels and casinos and collect protection from ones I don't. In a world of fixed odds, all of them stacked in my favor, my only excitement is getting to shake the dice and throw them into the unknown.

Nico slams the shot and pours out another. "You've fucked up."

"Yeah?"

He flashes me a shy grin. "Yeah. I slept with her at the bachelor party, so I already know she's mafia meat."

"Jesus," I mutter. "You and Benny are one Saturday night away from incest."

He laughs quietly, then picks up a stack of shot glasses with one hand and tucks the tequila bottle under his arm. His jovial whistle slips through the air like oil in water. In my peripheral, I see Griffin, the head of my personal security team, stop pacing the shadows to glare at him as he passes.

"Fucking idiot," he grunts, before returning to his hushed phone call.

I don't agree; in fact, Nico is one of the few cousins I wouldn't deem an idiot. He's just grown up with warfare hanging over his head like a constant storm cloud. He's not an idiot, he's just immune to things like explosions and bloodshed.

Left alone again, I eye the tequila shot Nico poured out for me. As a rule of thumb, I don't drink any liquor that's clear unless I'm trying to secure business with the Mexicans or Russians, but fuck it.

I slam it and wait.

To my mild disappointment, it burns down my throat and trickles into my chest, yet does nothing to extinguish the flame of unease that flickers there.

Dragging a knuckle over my jaw, I turn and rest my forearms against the bar. Mainly so Angelo doesn't catch the crack in my indifferent facade. Out of all the Viscontis, I'm the calm one. The voice of reason in a cesspit of ego and testosterone. The one that puts out their fires with an ice-cold bucket of reality and a plan. But I must admit, I'm struggling to adhere to that reputation tonight.

The Devil's Dip port is up in flames, and there's a niggling feeling in my chest that somehow, I'm responsible.

It was just a coincidence.

With a shake of my head, I roll the whiskey glass down my palm and press it against the inside of my wrist in an attempt to cool my blood. Of course, my brain *knows* it was a mere coincidence. Dante's been laying low for over a month now; it was about time he pulled his finger out of his ass and retaliated. And what better day to do it than Angelo's wedding?

The red-haired girl had nothing to do with it.

I close my eyes for a brief moment, suddenly aware of all the tension knotting in my back.

She's not my doom card.

Behind me, Angelo clears his throat. "Men, Cas's office in one minute."

I roll my neck on my shoulders. Smooth the band of my bow tie and realign my composure before turning around. Made men stride through a door at the back of the club in a line of tuxedos and crystal tumblers. Angelo fists Rory's hair and plants an angry kiss on her neck, before she joins her bridal party in the corner. A few of Gabe's men form a protective barrier around them, while Angelo turns his attention to me.

He stares at me, silent but expectant. Cocking a lazy smile, I hold my hand horizontally in the space between us. Both our eyes fall to it, and as usual, it's deathly still.

My brothers and I have played this game since we were kids. From breaking our mama's fine china by rollerblading in the kitchen, to realizing there's a security camera outside the house of our latest Sinners Anonymous victim—any time danger touched us, they'd turn to me to gauge the severity of it. I guess it's because I see things through a logical lens, or because I don't make any rash decisions.

The rule is and always has been that if my hand doesn't shake, their hands shouldn't either.

He swallows. Nods. But when his eyes travel back up to mine and narrow, I can tell he's not convinced.

"It's *Dante*, for fuck's sake."

My protest doesn't lighten the darkness on his face, and I look back down at my hand to double-check there's not even the slightest tremor in it. I can't believe I'm doubting myself, but I have to admit, the red-head has thrown me out of whack.

When she came into the bar last night, I heard her before I saw her.

Those muddy boots stomped down the stairs and up my spine, forcing me to read the first line of an email twice. That alone got my back up, and all before I'd even seen her.

And when I did, I'd be lying if I said I didn't look twice. And then a third time, because she slid up beside me at the bar and took her coat off like a fucking stripper.

Of course, the first thing I noticed was her copper hair. So messy and so *much of it*. I couldn't tell whether she'd just been fucked senseless on polyester sheets or been dragged through a bush backward. The second thing I noticed was the green dress that showed too much skin for a Thursday night. And the third? The security tag still fastened to the hem of it.

She was trouble and my gut knew it before she even opened her smart-ass mouth.

Usually, I find it easy to be a gentleman. I have a talent for laughing on cue, cracking a well-placed joke, then making a graceful exit when the small talk gets so dry it makes my eyeballs itch. At least one member of this family has to have manners, and I suppose that task falls on me.

But Penelope made me want to be anything but gentlemanly.

I'm wary of talking to women on this Coast, unless I'm on a one-and-only date with them. There's nothing less attractive than looking at a lady and seeing your last name flash in lights behind their eyes.

But hers were big and blue and lacked any spark of recognition—at first, anyway. Somewhere between her proposition and me taking a phone call from my brother, she figured it out, and I'd be lying if I said the sadist in me didn't rear its ugly head when I saw her trying to scurry up the stairs and out of my clutches.

The excitement had me throw my caution and self-control into the fire, so I shouldn't have been so surprised when I got burned. She hadn't cheated; she'd won my Breitling fair and square, and the way in which she did it only piqued my interest in who she was and what the fuck she was doing in Devil's Cove with a suitcase and a stolen dress. I slipped my timepiece into her pocket along with a Sinners Anonymous card in the hope I'd find her secrets waiting for me in the voicemail box by the end of the weekend.

I never thought I'd see her again. So when I spotted that red hair billowing in the wind from the other side of the lake, talking to my little cousin, unease crept under my collar, sticky and *hot*. It only got worse when she had the fucking nerve to try swindle me again. Talking about luck, of all things.

And then the explosion happened.

My molars grind on instinct, but when I feel Angelo's gaze growing sharper, I roll my shoulders back and pin him with my best look of indifference. "Would you like to see if my dick shakes, too, or shall we figure out what to do with our dumb-ass cousin?"

Without waiting for a response, I slap his shoulder and stroll into Cas's office. It has little more than a desk on one side and a long boardroom table on the other, where Viscontis gather like a pack of wolves. Angelo and I take our seats at the head of it.

I pull a poker chip from my pocket. Roll it between my thumb and forefinger. Suddenly, I'm fine with the fact I was unable to drown my unease in liquor, because the adrenaline of sitting next to my brothers at the head of this table by far overpowers it.

This is where I belong and I've always known it. Not in Vegas, but in Devil's Dip with my brothers. Despite all my success on the Strip, there's always been a black void in the hollow of my chest, an empty ache with the need to be home. I've waited nine long years for Angelo to return to the Coast. The moment I got the call he was moving back, I was on the next jet out, much to the dismay of my investors and security detail.

An electric silence cloaks the room. Three heavy beats pass before Gabe breaks it by slamming his fist against the table.

"Never liked the cunt."

The two younger Hollow brothers murmur in agreement, but not Cas. Instead, he leans over with his silk pocket square in hand and rubs the spot Gabe just punched. "This family is the reason I can't have nice things," he mutters.

"Nah. You can't have nice things in case your scary Russian fiancée throws them at your head," Benny quips. There's a ripple of snickers around the table.

"Enough."

Angelo's voice is sharp yet simple, cutting through the room like a steak knife. He loosens his bow tie and rubs a palm over his jaw. His wedding band glints under the recessed lights.

"It's my wedding night. I should be at home fucking my wife and looking up the weather for Fiji. Instead, I'm deep underground in Devil's Hollow with you bastard reprobates. I want a plan drawn up in the next ten minutes so I can get Rory out of here. Gabe, what are you thinking?"

Gabe leans back in his chair, snapping his bow tie like a whip.

"Grenades or a rocket warhead."

From the door, my latest recruit, Blake, calls upon Jesus under his breath. I hide my smirk behind my knuckles, before Gabe gets up and snaps his neck.

All of my men are ex-Delta Force or CIA, and they are bound to their instructions tighter than the laces in their combat boots. They are quiet, obedient, and stick to the shadows until I summon them to the light. Half the time, I forget they are there.

They are a far cry from Gabe's *soldati*, who all look like they've survived the apocalypse. Griffin was both pissed and bewildered with my decision to leave my shiny, gated compound in Vegas and move back to the Coast, and now that the port has been blown up, I'm sure I'll be hit by a gruff *I-told-you-so* the moment he catches me alone.

But he'll never understand me like these men around this table do. Being a Visconti is like a blood-type, you can't escape what you're born with. Wouldn't want to, either.

Angelo's jaw ticks in thought. He hisses out a puff of hot air, before jerking his chin to Cas and the other Hollow brothers. "And you guys?"

I stop flicking my poker chip and cut a look at Cas in anticipation.

When Angelo put a bullet through Uncle Al's head and started a civil war with Devil's Cove, the Hollow clan decided to stay out of it, despite their territory being slap-bang in the middle of us. *Think of Hollow as being the Demilitarized Zone*, Cas had said at the time. *We won't choose between family.*

Out of everyone in the Cosa Nostra, he's the most like me. A businessman first, a made man second. Now, though, I can see the dilemma biting at the edges of his conscience. Eventually, he steeples his hands and steels his jaw with resolve. "Smugglers Club is a global brand. We export over fifty-percent of our stock through your port, so Dante's little stunt has cost us millions." He swipes a thumb over his bottom lip, deep in thought. "He needs to pay."

"Yeah, with a grenade," Gabe grunts.

Cas shrugs. "Not the worst idea you've had, *cugino*."

"Rafe? What do you think?"

Feeling the weight of everyone's eyes on my skin, I turn to meet Angelo's gaze. I spin the poker chip in the air and catch it, before slipping it back in my pocket.

"I think it's boring."

Gabe snorts. "You think a grenade is boring?"

My gaze shifts lazily to him. "Only kids are entertained by things that go *bang*, brother."

Angelo huffs out a sardonic laugh.

The whole mafia cliché holds no appeal for me, and now that I'm finally back with my brothers, I refuse to be tied to archaic traditions and *sleeping-with-the-fishes* attitudes. We'll be wearing fucking fedoras next.

I check the time on my wristwatch, then rise to my feet. "Gentleman, we won't take up any more of your time, you're all free to go." I hold up my hand, slicing through the start of Gabe's gruff protest. "We'll keep you in the loop."

Suspicion flickers over Benny's features. "Free to go? We haven't agreed on how to take the fucker down yet."

I pin him with a tight smile. "It's a Dip issue; we'll handle it. In the meantime, if you need any extra men, talk to Griffin on the way out. I'll be happy to lend you a few members of my personal security detail."

"But—"

"He said we'll handle it," Angelo says, finality biting his tone.

Spines stiffen. The air crackles with words better left unsaid. Eventually, everyone rises to their feet, except Angelo and Gabe, whose glare is hot enough to burn a hole in the opposite wall.

"Fine. But we don't need your men," Benny grunts, grazing his shoulder against Blake's chest as he passes. "This one here looks like he wouldn't know how to use a gun even if it came with an illustrated instruction manual."

"Don't need a gun. These fists work just fine," Blake growls back, stepping in Benny's path.

I grind my back molars as Cas grabs Benny by the scruff of his collar and drags him from the room. I'm starting to wonder why Griffin thought Blake would be a good recruit. He should know the average Visconti would pop a cap in his temporal lobe just to prove a point.

The issue with my men following to the Coast is that they only know me as Raphael Visconti the businessman. They see the endless meetings, the VIP booths. They receive their elimination instructions in sealed manila envelopes and carry out the hits in quiet parking lots. They don't see the dark, violent underbelly attached to my family name. I've done well to keep both separate, and anything handled within the confines of the Cosa Nostra, I get Gabe and his men to carry out.

I've shielded them for so long, I'm concerned the likes of Blake think the Cosa Nostra is a figment of Francis Ford Coppola's imagination.

The door clicks shut, plunging us into silence.

That vein in Angelo's temple does a tap dance. "This is a game to you, isn't it?"

It's not really a question, because my brothers already know the answer. Gabe punches the table again, and this time, there's a loud *crack* from under his fist.

"Mama should have put you in anger management when she threatened she would," I muse.

"What, do you wanna challenge Dante to a friendly game of *Tic, Tac, Toe?*" Gabe's eyes find mine, furious and wild. *Unhinged.* "He blew up our port. Three confirmed dead already, and fuck knows how many more to come. Do us all a favor and leave the combat to me and my men, and go back to dry-cleaning your suits."

As I study him, it briefly occurs to me this is the most I've heard him talk since *that* Christmas. Shortly before our parents died, he came back to the Coast for the holidays with a haunted look in his eyes and a fresh scar running from his eyebrow to his chin. He was a whole different man.

Wouldn't say what happened to him—wouldn't say much at all, in fact. But something about plotting revenge has brought him to life, and I almost don't want to take it away from him.

And I wouldn't, except, my ideas are always better.

"Lay off the steroids, brother." I stride over to the desk, giving Gabe a patronizing pat on the shoulder as I pass. "They make your brain fuzzy and your dick small."

I sink into the armchair behind Cas's desk and drag his chessboard in front of me. With mild amusement, I realize it's the one I bought him last year for his birthday. Judging by the thin film of dust covering the pieces and the fact he owes me twelve grand, he hasn't been practicing.

Gabe stops behind me, casting a dark shadow over the board.

"Let me dumb it down for your 'roid-raging brain." With a flick of my wrist, I backhand all the chess pieces, sending them flying across the desk. "This is what you want to do. Immediate retaliation; total destruction. Sure, Dante rents his brain cells and only on alternate week days, but even he'll expect us to bite back tonight. At the very least, his men are guarding the perimeter of Cove as we speak." Slowly, I pick up all the pieces, taking my time to put them back on their rightful squares. Behind me, Gabe's impatient huff slithers down my shirt collar. "But you know what he won't see coming?"

"A Molotov cocktail?" he snaps.

"No reaction from us at all."

Angelo cocks his head. Strokes the stubble across his jawline. "Rafe's right. Dante's going to be sitting behind Big Al's desk, scratching his balls and waiting for a war." He jerks his chin at me. "What's the plan?"

I settle back in the armchair. "We play dumb and extend an olive branch. We tell him that *somebody* has blown up the port, and we need to put our differences aside to figure out who. Because surely," I add dryly, "nobody would be stupid enough to bomb the port that *they* fucking use."

"And then?"

With a smirk, I turn back to the chessboard. "And then, his luck begins to turn." I flick off one pawn. Then another. "Heart attack. Car crash. Drug overdose. All his associates and *soldati* meet their deaths in unfortunate, yet unsuspicious circumstances. One day, he'll look up and realize there is nobody left to fight with him."

We all look down at the board, where one black king stands alone, opposite an army of white chess pieces.

Gabe reaches over and snatches up the queen from the pile of discarded pieces. It looks comically small in his busted paw. "His *consigliere*, Donatello, has gone already. Last I heard, he's shoveling horse shit on a farm in Colorado with Amelia. A kid on the way, too."

I look up and flash Angelo a knowing wink. "You do crazy shit when you're in love, right?"

He scowls at me, picks up the rook and the knight, and slips them into his pocket. "The twins, Vittoria and Leo, we can leave out of it. They're barely sixteen and probably scared shitless."

Gabe reaches for the bishop, but instinctively, my hand shoots out and curls around his wrist. He glares at it like he's about to take a bite out of my flesh. I pick up the bishop myself and twirl it between my thumb and forefinger, before knocking over the black king and setting it down in its place.

"Tor stays."

The ice threading through my tone is a rare occurrence, and behind me, I feel Gabe stiffen.

"No."

"I'm not asking you. I'm *telling* you. He stays."

Torquato Visconti might be Dante's brother, new underboss, and the Coast's biggest dickhead, but he's my best friend and one of my finest business partners. Aside from turning up at the wedding, he's laid low ever since his father was shot.

But I have no doubt in my mind he'll come around.

"Yeah, he came to the wedding," Angelo says pensively, strumming his fingers against the table. "But it's funny that he was nowhere to be seen after the explosion."

"He left straight after the ceremony."

"That's because he's in on it," Gabe snaps.

"Nah," I shoot back.

Angelo's expression hardens. "I know you're five inches up Tor's asshole, but Gabe's got a point. We can't assume he's not backing his brother on this." He checks his watch, raps his knuckle against the desk, and straightens to his full height. "Fine. Cas and I will reach out to Dante and arrange a meeting. Gabe, you regroup your men and figure out an action plan based on Rafe's idea. And Rafe." His eyes rest squarely on mine. "Let me know when you hear from Tor."

Without another word, he strides around the desk and heads to the door. He stops within its frame. "By the way," he grunts, glancing at me over his shoulder. "Your new bar has been blown to shit. Secure another location, and fast. I want a joint so grand it makes the whole of Cove look like a children's birthday party at Chuckie Cheese."

Ah, yes. Construction was well underway for Devil's Dip's first casino and bar. Cut into the cliff with panoramic views of the Pacific, it would have pissed all over Cove's nightlife, especially with my name attached to it. But it was directly above the port, and well, shit happens, I suppose.

"Now that, I can do," I murmur, slipping the poker chip out of my pocket and tossing it in the air.

Gabe shakes his head. "We're going to war, and all you assholes care about is a good time."

Angelo's gaze darkens. "No. I want to show the cunt that a shitty little explosion isn't enough to take down the Dip brothers."

Amusement pulls at the corners of my mouth as he spins around and disappears into the main bar, calling Rory's name.

Now alone, blistering silence sizzles between me and my younger brother. I turn around and bask in the heat of his stare.

"Problem?"

"Yeah."

I glance at my watch and slowly rise to my feet. "That's a shame. I'd say take it up with the HR department, but I don't think the Cosa Nostra has one."

His glare burns into my back as I walk to the door. "Glad you're back, brother."

Nico's waiting for me as I step into the main club. He falls into step with me and lowers his tone. "About the money you owe me."

I roll my eyes, giving him a flick on the jaw without breaking pace. "Fuck off with the money talk, will you? You'll find that cash in the cracks of the sofa if you dig deep enough."

When he doesn't reply, I glance at his face. He wears a somber expression instead of his signature lazy grin, and the contrast makes me slow to a stop.

My gaze narrows. "What?"

Nico drags his teeth over his bottom lip, his gaze shifting over my shoulder.

"I'll wipe the debt if you do me a favor."

CHAPTER
Eight

Penny

B EEP. BEEP. BEEP.

The low, slow rhythm seeps into my subconscious, tickling a dark corner of my brain. It's not the sound of my alarm. Maybe it's my ringtone? I have no idea what that sounds like; not only because I usually have my cell on vibrate, but because no one has the number to my burner.

It's annoying, whatever it is.

I grunt and roll over to bury my head in the gap between the pillows, but something tugging on my hand stops me.

Only a few seconds pass before the pain starts. It sears from one temple to the other and snaps across my forehead like an elastic band.

What the—?

I pop an eyelid open and sweep the room. White ceilings, white bed sheets. Clinical and *sterile*. Even with blurry eyes and a pounding head, I know I'm not in my apartment. In fact, I don't remember getting home at all.

I was at the port.

The memory opens the floodgates in my foggy brain, and everything rushes back to me.

The orange sky.

The deafening explosion.

The *heat*.

The beeping gets faster, and I have just enough sense to realize it's because the clip on the end of my finger is monitoring my heart rate.

Light, quick footsteps approach, and then a woman appears in the doorway.

"You're all right, you're all right." She strides into the room with the gait of a leisurely Sunday stroll. She stops at the end of the bed and studies my chart, giving me a chance to study *her*. White hair swept into a tight bun, middle-aged, and plump in a way that makes the buttons down the front of her uniform sit in a zig-zag. She's the type of woman parents tell their children to seek out in the park if a creepy man approaches them.

She must be a nurse, which means I'm in the hospital.

"What happened?" Well, that's what I *try* to say. It comes out in a garbled groan and ignites a trail of fire up my throat.

Her gray eyes snap up to me, amused. "Save it, sweetie. I'll get you some water in a second. I'm Minnie, the charge nurse here at Devil's Hollow Hospital. And you are…" She glances back at the clipboard and her expression lights up. "Ooh! A Jane Doe! How exciting."

I blink. *Is it?*

She breezes over to the side table and pours a glass of water from a jug. "Easy does it," she says, watching me drink the liquid as fast as I can in an attempt to quell the fire. "All that screaming has made your throat dry," she tuts. "They could hear you in Canada."

My eyes feel like they're going to pop out of my head. *Screaming?* Why the hell would I be *screaming?*

"There was a little accident at the port, my dear. Your notes say you were struck by a stack of falling boxes, and you've taken a particularly nasty blow to the head."

She tugs a pen light from her breast pocket and does a quick sweep of my eyes with it. Pulls out the IV, and puts a fresh bandage on the back of my hand. "Doesn't look like a concussion, but we'll be monitoring you for a little while, all right?"

But I'm not listening. *Can't.* Because all I can feel is my own plea on my lips and all I can see is a hazy orange heat distorting the cold black sky.

I asked for a sign that I'd lost my luck and I received a full fireworks display.

I drop my head against the pillow, feeling the ice-cold hand of realization pressing down on my windpipe.

If I don't have luck, what do I have?

"Okay, sweetie. I need to do my rounds, but I'll come and check on you in a few. Rest up, okay?" With a soft pat on my shoulder, she bustles out into the brightly lit corridor, a hearty whistle floating after her.

Only one beat passes before a wave of guilt breaks over me. It snatches the air from my lungs and I slump down, resting my thumping head on my pillow.

Logically, I know my asking for a sign didn't cause the explosion, but I can't shake the feeling it was somehow my fault anyway. My brain forms an image of the port worker. One minute he was walking toward me in a halo of headlights, and the next, he was just gone.

Swindling and hustling are one thing; arson and explosions are another ball game entirely. Christ, these sins are stacking up like charms on a necklace, and I don't know how much longer I can bear that burden around my neck before I keel over from its weight.

Sitting upright makes my head spin, so I grip the side bars of the bed and stare at the ice-blue sky framed by the window, waiting for the dizzy spell to pass. As the wispy clouds and the soaring birds come into focus, emotion prickles in my throat, threatening to supply my eyes with a fresh wave of tears.

"Did you know two thousand frowns equal one wrinkle?"

My spine goes rigid at the sound of a sweet voice drifting in from the door. I turn, wincing as tightness tugs at my neck, and lock eyes with the girl it belongs to.

Silky blond hair and a golden tan that doesn't make sense in a blistering cold December. Her eyes are big and blue, filled with the type of innocence that only one girl on this coastline can truly claim.

Wren Harlow.

Grinding my teeth so my groan isn't audible, I force a dead-eyed smile. Of all the people I'd want to walk through that door while I'm having a private meltdown, Wren would be pretty low on the list. It's not because she's not nice—quite the opposite, in fact. She's *too* nice. So nice, she's known on the Coast as the Good Samaritan. Not a single Friday or Saturday night passes in Cove where you wouldn't find her trawling the strip and helping drunk people. She hands out Band-Aids and flip-flops to girls with aching feet. Hails cabs for the drunk and disorderly. She's so sweet it hurts my teeth looking at her.

Her gaze trails from my head wound to my feet and back again. Maybe it's the pain meds making me loopy, but I can't help notice her nail polish is the exact shade of pink as her shirt dress.

I have a feeling she did that on purpose.

She blows a bubble. Pops it. "You thinking about something bad?"

Frowning, I bite back the urge to tell her it's none of her business. Partly because I don't need any more bad karma, and partly because Wren is the type of girl who's probably never experienced even a dog barking at her, let alone a scruffy red-head going through an existential crisis.

"Maybe."

"When I have bad thoughts, I try to distract myself."

I rub the bridge of my nose, trying my hardest to keep my mouth shut. The last thing I need right now is an impromptu therapy session from a girl with a fast-pass to heaven.

"How? By cross-stitching your favorite Bible verses?" I mutter under my breath.

She sinks down on the foot of the bed, stretching her long, tight-clad legs across the floor tiles. "No, by going through the alphabet and thinking of a curse word for each letter." Her blue gaze comes to mine as she blows another bubble. *Pop.* "For example, A is for asshole," she says pointedly, a dark glint in her eye.

Despite the searing pain in my head and the sins weighing heavy on my chest, I can't help but let out a gruff laugh.

"Touché."

She grins, too, a beautiful smile that softens the planes of her face. She nods at the space above my eyebrow. "Looks nasty."

"Feels it."

"Want a candy bar?"

I blink. Before I can ask what she's on about, she jumps up, ducks into the hallway, and returns with a cart. "I've got all the classics, plus potato chips and cans of soda." She crouches down and squints at the bottom shelf. "I had some ham and cheese sandwiches too, but Billy in room eight took like *four*, even though they'll be serving lunch in an hour."

She returns to her full height and looks at me expectantly. When I don't reply, she grabs two Hershey bars off the cart and tosses one into my lap. Holding the other between her teeth, she drags the armchair across the room and sets it beside my bed.

I stare down at the chocolate wedged between my thighs. "You work here?"

"Nope, just volunteering."

Figures.

She flops down in the chair and swings her boots up to rest them on the end of the bed. "I work at The Rusty Anchor—been there for about a year now. What have you been up to, anyway? I haven't seen you on the Coast in a while."

I ignore her question because I'm still stuck on her job. "The *port* bar?"

"Uh-huh." My gaze instinctively cuts to the sparkly pink bobble wrapped around her high ponytail and she laughs. "It's not as bad as you think, really."

Mm. The last time I stepped foot in The Rusty Anchor, I left with six splinters and salmonella from the chicken burger. I'd assume that if a girl like Wren stepped into The Rusty Anchor, she'd spontaneously combust from the sins that lived inside of it.

She tosses her gum in the trash, tears open her candy bar, and stares at my wound. "What were you doing at the port, anyway? I'm sure I saw you at the wedding last night. Or did I have too many lemonades?"

"No, I was there." My fingers creep up to my pendant again. "But I went for a walk on my way home."

"Jeez. That's unlucky." *You're telling me.* "Well, it could have been much worse. Working at The Rusty Anchor means I know pretty much everyone who was injured." Her throat bobs. "And those who didn't make it."

My own throat dries up faster than the Sahara after a storm. "How many died?"

"Three. So far, anyway."

Jesus. "What the hell happened, a burst gas pipe or something?"

Biting off a chunk of chocolate, she chews thoughtfully for a moment. "Terrorist attack," she mumbles, all candy and teeth.

"I—*what*?"

"No idea who did it, though. Everyone was being pretty hush-hush last night."

Now, I'm starting to think these pain meds are making me loopy. "Why would somebody want to blow up that tiny port?"

"Because the Viscontis own it." *Visconti.* The name shoots from Wren's chocolate-filled mouth and hits my chest like a bullet. Of *course* the Viscontis own the fucking port. "It's too much of a coincidence that Angelo announces he's moving back to Devil's Dip, and then the port blows up on his wedding day."

My eyes slide to hers. "Angelo's moving back?"

"Of course. Rory won't leave the Coast." She sighs through another mouthful of chocolate. "Poor Rory. Doesn't look like she'll be going on her honeymoon after all."

Despite the cocktail of numbing agents taking the edge off my pain, the slow dread filling my stomach feels all too real. If Angelo's moved back to the Coast, then what does that mean for his brothers?

"On his own?"

"What do you mean?"

We lock eyes for a beat too long, then a knowing smirk stretches her pink lips. "Oh, I see."

"See *what?*"

She sinks back in her chair, that smirk widening to a grin. "If you've got your eye on Rafe, then you better get in line."

Heat rises to my cheeks, making my skin prickle. "I'm *not* interested in Raphael; I was just making polite conver—"

"Hey, hey, hey, I'm not one to judge." She holds her hands up in mock surrender. "They don't call him Prince Charming for nothing."

My laugh is bitter. "I must have grown up watching different Disney films."

"Aw, come off it. Rafe's lovely." Her hand touches her chest and the small smile that graces her lips suggests her mind has gone elsewhere. Somewhere Raphael Visconti isn't a raging asshole, presumably. "He's not my type, but I can fully appreciate the appeal. He's just...such a *gentleman.* You know, the type of guy in black and white movies that lays his jacket over a puddle of mud so his date doesn't ruin her shoes? Or, like, the kind of guy to send you a dozen roses, simply because it's a Wednesday."

I can't help it. "You seriously believe that shit?"

Her tinkling laugh floats across the room. "Seems like you've had a different experience."

I gnaw on the inside of my cheek to stop myself mentioning things like dicks in doors and guns in glasses.

When the silence lingers too long, Wren lets out another chuckle and swipes her boots off my bed. "Yikes. F is for 'fuck him,' am I right?"

Despite feeling like all the problems in the world are pinning me to this bed, I can't help but laugh.

Her gaze comes to mine, all sparkly and innocent. "If you're hanging around for a while, you should swing by The Rusty Anchor some time. You know, once we've cleared up the mess from the explosion, and once you don't look like Frankenstein." She prods the IV drip with a pink fingernail. "Rory and Tayce swing by every Tuesday night, and there's always room for one more at the bar."

Her offer is probably just in passing, a sweet gesture from a sweet girl. It shouldn't make the backs of my eyes burn like it does. Maybe it's because morphine makes me emotional, or maybe it's because I feel guilty about palming her off as just the weird girl who does good deeds.

I swallow the knot in my throat and nod. "I'd like that. Thanks for the chocolate bar and, you know," I murmur, my throat tightening, "being so nice."

Her laugh floats through the room like a welcome breeze on a warm day. "Nice is just what I do. See ya!"

And with that, she click-clacks down the hall, taking her cart with her. Left alone, I infect the sterile room with a loud groan. It seems like I've stepped out of one fire I caused and into another I didn't. How am I going to go straight when I'm surrounded by trouble?

I'd never expect this type of shit in Devil's Dip. It is—*was*—the sleepy town on the Coast. The one in the shadows of the flashing lights, where residents can close their eyes at night and not have to worry about getting caught in the middle of Cosa Nostra chaos.

Besides, if my luck really is waning...

I swallow the lump in my throat. Give a small shake of my head in an attempt to rid myself of the thought.

Luck is believing you're lucky. That's what the woman told me in the alleyway when she gave me her necklace. *This will help you, but you don't need to rely on it.*

My lids fluttering shut, I give in to the softness of the pillow under my head for a few moments. *I'm lucky. I am.* Still, I can't help but consider selling Raphael's watch, paying off whatever extortionate medical bill I'm slapped with, and then getting a bus over the border to Canada.

Eyes still closed, I reach out to the bedside table for my purse and realize it's not there. *Shit.* The last time I remember having it—remember anything, actually—was at the port. Groaning, I weakly wrestle with the wheelchair folded up beside the bed and slide my heavy limbs into it. I'll just wheel myself down the hall to the nurses' station and ask.

As I push myself out to the hall, white walls and silver doors pass in a cool, drug-fueled haze. A chill caresses my back and I realize I'm wearing nothing but a flimsy hospital gown, the type that ties up at the back. No bra, and my body is too numb and sluggish to assess whether I even have panties on.

The moment I turn the corner, my gaze locks with another and my heart drops on instinct.

Cold and brown as a slushy pile of mud on a winter morning, the man's eyes trail up from my muddy toes to the bandage on my head, before settling into a thin line of suspicion.

Silence screams, but the ghost of his gruff voice yells even louder in my brain.

Does a bear shit in the woods?

It's the man who was guarding the top of the stairs at the bar. Heartbeat jittering, my attention darts to the cluster of sharp suits and sour faces that loiter in the hallway behind him. Shiny shoes reflect clinical lights. Beefy hands curl around Styrofoam cups.

And then a familiar cashmere voice seeps out from the unknown and wraps its soft hand around my lungs. My wheels come to a slow stop.

"Thank you, Sheriff. Our family truly appreciates your help during this difficult time."

A shuffle of papers, then heavy footsteps grow louder. "Anytime, Mr. Visconti. Please send your brother my congratulations on the wedding."

"Only if you tell your mother those gingerbread cookies she sent over have changed my life."

There's a gruff chuckle, then black shoes and a beige uniform emerge from the door on the right. The Sheriff glances over his shoulder and grins. "She'll be happy to hear. Take care now, Mr. Visconti. And if you need anything, you know you can always reach me on my personal cell."

He strolls down the hallway in the other direction, trying to force a very thick brown envelope into the pocket of his slacks.

Annoyance prickles at my chest, because of course the Viscontis have the police under their thumbs.

For a few seconds, I'm torn between scrambling back to my room or continuing with my mission to get my phone. Stubbornness makes me settle on the latter. That, and my burning need to call my hotline and mull over my thoughts of moving to Canada.

I stare at the ugly geometric print of my hospital gown and keep pushing my chair, but as I grow closer and closer to passing the door on the right, unease slides under my skin like tectonic plates.

I peer into the hospital room to my right, and let my gaze settle on the man himself.

My heart hitches in my chest.

Black suit. White Shirt. Gold collar pin. I don't know why I bother checking his hallmark features off a mental list, because Raphael Visconti's outline is unmistakable.

The room is darker than mine, save for the lone sunbeam slicing a diagonal line across his profile. The bed is tightly dressed, and stacks of notes are wrapped in bands and piled high on the bedside table. More bribes, no doubt.

He's spilling out of an armchair in the corner, resting his elbows on his knees and subjecting the tiles underneath his Oxfords to an expressionless stare. He spins something between his fingers in a slow, hypnotic rhythm, and it takes four revolutions for me to realize it's a gold poker chip.

Thawp. Thawp. Thawp. The chip, diamond cufflinks, and his citrine ring wink at me.

Until they don't.

When Raphael's hands still and his shoulders tighten, the dust particles floating inside the sunbeam fall stagnant, as if they're holding their breaths on my behalf. Shadows shift to accommodate the planes of his face as he lifts his head and meets my gaze.

My pulse strums violently; my aching muscles brace for impact. For three loud heartbeats, I'm trapped in his glare.

Then, he does something I don't expect.

He laughs.

It's soft. Dark. As gentle as a kiss on a collarbone and no good could ever come from such a sound.

"Are you obsessed with me, Penelope?"

His tone is cushioned with amusement but there's something around its edges that tugs at my nerves.

"Yeah, that's exactly why I'm in the hospital," I reply sarcastically.

His gaze sparks with confusion, before turning a few shades darker. It carves a lazy path down my neck. My breathing stills as it crackles over the thin fabric of the hospital gown, and when it settles like a heavy weight in my lap, the warmth in my stomach simmers half a degree hotter. It's irritation—nothing more. Because, although I'm used to men staring at my body while wearing a lot less than this, there's something about the way he regards me—clinically, *objectively*—that makes my jaw stiffen.

"You were there." I catch the flare of his nostrils before they disappear behind his knuckles. When he speaks again, it seems to be just to himself. "Of course you were there."

"What, you think I bombed the port, or something?"

His eyes meet mine again. A pensiveness mars the ever-present amusement behind them. "Or something."

With a cocktail of frustration and annoyance flaming inside me, I huff out a shaky breath and turn my attention to harsh fluorescent lights lining the hallway ceiling. Obviously he knows I had nothing to do with the explosion—he wouldn't be sitting next to a stack of bribe money if I did—but I hate how the suspicion in his tone, even if fake, mirrors my own.

It's pathetic, but the idea that I've lost my luck is scarier to me than anything else in this world. Scarier than threats by Atlantic City casino owners, and scarier than the fear of my biggest sin catching up with me.

"Lucky charm?"

A voice flecked with ice-cold scorn slices the silence. My eyes skim down from the ceiling to find Raphael looking at my necklace with tight disgust. I didn't realize I was running the four-leaf clover up and down the chain.

"No," I lie. Then I straighten my spine and lie a little more. "I don't need a lucky charm. I'm lucky enough."

My voice is hoarse and sounds pathetic, thanks to the desperation woven within it. It's obvious I'm only trying to convince myself.

"So you said." He runs a slow tongue over his top lip as he nods to the bandage on my forehead. "You don't look so lucky to me."

I swallow the wedge in my throat. "I'm lucky to be alive."

His gaze slides to mine, dark and hot. "For now."

Silence eats up the oxygen between us. I can't stop *staring* at him. His threat was subtle, elegant, delivered on a velvet cushion upon a silver platter. I have no doubt he'd follow through with that thinly-veiled threat if provoked. So why the fuck does everyone on this Coast think he's a gentleman? That he's somehow different from the rest of his family, from his brothers?

Most people have an IQ big enough to spot a lion in sheep's clothing, surely?

My jaw tightens as I realize the truth. It's because he doesn't act like this around other people.

Suddenly, it clicks.

"This is about your watch," I announce, a quiet glee humming in my aching bones. "That's why you hate me so much. Your fragile male ego can't handle a woman getting one over on you."

I don't get the reaction I'm expecting. Just another laugh. "Nice, but still, no."

I watch the chip glint with every revolution, taunting me. When the last of my self-restraint dissolves, I jerk my chin toward the bunch of suit-clad idiots loitering in the hallway. "Do I get to choose?"

He cocks a brow, still spinning his chip.

"Which of your lackeys get to kill me, I mean? Because it'll be one of them, right? I know a gentleman like you would never risk getting blood on his pretty little suit."

He gives me nothing but a polite smile, and the darkness in his eyes suggests his mind is elsewhere. Medical machines beep through white walls and somewhere down the hall, a coffee machine bursts and sputters.

Eventually, he leans forward into the path of the sunbeam and the quiet calmness in his green eyes glitters under the light. "Rumor has it you're looking for a job in Devil's Dip."

My gaze narrows. What a left-field response. There's only two people who could have told him that: Rory or Nico. I discount Matt immediately, because I doubt he could hold a conversation with Raphael Visconti long enough to tell him this without jizzing in his pants.

"Yeah, but not with you or your family."

Dark amusement pulls at his lips. "Impossible."

My eyes itch as I force myself not to roll them. As much as his smugness grates down my spine, I know he's right. Even if the

Viscontis don't own the business directly, they sure as hell will have their sticky mafia fingers in the pie one way or another.

"You offering me a job, or something?"

"Or something."

What? The change of tune is enough to give me whiplash. I squint at him, trying to figure out what he's playing at. Maybe it's because my brain is damaged from the blow, but I can't tell if he's joking or not.

"Why do I feel like I'm about to get sex trafficked?"

Raphael lets out a short sigh. "I'm offended. All of my businesses are perfectly legitimate; thank you."

I open my mouth and close it again, trapping my insult behind my lips. I'm pretty hard up right now, so I'm not going to ruin my chance of finding employment if—and it's a big if—this isn't a joke.

"What's the catch?"

Now, something in Raphael's gaze flickers to life. "I thought you'd never ask." He run two fingers over his bottom lip, but it does little to conceal his soft smirk. "Play a game with me."

Despite my aching bones and jaded heart, the simple command stokes the embers in the pit of my stomach. A game?

Before I can ask about rules and wagers, he stands and closes the gap between us in two long strides.

My heartbeat skids to a halt. He's so close I'm entirely engulfed in his cold shadow. So close the soft fabric of his slacks nearly brushes against my bare knees, reminding me of how thin this stupid hospital gown is, and that I have almost nothing underneath it.

Instinctively, I grip the wheels of my chair, but when I jerk them backward, I don't move. *What?* I look south and find the toe of a shiny Oxford shoe pressing against the base of the tire.

I look up just in time to see Raphael slip his hand in his pocket and produce a deck of cards. He holds them just above my eye-line in a large, tanned fist with a *thawp* of his thumb snapping against the base of the deck, and I catch a flash of color up his sleeve.

Is that—

"Choose a card."

The demand knocks all suspicion of hidden ink out of my brain. "What?"

He fans the deck. "Choose a card."

"Well, what card?" I huff out. "What game are we playing?"

"You won't like it if I have to ask again."

His voice is butter-like, but by now, I know better than to be fooled by it. My front teeth capture my bottom lip, and I glare at the cards like they've done something to piss me off.

Think, Penny.

Right, well. There's a one-in-fifty-two chance that I choose the card he wants me to choose. And if I choose that card, I have no idea if it's a good or a bad thing. That's if there even *is* a card he has in mind.

Fuck it.

Without allowing for another thought, I tap on a card three in from the right end of the deck. Raphael stiffens, then, as if in slow motion, he slides it out. With a snap of his wrist, he straightens the remainder of the pack and slips it into his pocket.

I look up to his face and our gazes clash for five long, unbearable seconds. Eventually, he tears his eyes from mine and regards the card. He remains expressionless, disinterested.

A tick of his jaw. A flare of his nostrils.

Then he does something that takes me by surprise even more than his laugh did. He bends over, grips my throat, and snatches all the air from my lungs like it's his to take.

I part my lips to gasp, and when I do, something stiff slides between them.

The tangy taste of ink on my tongue. Sharp, cardboard edges on my lips.

But I'm too distracted by the heat on my earlobe and the rough jaw against my cheek. "Monday, six pm on the fisherman's docks," he whispers in my ear. His thumb grazes over the thumping pulse in my neck, sending an unwelcome shiver between my thighs. "Bring your resume and don't be late."

A cold breeze skitters over my chest as he returns to his full height. He side-steps my chair and strides down the hallway without so much as a backward glance. I watch in disbelief, my heart slamming against my rib cage, as his convoy of black suits follow after him.

When heavy footsteps cease and a door slams, I let out a choked groan. With trembling hands, I tug the playing card from my mouth and stare at it.

A few seconds pass before I allow myself a small, shaky laugh. *Triumph.* It hums in my blood, swirling with a cocktail of adrenaline and relief.

The Ace of Spades.
The luckiest damn card in the deck.
I'm back, baby.

CHAPTER
Nine

Penny

M ONDAY AFTERNOON, GOLDEN HOUR.
 THE towering cliff face of Devil's Dip looms over my shoulders, and in front of me, the orange sun sits low on the horizon, its rays reaching across the glittering sea to touch my face.

Despite the frosty weather burning the shells of my ears and turning my eyelashes crisp, I feel warm from the inside out, because today, I'm going straight. For real this time.

I spent the weekend in the hospital trapped under starchy bed sheets with nothing to do but glare at the white ceiling and eat Wren's Hershey's chocolate bars. It gave me the mental space to realize that when I'd returned on the Devil's Coast last Thursday, I'd hopped off the bus on the wrong foot. Committing one last grift before going straight is like a crackhead saying they'll have just one last hit before getting clean. I'd set myself up for a false start.

A second chance came in the form of the Ace of Spades and I'm grabbing it with both hands. I've even pinned that playing card to the door of my refrigerator, and every time I wander into the kitchen in search of a snack, I'm reminded of how lucky I am.

I'm, unfortunately, also reminded of Raphael Visconti's thumb grazing over the pulse in my throat.

A gust of wind breaks over the nape of my neck and sends a shiver down my spine. With frozen fingers, I tug my cell from my pocket and glance at the time on the screen.

5.55pm.

Mild panic twists my stomach in a knot. *Shit.* All Raphael had said was to bring a resume, be on the fisherman's docks at six pm, and not to be late. Well, I don't need to check Google Maps for the umpteenth time to know that's where I am; the stench of rotting fish and the blood staining the two wonky jetties protruding out into the water make that pretty clear. But there's no swanky bar or restaurant in sight, or even any kind of establishment I could work in, for that matter. To double check, I turn in a slow circle, taking in the charred remains of the main port to my right, the craggy walls of the cliff behind me, and then come to a stop right where I started—staring out at the Pacific in confusion.

Have I been played? Christ, not once did the thought cross my mind.

Annoyance and the seeds of humiliation grow in my belly, and I mutter a curse under my breath.

Fuck him.

I hate being reliant on a man. And of all men, why did I choose to rely on the one with the most shark-like smile?

Grinding out an icy sigh, I slide my gaze to the only sign of life: an old man tying up a rusting bay boat at the end of a jetty. I suppose there's no harm in asking him if he has any idea where I'm meant to be. As I teeter across slippery rocks and walk over the wobbly slats toward him, I make a new vow to myself. If Raphael Visconti has played me, I'll go through with my fleeting plan: cut my losses, sell his watch, and fuck off over the border to Canada.

"Excuse me?" I pause for a response. Nothing. I clear my throat and ball my fists in my sleeves. "Um, random question, but do you know if there's a bar or anything around here owned by Raphael Visconti? I'm trying to—"

"You've missed the boat."

His voice is gruff and barely audible, thanks to the blistering wind.

"I'm sorry?"

His shoulders slump in annoyance, and his rope goes slack. "You've missed the boat," he grunts again.

I frown at the back of his yellow raincoat. What does he mean, I've missed the boat? Like, I didn't arrive early enough for Raphael's liking and he's snatched back the job opportunity?

"I don't understand."

Another grunt. This time, he jerks his head to the left. "The staff boat left five minutes ago."

Oh. He means literally, not metaphorically. But—staff boat? I follow his gaze, and when I spot what he's looking at, I'm even more confused.

A yacht. A big, shiny white one, the type you see in rap videos and documentaries about rich people living it up in the South of France. It's merely a speck on the blue horizon, and impossible to spot from the mainland, thanks to the way the cliff juts out to the left. But from the end of the jetty, I can see it in all of its tacky, perplexing glory.

Slowly, it dawns on me that I never asked what job Raphael had for me. Because it was in Devil's Dip, I'd foolishly assumed it'd be some sort of humble service job, but now that I'm staring at a mega yacht bobbing over the Pacific, I'm not so sure.

Am I a boat stew?

"How the fuck am I supposed to know?"

I blink and glance down at the fisherman. I hadn't realized I'd said it aloud. Shaking my head, I glance at my cell screen again and panic. "Is there any chance you could take me over to it?"

The man stills. Swivels his head around like a fucking owl. He rakes a beady eye over my tights and dress and meets my gaze. Clearly, he likes what he sees, because he cocks a bushy brow and asks, "What do I get in return?"

I open my mouth but close it again, clamping down on the sarcastic retort on my tongue. Nope. I've been given a second chance to become a good, normal person, and that also means getting rid of my smart-ass mouth. So, instead of saying *I won't boot you into the water and pray you forget how to swim*, I force a smile and bat my lashes. "You get the joy of helping out a pretty woman in a bind." I clamp my fingers together and add. "Pretty please? With a big, fat, juicy cherry on top?"

His gaze holds mine for a beat before he rises to his feet, a move that makes his bones crack. "All right, get in."

Men. For once, I'm glad they're all the fucking same.

He roughly grips my forearm to steady me as I clamber into the boat. I slide onto a cold, wet bench while he untethers us from the jetty and fiddles with the console. A few moments later, the engine stutters under my ass and we're skating over the choppy waves. A mix of ice water and wind assault my face and hair, and I squeeze my eyes shut and curl myself around my purse in my lap in an attempt to keep it dry.

But it's fruitless; by the time the purr of the engine slows to a lazy chug, I'm soaked. Slug-like strands of hair stick to the back of my neck, and I'm pretty sure even my fucking panties are wet. Oh, and another glance at my cell tells me I'm ten minutes late.

Not a great start, Penny.

The boat pulls up to a swim deck at the back of the yacht, and the fisherman takes his sweet-ass time hoisting me up onto the ledge of his boat so I can reach the ladder. When his bony fingers inch a little too low on my hips, I bark out a nasty "fuck off." His response is something equally as unchristian-like, and before I can make it past the first rung of the ladder, he kicks the engine back into gear and tears off back in the direction of the dock.

Asshole.

Clinging to the slippery ladder, with my purse slung over my shoulder, I use all the strength in my puny arms to hoist myself up another rung. Now, I can just about see over the edge of the swim platform, and my eyes land on a pair of black, tight-clad feet. I run my gaze up further, taking in long, slender legs, a ridiculously short skirt, and a red mouth wrapped around a cigarette.

Eyes, familiar and feline, come to mine. It's Anna, the girl Matt is obsessed with. She takes a slow, final drag, before flicking the lipstick-stained butt past my ear and into the raging sea behind me. "You're late," she says coldly, before spinning on her bare heels and sauntering through a set of double doors.

Well, then. I guess she's still bitter about me interrupting her conversation with Raphael.

Huffing out yet another curse word, I army-crawl onto the deck and rise to my feet. I consider following Anna through the double doors, but the puddle of saltwater at my feet suggests it'll only get me into more trouble. Instead, I wander aimlessly along the side deck, peering into portholes, looking for someone, *anyone*, that can give me even the faintest idea why the fuck I'm on a yacht in the middle of December.

I find a girl further down the deck, bathing in the glow of the security light.

She's also puking over the railing.

As I approach, she glances sideways and wipes her mouth with a wad of tissue in her hand. "Please don't tell me you're Penny."

I look down at the green sludge sliding over the curve of the boat. "Is it a bad time?"

She huffs out a dry laugh and rips open a water bottle, then finishes it in five greedy chugs. "Sorry, doll. I'm Laurie, Raphael's right-hand-woman. I'd shake your hand but I think the movement will make me sick again. Do you have your resume?"

I fish it from my purse. Laurie is beautiful, even when she's spewing up her lunch. A Black girl with brown eyes, long lashes, and the sleekest ponytail I've ever seen. She looks a bit older than me, but definitely no older than late twenties.

"I'll survive without a handshake," I say, amused. I glance down at her hand married to the railing. "Are you okay?"

"Of course not; we're half a mile from dry land and I can't swim," she mutters, stepping away from the sea and gripping her stomach. "But I'll get used to it. I have to, because thanks to the explosion at the port, we'll be working on this damn yacht for the foreseeable future."

My gaze slides across the horizon, watching the last of the sun's rays dip behind the storm-gray horizon, cooling the sky's color palette.

"We will?"

"Come on, I'll get you up to speed."

I follow the wobbly path she cuts along the side deck and come to a stop at the open clearing at the front of the boat, where both side decks meet at a point. No doubt there's a fancier word for it, but the only boat I've ever stepped on is a ferry.

The wind feels sharper up here, relentlessly whipping through my wet hair and chilling my bones. Laurie slices through its howling with a dull clap of her hands. "So Coastal Events—"

"What's Coastal Events?" I interrupt.

Her gaze slants. "Seriously? How the hell did you get this job?" She shakes her head, as if she can't be fucked to hear my answer. "Coastal Events is the Devil's Coast branch of Raphael's events agency. The other branch is Vegas Events, and well, you can figure out where that's based. Anyway, at Coastal, we supply staff and entertainment for most of the Viscontis' parties up and down the coast. Poker nights over in Hollow, birthday parties in Cove, weddings in Dip...you get the idea." She slowly turns so she's facing out to sea, and I suddenly realize I recognize her from the wedding. She was the woman with the clipboard and the earpiece barking at wait staff for not moving fast enough. Her shaky finger rises toward the shore. I follow it to the jagged cliff face, veiled by a thin cloak of smoke rising from the port below it. Around halfway up it, there's a crater-sized hole, its edges charred black from smoke. "Rafe wanted to create a more permanent venue on his home turf, and *that* was supposed to be it. They'd just fitted all the glass when the explosion happened. Apparently, it caused loads of structural damage and weakened the foundations, so it's going to take ages to rebuild." We both stare at the gaping hole for a few beats. It makes the cliff look as if it is crying out in agony. "So, yeah, the yacht is the temporary solution."

"Christ, who's rich enough to have a yacht on-hand to use as a temporary bar?"

She laughs. "Rafe has two."

I shake my head in disbelief. I can't help but think I should have swindled him for much more than a Breitling when I had the chance. But no, that's not the mindset of a girl who's *gone straight.*

"Uh, Penny?" I swivel around to see Laurie glaring at the puddle around my feet. "Did you swim here?"

"The ride over was a little choppy," I mutter, wringing out the hem of my faux-fur jacket. Fat water droplets splatter against the deck. "Is there anywhere I can dry off?"

"Sure, there's a whole locker room for the girls onboard." Catching my raised brow, she adds, "Yeah, the yacht is huge. I'll grab you a uniform, make yourself presentable and then I'll give you a tour."

She bustles back down the side deck and disappears through a door. I follow her in and find myself in a small laundry room. She spins around and stabs a finger at my Doc Martens. "No shoes on deck," she barks. "Take them off. Your coat too. I'll dry it during your shift." I slip off my boots and shake my coat off my shoulders and hand both to her. She places the boots on a rack under the counter and tosses my jacket in one of the dryers. It whirs to life, and for a few seconds, she watches the drum spin before clutching her stomach. "Gotta go," she grunts, shoving past me and heading back out to the deck. "Uniform is on the counter, locker room is on the first door on the—"

Her instructions are cut off by a gurgle, and then her head dips between her shoulder blades as she feeds the fishes in the water below.

Well, then. Feeling my own stomach churn at the sound of Laurie's guttural moans, I skim over the row of bags on the counter, find one labeled with my size, and slip out of the internal door and into a narrow hallway. Plush cream carpet compresses underfoot; a glossy mahogany wall grazes my wet shoulder. Christ, if the servant quarters are this posh, I can't imagine how fancy the rest of the yacht is.

Halfway down the hall, I come to a stop in between opposite doors. Laurie's lunch decided to make an appearance before she could tell me whether the locker room was on the right or the left, so I suppose I have to guess. I go for the right, twisting the golden knob and breezing over the threshold. My tights-clad feet transition from soft cream carpet to polished wooden floors.

I blink under the yellow glow of recessed spotlights, and immediately the weight of a wrong decision clamps down on my chest.

Twelve pairs of eyes fall on me, but there's only one that has the power to stretch across the boardroom table and warm my frozen skin.

His gaze, green and indifferent, starts at my toes, skims over the hemline of my wet dress, then hardens on the four-leaf clover around my neck. As if meeting my eye is a reluctant favor to a friend, he slips the pen he's holding between his teeth and finally drags his eyes to mine.

"Yes?"

One simple word, but coming from Raphael Visconti's lips, it feels like a bead of condensation sliding down the side of an ice-cold glass.

What the hell is he doing here? Out of all the establishments this man owns, why does he have to be at *this* one? But now I feel like an idiot. He's got every right to be here; it's his fucking *yacht* after all. It's my own fault for assuming he wouldn't be and coming unprepared to be assaulted by that steady gaze.

A hot unease rises to the surface of my skin. It's not because I've burst into a meeting barefoot and soaking wet. Not even because it looks to be a serious one, judging by the sea of solemn faces and sharp suits.

No, it's because Raphael's presence is *electric*. Even when he's still and silent, it spills out from the head of the boardroom table and crackles between the four mahogany-clad walls. An invisible force, I don't doubt I'd feel his static even if I curled up in the darkest corner.

I can't take my eyes off him; I suppose he's used to that. His appearance, as always, is as crisp as his tone. Fresh fade, fresh shave. Tanned skin stretched over high cheekbones punctuated with a lazy stare that makes my blood burn. His suit is signature—black jacket, white shirt, gold collar pin—and he wears it like armor.

He cocks a brow.

I shake my head.

"Wrong room," I mutter, taking a squelchy step back and bumping my head against the door. The impact wasn't hard at all, but the way the *thud* echoes in the silence makes me cringe and someone in the room takes a sharp intake of breath.

Raphael's apathetic expression doesn't break. "Are you lost?"

"No." *Yeah.* I hold up the bag with my uniform in it. "I'm just looking for somewhere to get changed."

Only a man with real power can let silence marinate for as long as he does. Six drops of water drip from the hem of my dress and onto the wooden floorboards before he drags the pen from his mouth and uses it to point to a door over his shoulder.

Eleven pairs of eyes trail after me as I muddle across the boardroom toward the door on the opposite side. None of them belong to Raphael; he's too busy writing something down in a leather-bound notebook and pretending I don't exist. But as I pass, I catch his gaze dropping to my feet while a muscle tics in his jaw.

I slip through the door and click it shut. Inside, I rest my back against the cold wood with the intention of waiting for my heartbeat to slow. It doesn't get the chance to, because only a few seconds later, Raphael's deep, silky voice floats through the crack.

"My apologies for the interruption, gentleman. Clive, please continue."

Another voice, this one old and gruff. "Of course, sir. As I was saying, the major challenge we faced last quarter was the dramatic rise of input costs. We responded with pricing actions, delivering an underlying price growth of four-point-nine percent, which, I'm sure you'll agree, is quite impressive considering the current climate."

There's a ripple of awkward chuckles. I have no doubt none come from Raphael, and my suspicion is confirmed when I hear his voice harden. "I wasn't asking about the last quarter, Clive. I was asking about your outlook for the upcoming one."

A shuffle of papers ripples through heavy silence. Someone clears their throat. "Y-yes, of course, sir. Um, Phillip, would you like to take over? I think you're better placed for this..."

Painful excuses and numbers plucked out of thin air go in one of my ears and come out the other; the only thing that lingers within the space between them is the satin-like calmness of Raphael's tone. He sounds so normal. So...*businesslike.* I wonder if the men on the other side can see the truth, too, or if they think he's the perfect gentleman like everyone else on this damn Coast does?

I wonder if they know he carried a gun to his brother's wedding. I wonder if, while he's sitting there, reclined in his large leather chair talking business, that gun is tucked into the waistband of his bespoke slacks?

For some reason, the thought vibrates through my core in the most inappropriate of ways.

I squeeze my eyes shut to rid myself of it, and when I pop them open again, I squint into the dark room in search of a light switch.

My fingers find one just a few inches from my head, and when I flip it, soft yellow lights flood the space and what I see fills me with confusion.

There's a black marble vanity with two sinks carved into it. A large shower hugs the corner, and in the middle, there's a free-standing tub—the type I imagine someone like Marie An-toinette would bathe in.

I'm in a bathroom, not a locker room. A *private* bathroom.

I step into the center of it, cutting through moist air, heavy with the familiar scent of cedar.

The shower head behind me drips. As I glare at my distorted reflection in the misted-up mirror, my heart slows and a light lust spreads between my thighs. Not only is it a private bathroom, it belongs to Raphael Visconti, and he's *just had a shower in here.*

Christ. The thought shouldn't make my mouth water the way it does. Shouldn't sweep a thrill through me and tighten my nipples underneath my wet dress. Although I was invited in by the man himself, it feels dangerous to be in here. Too intimate. Like I've slipped behind enemy lines and have unprecedented access to what goes on behind.

And of course, it means I can't help but imagine what he looks like naked.

Trance-like, I slide my fingers through the condensation on the surface of the marble vanity. I ball the corner of a damp towel in my fist. I pick up expensive-looking bottles and skim the French labels attached to them, although I must admit, the *French for Dummies* book I read a few months ago does little to help me decipher them. Everything is neat and in its place—nothing like my bathroom at home. There's probably still a damp towel on the floor in my bathroom in Atlantic City.

When I find his aftershave, I bring it to my nose and take a long, deep huff from the nozzle. The scent makes me dizzy, affecting me like a shot of liquor on an empty stomach. I snort in disbelief, mentally scolding myself for being so fucking pathetic.

He's just a *man*, for Christ's sake. Not even one I like. Besides, all men wear aftershave and most of them, save for a few shitty brands they sell at the dollar store, smell pretty nice. Attracting women is literally what they are designed to do, and it's safe to say I'm not immune to that.

I step away from the counter, if only to clear my head.

Right, I need to stop examining Raphael's bathroom like it's a crime scene and get ready.

I shimmy out of my wet dress and bundle it into the sink. Thank god this job has a uniform, because it's the only smart dress I have.

I run my tights under the hairdryer, momentarily drowning out the boring business chat seeping through the door, then tug out my new uniform from the bag and slip it on.

It's another dress. A short black one, with wrap-around detail under the bust. *Signora Fortuna* is embroidered in silver silk on the chest, and I can only assume that's the name of the yacht.

It's a cute dress and feels expensive against my skin. Staring at myself in the mirror, however, I realize my hair and makeup are far too dowdy to compliment it. My hair is going to be near-impossible to save without a good wash and blow dry, so I settle for a quick blast of the hairdryer and then bundle it up into a high ponytail. After wiping away the mascara running down my cheeks, I fish out my makeup bag and add a slick of red lipstick and a pair of silver hoops that I'd forgotten I had.

I take a step back and admire the DIY job. A familiar pleasure ripples down my spine; I've always enjoyed the process of dressing up. I suppose it's because it was always a big part of my nightly ritual. I'd take the rollers out of my hair, step out of my robe, and slip on my newest stolen dress. Then I'd slick on some lipstick and spritz some perfume before leaving my shitty apartment and heading to a glossy casino with the intention of hitting men in their pockets.

Le sigh. Those were the days.

After kissing a tissue to remove any excess lipstick, I pause before tossing it in the trash. Something mischievous sparks in me, and instead, I leave it resting on the vanity. I don't know why I do it, but I know I won't remove it. In *Criminal Psychology for Dummies*, there's a whole chapter on how lots of serial killers, like Jack the Ripper and the Zodiac Killer, would leave calling cards at their crime scenes to taunt police. Well, despite the fact he's given me a job, I can't resist the urge to piss off Raphael, even just a little bit. It's harmless—just a red kiss print on a tissue—but the thought of him coming in here, seeing it among his perfect things, then scowling sends a wave of stupid, silly smugness over me.

I chase the high by looking around for something else to meddle with. My eyes are drawn to the mist on the mirror and with quiet glee, I drag my finger along it.

Still smirking to myself, I bundle my wet clothes into my bag and step toward the door. As my fingers graze over the doorknob, Raphael's low and slow voice floats through the cracks and touches my chest.

I swallow thickly, not ready to leave the humid room and the intoxicating scent of man that lingers within it.

My gaze falls to the aftershave bottle on the counter. Without thinking, I bring it to my neck and spray its cool contents over the length of my throat. On my wrists. Behind my ears. It sizzles against my warm skin, making me feel breathless.

Why I want to carry a reminder of this man around with me all night, I'm not sure. Perhaps like the kiss print and the artwork on the mirror, it's just a petty way to one-up him without breaking my vow to keep my head down and be good. It's another quiet notch of triumph on my belt.

Or perhaps the blow to my head has given me a delayed concussion.

Tucking my belongings under my arm, I steel my spine and enter the boardroom again. Keeping my eyes trained on the shiny floor and clinging to the wall, I pass the table of suits and tune out the dude droning on about shareholder expectations and profit-loss.

A stare burns the nape of my neck and I know it can only belong to one man. As I reach the door, he interrupts the suit's monologue without so much as an apology.

"Penelope."

My full name slides across the table and grazes my back. It makes me wince. Not just because the only person to ever call me by my full name was my father, often in a whiny, desperate tone when he wanted me to go to the liquor store to steal him another bottle of Jim Beam, but because it reminds me of hot Sambuca breath and silky threats and soft fingertips grazing my palm.

For some pathetic reason, I can't bring myself to turn around, so I glare at the grain of the wood door instead. "Yes?"

The click of a pen. The groan of a leather chair reclining. "My office, ten minutes before the start of service."

Please. The absence of the word echoes around the hollow chamber within my rib cage and forms a knot of irritation. I can't help but think I should have spat in his fancy French shampoo.

But, in the spirit of second chances and going straight, I simply square my shoulders and force a nod.

"Yes, *sir.*"

As I stroll out to the hallway, I glance over my shoulder through the narrowing gap in the door. A dent in his perfect brow, a tick of his square jaw. A spark in his pitch-black gaze as it caresses the backs of my thighs.

Another break in his facade and another notch of victory on my belt.

CHAPTER
Ten

Penny

T HE THEME OF PLUSH cream floors and rich mahogany walls continues throughout the yacht, and between them, obscene wealth thrives like bacteria on a Petri dish. Italian sofas draped with cashmere throws dominate the lounge. The scent of tobacco and secrets hangs thick in the cigar room, which is cleverly hidden behind a false bookshelf in the library. The bar itself, with its marble surfaces and tawny leather stools, could be mistaken for the lobby of any five-star hotel, if it weren't for the steam rising off the hot tub on the other side of the sliding French doors.

Below deck, a network of narrow corridors and oddly-shaped rooms make up the staff quarters, and a gleaming kitchen with enough pantry space and stove burners to feed a small country beats at the heart of it.

Laurie tells me there are two types of staff: service crew and ghost crew. We're service, in charge of making sure anyone who comes onboard has a good time, while the ghost crew make sure the yacht runs smoothly. They're the captain, engineers, and deckhands, and they all live onboard and, captain aside, way below deck.

"Pretty impressive, huh?" Laurie asks, flinging open a door and spilling light onto what appears to be yet another terrace. We step outside. Now, the night is dark and frosty and the coastline is nothing but an inky shadow peppered with twinkling lights.

Truthfully, I don't think it's so impressive. In fact, I think it's pretty gross that, for more than seven-eighths of the year, this boat probably bobs unoccupied in some glitzy European port, while there are millions of people who can't even secure a regular roof over their head. What's worse is that this asshole apparently has *two* of these things.

But I bite my tongue and manage a nod. "Yeah, impressive."

I follow Laurie as she dodges tables and heat lamps and heads toward a staircase in the shadows. I let out a small groan, because how the fuck is there yet another deck above us? We climb the stairs up to another patio, and Laurie tugs a key from her pocket to open the set of sliding doors leading back inside.

"Final stop, I promise," she says, rubbing the back of her hand over her mouth. "Thank *god,* because my stomach can't handle all this walking about."

Warmth and low jazz brush my face when we step inside. As I scan the room, an unwelcome sense of nostalgia and familiarity creeps over me.

Deep-seated chairs flanking green velvet tables. Black and red squares and the sensual purr of a spinning roulette wheel.

"There's a casino onboard," I say flatly, my eyes skimming up to the half-moon bar and the man cleaning glasses behind it.

"Of course there is; it's Raphael Visconti," Laurie replies in a blunt tone designed to squash any other questions. "We'll be working in here tonight."

My gaze slides to her, wide and flecked with mild panic. "In the casino?"

"No, in the toilets around the corner," she deadpans. "Of course in the casino! I'm going to put you behind the bar because I've just looked at your resume, and you definitely have the most experience." Mistaking my expression for nerves, she adds, "Don't sweat it. Tonight will be just friends and family, so think of it as a trial run. The real opening night isn't until the New Year, so there's loads of time for you to learn the ropes. Come on, let me introduce you to Freddie."

I converse with the bartender, asking and answering mundane questions that both float out of my mouth and over my head. I can't concentrate on pleasantries, because I can't shake the ominous feeling of dread looming over me.

My fresh start is taking the same shape of the life I left behind and I don't like the look of it. Soon, this room will be filled with oversized watches and overstuffed wallets, and temptation, in all of its hot, itchy glory, will drip from the walls like condensation. As part of going straight, I vowed to never step foot inside a casino again. Not because I don't want to—*Christ*, do I want to—but because the impulse to be bad is too great.

I swallow the lump clotting my throat. Force a smile when Freddie makes some shit joke about the Viscontis drinking the bar dry.

When the small talk finally fizzles out, Laurie checks her watch then leads me back down to the locker room—the first door on the *left*—to get ready for the shift.

As we enter, expensive perfume and laughter float over the tops of the wooden lockers. I turn the corner and find a gaggle of girls leaning against a row of marble sinks. I recognize some of them, including Anna, from the wedding, and others from childhood summers spent on Cove beach.

"What are we gossiping about, ladies?" Laurie drawls, sliding my bag off my shoulder and stuffing it into a locker with my name emblazoned on the front of it. Fancy. "And don't say 'nothing,' because Katie's face is as red as a tomato."

I lock eyes with a pretty blond and smile. Laurie's right; she's flushed something rotten.

Another blond pushes off the sink, jumping as she tugs a pair of tights over her tiny waist. "We're having a debate."

Amusement tugs on Laurie's lips. "Pray, tell."

"We can't agree on the type of girl Raphael goes for. Katie and I reckon he has the hots for blonds, but Anna thinks he only goes for brunettes."

She pronounces Anna like *Uh-Nah*, and based on that alone, I stop feeling even the tiniest bit guilty about interrupting her chat with Raphael.

Anna leans over the sink, reapplying her blood-red lipstick in the mirror. "I don't think; I *know*. My friend has worked as a shot girl in one of his Vegas casinos for over a year and she says he always has a brunette on his arm."

"Well, one thing is for sure. He goes for girls with at least half a brain, so that rules all of you out, anyway," Laurie mutters. A beat passes, then she doubles over, gritting her teeth. "Great, back to the bathroom I go. Meet me in the lounge for the start-of-service briefing in fifteen." Hurried footsteps thud on the tiles, then a door slams shut in the distance.

"Poor Laurie," Katie says, before turning her attention back to Anna. "Anyway, it sounds like you just have a bad case of wishful thinking."

"It *is* wishful thinking," Anna snaps back, far too quickly. "I have my eye on him, so whether he goes for brunettes, blonds, or"—her gaze slides to mine in the mirror with a spark of disgust—"even gingers, you better back off, because I'm staking my claim right now."

Soft laughter ripples between the girls. My cheeks burn and my tongue twitches with a nasty clap-back. Reminding myself of the Ace of Spades stuck to the refrigerator door, I busy myself with tugging my makeup bag out of the locker and rummaging around in it for my compact. *Nice* girls take back-handed compliments with a grain of salt, or bitch to their friends about it later. They don't start pulling hair.

"I think he has his eye on you, too," the other blond admits, spritzing herself with enough perfume to set off the fire alarm. "Not that it matters, because those rumors are definitely true."

"What, that he never goes on a date with the same girl twice?" another girl says, breezing around the corner in just her bra and panties. "I agree. He'll be a bachelor until he's eighty."

"And even then, we'll all still want to fuck him."

Girlish laughter rises up like shower steam and for some dumb-ass reason, irritation slithers down my spine. I couldn't give a flying fuck about Raphael Visconti's love life, but the fact that he fucks-and-chucks women is just the cherry on top of his obnoxious cake. It makes all the smooth talking and shark-like smiles seem even worse.

"You know what I think?" bra-and-panties girl says. "I think he's got the hots for the new girl."

The laughter stops, and the weight of five pairs of eyes falls heavy on my back.

Silence. Bitchiness crackles in the air like static, and then a retort from bra-and-panties girl flutters through it.

"Not a fucking chance."

It's low and syrup-like, but it wades through the locker room and steels my spine.

Sighing, I close my eyes and rest my forehead on the frame of my locker.

I'm not used to being around catty women. Being around women at all, actually. Good times spent with my mother only existed in pockets of sobriety. Outside of them, the only time she'd talk to me would be to drunkenly whine that my existence had ruined both her figure and her relationship with my father.

In high school, the girls I ate lunch with acted like I had leprosy after my parents were killed. The only group of girlfriends I've ever had were the strippers I worked with for a few months. They were kind and uplifting and would be the first to come to my defense with an eight-inch glass stiletto in hand when a patron stepped over the line. But strippers, like swindlers, follow the money. They'd bounce from bar to bar, even city to city, and it was all too easy to lose contact.

It's sad to say aloud, but it's all I've ever wanted. Maybe it's because when my parents would pass out on the sofa, exhausted from a day of strong liquor and loud arguments, I'd sit on the rug in front of the television and watch *The Sisterhood of the Traveling Pants* on mute. I longed to have friends like that. Friends I could complain about my parents to and who'd invite me to sleepovers on Saturday night so I didn't have to hear them fighting on the other side of my bedroom walls. Instead, all I had was a hotline, and, of course, Nico. While I love him, it's just not the same. Sure, I'm forever grateful to him for teaching me how to unbuckle a Rolex crown clasp with my eyes closed, but it would've also been nice to have someone teach me how to do winged eyeliner, or how to choose a bra that fits.

I learned how to insert a tampon from a YouTube tutorial, and I *still* don't know how to braid my hair.

There's a rustling beside me, and I pop an eyelid to see Katie sliding down the bench and coming to a stop next to my locker. She looks up at me with an embarrassed smile. "Ignore her; she's on her period."

I roll my eyes and cross over to the mirror above the row of sinks to touch up the concealer on my faint head wound.

I stand beside Anna, pretending like I can't see her gaze travel down the length of my body in the mirror.

She's thinking what all the other girls are thinking. I can see it in their sideways glances, but she's the only one to be so blatant about it. I don't look like them. I'm not six feet tall and I don't have the type of body that only eating leafy greens and doing a hundred crunches before bed will achieve. But I don't give a flying fuck, because I like how I look. Well, I'm *impartial* about it, at least. Worrying about the little pouch of fat that hangs over the waistband of my panties has never paid my bills. Obsessing over the fact that my thighs rub together has never given me a winning Blackjack hand.

And being judgmental about other women's bodies has never made mine miraculously perfect, either.

"Penelope, isn't it?"

Gritting my teeth, I slide my eyes over to Anna's reflection and nod. For whatever reason, she smirks and goes back to applying her makeup.

Skin stinging from thinly veiled insults, I focus on dusting powder over my nose and removing a mascara clump. It's easy to feign indifference, until the conversation turns even lewder and my cheeks turn crimson.

"Why do you think he only fucks from behind?" bra-and-panties chick muses.

"I'm guessing because he likes using hair as a leash," Anna retorts, swishing her own long locks over her shoulders for dramatic effect. "I've heard he fucks *rough*. Which is so hot, considering he's such a fucking gentleman."

Bra-and-panties eye's meet mine in the mirror. "What about you, new girl? What do you think?"

I think I'm thankful for low lighting and full coverage foundation. I snap my compact shut and hold her gaze. "I think I'll just ask the man himself."

"What?"

"Uh-huh. Where's his office?"

"But—"

"Where's his office?" I repeat, calmly.

Silence stretches from the lockers to the sinks. Katie's laugh slices through it. "Behind the bridge."

"Thank you, Katie," I say, walking over to my locker, tossing my makeup bag inside, and slamming it shut with more force than necessary. Before I stomp out, I pin Anna with a blistering glare. "Don't worry, I'll find out whether he prefers blonds, brunettes, or even *gingers*." Not waiting for her reply, I switch my wrath to bra-and-panties chick. "And what did you want to know again? Whether he gets off on pulling hair? I'll ask on your behalf, don't worry." I pretend to scratch my head in thought, ignoring the way her jaw drops open. "Oh, what was the other question you had? If he's into choking, right?"

"I didn't say—"

"Yes, that was it. Choking and spitting into girls' mouths. Got it. I'll report back. Toodles!"

I give an enthusiastic wave over my shoulder as I stride toward the door, ignoring the breathy "Wait!" coming from behind me.

Out in the hallway, I lean against the wall and take a deep breath. Christ, maybe there's a *For Dummies* book on how to deal with mean girls in the workplace without getting fired.

One thing's for sure; I won't be sharing a pair of Levi's with these girls over a long summer.

CHAPTER
Eleven

Penny

A s I PAD THROUGH narrow hallways and up spiral stairs barefoot, it's easy to put my new colleagues' catty comments to the back of my mind, because there's a much more pressing issue at hand, and it's waiting for me in the room behind the Captain's bridge.

My office, ten minutes before the start of service. He didn't say please, which would suggest I was in trouble, but, then again, in the handful of times I've had the misfortune to encounter Raphael Visconti, he's never used pleasantries, anyway.

My nerves vibrate against the walls of my stomach as I tap out a timid knock on the mahogany door. Almost immediately, his deep, velvet-clad voice floats from underneath it. "Come in."

I ball my clammy fists, remind myself to keep my smart-ass mouth shut, and step inside.

Raphael is sitting on the edge of his desk, forearms on his thighs and a poker chip spinning between his thick fingers. His gaze comes up from the floor, carves a laser-like path up my legs and over my chest, then narrows on my face.

The poker chip stops spinning.

"Is that the uniform Laurie issued you?"

Heart lurching, I only manage a nod.

His eyes fall down my body again, darkening with every square inch they cover. Why does it feel like he's silently rating each of my features out of ten? And why do I feel like I've scored pretty low?

And why am I disappointed about it?

Eyes coming to a stop on my thighs, he gives a tight smile, then he pushes himself off the desk and mutters something I don't catch. I can't be certain, but it sounded like *Christ*.

A prickle crawls up the nape of my neck as he walks to the far side of the room and stands with his back to me, facing the large French doors that frame the moody sea. He slides his hands into his pockets, the broad planes of his shoulders tense.

I can feel a cocktail of embarrassment and annoyance staining my cheeks, because with every heavy second that passes, it becomes more and more apparent what he's thinking.

He hires a type, and I don't fit that. Now he's wondering what the fuck to do about it without catching a discrimination case.

Just before the urge to tell him to go fuck himself overpowers my desire to hold down this job, he turns around and takes me off-guard with a much softer expression and a two-word command.

"Come here."

My natural instinct is to scowl and shake my head, because I'm still embarrassed about succumbing to the curl of his finger at the wedding. But at the same time, there's something so easy and charming about his tone that it makes my heart forget its next beat.

Ridiculous. I wonder if this is his real appeal. Not his looks or his easy wit, but the fact he has a talent for delivering crude commands in such a way that makes you want to follow them, instead of slapping him across the face.

Come here. Sit on my face. Moan my name louder, Penelope.

My feet move before my brain agrees to it. I come to a stop in front of him, close enough to feel the heat rolling off his body.

I didn't know warmth could radiate off an ice cube.

I freeze when he reaches out and gently cups my jaw. My head moves at his will, up and to the left, so I'm staring directly at the moon shining bright against the starless sky. His hand is large and hot, save for the ice-cold ring resting against my cheekbone. *Christ.* A warmth spreads to my lower stomach, and despite my attempt at keeping my expression neutral, I know he can feel my pulse beat a little faster in my throat; feel my breath grow denser as it skitters over the back of his hand.

"How's the head?"

"Fine," I bite back, before tugging myself out of his grasp. He lets me go easily, with little more than an amused smirk. I was definitely out of my mind when I thought I wanted him to treat me like he treats other women. I don't like this side of him. Hell, I don't like *him*. He makes me feel confused and out-of-sorts, like I've stepped outside on a February morning only to discover there's a blistering heatwave.

"Take a seat."

"I'd rather stand."

Acting like he hasn't heard me, he reaches for a piece of paper on his desk. He studies it.

"Penelope Price."

With a heavy heart, I realize he's holding my dog-eared resume. The one I knocked out in the early hours under the white lights of Devil's Dip's diner. It's a web of lies printed on one side of A4, and my fingers twitch to snatch it from his hands.

He takes a few leisurely steps across the room and tilts my resume toward the sliver of moonlight spilling through the glass.

Those green eyes glitter as they scan from left to right. "You spent six months as a cocktail waitress at the Hurricane casino in Atlantic City?"

Chest tightening, I nod. *Fuck.* Putting the casino I burned down in Atlantic City on my resume seemed like a genius idea at three a.m., when I was buzzing off coffee and chocolate cake. It no longer exists, so there's nobody there to fact check it. I mean; it's not the *biggest* lie on my resume, but it is the boldest. Technically, I did spend six months there, however it was on the other side of the bar, drinking tropical cocktails from coconut shells and swindling businessmen out of their company's travel allowance with stupid bar tricks.

"Interesting," Raphael muses, stroking his jaw. "The owner's brother is a good friend. Tell me, what was it like working under Thomas? I hear he's quite the tyrant."

He looks up at me, eyes shaded with a challenge. Despite my unease, prickly irritation nips at my edges, because I know he's trying to catch me out.

"Can't be that good of a friend, because his name is Martin."

The cool silver pendant around my neck sizzles against my clammy skin. Why do I know that? Because he growled it against my nose in the side alley of the casino, before slamming my head against the brick wall.

Raphael stares at me in dark amusement, before turning his attention back to my lies in his hand. "And so it is."

He paces the floor, continuing to read. I hate how hyper-aware I am of every slow, heavy footstep. How I feel every *thud* like a heartbeat under my rib cage. Seconds feel like minutes, and when the tension gets unbearable, my desperate voice slices the silence.

"What is this about?" I blurt out. "Am I in trouble already?"

He gives a tight smile, and, taking all the time in the fucking world, he sinks into his leather chair and spins it around to face me. Thanks to the sliver of moonlight cutting across his face, I have the displeasure of seeing him glance down at the hemline of my dress and run his tongue over his teeth.

A displeasure for sure. But still, being the subject of his attention makes me a little breathless.

"Penelope, I think we got off on the wrong foot." He leans forward, rests his forearms on his thighs and looks up at me with a half-lidded gaze. "If you're to work for me, then our relationship needs to be more..." He bites on his bottom lip and sweeps an eye over my thighs again. "Professional."

I feel myself blushing at the way he wraps those plump lips around the word *professional*. It drips with insinuation, like we've been secretly fucking for three months. Which of course, would never happen in a million years. Partly because I'd rather stick a knitting needle in my eye, and partly because I'm sure Raphael would happily source the sharpest one possible for me.

Plus, if that rumor is true, and he only fucks girls once...

I sweep the thought away with a breathless shudder. "I don't understand."

"Well, I fear I've given you the wrong impression of me."

"And what would that be?"

"That I'm not a gentleman."

My snort is ugly, loud and loaded with disbelief. It bounces across the dark office and lands on Raphael's perfect poker face. It's all sharp lines and thick lashes and if I saw it across a velvet table, I can't say for sure I wouldn't fold, even if I had a Royal Flush.

"You're not a gentleman."

His eyes flicker with the tiniest flame of amusement. "No?"

"You own two yachts."

"The Queen of England has eighty-three."

I blink. "You're a Visconti."

"So is Nico, and you seem to like him just fine."

"You carry a gun!"

He runs two fingers over his bottom lip, trying, and failing, to hide a smirk. "The gun is fake, Penelope."

"My ass."

"What about it?"

Our gazes clash. Mine burns with annoyance, his simmers with satisfaction. I tear myself out of its magnetic trap. It might make my blood a few degrees hotter, but I'll be damned if I'll be as easily fooled by it as the girls in the locker room below. Instead, I glare at the gold doorknob, wishing I could open it with the power of my mind.

"Penelope."

I grit my teeth at the way he delivers my name on a silk fucking cushion. I *hate* how it feels like cashmere against my ears, yet crackles and sparks like an electric current between my thighs.

I'd rather claw my eyes out than bring them back to him, but I do it anyway. Studying my face, he slides his hands out into the space in front of him. First, palm down, then with a slow, sensual roll of his wrists, his palms turn up toward the ceiling.

Smooth, tanned. Thick, long fingers, and a ring worth more than my fucking soul. Sure, I hate how he says my name, but I hate the sight of his hands more. Christ. My breathing shallows, and despite knowing better, my head swims with the thought of Raphael's fingers tugging at my strands. It's sordid, but I'm curious to know if the rumors are true about him pulling hair when he fucks. I can imagine the wining and dining part no problem—I'm sure he can turn on the charm like a tap, but he looks too polished to fuck so rough.

"Do you see blood on these hands, Penelope?" I scowl in response. When he cocks a brow expectantly, I force a small head shake. "You'll never see blood on these hands. You know why? Because I'm a *gentleman.*

Seemingly satisfied, he leans back in his chair and steeples his fingers under his chin. "Clean slate?"

His smugness cloaks my skin like a fever, and I want to douse myself in ice-cold water to rid myself of him. At this point, I'll say anything, *do* anything, to leave.

"Fine, clean slate. Brushed under the carpet. Line in the sand, whatever," I snap.

I move to side-step the desk, but as I pass Raphael, his hand shoots out and grabs my wrist.

Jesus. Feeling all the blood drain out of my head, I look down at where he holds me. His grip isn't hard like it was at the wedding, but it has the same effect of gluing me to the spot. It's firm. Secure. Sure, I could wriggle out of it with a shake of my hand, but when his thumb skims lightly over the pulse on the inside of my wrist and makes my vision jolt, I somehow know I won't.

Now, his voice has a rough edge when it touches my clammy skin. "If I'm a gentleman, I'm going to need you to be a lady."

I blink. "Meaning?"

"Meaning, no more stolen dresses and no more stupid quizzes."

His gaze bores a hole in my cheek and the lump in my throat thickens.

"Better pay me more, then."

Welp—vow broken. At least I bit my tongue for longer than usual, I suppose. My insolence reminds me that I don't even know what the salary is: I could be getting paid in *Reese's Pieces* and *way-to-go!*'s for all I know.

His grip tightens, confirming what I already knew. For the last five minutes, he's been in character, playing the Raphael he wants people to see. This cool, calm demeanor is a facade, and he's about as good at upholding it around me as I am keeping my mouth shut around him.

"Not every man that passes through this yacht will be as nice as me, Penelope."

"As nice as you? Are you forgetting you came at me with a hammer?"

"Could have been worse."

"Yeah?"

"Mhm," he drawls, gaze flashing black. "I could have whacked it on your fucking head."

Breathless from the unexpected venom in his tone, it takes me half a second longer than usual to regain my composure. When I do, I rip my wrist from his grip and clutch my chest, pouting like

I'm super offended by his sudden assholery. "Ouch. You're so big and scary that I think I just pissed my panties a little bit."

"Did you steal those, too?"

"It's probably best we don't talk about my panties—wouldn't want to give you a hard-on in the middle of your work day."

His glare narrows, but amusement now softens its edges. "You talk a lot of smack for a girl that needs a job."

I falter. Despite the seeds of fury spouting in my stomach, my better judgment tells me I should shut the fuck up. He's still my boss, after all, and although I'm not happy with that, I really need the money.

Fine.

I straighten my spine. Pin him with a docile smile and pretend like the triumph humming behind his expression doesn't piss me off.

"You're right," I say as sweetly as I can muster. "Forgive my insolence, gentleman. I'll take you up on that clean slate, starting from right now."

I catch a glimpse of the small smirk tilting his lips before I turn toward the door. I'm twisting the doorknob when his low, syrupy words trickle along my nerve endings. He mutters them from the shadows, but I hear them like he yelled them into a megaphone.

"Bet you don't last the night."

My shoulders hitch, and a familiar thrill coasts down my spine. "Bet you twenty bucks I do."

"Bet you fifty."

I run my tongue over my teeth, hot, bitter annoyance swelling inside of me. "Yes, *sir*."

The lure of freedom and an orange glow wash over me as I open the door to the bridge.

"Penelope."

My lids flutter shut. *So close.*

"It's yes, *boss*."

CHAPTER
Twelve

Rafe

W ARM WHISKEY, HIGH STAKES, and the occasional kiss from Lady Luck are the hallmarks of a Raphael Visconti party, and tonight is no different. Despite the rumors and the fan-fare that surround any event I tack my name onto, it's this simple Holy Trinity that has amassed me a fortune within the nightlife industry. Everything else is just fluff and elaborate marketing.

It's the first trial night. The crowd is tight-knit, the atmosphere is electric and care-free. Drinks flow and laughter floats. You'd never know the Viscontis were on the brink of a civil war, or that less than an hour ago, I made the decision to liquidate my majority stakeholder shares in Miller & Young, the logistics company that has been my third largest source of income for the last five years.

But I suppose us Viscontis have always had a talent of burying our problems underneath velvet tables while we piss away our ill-gotten gains with ridiculous bets over the top of them.

Talking of ridiculous bets. Across the table, Benny and Gabe are playing Vegas Rummy. When we were kids, they'd play it under the back pew of our father's church during Sunday service, but now, the stakes are a little higher than a couple dollars and a pack of Big Red gum, and, well, Gabe is a lot less forgiving.

If Gabe loses, Benny gets his Harley. If Benny loses, Gabe gets to break three of Benny's fingers.

Of his choosing.

Usually, I'd be head-over-ass invested in such a show, probably throwing a few bricks of my own into the ring for pure entertainment value. But not tonight. Because tonight, a certain copper-haired brat with sticky fingers and an attitude problem keeps stealing my attention.

Penelope Price.

She's working behind the bar and it's safe to say it's the first one she's ever been behind, regardless of what her resume says. She's been on shift for just over an hour and already three crystal tumblers have met their demise on my mahogany floors. *Three.* Each time I hear a smash, another spark of annoyance zaps down my spine, and it gets a little harder to maintain a gentlemanly composure.

She wasn't buying it, anyway.

Every time I glance in her direction, she meets my scowl with one of her own and I remember yet another thing I dislike about her.

I dislike the massive dick she scrawled on my mirror; dislike that I laughed aloud when I saw it. That obnoxious lipstick print she left on a tissue in my bathroom, too.

But what irks me more than anything is how she looks in her uniform, and worse, how every red-blooded male on board—with the exception of my pussy-whipped older brother, of course—is clearly thinking the same thing.

Never in my life have I seen these men *get up and go to the bar* to order a drink, like commoners at a local pub. These are men that don't even need to look up when the whiskey in their glass dips below a certain level, because another will just magically appear on a silver serving tray. But right now, there are two Viscontis and three of my former business associates forming a line at the bar, waiting like simps for Penelope to serve them.

I'd chalk it up to her being fresh meat on the Coast, but as my gaze, once again, slides reluctantly to her, I'd be lying if I said I didn't understand the appeal.

Earlier on the terrace, I overheard one of my men comment that she looks like Jessica Rabbit, and while I don't pay him to perv on my girls, he's right. She's got these big, blue eyes that seem to fool everyone but me. Pale skin that flushes crimson at the slightest insult. Freckles on a button nose that merge into a single mass every time she scrunches it.

And that body—don't even get me started. It's like she's jumped right out of a 1950's pin-up poster. On every other girl circulating the room, the uniform looks like a *smart black dress*. So why does it make her look like a stripper role-playing a slutty cocktail waitress at a bachelor party?

But it's not just her looks, it's the way she uses them to her advantage. Like right now, for instance. She's resting her palms against the bar and gazing up at Marco with a smirk on her lips, like there's a million dirty thoughts racing behind that innocent gaze. Of course, my idiot second-cousin is lapping it up, no doubt convinced he's getting into her panties tonight. But I know the truth—she's not interested in what's under his suit, she's interested in what's in his wallet.

How do I know? Because when she slid up next to me at the bar last Thursday night and peeled off that fur coat like she couldn't wait to show me every inch of her body, I almost fell for her act too.

Not almost—I did. Gave her my beloved watch, didn't I?

It makes sense, I suppose. Made men are attracted to trouble and this girl epitomizes it.

I slip the poker chip from my pocket and flick it between my thumb and forefinger, as if it'll save me from the claws of irritation digging under my skin. I don't get irritated—I pay people to get irritated for me. But something about the way my newest member of staff is gazing at my dumb-ass cousin rubs me the wrong way.

Despite Nico asking so nicely for a favor, I hadn't planned on giving her a job. Nothing about a loud-mouthed girl in a stolen dress screams employable, but while I was on damage control duty at the hospital, she'd rolled into my room with a nasty gash on her head and my lungs had tightened.

She'd been there, at the port, and suddenly, the word *co-incidence* had lost its calming edge. Every ounce of logic that has gotten me this far in life tells me the whole doom card thing is bullshit. Even if it isn't, there's no chance in hell Little-Miss-Hot-Mess-Express is it. But logic only stretches so far, so, under the pretense of changing my mind about my favor to Nico, I'd offered her a job. It was purely a selfish decision. I'm a busy man, and I need to squash this paranoia that this five-foot-nothing redhead is going to lead to my downfall. I need confirmation that the loss of my watch and the port explosion really were just coincidences. Despite knowing I was being ridiculous, I couldn't help but get her to draw a card from my deck.

Bullshit or not, if she'd drawn the Queen of Hearts I'd have put a bullet between her eyes. But she didn't. She drew the Ace of Spades, of all things. The luckiest card in the deck. I was part relieved and part pissed off that I'd only fueled her egotistical belief that she was *lucky*.

With a sideways glare at the four-leaf clover around her neck, I roll my shoulders back and take a sip of whiskey. Yeah, she's not my doom card. If she was, my world would be going up in flames right now. Sure, I'm down fifteen G's tonight because I've lost every hand I've picked up, and after that shit-show meeting in the boardroom, I'm cutting ties with one of my most lucrative investments, but these things happen.

"Shit."

A dark hiss shoots across the table from Benny's lips and I smirk into my whiskey glass. Gabe's just thrown down a Joker, and now, Benny's staring at the back of his inked hands, as if he's weighing what fingers he could cope without for two-to-eight weeks. Clearly unable to decide, he shakes his head and scoops up the fanned cards.

"Best of three."

"It'll cost you," Gabe retorts. He's feigning boredom, but I know he's itching to snap a couple of Benny's bones.

"Cost me what?"

"Another finger."

Benny pauses, before grunting out a monosyllabic agreement and dealing out another round.

Idiot. He should know by now Gabe doesn't just break fingers; he smashes them with his favorite hammer.

Out of the corner of my eye, the women's restroom door swings open and Rory staggers out of it. She stops, blinks at the five-deep line of girls waiting to pee, and holds her hand up in an awkward apology. A few seconds after, Angelo strides out after her, straightening his tie with one hand and raking his tousled hair with the other.

I give a small shake of my head. Even Benny can keep his cock in his pants longer than Vicious these days, and that's saying something.

He's a fool in love, not a capo on the brink of war.

Angelo catches my eye and drops me a wink, before slapping his wife's ass and sauntering through the French doors, where Cas smokes a cigarette under a heat lamp. Rory smooths down her red dress and weaves between tables, making a beeline for the chair next to me.

"Oh, swan," she mutters as her stiletto buckles underneath her. Before she can face-plant on the table, my hand shoots out to grab her forearm and I gently lower her into the seat. "It's these darn shoes. I'm more used to running sneakers than heels these days."

"More used to OJ than white wine spritzers, you mean?"

She squints up at me like she's looking into the sun, a lop-sided grin on her lips. "White wine spritzer, you say?"

Amused, I beckon the nearest server and order another round, plus a large water.

Rory slumps against the chair, twirls a curl around her finger, and studies me. I gulp the last dregs of my whiskey in preparation. *Here we go.*

"So...are you feeling lucky tonight, Rafe?"

"No more Blackjack, Rory."

"Aw, come on. Just one round." Her eyes dart up to Angelo out on the deck, then come back to me with a mischievous spark. "Or are you a chicken?"

My lips tilt. "I'm scared shitless, darling."

Last month, Rory started playing Visconti Blackjack with Angelo's men. It's similar to regular Blackjack, but you play against an opponent, rather than the house. I guess she didn't connect the dots between her winning every round and her opponents being on my brother's payroll, because when she asked me to play with her, she was shocked that she lost. She lost the next game, and every game after that. Now, she owes me three-hundred grand of her husband's money and can't seem to get enough of trying to claw it back.

Of course, I'd never actually cash the debt in, but it's been mildly amusing to watch her squirm about it.

"Fine," she sighs. She sweeps a curious gaze over the Venetian chandelier about our heads. "Nice yacht. Does it count as a business expense now that you're using it as a party venue?"

"Are you working with the feds, Rory?"

She lets out an easy laugh. "Nope, just trying to make conversation with my new brother-in-law."

"Brother-in-law? You were due to be my aunt up until a few months ago."

A server places two drinks in front of her and a fresh whiskey in front of me. She reaches for the wine glass, but I push it out of reach and rap my ring against the water bottle. "This first."

She scrunches her nose but doesn't protest. Three glugs later, she slams it down on the table and basks me in her attention again. "Well?"

"Can't you get to know your other brother-in-law, instead?"

She lunges over and clumsily slaps Gabe's shoulder. He doesn't flinch. "Me and Gabe? We're already as thick as thieves."

"Yeah?" I can't imagine Gabe bonding with anything except his motorbike or a new gun, let alone Angelo's blond, bird-loving wife.

"Yeah. He helped me build the bird hide in his garden. Dug the pond out for me, too." She leans in, wide-eyed and whispering. "And just last week, he let me shoot his—"

"What did I tell you?" Gabe cuts in, glancing up from his cards with a scowl.

Rory pretends to lock her lips with an imaginary key. "Oops, I forgot. Gabe says you're a snitch."

Mild amusement tugs on my lips; I throw my arm over the back of her chair and settle into the conversation. "Did he now?"

"Uh-huh." She gulps her wine. "Says you'll squeal to my husband like a little pig."

"Is that right?"

"Yup. And we don't talk to snitches."

Gabe nods in approval, tosses the Jack of Diamonds on the table, then holds his fist out for Rory to bump. She does so, but immediately winces and tucks her balled hand into her lap when she thinks nobody's looking.

I sip my whiskey and set it down with a dark chuckle. It soon evaporates into thin air, however, because a loud laugh shoots through the casino and sucker-punches my jaw. Gritting my teeth, I cut a reluctant look to the bar and find its owner.

Another thing to add to my list of dislikes: The fact that her laugh is the loudest thing in the room. What's so funny, anyway? She's only talking to Nico. He barely says three words in the same breath, and he couldn't tell a joke even if he read it on the back of a Laffy Taffy wrapper.

I regard her through a lens of mild contempt. Strands of her red ponytail fall off her shoulders as she tosses her head back to laugh again. If I hadn't hired her to satisfy my superstition, the girl would be out on her ass before the end of the night, and not just because I bet her fifty bucks she would be.

I'll let it slide, but only until I've confirmed she's not my doom card. Then she can crawl back into whatever hole she escaped from. For the sake of keeping the peace for the short time she'll work here, I brought her into my office in an attempt to extend an olive branch, but the moment she sauntered in and scowled at me—in *that uniform*—I practically snapped that branch in half.

She's irritating, but I'd be lying if I said she didn't pique my interest. Aside from her penchant for outdated bar tricks and her egotistical belief she's lucky, I know barely anything about her. Nico only told me her parents worked at the Visconti Grand when he and Penny were both kids, and she left town when she was eighteen.

I run a thumb over my bottom lip and give a small shake of my head. Eighteen, Christ—that was only three years ago. She's still a kid, so fuck knows why I'm even looking at the length of her skirt, let alone wondering what's underneath it.

I shift my brain to a topic less X-rated. No one turns up in Cove in a stolen dress with a suitcase on a Wednesday night. She's running from something, and my blood is itching to know what. I slipped a Sinners Anonymous card in her coat pocket, and another between the pages of the Bible in her hospital room in the off-chance she's a God-fearing Catholic girl, which I highly doubt. I'm hoping when I check the voicemail on Sunday, I'll find a naughty secret in the inbox.

As if suddenly aware I'm glaring at her, Penelope's laugh comes to an abrupt stop. The doe-eyed darling pretense melts away, and she meets my eyes with annoyance.

I'm not the type of man who averts his gaze, even if he doesn't like what he sees.

She doesn't flinch. Doesn't back down, either. I'm not usually one for insolence, but *Jesus*, it's kind of hot. Nico is leaning over the bar and talking shit in her ear, but she doesn't take her eyes off mine. We glare at each other for what seems like minutes—but surely can only be seconds—before she slowly lifts her hands to her high ponytail, splits it in half, and pulls.

A little huff of air escapes my lips. Fuck. It's an innocent enough move. I've seen lots of girls adjust the tightness of their ponytail like that, but for some reason, when she does it, I feel it like a white-hot bolt of lightning in my groin.

She might as well have tugged on the end of my dick.

I grind my molars and glance at the liquor wall behind her head for a split-second's respite. When I look back, she's still staring at me, a smug smirk dancing on her lips, and irritation, itchy and hot, creeps down the back of my collar.

It was a short, silent game, and she just played dirty to win it.

Irritation is chased by a dark, electric thrill.

Silly girl. If only she knew I don't just play games; I create them. I can't wait until she finally picks up the phone and plays my most exciting game of all. I make a mental note to slip another Sinners Anonymous card into her locker, then turn back to my sister-in-law while a server tops off my glass.

Back to being a gentleman.

"I'm sorry you're not in Fiji right now, Rory."

"Eh," she says with a shrug. "I'd rather stay on the Coast and watch Dante get his head blown off."

My glass halfway to my lips, I still. Benny flashes me an *I-told-you-so* look. I know what he's thinking: the Hollow brothers have a theory that Vicious's new wife is a secret psychopath. Said theory only strengthened a few nights ago at a private game over in Whiskey Under the Rocks, when Castiel told us that he and his Russian girl went over to dinner at their house just before the wedding. Cas had made a comment about them needing a new chef, because the lasagna was dry, and it turned out Rory had cooked it herself.

She'd smiled sweetly and told him there was no need to apologize, but after dessert, Cas went out to his Lambo to find all but one tire slashed and a little angry face scratched into the rear window. When he mentioned it to Angelo, he brushed it off with a hard flick of his finger and an ice-cold threat. Told Cas his *darling wife* would never do such a thing, and if he mentioned it again, they were going to have a problem.

Rory's all right in my books. She brought my brother back to the Coast, hates Dante as much as I do, and if she did slash Cas's tires, then that's pretty funny. It's a well-known fact that, although made men are attracted to trouble, they marry meek. It's refreshing to sit next to a Cosa Nostra wife who doesn't stare at the napkin in her lap and speak only when spoken to.

"Did Penny pee in your Cheerios?"

Only when Rory's question grazes my right ear do I realize I'm staring at Penelope again. Half the room is staring at her, because she's going at it with a cocktail shaker with such vigor, her tits are threatening to pop out of that low-cut dress.

Heat instantly rushes to my groin, and images of her bouncing up and down on my dick with the same enthusiasm flash in front of my eyes.

Christ. I lean back in my chair, grip the poker chip with one hand, and drag the back of the other over my mouth in an attempt to conceal my annoyance. It irks me more than it should knowing my dick is just one of a dozen in this room growing hard at her little stunt.

I slam the rest of my glass and pin Rory with a tight smile. "Ah, you know my newest recruit."

"Uh-huh. Penny's real nice. Used to keep me company during my night shifts at the diner."

I cock a brow. "Night shifts? Did I hire a vampire?"

Instead of laughing, Rory looks down at the table. She traces a finger over the white grid markers and swallows. "She didn't sleep much after her parents were killed."

My eyes narrow. "What?"

"Yeah, we were around fourteen when it happened. I started working at the diner at sixteen, and she was still coming in most nights." She rubs a hand down her arm, like she's suddenly cold. "I was the same when my mom passed, but only for a few months. Guess you can't put a timeline on grief."

Nico didn't tell me that.

I chug down this new information with a gulp of whiskey, but the liquor doesn't make it any easier to swallow. It doesn't sit right in my chest. People only get killed on this Coast if a Visconti pulls the trigger, and our staff only get killed if they are traitors or thieves.

I'm sure the apple doesn't fall too far from the tree.

"Why are you glaring at her, anyway?"

I huff out a breath. "I'm not glaring, Rory. It's her first shift; I'm simply observing her to make sure she's not"—*my doom card*—"bad at her job."

Rory shrugs, a cheeky grin splitting her face. "She seems to be doing just fine to me."

I follow her gaze and watch as Penelope pours a slushy yellow liquid into a glass and slides it over to one of my now-former business associates at Miller & Young. She lets out a girlish giggle and slips an umbrella and a curly straw into the drink, and, in return, Clive hands her a fistful of notes and a business card.

My stomach tightens. Christ, I'm in a shitty mood tonight.

"If you'll excuse me, sis."

Before Rory can beg for another game of Visconti Blackjack, I'm on my feet and striding toward the French doors. I need a cigarette somewhere dark and cold to collect myself.

Somewhere Penelope's laugh doesn't heat my blood.

CHAPTER
Thirteen

Rafe

I PASS CLIVE'S TABLE just as he's sinking into a seat with a sleazy smirk on his face. It's not my intention to talk to him, but I find my feet slow to a stop anyway.

I rest my knuckles on the table, lowering myself until my body casts a black shadow upon his cautious gaze.

Next to him, Phillip shifts three inches to the left.

"Uh, is everything okay, Mr. Visconti?"

Fear grips his voice, because although Clive exists in the legitimate side of my life, which is filled with boardroom meetings, red ribbons, and oversized checks, he's well aware of what happens on the other side. The darker, seedier side, where hot, Italian blood runs deep and impulsive. Where made men wager broken fingers, and one can get their neck snapped for seemingly trivial matters, such as ordering shaken cocktails from busty bartenders.

"What are you drinking, Clive?" I ask calmly, my smile unwavering.

A drop of condensation slips off the glass and lands on the table with a loud *plop*. "Frozen margarita."

My jaw ticks, and two trains of thought pull into the station.

The first is, no bartender with more than a day's experience would dream of putting a margarita in a wine glass.

The second is, out of all the years I've known Clive, I've never seen him drink anything but vodka soda. I've certainly never seen him drink a cocktail—definitely not one that needs to be shaken by hand.

We stare at each other for a few beats, and I find myself biting back the surprising urge to connect my fist to his jaw. It's a fleeting feeling, but my hand twitches in agreement. Jesus. I haven't hit anyone with my bare hands since I bought my first casino almost ten years ago. I walked into a meeting with a potential investor, and he took one look at my busted knuckles and stood.

What he said over his shoulder before he left has stuck with me for life.

There's only a small difference between a thug and a businessman, kid. One has blood on his hands, while the other has blood on someone else's.

A month later, I hired Griffin. I've never felt the satisfaction of bones cracking under my fist since.

Above Clive's balding head, a set of eyes rest heavily on me. I skim my gaze upward and find Gabe glaring over the top of his cards. He cocks a brow. It's barely a twitch of a muscle, but coming from him, it's enough to end a life.

I pause. Chew on the inside of my cheek and consider his silent offer. It's a given all the big-wigs at Miller & Young have earned their place at the top of my hitlist today. Last Thursday, their stock price started sliding south and hasn't recovered all week. It took me hauling the board of directors all the way to the Coast to find out why. The CFO is secretly being investigated for embezzlement, and not a single one of the idiots was brave enough to pick up the phone and tell me.

They'll each meet their demise in due time, but in true Griffin fashion, they'll go out with a whisper, not a bang. A silencer pressed to a temple in an empty parking lot. Faulty brakes on a freeway.

It's not because I'm above the whole sadist thing. I really am not. I just keep that side of me well-groomed and tethered on a tight leash. I let it loose only for one week a month, when my brothers and I play our game. Once it's over, I put a muzzle on it and go back to outsourcing my problems.

Go back to eliminating with efficiency, rather than killing with flare.

I give Gabe a reluctant shake of my head. Without a break in his expression, he carries on with his game and I turn my attention back to Clive, a smile as fake as a three-dollar bill stretching my lips.

"Enjoy."

The sound of my ring rapping against the table makes him flinch.

Outside on the terrace, I stick to the shadows until I reach the farthest end of the empty seating area, where the sound of a good time barely reaches my ears.

The sky is dark, the ocean darker. Its waves are rugged, relentless, and every time they slap against the hull, a light mist rises up and sizzles against my skin.

I lean back against the railing, light a cigarette, and exhale its smoke into the orange glow of a security light. Each drag loosens another knot between my shoulders, and now that I've put distance between myself and the...issue, I can see just how trivial it is. Ridiculous, even. Across all of my establishments, I have a staff of over twelve thousand and have never seen any of them as anything but a number on an expenses form. And that's all Penelope is—an expense. A number on an Excel spreadsheet, just like all the other girls. With another drag on my cigarette, I make a vow that, for the very short time the little red-head will work for me, she'll cost me only a dollar amount, and not my fucking sanity.

Even if she tightens her ponytail like *that*.

"Oh, for goose's sake, I'm not a child, Angelo!"

Rory's soft, white wine-tinged voice floats through the night and steers my attention to the French doors on the other side of the terrace. A few moments later, she stomps through them, my brother looming over her like a dark, protective shadow.

"There's not a chance in hell I'm letting you watch, Magpie. You cried for three days straight when a pigeon flew into my car windshield. Remember that? You didn't sleep a wink because you were traumatized by the sound of its bones breaking. You know how much louder human bones sound?"

"Benny's not exactly an innocent little bird," she snaps back. She attempts to stomp off toward the side deck, but Angelo grabs her wrist and spins her into his chest.

"But *you're* an innocent little bird," he mutters, bending down to kiss her forehead. "My little bird, and I don't want you to be upset."

"Okay, fine," Rory sighs, leaning against his chest. They stand like that for a few moments until Rory snaps her head back and points toward the ocean. "Holy crow, did you see that?"

"See what?" Angelo growls, brushing his hand over the back of his slacks, where I know he keeps his gun.

"I'm pretty sure I just saw a humpback whale."

"Really?"

"Uh-huh, look."

She points over the railing and out to the inky abyss. My brother untangles himself from her and squints to the horizon.

"I don't see—fuck's sake."

He realized too late that Rory's got her heels in her hand, sprinting down the side deck toward the bow. The strong wind carries her gleeful, parting retort.

"Humpback whales in December? Don't be an idiot, baby."

I laugh aloud, and from across the terrace, Angelo's eyes find mine and darken with annoyance. I crack an imaginary whip, which only pisses him off even more. He mutters something bitter under his breath, before flipping me off and storming down the deck after his wife.

Still grinning, I turn around, flick my cigarette butt into the ocean and rest my forearms on the railing. Only a few beats of peace pass before the crash of another glass snaps my shoulders into a tight line and wipes the smirk off my face.

I palm my jaw. *Four.*

To my right, the staff door connecting the bar to the outside seating area bursts open. White light and irritation flood out of it.

"Just get out of my way for a little while, yeah?" Freddie hisses. My gaze slides sideways. He holds the door open and glares at Penelope as she slinks past him and out onto the terrace.

She peers around, regarding the empty tables and chairs with bewilderment, before whipping around to face him. "And do *what*, exactly?"

"Oh, I don't know, Penny. Collect glasses and empty the ashtrays, perhaps? You know, things that *real* bartenders do?"

Penelope steps toward him, but he slams the door in her face. Slams it a little too hard for my liking, and a strange sheet of irritation slides under my skin, cold and rigid. I suppose it's the gentleman in me. By nature, I dislike watching a man—especially one on my payroll—talk to a woman like that, even if she's one I'm not a fan of.

My own hypocrisy is not lost on me, because hell, only a few hours ago, I told the same girl I should have whacked her over the head with a hammer. Just like whipping out my Glock at a wedding, it was very out of character for me. Self-control sits at my very core, tethering me like an anchor, and yet, it seems to defy gravity the moment she steps into my vision.

An uneasy possessiveness creeps over me and settles in a noose around my neck. It's almost as if she's mine to be pissed off at. Nobody else's. Definitely not Freddie the fucking barman's.

She pushes off the door and weaves through the tables, picking up beer glasses and tucking them into the crook of her arm as she goes. My torso twists like it's tethered to her, forcing me to witness her hemline slip up her thighs and the fabric of her neckline gape away from her chest every time she bends over to pick up another glass.

Irritation flares in my chest with every dip. With every glimpse of tights-clad thigh and every flash of black bra. *Black.* Of course her bra is black. Bet it's lace, too. Bet she never matches it to her panties, and, speaking of panties, I bet they are obscene. Dental floss things I could snap off with my teeth, or, at the very least, the type that barely covers her pussy.

Fuck, she's annoying. I have half a mind to throw her overboard based on my assumption of her underwear preferences alone.

Stop it. She's barely old enough to drink. I'm burning up and just about to light up another cigarette in an attempt to short-circuit the semi forming in my slacks when she suddenly stops collecting glasses. Balancing them precariously in her arms, she crosses the seating area to the railing and stares out to the black silhouette of the Coast.

Her eyes close and she tilts her head up to the moon. I can't take my eyes off her. Thick lashes rest on pale, round cheeks. Rhythmic puffs of condensation escape plump, parted lips, before being carried away by the same wind that makes her long, red ponytail dance.

Something unwanted, unsavory, burns in my chest, but common sense snuffs it out like a hard blow extinguishing a candle.

She's not the Queen of Hearts; she's far too uncivilized for that. No, just a red-herring with a killer body. Dangerous, sure, but only to weak-willed idiots like my cousins and security detail, not to a man like me.

The decking groans under my feet as I step out of the shadows, and immediately, Penelope stills. Her eyes pop open, but they don't come to me. Instead, she glares out to sea and hardens her jaw, as if she knows, just by the sound of my footsteps, that the silhouette looming beside her is me.

Petty amusement fills me as I stroll in her direction. I have every intention of ignoring her and heading back inside. Treating her like an expense on a spreadsheet and not like a woman whose panties have me intrigued. But as I pass, I make the mistake of stealing a glance at her arm, and notice her skin is coarse with goosebumps.

And then I hear her teeth chatter.

Fuck's sake.

When her pathetic shivering doesn't stop, I slide my suit jacket off and slip it over her shoulders.

Despite the dramatic trembling, she falls still and silent under my touch. Perhaps it's because I've threatened to snuff the life out of her more than once, or perhaps it's because my hands are curled into fists around the lapels of the jacket, and my knuckles are resting lightly on the soft curves of her breasts.

A firework fueled with both annoyance and lust explodes inside my rib cage as I feel the textured fabric underneath her thin dress against the back of my hand.

Lace. I knew it'd be fucking lace.

I'm hotter than a furnace and the warmth of her back brushing against my chest only stokes the fire. *Did she take a step back, or did I take one forward?*

I don't know whose fault it is, but now I can feel her heartbeat thumping on the other side of her spine, and I don't like the way its rhythm matches my own. There's a voice in my head telling me to step back. Telling me I'm no better than my pervert cousins, because masquerading as chivalrous only to cop a feel is something Benny would do.

But I don't. Instead, I watch over Penelope's head as her parted lips paint the night's sky with white, shallow breaths. One. Two. Three. Each ragged and raspy, crackling like static along the length of my dick.

I can only imagine what those hot breaths would feel like against my throat as I railed the insolence out of her.

The thought makes my grip tighten around the fabric of my jacket. My knuckles press harder against her tits, and suddenly, the white puffs against the night's sky grind to a halt.

Silence, heavy and tangible, swirls us. Somewhere near the bow, Benny screams and Rory laughs. I don't even have it in me to smirk, but the sound makes Penelope flinch against my chest, and her head whips to the right so fast, strands of her ponytail slap against my lips, giving me an unwelcome taste of her strawberry shampoo.

"What was that?" she whispers.

My jaw grinds shut. "Benny getting his fingers broken."

"Oh."

A beat passes, before she slowly turns back to face the ocean. As she does, I can't help but lower my mouth to the base of her ponytail so her hair brushes against my lips again.

Christ, I'm more of a simp than Vicious.

I steal another huff, and this time, something other than strawberry and hairspray assaults my nostrils. Something familiar. *Mine.*

The realization has claws and they dig under my skin; she's wearing my aftershave.

She must have sprayed it on herself in my bathroom, sometime between drawing dicks and kissing tissues. For some unknown reason, it makes my blood boil hotter than it should. Maybe it's because she's been swanning around all night, giving every man on my yacht googly eyes while wearing my scent on her skin.

Maybe it's because, now, she smells like a one-night stand. Women always do weird stuff like that the morning after. Use my products or steal a hoodie, something to keep the night alive a little longer.

Why the fuck does she want to smell like me?

My fingers twitch with the urge to curl around her pony, yank her head back and smell it at the source—the soft curve of her neck. But suddenly the image of her tugging at her own hair from across the bar slides into my muddy thoughts, followed by the look of triumph that curved her cupid's bow when I looked away.

She's not wearing my aftershave because she wants to smell like me. No, she's wearing it because she knows it'll piss me off.

She's playing another silent, dangerous game. Only this one, she's not going to win.

Amusement in its darkest form fills me, and I slowly inch my fists down the opening of my jacket, and uncurl them so my palms are lying flat just under the swells of her breasts.

Fuck. I can't pretend like this isn't the ultimate exercise in self-control. I've already touched her far more than I should any employee, and I know the ghost of her warm, soft flesh under my palms is going to haunt me well into the early hours.

But when her lungs expand under my palms and her head drops back against my chest with a little *thud*, I know I have her. And now, it's time to ignore the maddening pulse throbbing in my cock, and swing for a home run.

I focus on the murky silhouette of the Coast in front of us and slide my fingers upward, brushing over the band of her bra, feeling the weight of her heavy tits in the space between my thumbs and forefingers.

And then, as gently as my impulsive Visconti blood will allow, I *squeeze.*

It's barely a twitch, but Penelope gasps, and a few seconds later, the sound of four beer glasses hitting the lower deck below rips through the air.

Eight.

She curses roughly, yanks herself from my grasp, and leans over the railing.

Grinning, I close the gap between us again, curling my fists over the railing on either side of her and trapping her in.

I stoop low enough to brush my lips over the soft shell of her ear and to see the flush of red staining her neck. I fight the urge to sink my teeth in, and instead, focus my energy on controlling my voice as I deliver her a final parting word.

"Even the way you shiver is annoying."

And with that, I push off the railing and leave her there, wrapped in my jacket.

I don't need it anyway. I'm so hot and worked up that as I stride back into the casino, I'm tempted to pop off my dice cufflinks and roll up my sleeves, but I *never* roll my sleeves around business partners.

Laurie bustles past with a clipboard, and my hand shoots out to grab her wrist. Her eyes come to mine, wide and wary. "This can't be good," she sighs.

"Change the uniform."

She frowns and glances down at her outfit. "To what?"

To something that covers Penelope's ass cheeks.

A vein throbs in my temple. "It's not appropriate for winter. Get pants or something."

She shrugs. "Uh, okay. With the boat logo and everything they'll take me about four days to source, but they'll be here for opening night."

I leave her with a curt nod, before making a beeline for Gabe. He's leaning against the end of the bar, taping up Benny's broken hand. As I approach, his eyes meet mine, brimming with amusement.

"Good chat?"

Fucking Gabe. I swear, sometimes I think he disappeared for so long because he went and got eyes surgically attached to the back of his head. I've never known anyone else who can be in everyone's business, yet not give a flying fuck about any of it at the same time. I ignore his question, instead reaching for his whiskey and finishing its contents in two large gulps.

"I've changed my mind, brother."

He stares at his now empty glass, then shifts his gaze to Clive slurping on his margarita.

"I bet you have," he murmurs. Then, with a quiet smirk, he goes back to taping Benny's pinky to his ring finger.

CHAPTER
Fourteen

Penny

"**Y**OU OKAY, PEN?"

LAURIE SLIDES across the locker room bench and into view, her question cutting through the girlish chatter around us.

"Never better."

"Hey." Her elbow slams my locker shut. "Don't give me that shit. What's wrong?"

Oh, I don't know, Laurie. Maybe it's because the ghost of our boss's hands squeezing my tits feels like a third-degree burn?

Of course, I don't say that. Partly because I have no idea how Laurie would react to such a ridiculous claim, and partly because I'm not entirely convinced it wasn't a fever dream.

He'd slunk out of the shadows like a black panther, steeling my spine and snatching my breath. By the daggers he'd been shooting me all night, I expected him to toss me overboard, or at the very least continue walking. I never expected him to stop and drape his jacket over my shoulders.

I don't know what was more surprising: his chivalry or the fact his hands had...*lingered.*

Christ, who am I kidding? They did a whole lot more than linger, and a cold sweat coats my skin at the mere memory. His knuckles grazing my breasts could have been accidental, sure. Not that the possibility of it being innocent stopped my nipples from tightening. But when those large fists skimmed to just below my bust and *gripped me there*, I almost lost my fucking mind. His large palms burned like hot irons against my rib cage, and fuck, it was barely a squeeze, but just from that pressure alone, I know, I just *know*, that no girl could fall into that man's bed and make it out alive.

A cold hand slides over my wrist. I look down and meet Laurie's concerned gaze. "Are the girls being bitches?"

I choke out a laugh and slip my dress off over my head. "They're fine. Don't think Freddie likes me, though."

"Doesn't matter, Rafe just fired him."

I fist the fabric in my hand. "*What*? Why?"

Laurie shrugs, already distracted by something behind me. "One thing I've learned working for the Viscontis is that they do whatever the fuck they want. Sometimes there's no rhyme or reason; other times, it can be over something super petty. He probably added ice to a whiskey, and you know around here that's practically sacrilege."

I busy myself with folding my dress, but inside, my heart is pounding. *Shit.* The moment Freddie asked me to knock out a vodka martini and I responded with nothing but a blank stare, he knew my resume was a lie. He got increasingly more pissed with every cocktail I hadn't heard of, and with every tumbler that slipped through my fingers, until he eventually demoted me to glass-collecting duties.

He's a bit of a dick, sure, but he's good at his job and picked up my slack all night. So, I wonder why Raphael fired him?

"You coming, Pen?"

I glance up and realize Laurie and the other girls have already changed into their regular clothes, with their bags and coats slung over their shoulders.

"To where?"

She jerks her chin toward the ceiling. "We're having a few drinks in the sky lounge before the staff boat leaves."

"Oh." I glance down at my bra and tights. "I'll be up in a minute."

The girls filter out, and when left alone, I close my eyes and drop my forehead to the cold metal frame of my locker. It does nothing to extinguish the flames licking my skin.

What's wrong with me? Anger twists a knot in my stomach but for all the wrong reasons. I should be angry he groped me without permission, and it's crazy that I'm not, because when I was ten, I made a vow in the alleyway behind the casino that if a man ever groped me again, I'd bite down on his hand until I tasted blood.

But no, I'm angry because I liked it. Wanted it. Wanted *more.* Angry because the moment his pinky fingers skimmed under the band of my bra, I dropped the four beer glasses I was holding and my iron-clad wall fell with them.

His hands on my body made me vulnerable, and that's what he wanted. He didn't gloat but I felt it anyway, trickling over my shoulders, hot and sticky like syrup and just as hard to wash off my skin.

I sigh into the silence. Somewhere beyond my closed eyelids, a shower head drips onto marble tiles and muffled laughter floats down from the ceiling.

Jeez, the thought of conversing with Anna and Claudia—the *not a fucking chance* bitch—over a vodka soda without putting at least one of them in a headlock seems near impossible. I'm going to take as long as I can to get ready and hope nobody comes down to find me.

I push off the locker, head to the sink, and splash my face with ice-cold water. Some of the girls have left their toiletries by the mirror, so I rummage in Anna's sparkly makeup bag and find a cleanser that appears to be more expensive than my rent. I squirt six pumps into my hand, another ten down the drain, and scrub my makeup off. As I dry my face with a towel, heavy footsteps cut through the sound of running water, making the hairs on the back of my neck stand to attention.

No shoes on deck.

Unless you're a guest. Or, you know, the man who makes the rules.

I tense. Drag my gaze up to the mirror just in time to see a dark silhouette emerge from behind the row of lockers.

White shirt. Gold collar pin. Carved-from-stone features.

Raphael Visconti strides around the corner, looking at his cellphone. He takes three steps toward the sinks, before his eyes shift to my tight-clad feet and he stops in his tracks.

Click. The sound of his cell phone locking. Displeasure coasts over his perfect features, but by the time he slides his phone into his pocket and lifts his gaze up to mine, it's dulled with that all-knowing, all-seeing amusement.

We stare at each other for three restless heartbeats, and the ghosts of his hands flare up below my bust like a nasty rash.

"This is the women's locker room."

"I have eyes, Penelope."

"Well, it's not very gentlemanly to burst into the women's locker room, is it?"

His stare darkens to a stormier shade, and slowly his eyes carve an electric trail down my throat, across my collar bone, and settle on the pendant around my neck. They snap down to my cleavage for half a breathless second, before moving back up to the four-leaf clover. If I'd blinked, I'd have missed it.

Christ, this time I wish I'd blinked.

"Lucky girls don't drop eight glasses on their first shift."

Well, then. I suppose we're just going to ignore the fact I'm next-to-naked. I'm in nothing but my bra, panties, and a pair of black tights, yet Raphael's expression suggests he could be waiting for a fucking bus.

Well, two can play apathetic, even if only one of us actually feels it.

Despite my body buzzing with anticipation, I give a well-practiced eye roll and pluck out Anna's moisturizer and slather it all over my face. "Did you get lost?" I ask, tone dripping with boredom.

He leans against the locker behind me and gives a lazy glance at his watch. "I was looking for someone else."

Someone else. Annoyance grates my chest like sandpaper, and I slather cream over the area, as if it'll help soothe the burn. "She's not here," I snap.

His eyes spark. "Who's not?"

Silence. I bite my tongue to stop myself from exposing the chink in my armor of indifference, because I'd hate for him to catch sight of the raging green monster underneath. It shouldn't even be there, anyway.

Of course, I can only assume he's here to meet Anna, and the thought of him coming into the locker room in hope of finding *her* in her bra, panties, and tights, makes the idea of putting her in a headlock all the more alluring.

Seconds pass, each one *drip, drip, dripping* onto my skin like Chinese water torture. It's near impossible to feign nonchalance when there's a six-foot-four man with large, hot hands standing less than a meter away from me.

It annoys me how polished he always looks. It's nearing midnight; he's nine whiskeys down—I counted—and his suit jacket is currently stuffed in the back of a kitchen freezer. I know, because I put it there. But still, he looks as crisp as a winter morning. The crease down the front of his trousers is sharp enough to slice my skin, and even with a magnifying glass, I doubt I'd find a wrinkle in his bright white shirt.

Bet he irons his bed sheets. Well, has one of his minions do it for him, anyway.

I pump even more cream into my hands, desperate for something to do. Just as I'm about to conjure up a smart-ass remark, simply to poke a hole in the heavy tension weighing down on my head, a dark shadow shifts over the sink.

Self-preservation kicks in. Raphael's quick, but I'm quicker, because the memory of him trapping me against the railing from behind is as raw as an open wound, and I refuse to put myself in such a vulnerable position again. I spin around and press my back against the counter, just as his hands touch down on either side of me.

Our gazes clash. His mouth curves. My lungs tighten.

This was a bad idea.

I suck in a shaky breath and a satisfied smirk deepens his dimples. His amused gaze searches mine. "How was your first shift?"

I recoil at the polite and professional tone tickling my nose; it's at odds with the dizzying warmth of his body brushing against my chest. I can't say I've stood this close to a man while being half naked and had him make *pleasantries*. Especially not as my breasts graze against the cold buttons of his shirt every time I breathe.

Fuck. Of all the days not to wear a padded bra.

"It was fine."

"Fine?"

I swallow and steel my jaw, trying—and failing—to ignore the static crackling against my nipples. "That's what I said."

He licks his lips, slowly nodding. Then, with a steadying glance to the ceiling, he dips his head and looks at my chest.

Finally. The word pops into my head, unwanted and pathetic, and I clench my teeth in an attempt to rid my brain of it. Since when was I the type of girl who craved men's attention for any reason other than to get money out of them? But no amount of rationale can stop my head from spinning.

I try to slow my breathing while he runs an objective eye over my breasts, from the hem of my lace bra to my tip money poking out of it. When he lets out a small breath of amusement, I feel its heat flow between my cleavage and settle like a weight between my thighs.

"My patrons seem to like you, at least," he says softly, dragging his gaze from the faces of Hamilton and Jackson peeking out from beneath my bra to my own. It hardens with something unreadable. "I wonder why."

Annoyance flares up against the walls of my stomach. *What an asshole.* I'd rather he just called me a slut than insinuate it in that velvet-and-nails way. He straightens to his full height and takes a step back, but not before turning his palm inward and brushing it over the dip of my hip as he pushes off the counter.

It's barely a touch, but it snatches my next breath and I press my back harder into the counter to stop myself from swaying. He says something, but I don't hear it—I'm too distracted by how the ghost of his palm *burns*.

"What?"

He cocks a brow. I look down to see he's holding out a fifty-dollar bill in the space between us.

"What's that for?"

"You lasted all night." His gaze comes to mine, bored. "Against all odds."

Jesus, and so I did. It's very unlike me to forget about a bet, especially one I was certain I wouldn't win. I should feel a lot smugger about finessing money out of Raphael Visconti, but the triumph doesn't taste as sweet on my tongue tonight. I'm too distracted, too feverish.

I lean against the counter in an attempt to cool my sizzling skin. "Told you I was lucky."

There's that displeasure again. Raphael wipes it off his bottom lip with a swipe of his thumb, and shoves out the bill with the other. "Take it," he says sharply.

A beat of tense silence passes. Swallowing, I lift my palms up on either side of myself. They are coated in Anna's expensive face cream.

Raphael's brows draw together in his confusion as his focus darts from one hand to the other, before settling on the money in my bra. Then realization settles on the planes of his face like a thick blanket of dust.

His jaw tightens. He rakes a hand through his hair and lets out a huff. I, on the other hand, don't dare breathe. *Can't.* I'm too stupefied under the weight of *what if* and *maybe so*. My nipples tingle in anticipation, and there's suddenly a new pulse in my clit, its throb fast and *maddening*.

But then he gives the tiniest shake of his head. He skims his stare up to meet mine. It's dark and dangerous, void of any light or humor.

I doubt any good could ever survive in there.

"That wouldn't be very gentlemanly of me, Penelope."

"You're not a gentleman," I whisper back.

Tension crackles like static. It's so heavy I could stick my tongue out and fucking taste it.

Raphael rakes his teeth over his bottom lip, stare intensifying. "You seem to be obsessed with the idea of me not being a gentleman." He takes a slow step forward, still holding the bill out between us. "It'd be wise of you to get that notion out of your head."

The buttery drawl doesn't fool me; I know it's a threat rather than a suggestion.

Still, it slips from my lips before I can consider the consequences. "All right, you are a gentleman then." My eyes narrow. "To everyone but me."

He stills. His free hand curls into a fist just before he slides it into the pocket of his slacks.

"Do you want me to be a gentleman to you, Penelope?"

My heart skips its next beat. I can't focus, can barely fucking see. The air is too thick and my pulse is too loud. I feel drunk and high at the same time, like I'm spiraling out of control. Maybe that's why I'm stupid enough to shake my head.

A hiss escapes Raphael's parted lips. It's low and slow, and I don't like the way it sizzles against my skin. But then he swallows. Glances at the ceiling, and lets out a bitter laugh. It rains down like an icy mist, spraying me with both disappointment and humiliation.

He tosses the note on the counter beside me, and my heart drops with it.

He steps away, looking at himself in the mirror behind me. "Nice dick by the way."

I blink, snapping myself out of the lust-induced trance. "What?"

"On my mirror," he says with a dry, sardonic smile. "It was true to size."

My throat clots. "Was it?"

Don't look, don't look, don't look.

My gaze drops to his slacks.

Fuck's sake.

His laugh washes over me, but there's nothing smooth about it. It grates me in places it shouldn't, and I know when I'm staring at my dark bedroom ceiling at five a.m. I'll still be thinking about it.

With a tight smirk, he turns and strides toward the door. I hate the feeling that he's won this round—as well as the last—and in an attempt to level the playing field, sarcasm shoots from my mouth before I can stop it.

"Is that all, *boss*?"

He slows to a stop. Pops his knuckles.

Triumph. But it only tastes good for a second, before his calm, smooth voice slices through the locker room and assaults me.

"Careful calling me boss when you're half naked, Penelope," he drawls. "I might just get the wrong idea."

The door slams shut louder than usual, and its echo reverberates around the hollow cavity in my chest.

Scratch the laugh. *That's* what I'll be thinking about at five a.m.

CHAPTER
Fifteen

Penny

T HE DEVIL'S DIP DINER is open twenty-four seven, a haven of burgers and bitter coffee for someone who doesn't sleep at night. It's been three days since my first shift on the yacht, and every night since, I've sat in a sticky booth under unforgiving strip lights with a copy of *Real Estate for Dummies* in front of me.

I've re-read the first line of the first chapter more times than I can count. I can't get into it—not just because I know I'm never going to be the type of woman to wear a suit to work and have her face plastered on a bus stop bench, but also because, as I predicted, Raphael's parting words are playing on a loop in my brain.

Don't call me boss when you're half-naked, Penelope. I might just get the wrong idea.

The curl of his fist. The set of his shoulders. The sharp line of his jaw as he glanced back at me. The image is so visceral that if I stare at the sheet of darkness through the window for long enough, I can see his silhouette against it.

I got under his skin for the briefest of moments, but nowhere near as deep as he's gotten under mine.

Pathetic, really. Am I so immature and sex-starved that a squeeze of my breasts, a touch of friction, and a mild-mannered threat are all it takes for the butterflies in my stomach to brush the dust off their wings?

A server fills up my coffee cup, and I take a gulp before letting it cool down, in the hope that the burn will distract me from the nervous energy buzzing in my chest.

It doesn't.

Behind me, the bell above the door chimes, ice-cold wind brushes my back, and warm laughter chases after it. I twist around to see a group of girls pour in. They're around my age, and judging by the Santa hats and off-beat clatter of stilettos across the lino floor, they've just come from a Christmas party.

The one in the sparkly dress slams her palms against the counter. "Gimme everything you've got!"

Laughter ripples through the diner, tilting the lips of servers and the three lone diners occupying the other corner booths.

"But seriously," a girl in a red skirt groans, coming up behind her friend and wrapping her arms around her waist. "We start work in three hours, and the only things that'll soak up the vodka are burgers and fries."

Feeling like an orphan peering into a family's living room on Christmas morning, I watch the exchange over the back of the booth seat, until my smile fades and the hollow void behind my sternum grows denser. It's like I've watched them open their presents in front of the fire and have gradually realized the warmth and happiness inside won't reach me through the glass. The reality is that I'm left outside in the cold with nothing.

I bet they share jeans and confess their odd obsessions with men who hate them.

Sucking in a breath to anchor myself, I turn back to the wall of the diner. Ignoring a pitiful smile from an old man in the corner booth opposite, I study the signed football shirts behind Plexiglas, and grainy photographs of Z-list celebrities shaking hands with the owner.

"Wait—turn this up!"

I glance behind me, just in time to see red-skirt girl lunge over the counter and grab a remote control. My gaze follows where she's pointing it to and lands on the chunky television mounted on the wall.

Breaking News. The words flash red and white below a somber-looking woman. She's wrapped up in a cashmere scarf and stands in front of a charred building with a padded microphone grazing her lips.

The girl behind me stabs at the volume button.

"I'm standing outside the former Hurricane casino and bar tonight, shortly after news broke that the owner has asked the Atlantic City Fire Department to cease their investigation into the fire." The reporter glances at the paper in her hand. We're here with the owner himself, Martin O'Hare." The camera pans to reveal a man standing beside her. "Martin, could you tell us why you've decided to call off the investigation?"

An icy awareness spreads over my skin, chilling everything that lies beneath. It feels instinctive to get up and run, but I'm frozen to the plastic booth. I can only stare at familiar eyes and listen to a familiar voice, as panic climbs up my throat.

"First of all, we'd like to extend our highest gratitude to the men and women of the Atlantic City Fire Department; they've worked tirelessly on this investigation over the last few days. However, being mindful that public services are overworked and funds are overstretched, we've decided to pursue other methods of justice that don't burden the taxpayer."

"Are you saying you're taking the law into your own hands?"

Martin lets out a gruff laugh. "You make us sound like thugs, Claire."

"Well...it does sound a little sinister; don't you think? Why not let law enforcement handle the issue? There's a suspected arsonist on the loose, after all."

He smiles tightly. "As I said, we don't want to waste any more inspectors' time or taxpayers' money. We're fortunate enough to have the resources to hire private investigators, and out of respect to the residents of this great city, that's what we'll do."

"And when your private investigator catches him?"

His stare shifts to the camera. It reaches through the television and singes my clammy skin.

"Who said it's a *him*?"

My vision wavers like it has its own pulse, but at the heart of it, Martin O'Hare's all-knowing glare is as sharp as a knife. The news cuts suddenly to an orange inferno lighting up the night's sky. Vicious flames licking red bricks until they turn black. There it is: the epitome of my personality—impulsive and bitter—in all of its blazing glory. And here I am, watching it from a fucking diner over a cup of coffee.

Christ, what the fuck is wrong with me? I've been here obsessing over a satin-wrapped monster and feeling sorry for myself because I have no friends, as if I'm *not on the fucking run*. As if I didn't stuff my life into one suitcase and hop on the first Greyhound heading in the opposite direction of the mess I'd made.

Martin O'Hare knows. He knows I set fire to his casino, and all I can hope is he doesn't know where I went after I lit the match.

"Hey girl—you okay?"

Sequins, stilettos, and loud voices graze over me, and only when I slam a twenty on the counter and catch the concerned eye of a server do I realize I'm on my feet and heading toward the exit.

"Never better," I croak, before bursting out onto the street.

The night is lit by tacky Christmas decorations. Candy canes glow red and white in shop windows, and blow-up Santas tied to street lamps wave at me under a film of frost. As my boots slip over the icy ground, I slow to a stop and sigh out a streak of white against the sky.

Damn it. The last place I want to be is my apartment, because the rooms are too small and my panic is too large.

Your sins will catch up with you eventually. They always do.

I suppose I already knew that, long before I struck a match, dropped it in a vodka bottle, and left it on the doorstep of the Hurricane bar.

That's why I started my Grand Quest in the first place. Not because I truly wanted a career more high-brow than swindling, but because I knew it was like a gateway drug. Once I got hooked, I'd only spiral into deeper, darker depths of sin. And look at me now; within the span of three years, I've gone from making men's wallets a little lighter to burning down buildings.

I should never have let myself get this deep. I should have gone straight a long time ago.

A crackle of static prickles on my skin, and as I glance up to the sky, the first drop of rain lands on my top lip with a heavy *plop*. Another falls, and then another. Within seconds, a storm is cascading down from the heavens like God has dropped his marble collection.

And then a bolt of lightning illuminates the sky, startling me.

Shit. That's all I need.

Holding my breath, I hug my book to my chest, tuck my chin into the collar of my soggy coat, and break into a run toward the closest source of shelter—the oversized phone booth in front of the bakery. I slip inside and slam my back against the door.

The rumble of thunder rolls in seconds after, vibrating the glass walls of the booth. I gasp in a lungful of stale, humid air and will my legs not to buckle underneath me.

Of all the moments for a rare coastal thunder storm, it has to be *now*?

As another sharp flash of light fills the booth, I desperately scrabble for something to distract myself. I wring out my hair and then, under the flickering glow of the light bulb, inspect my book for water damage. Thankfully, it's covered in protective plastic because it's a library book. The irony of me caring brews a bitter laugh which melts into the next roll of thunder.

I'm losing my fucking mind.

I close my eyes and lean my head against the door for a few seconds.

Inside the booth, my ragged breaths sour into carbon dioxide, and beyond the box, sheets of rain distort red and white lights. I squeeze my eyes shut for the next flash of lightning. When it passes, I open them and my bleary gaze lands on something stuck on the back wall of the payphone. Something familiar. I blink to sharpen my vision, then I lunge forward and snatch it from its thumb tack.

A matte-black card, gold embossed letters, and a number printed in silky black numerals. Another laugh escapes me, only this one doesn't taste as bitter.

Sinners Anonymous.

The night I found my first Sinners Anonymous card is burned into my memory. I was thirteen, hiding in the Visconti Grand Bathroom because Nico hadn't come to the casino that night. The card was tucked into the mirror a foot above my reflection. I don't know what possessed me to slip it into my pocket, but I did.

That night, as I glared at the glow from car headlights passing over my bedroom ceiling, I suddenly remembered I had it. So, I crept downstairs and sat on the armchair opposite my father passed out on the sofa, and I called the number.

The woman's voice was robotic but it was still the softest I'd ever heard. She didn't cut me off like my mother did. Didn't shout at me like my father. She made me want to open up. Made me feel like I finally had someone to talk to.

For the next five years, I used the hotline like a diary. It was my anonymous safe haven, a space to moan about my parents' drunken fighting and discuss the new tricks I'd learned from Nico.

I know she's not even real, but I feel kind of guilty for leaving her behind when I left for Atlantic City.

I rub my thumb over the textured header and catch my bottom lip with my teeth. This is the third card I've seen since arriving back on the Coast. The first was in my apartment, and the second was tucked into the pages of the Bible in my hospital room.

As it fell out onto my starchy bed sheets, I'd had a thought, and the same one creeps into my head again now.

Religious people confess their sins, right? Maybe if I did the same, I wouldn't feel them tugging at my ankles, attempting to drag me into the fiery pits of hell below. Maybe if I use the hotline for its intended purpose, I won't hear the roar of fire echoing around my brain between every heartbeat, or maybe I won't catch a whiff of smoke every time I turn my head too quickly.

But I don't believe in God. Where was he when my mother got her head blown off? When my father was crying out for him in the corner of the kitchen?

God didn't save them that night, and he didn't save me, either. Luck did. I felt it in the warm and weighty charm around my neck. My whole body buzzed with shooting stars and horseshoes and the number seven, not with the voice of the big man in the sky.

But that doesn't stop me from reaching for the receiver or squeezing it against my ear as I flinch under another bolt of lightning. Before I know it, I'm squinting at the keypad, punching in a familiar number.

I hold my breath for all three rings.

Click.

"You have reached Sinners Anonymous," my old friend says. "Please leave your sin after the tone."

I pause. Exhale heavily down the mouthpiece and rake a hand through my sopping-wet hair. My sin is *right there*, stuck in the back of my throat, too thick and damaging to travel any farther. It grows bigger, denser, and my breath grows labored in an attempt to get around it.

Why do I feel like she'll judge me? She's not even real, for fuck's sake.

My eyes drop to the book in my hand. To the label glued to the spine: *Property of Atlantic City Public Library.*

I choke out a shaky laugh and lift my gaze toward the rain hammering on the roof.

"I borrowed three library books, and I'll never get to return them."

CHAPTER
Sixteen

Rafe

"HAVE YOU EVER BEEN in love?"

Staring at the sheet of rain sliding down my windshield, I bite back a sigh. This woman has been asking me stupid questions all night.

What would you choose as your last meal if you were on death row?

If you were a pizza topping, what would you be?

Would you rather be a strawberry with human thoughts, or a human with strawberry thoughts?

Right now, I'd rather be a human who is anywhere but my own car. But of course, I offer a small smile and shake my head. "Afraid not, Cleo."

I catch the spark of excitement in her eyes before I turn my attention back to the road. *Wrong answer.*

The glow of her cellphone reflects off her face, and the sound of her frantic typing cuts just above the hum of the eighties Christmas song on the radio. No doubt she's updating the group chat with the latest installment about our date.

Sometimes I wonder if it'd just be easier to do what every other man in my family does—fuck and chuck without mercy. But the idea of plunging my cock into a woman whose last name I can't remember feels...uncivilized. It's something zoo animals and my cousins do, not real men.

No, I prefer to torture myself with wining and dining a woman before taking her to bed, even though, more often than not, I couldn't give two flying shits about the conversation floating over the dinner table.

Angelo thinks by drawing out the run-up to getting my dick wet I'm giving women false hope that it'll turn into something more. I don't agree; I'll never take a wife, and I'm *very* transparent about my intentions from the jump.

Every woman I take out gets the same fair warning. They'll get one candle-lit night, where I'll play their Prince Charming and suffer through their vapid monologues with an intrigued smile. Then, after they sweat against my silk sheets and moan ill intentions in my ear, they'll never hear from me again.

One night never turns into two. Not in a million years. But still, this hard-and-fast rule seems more like a challenge than a boundary for most women—this one in my passenger seat included.

I slow the car to a stop outside Cleo's walk-up on Main Street and kill the engine. In the silence, the thunder rolling over the roof of my car sounds even louder.

"Thank you for a delightful evening," I say dryly.

Anticipation crackles and pops off my date's Little Black Dress. My gaze slides down to her hands curling around the hem of it. I stifle another sigh.

Usually, here's where I'd lean my forearm against her headrest. Slide my hand up her thigh as I murmur something about being invited up for coffee against her lips. But for some odd reason, the thought of doing that tonight fills me with dread.

Maybe it's because I'm wiped out from a week of bad business, or maybe it's because I really don't care what she's got going on underneath that dress.

Under her wide, watchful eyes, I drag a palm over my mouth and drop my head against my seat. Maybe I just need to switch up the type of women I date. For nine years, I've been seeking out cookie-cutter brunettes that I probably couldn't pick out of a police line-up if you held a gun to my head. But I choose them because they *aren't* my type. They are easy to fuck and forget about. If I actually chose my type, well...that'd be dangerous.

The next lightning bolt brings a flash of red hair and lace lingerie with it.

Jesus. Suddenly feeling hot under the collar, I shove open the door and step out into the rain. As I round the back of the car, Blake catches my eye through the windshield of the armored sedan parked behind me. He winks, then creates a hole with one hand and slides his finger in and out of it. Ah, the universal sign for getting laid.

I'd laugh if it'd come from Griffin or one of my other men, but this dick is already on thin ice after the whole Benny fiasco. I open the passenger door for my date, and her breathing stills as I lean over her, but I pretend not to notice.

I'm only reaching for an umbrella.

I hold out my hand and force another smile. "Allow me."

Shielded from the storm, we take the five steps to her front door in silence.

"Well," she whispers, staring up at me like an anxious deer in headlights. "This is me. Unless, uh...you know, you want to come up for coffee, or something?"

It's already three a.m.—seriously, this woman *wouldn't stop* with the dumb questions—and I'd be lying if I said the idea of railing her doggy-style on her polyester sheets while staring at the floral-feature wall behind her headboard turned me on.

I shift my focus over her head and across the road. Annoyingly, I know the real reason I don't want to go upstairs, and it's got nothing to do with business or being bored of brunettes. But *that* reason is so ridiculous, I almost want to go inside to prove to myself that it's not real.

Another zap of lightning illuminates Main Street. It bounces off shiny surfaces, like the puddles in the road, shop windows, and the glass of the large phone booth opposite. A flash of red—real this time—catches my eye, and my gaze narrows on it.

Surely not.

"Rafe?"

My attention drops back to Claire. Clara? Whatever. When I can't remember their names, I just call them darling. "I'm so sorry, darling, but I've got a very early start tomorrow."

Her hopeful smile falls. "You're not coming up?"

No, I'm going to forgo getting my dick sucked in favor of crossing the road and making sure I'm not hallucinating. "Believe me, darling, I'm more upset about it than you are." Another flash of lightning, another glimpse of red hair and glaring blue eyes. I'm blaming the split-second distraction for why I say something beyond stupid. "Let's do it again some time."

I regret it the moment it slips from my lips, even more so when her eyes light up like the Vegas strip. I quickly make my excuses, wait until she's safely behind her front door, then stride across the road.

As I approach the phone booth, my gaze locks with another through the rain-streaked glass. For some reason, irritation sparks in my chest. What's that saying, again? Something about if you think of the devil, it'll appear?

Well, tonight the devil is dripping wet and clutching a yellow book to her chest.

Closing the umbrella, I reach for the handle. On the other side of the glass, I see Penelope reach for it, too. Her attempt to hold the door shut is pathetic, and I'm barely met with any resistance as I fling it open.

Wedging the door open with my foot, I lean my arms against the top metal frame and let my eyes climb her body. She's soaking. Her furry coat looks like a stray dog from one of those ASPCA advertisements, and her hair is so wet it's gone from copper to rust.

"What are you doing out so late? Working the street corner when you got caught in the rain, were you?"

Silence.

My gaze narrows on the panic carved into her face. "What's wrong?" Again, no answer. I sweep an eye over the empty street, then step inside, slamming the door shut behind me. I grip her chin. "I'm not in the business of asking twice, Penelope."

A gasp escapes her lips as a bolt of lightning floods the space with light. Her jaw flexes against my thumb pad, and realization washes over my unease like a cold bucket of water.

I let my fingers slip off her face and laugh. "Scared of a little lightning? Please, the chances of getting struck are one in a million."

It's her turn to laugh. It's loud and bitter and when it bounces off the walls, I'm suddenly aware of how small it is in here.

"I'll walk you home."

"I don't want to walk."

"I'll drive you home then. We're thirty seconds from your apartment, lazy bones."

"Go away."

Wiping the amusement off my face with the back of my hand, I lean against the door and study her. When lightning illuminates the booth, her shoulders tense in anticipation, and her fingers curl into fists by her side. Her lips part to count in breathy whispers, and when she gets to seven, thunder rolls over her hunched shoulders.

Her shaking makes the silver around her neck glint.

I groan. "You're not serious."

She pops one eye open and glares at me through it. "What?"

I nod to her necklace. "You think you're one in a million." I don't even bother trying to hide my eye roll. "How self-absorbed to do you have to be to believe—"

"I'm *not* self-absorbed." Her trembling fingers fly to her necklace in defense. "I'm lucky."

"Yes, because getting struck by lightning is real lucky."

She shakes her head, running the four-leaf clover up and down the chain. "Luck isn't just about good things happening to you, it's about having the odds stacked on your side. Every dice has a six, right? Anyone can land on it, but lucky people are more likely to land on it than most."

"And with that logic, lucky people are more likely to get struck by lightning," I reply dryly.

She nods, and I huff out a sardonic breath. "No such thing as luck, Penelope. Good, bad, or otherwise. Not sure how many times I have to prove it to you."

Now, her other eye pops open, and she treats me to an incredulous stare. "You're the king of casinos. How do you *not* believe in luck?"

"Because I'm a logical person." *Lie.* "I believe in the proven science of probability and statistics. Every single person on the planet has the same odds of rolling a six. It's *math.* Jesus, I bet you also match your nail polish to your horoscope and don't leave the house when Mercury is in Retrograde."

She scowls. "Funny." Her eyes slide down to the umbrella at my side and something mischievous dances behind them. "Open it, then."

"What?"

"If you truly don't believe in luck, *good, bad, or otherwise*," she mocks, in a gruff voice I assume is meant to mimic my own, "then open the umbrella."

I run my tongue over my teeth. Glance up at the rain hammering on the roof. Fuck, she's got me there. I'd rather play Russian roulette against my own temple than open an umbrella inside. I'm not even sure if a phone booth counts as inside, but I'm not going to find out.

The next strike of lightning couldn't have come at a better time. Too distracted by talk of superstition, Penelope forgot to count until the next roll of thunder and it catches her off guard. She yelps. Slams a hand against my chest to steady herself. My muscles tense under the weight of her warm palm. Maybe it's because it's past three in the morning, or maybe I'm just out of my fucking mind, but I slide my hand over hers.

"Shh," I murmur, curling my fingers over her palm. "It'll stop soon."

Wide-eyed, she slides her attention down my shirt to where my hand grips hers. Her heavy breathing fills all four walls of the phone booth. Steam rises off our bodies and crawls up the glass, and now I can't see what's on the other side of them. It's just Penelope in here with me, cautious and wet, trembling too close to me for comfort.

A light venom swirls under my skin, itchy and hot.

What was I thinking? I strolled into this phone booth like I was going for a Sunday walk. Like I wasn't trapping myself into an eight-by-four box with a girl whose half-naked body I'd thought about at least once an hour for three days straight.

Now what stands between me and that lace bra? A couple layers of wet clothes I could have off her body in under ten seconds. Under five, if I was feeling...*reckless.*

Lust crackles and pops like an electric current running down to the tip of my dick. Fuck the whole Queen of Hearts nonsense. Even if she's not my doom card, she's bad for me. Bad for my self-control, and for my image. Just the spark of defiance in her big, blue eyes makes me want to tear off my gentlemanly mask and devour her whole.

I clear my throat and drop her hand, partly because this shirt is Tom Ford, and partly because the softness of her palm against my chest is giving me a semi.

"If you think you're so lucky, let's play a game."

Her eyes narrow, caution warring with interest. "What game?"

Biting back my amusement at her inability to hide her excitement, I pull a dice from the pocket of my slacks. I toss it in the air, catch it, and turn my palm upward with my fingers closed. "Guess the number. If you're right, I'll admit you're lucky."

She cocks a sarcastic brow. "That's all it'll take for you to believe me?"

Of course not. But another flash of lightning has just lit the glass pane by her head, and she didn't flinch.

"Sure."

"And what do I win?"

"Bragging rights."

She rolls her eyes. "And?"

I laugh. "A hundred bucks."

Another rumble and she doesn't even notice. "Four."

"Sure you don't want to think about it?"

"I don't need to think; I *know*."

It suddenly occurs to me what makes this girl so attractive. Physically being the dictionary definition of my type aside, it's her confidence that claws under my skin. She's borderline cocky, which presents a challenge within itself. It seems I crave the satisfaction of knocking it out of her with any means possible.

I uncurl my fingers.

Our eyes clash, hers dancing with glee, mine tinged with disbelief.

You've got to be shitting me. With a sly grin I want to wipe off, maybe with my own mouth, she holds her hand out between us.

I slap the bill into her palm with more force than necessary. Thankfully, she slides it into her pocket and not her bra.

The air is thick with her excitement. She leans back against the glass, exposing the soft curve of her throat, then she looks up at me through thick lashes. "Best of three?"

I laugh. "You're pushing it, girl."

"Aw, come on. You can afford to lose a few more bills. You're a billionaire with two yachts and a whole-ass island in the Caribbean." She jerks her head toward the street. "You probably have a grand in change in the center console of your car alone."

My eyes slant. "You been Googling me or something?"

The air shifts at the sound of her breathy laugh. I don't like how it tastes; how it feels in my slacks.

"Or something," she whispers.

Fuck.

She holds my eye for longer than she should. Her sly smile slowly slips off her lips, until there's no trace of humor left on her pretty little face.

She looked me up? Why does that send a dark ripple of pleasure through me? I guess because it means she's been thinking about me.

I doubt she's thought about me in the same way I've thought of her, though.

Half-naked and covered in that cream.

The image flashes behind my eyelids for the millionth time today. Before I can stop myself, I close the gap between us, resting my palm against the wall above her head.

She tenses as I move closer. Then, as another rumble of thunder rocks the booth, she lets out a hot, shaky breath against the base of my throat. I feel it like a lead weight in my balls, and I push my hand a little harder into the wall.

Glaring at the dog-eared calling cards of taxi-drivers and cheap hookers, I ask her a question I know I shouldn't.

"Have you ever been in love, Penelope?"

I don't know why I ask it. A mix of it being one of the last questions my date asked me, and mild curiosity, I guess. Sometimes, when a girl moves back to their small hometown, it's because they've had their heart broken—according to most of the shitty Hallmark films my mama used to watch around this time of year, anyway.

Penelope's eyes slide up to mine, searching them with a guarded expression. "Is this another game?"

I shake my head.

"Then, no."

A small flicker of relief dances like a candle in the darkness of my chest. Ridiculous. I shouldn't give a flying fuck if this girl has been in love or not. I don't.

"Why not?"

I think I know the answer. Twenty-one is no age to fall in love. But to my surprise, she tilts her chin, stares me dead in the eye, and tells me something I don't expect.

"Women don't fall in love; they fall into traps."

Letting out a breath, I push myself off the wall in an attempt to get away from the intoxicating scent of her strawberry shampoo. Away from the damp heat of her coat brushing against my chest. But even as I lean against the cold glass door, it's impossible to get away from *her*. She might be five-foot-nothing, but she fills every inch of this space, making the air so thick and sweet that it might just burst at the seams.

I wonder who hurt her? A boy her own age. Some spotty kid in his basement, no doubt. Briefly, stupidly, I wonder if I should hurt him, too.

"That's a very jaded view of love, Penelope."

"And you?" My gaze falls down from the rain-stained roof at the sound of Penelope's voice. "Have you ever been in love?"

I laugh. I can't tell her the truth. I can't tell anybody the truth, not even my own brothers. Because if I did, I'd have to admit something else, something bigger.

I chose the King of Diamonds, not the King of Hearts.

It's easier to go with the same answer I gave Callie. Or was it Cora?

"Afraid not, Penelope."

She breathes out a low and slow breath that crawls under my ribs and fills the hollow cavity there. Her expression is indifferent, unreadable, but her eyes spark with something hotter.

When they lock onto mine, my heart slams against my ribs.

Rain falls from her hair onto my loafers in loud, sticky *plops*. Outside, cars glide over the wet cobbles of Main Street, their tires creating a frictionless hiss and their headlights washing over rain-soaked glass. They shift a fragmented yellow glow over the planes of Penelope's face.

My gaze crawls down to her plump, parted lips, then down the curve of her throat as it bobs.

"The storm has stopped," she whispers.

"Five minutes ago."

She takes a step toward me, tucking her book under her arm. "I should go."

My jaw tightens as her chest grazes against mine. When she realizes I haven't moved, she tenses and looks up at me warily.

A familiar feeling swirls through my veins. It's dark and dangerous and has no place in my blood on a random Thursday evening. The sadistic thoughts creeping out from the shadows in my brain shouldn't be there, either.

I tilt my head to the side. Slide my hands into my pockets and curl them into fists.

"What if I don't let you go?"

It's a question, not a threat.

Maybe.

Whatever it is, it shouldn't be leaving my lips.

Her frown does little to hide the fear that passes through her doe eyes in a wave. She tilts her chin and says, "I'll fight you off."

My thumb sliding across my mouth conceals my dark amusement. Where does this chick get her confidence from? The top of her head barely reaches the third button on my shirt, for god's sake. If I wanted to...*have my way* with her, there's nothing she could do to stop it.

Both excitement and unease hum under my skin. "And how would you do that?"

What the fuck are you doing, Rafe? It seems like every interaction I have with this girl turns into a game. This one feels like revenge. For wearing my aftershave. For shaking her head when I asked her if she wanted me to be a gentleman. I want to make her as uncomfortable as she makes me. Only, this game feels riskier than a roll of a dice or a halfhearted bet.

And I can't say for sure I'll be the one who wins.

Fuck this.

I'm not in the business of scaring women for my own amusement, anyway. Not like this. I'm just tired and horny and probably growing delirious from the lack of oxygen in here. I'm about to step aside with an easy laugh when Penelope's eyes dart below my belt.

My blood heats. Silly girl. The first rule of playing any game is to never let your opponent see your next move. I'll give it to her—she's quick. I'm quicker. As her knee comes up to meet my groin, my knee comes up too. I slide it between her legs and pin her to the back wall with it.

Heart slamming with the adrenaline that comes with a win, I press my body into hers, a triumphant laugh humming deep in my throat.

"Too slow, Penelope. Now what?"

She doesn't reply, and with every heavy second that crawls past, a hot, prickly awareness creeps through me. The sharpness of her fingernails digging into my biceps. Her steam-like breath against my Adam's apple. The warmth of her pussy mound against my thigh, and the fast, flickering pulse that beats in the middle of it.

Fuck.

Glaring at a raindrop as it fights its way down the glass, I take a slow, deep breath. It does little to cool the lust searing through my veins.

Don't do it, Rafe.

I won't. I won't push my thigh deeper between her legs in the hope that she'll moan from the friction. I won't grab her by the nape of the neck, tilt her lips to mine, and explore the taste of her smart-ass mouth.

It'd be all-too-easy, sure. A heady cocktail of body heat, rain, and darkness shield us from the outside world. I could have this girl in a heartbeat, no wining and dining necessary, and no one but me, her, and my own conscience would know about it.

Suddenly, Penelope's hips tilt forward, her pussy sliding half an inch down my thigh.

My stomach tenses. "Don't."

It's a sharp warning, delivered through the gap between my clenched teeth.

She shifts again, more deliberately this time. Her wet hair tickles my throat as she tilts her chin.

"Or what?"

It's barely a whisper, but it's loaded with an insolence I want to rip from her vocal cords. What that tone does to my dick should be illegal.

Blood thumping in both my temples and my cock, my mind swims with bad thoughts and my tongue is bitter with the taste of bad decisions.

I should step away from this chick. No good could ever come from her, doom card or not. But if I do, then I lose the game I started.

And I *don't* like to lose.

No. She's a kid, and I'm her boss. Gathering all the self-control I have, I tear myself away from her and shove out to the street.

Glaring at a deflating Santa bobbing lazily against a lamp post, I readjust my slacks and smooth down my shirt. I take a deep breath of damp, December air. With the rain falling from the sky cooling me down, my head clears and my common sense crawls back to me.

Jesus, I definitely stepped over the line. I guess forced proximity and bratty behavior will do that to even the most level-headed man. Still, I should apologize; that was no way to behave to a lady, even this one.

Behind me, the phone booth door slams shut, and heavy footsteps stomp off in the other direction. Sliding my hands into my pockets, I fall in step with Penelope as she bulldozes in the direction of her apartment.

"Penelope."

She ignores me in favor of glaring at the puddles beneath us.

"You don't have to walk me home, you know."

"It's three a.m."

"I'm not your date." She grinds to a halt, whipping around to face me. I search her eyes for any kind of fear, but surprisingly, nothing of the sort swirls behind those big, blue irises. "What happened, anyway? Didn't get invited up for coffee?"

Despite my cock throbbing in my slacks, amusement fills me. "Is that what ladies do? Invite men up to their apartment for coffee?"

She swallows. Tightening her grip on her book, her eyes crawl down the front of my shirt, past my belt, and land on my dick. The heat of her gaze makes my fist curl tighter around the poker chip in my pocket. *God help me.*

"I wouldn't know," she whispers, stopping outside a green door. "I'm not a lady."

And then without so much as a goodbye, she disappears behind the door and slams it shut behind her.

I stare at it in disbelief for a few moments, then turn my head to the sky and let out a humorless laugh.

This chick can't be real.

I turn on my heel and stroll back down Main Street, Penelope's warm pussy still branding my thigh, her insolence still dancing in my ears.

As I pass the phone booth, something slow and instinctive creeps underneath my collar, slowing me to a stop.

Surely not?

Before I can put weight to it, I slip back inside the phone booth and pick up the telephone receiver. Stab the star key, followed by the six and the nine.

And when a familiar voice of my own creation floats down the line, my laugh fills the space more than Penelope's breathless whispers ever could.

Let the games begin, silly girl.

CHAPTER
Seventeen

Penny

A S MY APARTMENT DOOR clicks shut behind me, a pair of battered Chucks step out onto the punny welcome mat across the hall. My gaze skims up to meet Matt's lopsided grin.

"There you are." He tugs on a beanie. "Thought you might've had enough of your sticky carpets and 8B's rock music and skipped town again. How have you been?"

I wouldn't say I've been avoiding Matt, but I'd be lying if I said I didn't hold my breath and mute the television when he's knocked on my front door a few times.

The moment he found out I was at the hospital, he turned into Florence Nightingale. He feels guilty because he didn't know I'd left the wedding, even though it's my own fault because I didn't tell him. Although I'm back to my usual self and my wound is barely more than a mark, he's still checking up on me and bringing me dinner. I'm definitely not complaining about free food.

I decide to move the subject away from my head for once. "What's up with 8B, anyway?"

It's a good thing I don't sleep, because the neighbor sandwiched between Matt's and my apartments blares out shitty music at all hours.

His eyes light up as we descend the staircase. "Wanna know something crazy?"

"Always."

"I've lived here for almost five years, and I have absolutely no idea who lives there."

We step out onto icy cobbles under sunny skies. I slow to a stop and squint up at him. "For real?"

Matt slides a pair of Ray Ban's up his nose. "Uh-huh. Never seen them in the hallway and never seen any letters or parcels get delivered to their mailbox." He glances up at the building then drops his voice. "Get this. Once, I came home from a night out pretty fucking high, and the music was psyching me out. So, I took a glass and put my ear to the wall. You know that trick, right? Makes everything louder?"

I nod.

"Yeah, well underneath the blaring music, I could hear *drilling*."

I bite out another laugh. "No you couldn't."

"I'm being serious, Penny. And this was at three a.m. What the fuck are you drilling at three am?"

We fall into step, fighting against the blistering wind as we walk down Main Street. The sun is already sinking toward the horizon, creating a sharp orange glow over the cobbles. "I think you need to lay off the weed."

"I think you're right. Anyway, how's work going? Has Anna said anything about me yet?"

I haven't had the heart to tell him she's a massive bitch yet. Especially not when he's been leaving pizza pockets on my doorstep.

"Ah, you can do better than Anna," I say breezily. "A guy like you could get Beyonce, if he wanted."

He rolls his eyes. "Yeah, I'll cross my fingers she swipes right on me on Tinder."

I'm still laughing as we reach the end of the road. We're about to part ways, when his attention drops to my wrist. "Hey—nice watch!"

I stretch out my arm and the Breitling winks at me, like we're in on a private joke.

After a restless sleep, I woke up late this afternoon filled with the hot flames of vengeance. Last night, Raphael had made me feel a whirlwind of emotions. I was irrationally pissed he was with a woman, conflicted that he calmed me down during the thunderstorm, and then *crazed* when he slid his thigh between mine. His presence filled the phone booth and soaked into my skin, and I hate that it doesn't wash off as easily as his aftershave.

I'm wearing his watch and I know it's not just to annoy him, but also because if I'm playing this dance with Raphael, I'm not thinking about Martin O'Hare and him telling national news he's going to take matters into his own hands. I'm good at shoving bad things right down to the pit of my stomach, as long as I have something to distract me.

Raphael Visconti is a very welcome distraction.

Thanks to my newly acquired timepiece, I'm punctual today, so the sleek staff shuttle is still bobbing at the end of the jetty when I arrive at the dock.

As I'm hoisted onto the craft by one of Raphael's steroid-induced flunkeys, I'm all sunny smiles and small talk.

Anna's scowl melts into a smirk as Claudia whispers something in her ear, but then the engine bursts into life under the bench and I find it impossible to give a flying fuck. I close my eyes and bask in the salty assault, finding freedom in tangled hair, wet cheeks, and a numb nose.

There are worse commutes, I suppose. And besides, Martin O'Hare isn't going to find me in the middle of the Pacific, is he?

The roar of the engine simmers to a shuddering idle, and when I open my eyes, I'm met with a gaze sharper than a needle and just as capable of popping my helium-filled heart.

Raphael stands on the swim platform, a contrast of crisp black lines and gold accents glinting under the winter sun. He's broad and tall and, even with fifty feet and a strong current between us, his presence touches my soul like a Zippo flame dancing too close to an oil spill.

The boat bumps against a fender, the suit-clad skipper secures the mooring line, and Raphael takes a smooth step forward. Dice cufflinks wink and a gold poker chip disappears into the pocket of his slacks.

"Good afternoon, ladies," he says smoothly, a satin smile carved into his dimples.

A giggly chorus floats around me. I turn my back and sigh into the wind, wishing it'd carry me back to shore. Maybe even over the border to Canada.

"Allow me."

A silky tone and my own curiosity turn my head just enough to see Raphael hitch up his slacks and extend a large hand to Katie. He pulls her up onto deck with ease and chuckles when she falls against his chest.

"I'm sure there's something in the staff handbook about drinking before a shift, Katie," he jokes. "I'll let it slide this time, all right?"

He winks, she blushes, and I wonder if drowning really *is* as bad as everyone makes out.

Claudia elbows her way to the front and extends her hand. "My goodness, who's the lucky man?" Raphael drawls, swiping a thumb over her diamond ring.

"That's not my ring finger, Mr. Visconti." She giggles and waves her other hand in the air. "*This* is my ring finger. And as you can see, it's *very* much bare."

Raphael pins her with a lazy smile. "Phew. I thought you were about to break my heart there, Claudia."

With an itch in my blood, I glare out to sea and try my best to tune out plastic pleasantries and shameful attempts at flirting. Laurie aside—she'd simply patted him on the shoulder and fled for the nearest bathroom—these girls must have three brain cells between them if they are gullible enough to fall for Raphael Visconti's act.

His charm is like his aftershave—intoxicating. But when you get too close to the source, like I did last night, you can see it for what it really is: a thick satin veil hiding the danger that lies beneath.

"Penelope."

His voice is colder when it touches my nape, making my lids flutter shut. A nervous energy hums under the surface of my skin now. I'd thought it was a genius idea to slip his watch on when I passed my suitcase this morning, but now, with its former owner just a few feet behind me, I'm a little less brave.

I galvanize my spine and turn around. Unfortunately, I'm the only girl left on the boat, and unless I fancy swimming back to shore, there's only one way off it.

Raphael glances over his shoulder at the sound of the door behind him clicking shut. When his gaze comes back to mine, it's five Pantone shades darker.

"I don't have all day."

"And I don't have a broken leg. Don't need your help, thanks."

He glares at me for a beat too long, then shifts his attention to something above my head and extends his hand. He can feign apathy all he fucking wants, but the tick in his jaw suggests he'd rather get his teeth pulled than have me grab hold of it.

"Wouldn't be very *gentlemanly* of me not to help you," he says dryly.

Like he suddenly remembered something else he's forgotten to be pissed off about, he runs an eye down the side of my thigh, lets out a hot hiss, and returns to glaring above my head. "And it wouldn't be very *ladylike* of you to get off the boat with your ass hanging out."

"Not like you haven't seen it already," I snap back. My heart flutters at the memory of his staring at me in the locker room.

"Yes, but my men haven't," he says icily. "And we're going to keep it that way."

Only now do I realize he's not staring into the distance merely to avoid looking at me, but rather, he's staring at something. Some*one*. I turn around and catch the skipper looking at the backs of my thighs, as if lost in thought. Feeling the weight of two pairs of eyes, he looks up, flinches, and quickly turns away.

I sigh. *Men.*

"Up. Now."

Jeez. I look down at the large hand under my nose. Blue rivulets under olive skin and neat, blunt nails. A shuddering breath escapes me as my mind floats to two scenarios:

That hand sliding over the dip of my hip.

It tightening around my throat.

Soft. Hard. Each, unfortunately, as enticing as the other.

Clearing my throat in an attempt to regain some sort of control, I slip my thumb and forefinger around his wrist, between his watch strap and cuff. I slide his sleeve up an inch and reveal what I already knew would be there.

Ink, and lots of it.

Just like his charm and his aftershave and Sunday morning smiles, his bespoke suits are yet another veil, disguising the darkness that leaks from the inside out. The private security. The yachts. The autonomy over a whole fucking coastline. It's so blatant that Raphael is a bad man, and I wonder if all the women who look at him with hearts in their eyes just choose not to see it.

How am I meant to be good when I'm obsessed with something so bad?

Heart beating in my throat, I graze my thumb over Italian script. Stroke the corner of a Joker playing card. A cocktail of curiosity and lust blooms hot between my thighs, partly because he doesn't stop me from pushing up his sleeve a little farther, and partly because I ache to know how far up his tattoos go. Half sleeve? Full sleeve? Or do they cover every inch of his sculpted, tan skin, like sinful secrets under a blanket of Brioni?

I look up to find him watching me, his own curiosity softening the planes of his face.

"You don't fool me," I murmur.

My smugness is short-lived, swept away by a flash of green and two strong hands hauling off the shuttle. They slip under my arms and carry me like a rag doll across the swim platform and into the jet ski garage. My back slams against something hard and I brace myself for the moment my head meets the same fate.

But the *crack* doesn't come, because Raphael's hand slips behind my crown and cushions the blow, while the other hand claps down on my mouth and absorbs my scream.

Oh shit. I'm pressed up against the darkest, quietest corner of the yacht, and despite its sophisticated silhouette, I'm not entirely sure the animal trapping me in is domesticated.

My pulse whooshes in my ears, the sound almost lost to the roar of adrenaline licking my body wildfire. I'm panting, and the wry amusement swirling through Raphael's gaze suggests he's enjoying how each of my ragged breaths dampen his palm.

"Let me—"

Uncertainty flares up behind his ice-cool demeanor and his grip tightens around my jaw, ending my protest with a full stop. It's barely the twitch of a muscle, but just like the squeeze of my breasts and the flex of his thigh against my pussy, the insinuation feels so much heavier.

He takes a leisurely step closer, obstructing my view of the only exit.

"Haven't you heard, Penelope?" he muses. "Red heads should never speak first when they step onto a boat. It's—" He stops himself. Rolls his shoulders back and corrects his smile. "Inappropriate."

My pussy clenches around the word *inappropriate*. He must have noticed, because he punctuates my moan against his palm with a sharp tug of my hair. *Christ*.

With a lazy smirk, he searches my half-lidded gaze, as if admiring the frenzy he's sent me into. His eyes travel further south, grazing over my neckline, before coming back to meet mine with an edge of approval.

"As much as it pains me to admit it, you're rather hot when you're gagged."

Sweet, holy hell. My clit beats to the tune of his flippant taunt; my nipples ache for the friction of his chest against mine.

A hot palm against my mouth, thick fingers in my hair, and the smell of chlorine mixed with his signature scent assaulting my nostrils: I'm falling into the black abyss of sensory purgatory, and Raphael Visconti is peering over the edge, waiting patiently for me to hit the bottom. It feels like if I don't claw my way out immediately, I'll die at the mercy of his large hands and smug smirk.

I push back against his hand behind my head, creating a millimeter of space between my mouth and his palm. I stick my tongue out flat and I *lick*.

Slowly. Sloppily. Steam rises from my blood with every inch of his palm I cover.

Realization crawls over the hard planes of Raphael's face, and then the humor in his gaze flicks off like a light switch, plunging us into the ice age.

My breathing slows. My triumph sparks.

A smile curves his lips again but this time, it's cold and calculated. Loaded with ill intentions, each of them meant for me. Before I can twist my head out of his grip, he removes his hand from my mouth and drags it down the side of my cheek, *hard*, coating my clammy skin with my own saliva.

What the fuck? It's a childish retaliation, but the wet weight of his palm gliding frictionlessly over the angle of my cheekbone sends a violent shiver to the nerve endings in my clit. Christ, it feels so sordid, so *obscene*—a dirty kink I didn't know I was into. Before his palm slides off my chin, he hooks his thumb over the curve of my bottom lip to keep it there.

I forget to breathe. Forget to *feel*. I'm too focused on the dark fascination clouding his eyes as he glides his thumb from one side of my lip to the other. I might have my own fucking saliva dripping down the side of my face, but a nasty flare of satisfaction spreads behind my aching breast. I've stood in front of enough hungry men to recognize that look. Sinful ink, yachts, and fat wallet aside, I'm the one with the upper hand here.

I'm winning this game.

I prove it to myself by clamping my teeth down on his thumb as it comes back to the middle of my lip. A blaze of annoyance, a hot hiss of breath, and then Raphael's gaze snaps up to mine.

Three irregular heartbeats pass before he gains enough semblance to drag his thumb from my mouth and rest it lightly on the indentation of my chin.

"I bet you bite when you fuck," he says pensively, as if talking to himself rather than me.

My heart hitches. "And I bet you a hundred bucks you're hard right now," I answer.

I don't know why I say it. Drunk on lust and wishful thinking, perhaps. But something in my words seems to be the antidote Raphael needs to regain his composure. He untangles himself from me and takes a step back. He looks at his wet hand in mild amusement, plucks out the pocket square from his suit jacket and wipes it between his thick fingers.

With one last lingering look, Raphael tightens a cufflink and turns on his heel.

"You're a dog, Penelope," he says breezily over his shoulder. "I should look into putting you down."

"They already tried."

His footsteps slow to a stop and he glances back at me. "And?"

"I bit the vet."

Silence. Then his laugh, dark and dangerous, floats over and caresses my skin like a long-time lover. The pleasure of it ripples through my center and settles like a weight in my already soaked panties.

Just as Raphael strides out of the garage and out of sight, a light thump hits the deck. On shaky legs, I walk over and see what he dropped.

Now it's my turn to laugh, although it has a more nervous undertone than Raphael's did.

Five twenty-dollar bills in a silver money clip.

CHAPTER
Eighteen

Rafe

B ENNY STANDS ON THE boat tender, arms outstretched and his legs shoulder-width apart. An unlit cigarette dangles from his lips, and his glare is almost hot enough to warm up this icy December day at sea.

"*Cazzo*," he growls as Griffin slides a beefy hand up the inside seam of his slacks. "If you wanted to touch my dick, all you had to do was ask."

"I'd have to find it first," Griff grumbles back.

Amusement leaves my lips in a puff of condensation, which only makes Benny's scowl darker. "You don't trust me, *cugino*?"

"Standard protocol, Ben."

"You want me to squat and cough next?"

I smirk. "Depends. Got anything up there I should know about?"

Griffin gives me a curt nod and steps back, clearing my cousin to embark the yacht. I yank him up onto the swim platform with one hand and clap him on the back with the other.

He smooths down the front of his shirt and cracks his neck. "I haven't seen you on dry land for a while. You living onboard?"

I nod. "It's a bit more luxurious than any hotel in Dip, don't you think? Besides, it means you can't turn up unannounced as usual, with your hookers and your whiskey."

He laughs. "Unfortunately, the only thing I've brought today is bad news."

My heart sinks three inches in my chest. *Of course it is.* Seems like all news is bad news these days. Every time I pick up the phone or open an email, another brick of my empire crumbles away.

Benny saunters into the lounge, swipes a bottle of *Smuggler's Club* from behind the bar, and disappears down the spiral staircase. I find him in the crew mess, poking his bandaged hand around the pizza boxes and the sandwiches laid out for my men.

"You can't tell me you have bad news and then proceed to stuff your face," I say dryly, beckoning him over to the corner booth.

Gnawing on a slice of pizza, he strolls over and drops a thin manila folder in front of me. I flick it open, then run a wary eye down the list of familiar names. Half of them are scratched out with a sharp stroke of a fountain pen.

"What's this?"

"This V.I.P guest list for Thursday's poker night." He kicks out a chair and slumps down on it. "Ten of our biggest hitters have pulled out."

Benny, Tor, and I have held a joint poker night in Hollow on the last Thursday of every month for years. It's a partnership that's always worked seamlessly. Tor brings the big-hitters from Cove, I bring them from Vegas, and Benny brings anything that billionaires with too much money and not enough morals could possibly want. Since Tor has disappeared off the face of the planet—I *still* haven't heard from that fucker—Benny and I have decided to go it alone for the first time in forever.

My back molars grind together, but I keep my expression indifferent. "Let me guess; they've all caught that nasty flu going around."

He smirks at my sarcasm. "You're not too far off, *cugino.* Dante always has been a fucking germ."

My gaze snaps up from the list to meet his. "What's he done?"

"Apparently, he's holding a poker night to rival ours in Cove. Same night, same time. Called up all of our big-hitters and offered them half-price buy-ins and double the winnings." He leans back on his chair, watching for my reaction over his pizza slice.

I give a small shake of my head. "Not a single one of these men would take him up on that."

I can say that with full confidence. Our clients don't come to our poker nights for cheap buy-ins, they come because I'm there. These men fly from all around the world to have the chance to sit at the same velvet table as me. I spend most of the night signing chips rather than playing them.

"You've got that right. Obviously, none of them are going to Dante's poker night, either. But him calling everyone up and begging them to change their plans makes it obvious there's a Visconti family rift. Seems like everyone wants to stay away in case they get caught up in the middle of it."

I strum a finger against the cleft of my chin, glaring at the strip lights above Benny's head. "Where's he holding it?"

"*Portafortuna*. It's his new joint up on the north headland."

"We could always blow it up."

It's little more than a musing, out of my mouth before I can put weight to it.

Benny lets out a low whistle. "*Dio mio*. Who am I talking to, Rafe or Gabe? Hell, I'm surprised you haven't strolled over to Cove and forced both Vicious and Dante to sign a peace treaty, just to smooth things over."

"This is a little more serious than a drunken argument at Whiskey Under the Rocks, Ben."

"Mm. You wouldn't get into Cove even if you want to, anyway. My eyes and ears tell me Dante's put airport-style security at the borders. Full pat-downs, bag checks, the lot."

I turn around at the sound of Benny gagging. He pulls something out of his mouth with his bandaged fingers and dumps it on the table. "Is that a piece of fucking *pineapple*?" he exclaims, looking down at the yellow lump in disgust. "On fuckin' *pizza*?"

I smirk into the back of my hand. "Wasn't bought for your consumption, fat-ass."

Benny's phone buzzes, and he takes the stairs two-at-a-time to take the call.

Once again, Penelope proves the age-old adage of, if you think of the devil, it'll appear. Through the door on the other side of the seating area, I see her saunter into the kitchen and slow to a stop as she approaches the sinks. Her eyes slant at the mountain of dirty dishes.

"Is this all from last night?"

Chef Marco saunters over and tosses her an apron. "Yeah. Usually gets done after the shift."

"So why's it still here?"

He shrugs. Taps a cigarette out of a carton and tucks it into the crook of his mouth. "Boss's orders."

She rakes her fingers through her ponytail. "Son of a bitch," she grunts.

I lean my elbows on the table, warm satisfaction filling my center.

"I've killed men for saying nicer things about my mama, Penelope."

Her shoulders snap into a tight line, her gaze roving around to find mine. The surprise of seeing me in the shadows of the next room melts into hatred, which then crystallizes into something more mischievous.

Still holding my eye, she flicks on the hot tap, squirts dish liquid into the sink, and bends her elbows, pretending to roll up imaginary sleeves. My gaze drops to the watch sliding up her forearm—*my fucking watch*—and my mood darkens.

"I'm sure she was an absolute *doll*," she says sweetly, before plunging her hands into the soapy water.

Leaning back against the booth, I hide my amusement behind my knuckles. I'd insisted Laurie put Penelope on back-of-house duties under the pretense that all newbies should learn the ropes of every department, but really, it's because the new, more *modest*, uniform isn't coming in for another few days. It's less of a punishment for making me question my morals last night, and more of a stupid, self-preservation thing. With so much shit going on with my business, I'm not sure I have the restraint to spend another evening glaring at her over my poker hand while she shakes up cocktails for my guests.

Still, giving the regular pot-washer a paid night off was a petty chess move. And fair play to her, shoving my Breitling into a bowl of suds with a sexy smile is excellent retaliation.

But she'll never win the war against me. Not now that I know she calls Sinners Anonymous.

Right on cue, steel-capped footsteps thunder above my head and down the stairs.

My men appear like a pack of hungry wolves in the crew mess and make a beeline for the pizza and sandwiches laid out on the dining table. I nod politely as a slew of thanks come my way. Blake chomps off a huge chunk of a sub and grunts approvingly in my direction.

"Is it your birthday or something, boss?"

Is this idiot for real? I celebrated my thirty-fourth birthday three months ago on a private island in the Maldives. Eyelid twitching, I manage to give him a tight-lipped smile. "Just getting into the Christmas spirit of giving."

Through the sea of broad shoulders and suits, I watch Penelope scrub at the dishes from last night. She pauses every few minutes to huff strands of hair out of her eyes and wipe her brow against her shoulder.

After reverse-dialing the last number called from the phone booth last night, I couldn't get back aboard my yacht quick enough. I'd intended to settle down behind my desk with a glass of whiskey in one hand and my dick in the other and let Penelope's sins unravel through my Bose speakers.

They didn't come. Turns out, Penelope has been using the hotline like a fucking *diary*. Talking shit for the sake of talking shit. Vapid tidbits about her day, random musings about whatever book she's reading, or recaps on conversations she's recently had with her neighbor. Ironically, the only call that mildly piqued my interest was the one she made in the phone booth: *I have three library books, and I'll never get to return them.*

The three, drawn out breaths that had preceded it suggested it wasn't what she'd originally planned to confess.

Still, skimming through the most boring inner workings of her brain hasn't completely been in vain. One interesting fact I learned about Penelope is that she detests ham and pineapple pizza, and tuna sandwiches make her gag.

Which is why I bought my men both for lunch.

"Where do you want us to put the plates, boss?"

I run my tongue over my teeth, amused. "Just dump them in the sink."

A stampede of suits and steroids stomps through the door to drop mounds of dirty dishes into the sink. Penelope stares in disbelief as each plate breaks the surface of the water with a loud *plop*. Rivers of suds run down the cabinet and pool on the floor. Her eyes trail it, before darting to the row of shiny shoes stomping back out into the crew mess.

"Hey! Where are you going?" Her bark receives little more than a few smirks and sniggers. "I'm not washing your shit up! Come back and do it yourself!"

As the crew mess clears, there's only one of my men left. Blake. He pushes off the doorframe and saunters into the kitchen, holding his plate high above the water.

Penelope takes a step forward. "Don't be a dick." Another step. "Seriously."

The plate falls, landing in the water with such force that it sloshes all down her dress.

The walls of my stomach tense, but I don't move from my corner. Penelope's and my eyes run down the front of her dress and tights. Both are soaked. She sucks in a shaky breath, curls her fists, and turns back to my lackey.

"Were you born a cunt, or were you turned into one by school bullies and a father that didn't love you?"

My lips tilt, a dark chuckle filling my chest. Where does this girl get her smart mouth from?

Blake takes a step forward. "You could always take it off, *sweetheart*."

My vision darkens around the edges, but I will every muscle in my body to stay in this fucking booth. I run two fingers over my mouth and watch how Penelope handles it.

She blinks. "What?"

"Your dress, sweetheart. Take it off if it's wet. I won't mind."

My ears ring with all the blood rushing to my head. And why the fuck is my hand brushing against the grip of the gun tucked into my waistband? Ridiculous. *That's not me.*

Clamping my jaw shut, I ball my hands into fists and lay them on the table. My glare is so hot on the side of Penelope's face, I'm surprised she hasn't caught fire, let alone felt its heat. She licks her lips, like she's considering something.

Eventually, she swallows, and looks up at him through half-mast lashes. "What'd you say your name is again?"

"Blake. I'd ask you the same, but every man on this boat knows who you are."

Penelope laughs. *Laughs.* It bounces out of the kitchen, across the crew mess, and zaps me in the dark corner like a fucking cattle prod. I clench my fists tighter, the weight of my gun growing heavier, like it's reminding me it's there.

"Shut up, no they *don't.*"

A grunt leaves my lips as she playfully swipes at his chest.

"No seriously," he drawls, slipping his hand under her chin and tilting it toward him. "You're gorgeous. Anyone ever tell you that?"

Red mist rolls through the crew mess like a sand storm in a desert. *Fuck this.* It'd be all too easy to pop a bullet in his head and toss him overboard with a couple of bricks tied to his ankles. But as I'm half-way to my feet, Penelope's hand sliding into the pocket of his pants stops me in my tracks.

"Gorgeous? I've heard it a few times," she says sweetly, never taking her eyes off his. As he laughs and says something about loving a chick with confidence, she slides out his wallet between her thumb and forefinger.

She presses it against the small of her back and side steps him. "Welp, I better go clean up!" She turns and slinks through the door on the other side of the kitchen, ignoring Blake's pathetic *will-I-see-you-later?* trailing after her.

Rubbing a hand over his buzz-cut, Blake lets out a sleazy laugh and strolls out of the crew mess and up the stairs.

Alone with my heart slamming against my chest, I can't decide who I'm going after first.

CHAPTER
Nineteen

Rafe

NICOTINE AND SEA BREEZE do nothing to dull the irritation searing the nape of my neck.

Doesn't matter. I'm not smoking to calm down, I'm smoking to procrastinate. Wiping mist from my jaw, I suck in a lungful of chemicals no worse for me than a red-head moaning into my palm, and exhale them toward the denim horizon.

I'm annoyed for a million reasons, only half of them rational, and only one that needs my immediate attention.

I tug Blake's cheap wallet out of my back pocket, flick it open, and sneer at his driver's license photo. It was lying at the bottom of the spiral staircase, no doubt from where Penelope tossed it. There was nothing left in it except a prepaid credit card and a condom.

As I flick it into the sea, the impulsive thought simmering at the back of my brain still lingers: I should throw him in with it. That's why I'm going after Penelope and not him right now. Embarrassingly enough, I can't say I wouldn't shove my Glock in his slimy-ass mouth if I did.

Images of Penelope on her fucking tippy-toes, gazing up at my newest recruit like laying one on him was at the very top of her bucket list, burns bright behind my retinas. The way my hand had twitched toward my gun was wild, and for a moment, I had a glimpse of what it must be like living in Angelo or Gabe's head, where violence follows impulsion and consequences are a foreign concept.

I already knew she was a dirty little thief, but now I know it's worse than I thought—she's *good* at it. Well-seasoned. If I was in my early twenties and still chased trouble, I'd be losing my mind at the sight of it. And although I'd be lying if I said I wasn't a little impressed, and more than a little turned on, I'm running a business, not a juvenile detention center.

I drop my head against the side of the yacht. Slide another cigarette out of the carton and bring my Zippo to the tip.

No. I snuff out the flame with a flick of my wrist. If I smoke one more cigarette, she might have put her dress back on.

Below deck, the faint hum of a hairdryer seeps under the locker room door. Galvanizing my self-control, I push it open and stride down the row of lockers toward the sinks.

I slow to a stop. Drag my hand over my throat. Greasy burgers, weed, Sunday morning lie-ins. Just because I crave things that are bad for me, it doesn't mean I give in to them. I should have applied the same hard-and-fast rule to seeing Penelope in her underwear and tights, because that's the epitome of bad for me. As I slow to a stop behind her, the weight of a bad decision throbs inside my slacks.

Christ. The last time I saw her like this, I went on to sit behind my desk with a rock-solid erection I refused to relieve, and almost managed to convince myself that it *simply wasn't real*. That nine whiskeys had romanticized my memory of her next-to-naked.

Unfortunately, as I roll a heavy gaze over the curve of her ass, the paleness of her skin, and the outline of her thong shaded by her tights, I realize it was wishful thinking. She doesn't flinch when I enter the room and it both turns me on and pisses me off. I wonder; would she still stand there in her panties with that indifference carved into her face if it was one of my men who'd strolled in here?

I steal another glance at her ass. Confirmed: she wears thongs. Unconfirmed: whether they're lacy like her bra. Whether I could rip them off with my teeth.

The buzz of the hairdryer stops. I lift my attention to the spotlights in the ceiling and run a finger over my pin collar. A slow, deep breath, and only then can I feign enough nonchalance not to look like a pervert.

She meets my gaze in the mirror. "You know, in a conventional workplace, a boss following their employee into the locker room would be considered sexual harassment."

My dry laugh doesn't tilt my lips. "In case you haven't noticed, this isn't a conventional workplace."

Her eyes spark with amusement. "Do you pay taxes?"

I glance at the bills peeking out of her bra cup. "Do you?"

When she laughs, a delicate flush stains her neck, and despite the fact that both the sight and the sound of her hum like a live wire down the length of my dick, I don't return her smile.

Draping her dress over her arm, she pushes off the sink and saunters toward the cubicles behind me. "Touché, boss."

Impulsion. Violence. Her sass falls off a cliff because I can't stop myself shooting out a hand and hooking a finger into the waistband of her tights. She wobbles to a stop, and her next breath fizzles through the part of her mouth.

My cock pulsates to the rhythm of a dripping shower head.

"What did I tell you about calling me boss when half-naked, Penelope?"

Her *gulp* stokes the flames of my annoyance. Only when I'd acted on it, did I realize the sight of her was pissing me off. Bending over the counter, prancing around with a bounce in her step. She knew exactly what she was doing and has made it near-impossible to be serious with her.

I'm a dirty hypocrite; I know. I purposely smoked a single cigarette to make sure I caught her half-dressed. Besides, deep down I'm more pissed with myself than with her, because if I'm fooled by the way her body moves and the way her laugh sounds, then I'm no better than my lackey.

Despite the heat of her soft hip burning between my first and second knuckles, I regain enough composure to look at her. "Tell me, where did you learn to be such a dirty little thief?"

Her eyes widen. "What?"

"I saw what you did to Blake. What did I tell you, Penelope? You want to work here, you have to be a lady. I said no more grifting, no more stolen dresses. I'd have added no more stealing wallets to that list if I'd known you were into that shit." My mood darkens a shade. "What are you, feral?"

She glances down at my hand, as if only now realizing I have her hooked like a fish on a line, and she didn't stop by my side on her own accord.

When her blue eyes come back to mine, they're wide and soft around the edges.

I'm more sadistic that I thought. Only the tiniest flare of vulnerability reminds me that she's five-foot-nothing and wouldn't make it farther than the lockers if I decided she wouldn't. Just like she wouldn't have made it out of the phone booth if I hadn't stepped aside.

This girl may look the part, and my business might be falling to shit, but she could never be my Queen of Hearts. Her quick mouth, sticky hands, and hard stare are annoying, but they couldn't bring me to my knees. I'd snuff the life out of her before I let them.

One day, she'll play her games on a man that isn't as...sportsmanlike as me, and they'll do just that. The thought slides a sheet of unease under my skin.

"Answer my question." My tone has lost its edge. "Where did you learn to pick a pocket like that?"

Hot, shallow breaths leave her lips and graze my throat. Curling my free hand into a fist around my poker chip in my slacks, I tear my gaze from hers in an attempt to thin the air. *She's too naked for this.*

As I'm glaring at Laurie's locker behind Penelope's head, her soft voice touches my ears, its contents as unexpected as its tone.

"I'm trying," she whispers.

My eyes skim to hers, and dammit, I wish I hadn't looked, because I don't find the sarcasm I was expecting. Instead, her face is flushed a pretty pink and her bottom lip sticks out. I shouldn't know how it feels to run my thumb over it. Shouldn't want to do it again, either.

"Trying?"

"To stop with the whole swindling thing. You were supposed to be my last..."

My eyes slant on hers as her sentence trails off. Gritting my teeth, I say coldly, "Call me a mark, Penelope, and it'll be the last word that comes out of your mouth."

She flashes me a lop-sided smirk. "*Target,* then."

I snap the waistband of her tights, hard, in an attempt to shock her. More fool me—the moan that escapes her lips tugs on the tip of my cock. I dig my finger back in, deeper this time, a darkness filling me as my fingertip grazes the band of her thong.

Dead parents, bratty behavior. That's a recipe for a sinner if I've ever seen one. What I'd do to sink my teeth into that dough-like skin and taste those sins of hers. To pull on her red ponytail and relish in every confession she makes against my pillow as I fuck her from behind.

Lust crawls under my skin like an itch I can't scratch. I clear my throat, trying—and failing—to ignore the heat of her gaze shining up at me.

This is ridiculous. That's what I thought earlier too, when I left the jet ski garage a hundred bucks lighter. This girl has a way of luring me into quiet places and sending me into so much of a spin I forget where the exit is.

Being a dick is the only way I know how to stand up straight around her.

"Try harder," I grind out. I drag my finger out of her tights again, and the satisfying snap of elastic reminds me of the crack of a belt. "Keep your sticky fingers to yourself, Penelope."

"Yes, boss—"

I grip her jaw rougher than I intend. I'm too worked up, too *hot*, to feel any regret. "Don't get smart with me. Blake's an easy target: dumb as a bag of rocks. You won't get away so easily if you try that shit on anyone with half a brain and a Glock in their waistband."

She frowns, her jaw muscle flexing against my thumb pad in defiance. "Bet I could."

I stare at those lips a beat too long. *Bet I could.* Christ, I've known her for a week and she already knows what buzzwords will dig her red fingernails under my skin. Years of conditioning makes it instinctive to bite back with a wager, but in the interest of being professional, I clamp my mouth shut and drag my hand away from her face.

I take a step back and flex my fist. Stride toward the exit. I don't intend on stopping until I'm in the darkness of my office, where the heat of her skin and the scent of her strawberry shampoo can't mar my restraint, but her voice comes in a low, sultry rasp, my name wrapped within it.

My stomach tightens. I turn and look at her face. Her stupid, pretty face, punctuated with features that make men do silly things, like follow her into locker rooms knowing she'll be in pantyhose and lace.

"If Blake's an easy target, what does that make you?" She pulls a wallet out from under her dress.

Son of a bitch.

She holds it up like a trophy, and the initials RV glint in gold under the spotlights. My own name, taunting me with how fucking complacent I've become.

With a lazy smirk, she flips open my wallet and peers inside. She tugs out a hundred-dollar bill and slides it into her bra.

"That's for winning the bet." She pulls out another hundred. "Plus VAT." She cocks her head in thought, then pulls out another. "Plus tip."

I watch in dark amusement as she tosses my wallet onto the bench and flashes me a sickly-sweet smile. "Pleasure doing business with you, *boss.*"

She slinks off into a cubicle, leaving me with an unwanted thrill under my skin and the threat of a hard-on in my pants.

I bite out a laugh.

This girl isn't the Queen of Hearts, but the Devil in disguise.

Unfortunately, I can't say for sure I wouldn't follow her into hell.

CHAPTER
Twenty

Penny

T HE RUSTY ANCHOR BAR *and Grill.*

The sign above the door is missing most of its vowels, and the way the 'R' flickers violently is giving me a migraine. Frowning, I pull out my cell and open *TripAdvisor* again.

Nope. Not hallucinating. This really *is* the highest rated bar in Devil's Dip. Jeez, I know you shouldn't judge a book by its cover, but I'm pretty sure I remember its pages being as shoddy, too.

Wren really works here? It just doesn't make sense. She's all sunshine and smiles and this place is, well...

I cast a weary gaze over the parking lot, which is just a gravel road with two beat-up Chevy pickups parked under a broken street lamp.

...the setting for a true crime podcast.

Stop it, Penny. I don't know why I'm being such a snob about aesthetics. My apartment in Atlantic City had a family of spiders living under the sink.

My gaze slides up to the black sky. Truth is, I'm just using it as an excuse not to go inside. Because the thought of walking through that door and putting out the nicest version of myself in order to make friends feels...*sad.*

Still, what other option do I have? I need friends. Normal girls have friends. Can't fake it with the likes of Anna, and I can't spend all my days off glaring at the stark white walls of my apartment.

Christ, yesterday I called the hotline four times, simply to have somebody to talk to.

And Wren invited me, right? At the hospital, she said there was always a seat at the bar for me on Tuesday evenings. But she was probably just being nice…

Well, Rory invited me, too, I guess. On the night of my first shift. I'm not sure it counts, though, because she got so drunk, she had to be put to bed in one of the cabins. Maybe it was just the liquor talking.

Ah, fuck it. I'm going in.

As I step inside, warmth wraps around me like a hug. For a brief moment, my lids flutter shut, but then I force them open and scan my surroundings.

If this bar was in the heart of a big city, the interior would be described as *shabby-chic*, or *rustic*. But I highly doubt the hole in the ceiling or the tin bucket directly underneath it was a design choice. Or the suspicious looking stain on the floor, for that matter.

The Rusty Anchor still has the same old pages; they're just covered in gaudy Christmas decorations.

Heaving a nervous sigh, I walk past the handful of pot-bellied men slumped over half-drunk beers and slide onto a stool at the bar. There's nothing behind it apart from a few liquor bottles, and nobody in front of it but me.

No Wren or Rory, and definitely no other girls I could share jeans with.

I strum my fingers on the wooden bar. Chew on my bottom lip. Looking around for any sign of life under seventy, my eyes settle on the tip jar and my strumming stops. Years of morally-gray conditioning make my fingers twitch to fish out a few bills, but instead, I curl my hand into my lap and huff out a bitter laugh.

This is ridiculous.

I'll just go back to the diner, grab a burger, and get started on HTML *for Dummies*—

"Penny!" My name in squeal form shoots out from behind me and pierces my jacket. I turn as Wren emerges from a back room, a crate of glasses balancing on her forearms. "Oh my goodness, so good to see you!"

Relief fills my chest as she buries me under a pile of questions, like where I've been, how's my head, and how I'm finding the Coast. Once they taper off, she drops the crate and beckons me over. "Come, Rory and Tayce are over here."

I follow her golden glow around to the farthest corner of the bar, where Rory and a girl I don't recognize sit on stools on the other side of a Christmas tree. A deck of cards, a bowl of candy, and two beer bottles sit between them.

"Penny!" Rory jumps off her seat and slings her arms around my neck. Even with a messy bun and wearing Nike sweats, she looks as beautiful as ever. "So good to see you." She grips my shoulders, pushes me to arms-length, and searches my eyes. "Last Monday, I didn't do anything...*embarrassing*, did I?"

I mean, I walked in on her sucking her husband's dick in the storage room, but there's no need to bring that up. "Not at all."

She looks relieved, then ushers me over to where they're sitting.

"This is Tayce," Wren says. As I sit down, I meet the gaze of the dark-haired girl. She's wearing a beanie and a leather jacket, and, actually, I recognize her from the yacht, too.

"Tayce is a tattoo artist, lives in Devil's Cove, and is...um..."

"A mystery," Tayce finishes for her, flashing me a wink. "And what about you, red-head?"

Under the weight of three pairs of eyes, my brain whizzes in a circle, trying and failing, to come up with anything good. *I'm Penny, I'm a thief, and I set fire to a casino in Atlantic City because its owner forced me out of the state.*

Yeah, that might be appropriate if I were trying to make friends in jail—which might be the case soon, considering Martin O'Hare knows the arsonist was a *she*. I've buried the panic under all my organs and refuse to turn on the television so it doesn't get the chance to rear its ugly head.

"Uh, I'm Penny, I'm twenty-one, and I work onboard *Signora Fortuna*."

Pathetic, I know.

"Ah, so you're working with Rafe now," Wren says, the twinkle in her eye hinting that she remembers our conversation from the hospital. "Do you think he's a gentleman yet?"

Gentleman. That word is an emotional trigger these days, giving me flashbacks of muffled mouths, snaps of elastic, and silk-wrapped threats. I'm growing clammy under faux fur, so I slip off my coat and drape it over the back of the stool.

Rory grabs a fistful of peanut M&Ms, shoves a handful in her mouth, and slides the bowl over to me. "What's it like working for my brother-in-law?"

I grit my teeth. "I barely see him."

She laughs through rabbit-like crunches. "Really? 'Cause he sees you."

Five words of little importance, and yet they sweep my next breath from my lungs. The smartest thing would be to say nothing, I know. But the itch in my throat won't let that happen. "What do you mean?"

"The night I was on the yacht, he couldn't take his eyes off you."

My cheeks sting, putting a dent in my nonchalant facade. Thankfully, Wren lunges over, whacks Rory on the arm and says, "Stop it! She's turning red."

"Uh-huh," Rory says with an all-knowing smirk. "Fine, change of subject. What's it like working with the mean girls?"

I laugh, thankful for the change of subject. "Laurie's nice, and so is Katie. But there's this one girl..."

"Anna," Rory and Wren say in unison, sharing an eye roll.

"You know her?"

"We went to school with her." I frown. *That's strange.* I'd think I'd recognize her too, then. "She was horrible then, horrible now." Rory leans in, a secret swirling in her amber eyes. "Wanna know something cool?"

"Always."

"Her front two teeth are fake."

I blink. "Really?"

"She was bitching about me in the toilet of a club, and Tayce overheard. Punched them straight out of her mouth."

They all laugh, and I turn to Tayce in surprise. She runs a thumb over the side of the card deck and hitches a shoulder. "Talk shit, get hit," she says, breezily.

I stare at her for a beat too long, something between amusement and curiosity sitting in my stomach. Before I can put weight to it, Wren pipes up.

"Beer anyone?"

I nod, and her gaze narrows on me. "Did you drive here?"

"No?"

"Okay, good."

She strides into the back room, and Rory meets my confused gaze with a smirk. She cocks her brow to a paper sign above the liquor wall, and I squint to read it. It's yellowing, with curling corners, but I can just about make out the faint message:

More than two drinks will require handing over your car keys to a member of staff. No ifs, no buts, no exceptions.

The last line is in bold, underlined, and followed by a row of exclamation marks.

"Wren's a goody-two-shoes. It's not even the legal limit."

"Hey, I heard that!" comes a yell from the back room. A few moments later, Wren emerges with a mock scowl, holding three beers between her fingers. "Nothing wrong with being good, Rory. You should try it some time."

Rory's chuckle is dark, and I like the way it feels against my skin.

"All right, gotta pee."

As she slides off the stool, a dark mass shifts in the shadows beyond the glow from the Christmas lights. My heart leaps an inch up my throat, and my hand shoots out to grip the edge of the bar.

"*For flamingo's sake*, Gio. I can use the bathroom without getting my throat slit, you know?"

A beefcake of a man steps out into the low lighting, suit-clad and stony-faced. "Boss's orders, I'm afraid."

Rory sighs. "Don't marry a made man if you enjoy peeing in peace, ladies." She shoves through the swinging door, and I'm pretty sure I see her push it from the other side so it swings back out and hits her guard on the ass as he comes to a stop and turns in front of it.

Heat brushes over my fingers, and when I look up, I realize Tayce is staring down at them. I follow her gaze.

My hand is still clutching the edge of the bar, knuckles white.

I slip it off and tuck it into my lap, but it's already too late. Tayce sits up straighter, runs her tongue over her teeth and cocks a microbladed brow. Instinctively, my eyes sweep the bar for Wren, in desperate need of her sunny disposition to crack the tension, but she's on the other side, serving an old-timer.

"You're running from something."

I knew it was coming. Could taste its thickness in the air before it floated out of Tayce's mouth. But the premonition doesn't stop my heart from skipping like a rock over a lake.

I take a cold swig of beer. Set it down. "Don't know what you're talking about."

Clink. I look down to see the neck of her beer bottle connect with mine. "Cheers to that."

Confusion and heat swirl my veins, and although I can't bring myself to look at her, I feel tethered to her by an odd sense of comradery. We've said about three words to each other, but in the thick silence, I can hear the unspoken. Sins, regrets, dirty pasts, and plastic names. The story in her brown eyes reflects my own.

The distant flush of a toilet. The running of a tap. A door crashes against the wall behind me and then Rory slides in between Tayce and I.

"You don't happen to be a master of Blackjack, by any chance?"

Her question catches me off guard. I clear my throat and cast a suspicious gaze over the deck of cards in Tayce's hands, as if the King of Spades will suddenly grow a mouth and tell them all my secrets. "No, why?"

"Darn it. I need to win against Rafe."

Something nasty flares up in my chest, and I force my expression not to reflect it. "How come?"

"He's the only one who doesn't let me beat him."

I bite out a laugh. "Why would anybody *let* you beat them?"

She frowns, like I've asked the stupidest question possible. "Because I'm married to Angelo Visconti."

My gaze cuts to the wall of muscle still looming a few feet behind her. *Fair.*

"But obviously, Rafe isn't scared of his brother and he plays to win. Now, I owe him almost three-hundred-thousand dollars."

"*Angelo* owes him three-hundred thousand dollars," Tayce corrects.

Rory winces. "Yeah, but he doesn't know that yet. I was hoping I wouldn't have to tell him, either. My plan is to get super good at Blackjack and win it back before Rafe tries to settle the debt." Her amber stare darkens, and I see a flash of something more sinister than her angelic silhouette portrays. "And besides, what I'd give to wipe that smirk off his face. Just *once.*"

Same.

Mischief creeps up my back. Impulse thrums in my temples, and my mouth works before my brain can tell it not to.

I slide the deck from Tayce's hands. Cut it in half, and shuffle. The *thawp* feels like a hit of heroin.

"Are you any good at math, Rory?"

Her eyes narrow on my hands. "Yes, I'm in aviation school."

"And what about keeping secrets?"

Her lips tilt. "Like you wouldn't believe."

"Well, then. I'll teach you how to win every time."

CHAPTER
Twenty-One

Penny

T WO HOURS PASS IN a blur of beers and bets. With every flick of my wrist, Kings and Queens welcome me back to the dark side with vapid smirks. As the night blackens against the windows, they reflect only us, the colorful Christmas lights, and the life I left behind.

I have to remind myself that I'm merely visiting.

The door opens and a suited figure strolls through it. He brings in something colder than the December wind.

"Husband alert," Rory mutters under her breath, sweeping the cards up and greeting him with a charming smile.

Angelo Visconti strolls up behind her, wraps his hand around her throat, and pulls her head back against his chest. I stare at his busted knuckles and my eyes itch to look away, because it feels too intimate for my viewing pleasure. His lips drop to her bun and his attention slides up to me. "You made a friend."

"We were already friends, silly." Sadly enough, this admission makes the pit of my stomach warm. "This is Penny."

"I know, we've met."

"You have?"

We have?

"Yeah, she walked in on you sucking my dick in the storage cupboard of Rafe's yacht."

Turning beet red, Rory attempts to twist out of Angelo's grasp and claw at his face. Angelo laughs, easily pinning her arms to her side, and lands a gentle kiss on the crown of her head.

"I'm going to get you back," Rory hisses, biting back an embarrassed smile.

"Look forward to it."

Why the fuck am I grinning like an idiot? But then my amusement twists into something resembling jealousy and I don't even know why. I don't know what my Happy Ever After entails yet, but it won't involve a *man*, of all things. Still, I can't stop a single bitter sentence flashing behind my eyelids. *Must be nice.*

I stand and shove my coat on, and when I look up from the faded carpet, Angelo is still staring at me, dry amusement lurking in his dark gaze. An uneasy sense of *deja vu* crackles under my skin. Not because I've lived this moment before, but because he looks so much like his brother. A rough outline to Raphael's meticulously drawn portrait.

Angelo is everything Raphael Visconti pretends he's not.

Dominance and danger ooze from every pore, but, unlike his brother, he embraces it. He doesn't attempt to distract you from it with a silver tongue and diamond cufflinks.

No. He's raw, rugged. All shadowy stubble and open-spread collars. In theory, his version of a made man should be scarier, but it's not. At least not to me, because if Angelo wanted to kill me, he'd put a bullet in my head and move on with his day.

Raphael would turn it into a game. Like a cat with an injured mouse, he'd toss me from paw to paw, before outsourcing my death to someone on his payroll once he got bored.

Despite my father's final calls to God haunting my memory, I know how I'd rather die.

Angelo looks over my shoulder. "Tayce, one of our men will take you home."

"Yes," she hisses, sliding off the stool and slinging her leather jacket over her shoulder. "There's nothing better than a Visconti Uber. Blacked-out windows, reclining seats, and those mini water bottles in the center console. A dream."

Rory frowns. "We don't have any mini water bottles in our car?"

"Because you've filled the center console with candy, baby," Angelo replies. Looking back to me, he adds, "My men will take you home, too."

"Sweet, but no need." I pick up my purse and hoist it over my shoulder. All eyes fall on me. A few beats of silence, then I crack under the awkwardness. "I'm only ten minutes away. I'll just walk."

Angelo's gaze thins. "You won't. It's past midnight."

I can't help but laugh. "I'll be fine. Thanks though!"

Rory clamps down a smirk, as if she wants to say something but thinks the better of it. Under the heat of Angelo's glare, I exchange pleasantries and numbers with all three girls and head toward the door with pace to my step. Partly because I'm buzzing off the high of a successful night making friends, and partly because I have a feeling one of Angelo's men is going to reach out from the shadows and snatch me up at any moment.

There are more of them in the parking lot, too. Suits leaning against sedans and blowing cigarette smoke up into the night sky. Avoiding their gazes, I tuck my chin into the collar of my coat and walk to the main road. Tonight, the streets are stiff with frost, and the impending threat of rain crackles down my spine.

Despite not being dressed for rain—my faux-fur coat smells like dog when it gets wet—I decide to take a walk. Why not? I know tonight, of all nights, won't be one in which I experience the miracle of sleep, anyway. Instead of turning down toward main street, I take a left, climbing higher up the cliff-face.

I bow my head in an attempt to stop the wind stinging my eyes, instead focusing on the sidewalk under my feet. Soon, it tapers off into a rough, narrow lane, and the orange haze from the streetlamps cuts off.

Then the rain starts.

It's not the romantic mist I was hoping for, but cold, glassy needles, arrowing down from the heavens without mercy. The type that penetrate your skin and chill your bones, making you shiver at the memory of being caught in it even weeks later.

As another icicle fights its way down my collar, I bite out a curse and slow to a stop.

The road ahead has somehow morphed into a black hole since the last time I looked up from my Doc Martens. There's not a streetlamp, house, or car in sight, and carrying on feels like something only the dumb bitch who dies at the beginning of every horror movie would do.

I turn my back on the wind and retreat. Maybe the four stark walls of my apartment aren't so bad, after all.

I'm less than three steps into my descent when a white glow washes over my back and stretches my shadow. It illuminates the puddles underneath my boots, and when the roar of the wind clashes with the angry growl of an engine, I know I'm in trouble.

An enormous dark sedan passes around my shoulder. It comes to a sudden stop ahead of me, swinging round at the last minute to block both sides of the road.

Well, that's not good. I reluctantly stop and swallow the panic clotting my throat. In *Self Defense for Dummies*, there's a whole chapter on opportunist kidnappings. One of the stats that really stuck out for me is that if a kidnapper manages to get you off the street and into their car, your chances of survival drop to less than three-percent.

Three-fucking-percent.

My luck hasn't been sharp enough recently to be happy with those odds.

Heart slamming against my ribs, I scramble in my purse for something, *anything*, to defend myself. Somehow, I still have the semblance to curse myself for being so stupid. In Atlantic City, I *always* had a knife on me. Nothing fancy, just a small switchblade I could wave around if danger came too close. But it lies abandoned in my bedside dresser in my old apartment, and all I have in my bag are my keys and a book.

The driver's side door flies open and a dark figure steps out of it. I sigh, knowing I don't have the hand-eye coordination to guarantee I'd jab my key anywhere near a vital organ. I pull out *HTML for Dummies* and hope it's heavy enough to knock out my attacker if I crack them over the head with it.

A black silhouette parts the rain and storms toward me. As it crosses the path of the car's wide-set headlights, I realize it's Raphael.

A cold sweat drifts through me. *Is it really him?* Looks like him, but bigger, scarier. Not just because the backlight of the beams highlights his stature and darkens his thunderous expression, but because he's only wearing black slacks and a white shirt, with his sleeves folded up to his elbows.

My eyes fall to the space between his sleeves and wristwatch. Shapes and script shift on his forearms as he clenches his fists at his side. The sight alone makes a heady thrill sweep through my core.

There won't be any gentlemanly pretense tonight.

He stops a few feet away. Stabs a thumb over his shoulder. "Get in the car."

The venom in his tone spins me sideways. "Your car? Not a chance. I'll end up in a ditch somewhere."

"You're walking around at midnight, Penelope. Seems like you *want* to be in a ditch somewhere."

"Don't worry about me, I'll be fine."

He takes a step forward; I take one back.

"Get in the car."

"Say *please*."

I'm shivering from the inside out and my toes are swimming inside my boots, yet, I'm standing here, the dictionary definition of a girl cutting off her nose to spite her face.

Raphael's head dips between his shoulders, and he pinches the bridge of his nose. Then his hand shoots out and grabs my throat so fast it steals my next breath.

"Penelope. You're five-foot-nothing and probably can't throw a punch to save your life. Get in my car before I toss you over my shoulder and spank your ass for the inconvenience of getting me wet." A tight, mocking smile flashes through the rain. "*Please.*"

He lets go with an angry shove, then steps aside to let me pass. *Well, then.*

Blood drumming in my ears and slightly stunned, I move toward the car. My ass is barely touching leather when the door slams shut behind me. As Raphael moves in a blurry shadow across the windshield, the weight of a bad decision pushes down on my shoulders.

I can pinpoint its source immediately. The warm, masculine scent that lingers within the four walls of the G-Wagon. After making the mistake of spraying it on myself last Monday, I spent an hour in the shower scrubbing it off, and I *really* don't want to be intoxicated by it again. It smells like danger, and I don't like the heat it spreads in certain parts of me.

My unease only heightens when Raphael slides into the driver's seat. He stares straight ahead in silence, but the anger rolling off his inked skin *roars*. I push up against the cold window in an attempt to get away from it.

"Seat belt."

It's all he says before shifting the car into gear and tearing off through the rain.

You know, perhaps I should have taken my chances and run. Now that I'm sitting here with the throb of his hand around my neck, it feels like it would have been the safer option.

Instead, I clutch onto the book in my lap and focus on the wipers working overtime.

A Christmas song crackles on the radio, barely audible. My hair drips onto the armrest in rhythmic *plops*. In my peripheral vision, I see Raphael's irritated gaze fall to the small puddle I've created.

"These seats are Nappa leather."

"And my sweater is cotton."

"What?"

I hitch a shoulder. Glare at the glow of fragmented headlights through the windshield. "Thought we were naming fabrics no one gives a shit about."

A beat passes, then he huffs out a dark laugh and shakes his head. A few more of my heartbeats thump before his voice touches my skin again. This time, it has a calmer undercurrent.

"Seriously, Penelope. Don't walk the streets alone at night. Pretty girls don't always get to see the next day."

I blink, completely ignoring his safety message in favor of indulging the light thrill creeping under my skin. "Did you just call me pretty?"

His jaw ticks. "You know you're pretty."

"I do?"

He has my full attention now. I stare down at his knuckles tight on the steering wheel, and the way his grip makes the King of Diamonds on his forearm flex squeezes my lungs.

"Of course you do. You wouldn't be prancing around in your panties trying to tease me if you didn't," he mutters bitterly.

Despite the unfortunate circumstances I've found myself in, I can't stop the hot triumph licking the walls of my heart.

I curl my fingers around the plastic edge of my book and feign nonchalance.

"You barely looked."

"Because I'm a gentleman, Penelope."

My gaze falls down his chest. His shirt is soaked through and I can just about see the dark shadows under its expensive fabric. A chink in his bespoke armor, and I'm breathless at the mere idea of what's underneath.

The car slows. Confused, I look up and find myself trapped in Raphael's intense gaze. "Would you have wanted me to look?"

"I—what?"

He licks his lips, a new wave of darkness to his expression. "You said I barely looked," he says quietly. "Would you have wanted me to look?"

A shiver rolls through me, slowing my next breath. The goose-bumps rising on the back of my neck have nothing to do with getting caught in the rain and everything to do with the hot, heavy expectation swirling inside the four walls of the car. It soaks into my skin, permeating my lungs and making it harder to feign indifference.

I settle with changing the subject. It feels safer.

"How did you know where to find me?"

A few seconds pass, before Raphael's gaze stops burning my cheek, and the car engine purrs under my ass again.

"My brother told me one of my girls was on the loose."

My girls.

Two words that both please me and annoy me at the same time. I'm not sure how I'd feel if it had been singular.

Unable to shake the uneasy awareness that comes with im-minent danger, I glance between the seats, as if expecting a suit-clad lackey to emerge from the trunk. "No minions tonight?"

Raphael smirks and glances in his rear-view mirror. "You don't think I can handle myself, Penelope?" He looks at me sideways, eyes dropping to my chest and back up again. "You think I can't handle *you?*"

There's a toneless edge to his questions. It rolls through my blood like oil in water, sliding around and making me squirm. It's unreadable, unpredictable, and for once, I wish he'd just make polite small talk with me like he does with everyone else.

"Well, your gun is fake, right?"

He laughs coarsely. Drops his head against the headrest. "Ah, yes. And so it is."

He turns the wheel with the heel of his palm and I realize we're pulling onto Main Street. Disappointment prickles at my chest. Ironic really, considering minutes ago, I didn't want to get into his car at all.

Suddenly, the seat belt cuts into my collarbone as I'm thrown forward. I gasp, reach out to the dashboard, and whip around to Raphael.

"If that was an attempt at killing me, it was pathetic."

But he's too busy glaring out my window to reply. His expression is treacherous, not an inch of gentleman remains on the sharp planes of his face.

"Why is the front door to your building open."

It's not a question and he's not hanging about for an answer. Hissing something ungodly under his breath, he pulls his *fake* gun from his waistband and lunges for his car door.

I grab his forearm and he freezes. We both look down at my fingers; his expression tightens with irritation, and I can feel the embarrassment burnt into mine.

I shift over Nappa leather. "Relax, it's always open."

His gaze slides up from my fingers to the watch around my wrist. I don't know why I'm still wearing it, but I'd be lying if I said it's because I forgot to take it off. It's warm and weighty and impossible not to notice. "What do you *mean*, it's always open?"

"What I said—it's broken." He looks up at me like I've just called his mother a whore. "But it's fine, my apartment door has a lock."

"Your apartment door has a lock," he repeats, mockingly. "Christ." He scoops up his cell from the center console and the screen illuminates the fury etched into his face. My fingers bob over the tendons flexing and contracting in his forearm as he types out a text, and suddenly feeling drunk on the knowledge it shouldn't be there, I drag my hand away.

He doesn't notice. Instead, he tosses his cell into the cup holder and continues driving past my apartment. "It's getting fixed."

I blink. "What, now?"

He nods, barely listening to me.

"Yeah, right. No locksmith is coming out in the middle of the night."

A sardonic smile deepens his dimples. The way he rakes his teeth over his bottom lip feels like a breathy whisper against my clit. "One of the perks of being filthy, stinking rich, Penelope."

Well, there it is. We're back to smug smirks and quick-witted comebacks, and although I roll my eyes, I'm secretly relieved to have safer ground under my feet.

I rest my head against the window. "Well, thanks, I guess. You can just drop me off at the diner and I'll wait for it to get fixed."

He glances at the time on the dash. It's nearly one a.m. "You hungry?"

I'm always hungry. "Little bit."

With a lazy shrug, he palms the wheel again, turns in the street, and parks haphazardly on the sidewalk outside the diner.

"Pretty sure this isn't a parking spot," I mutter under my breath, bringing a dark smirk to Raphael's lips.

The diner's yellow glow seeps through the rain on the windshield, and safety in the form of salty French fries and sugary milkshakes awaits.

I pop open my door, and unfortunately Raphael opens his, too.

My shoulders tense. "You're coming in?"

"No, I'll just sit here and play with my balls."

His door slams shut behind him, and a few seconds later he appears in the frame of mine, wearing his suit blazer. He rests his palms against the top of the car and leans in with half-lidded impatience. "Don't have all night, Penelope."

Well, then.

In the diner, the doorbell chimes above my head and warmth brushes my face. Standing on the welcome mat, I squint under the harsh strip lights—they're a stark contrast to the darkness that shrouded me outside.

Speaking of darkness, Raphael's wet chest presses against the back of my head as he steps in behind me. His lips graze over the shell of my ear and fill it with a hot demand. "*Move.*"

I sigh into the diner and squelch across checkered tiles. Eyes follow me, but only until a certain point, then they snap to the six-foot-four gentleman darkening the doorway.

A glance over my shoulder confirms he's never stepped foot in this diner in his life. Or any food joint that serves food on a plastic tray, probably. He stands on the welcome mat, hands in his pockets, regarding his new surroundings with badly concealed amusement.

A blond girl slides up behind the counter and pins me with wide eyes. "Hello! I'm Libby and I'll be your server for today." She's talking to me, but the angle of her body is tethered to the asshole over my shoulder. "Are you eating or taking away?"

"We'll eat—"

Raphael's smooth demand sweeps my answer away. "Takeaway."

My jaw ticks in annoyance, and a thick dread coats the walls of my chest. Eating in is...safer. The bright lights and the people and cameras make bad things less likely to happen. Instinct and self-preservation tell me I shouldn't disappear into the dark with

Raphael Visconti, even if the nervous excitement buzzing inside me suggests otherwise.

"Takeaway, then," I grind out.

Libby taps a few keys on the computer. "And what would you like?"

I rattle off the order I've made almost every night since moving back to the Coast. With a tiny gulp, the server drags her gaze upward and practically whispers, "And you, Mr. Visconti?"

"Nothing, thank you—"

"He'll have the double cheeseburger combo. Extra bacon, extra cheese." I bite my lip in thought, sweeping the back-lit menu above the counter. "And a chocolate milkshake. Extra-large."

A breathy grunt touches the nape of my neck, making me smile.

"Uh, okay…" More tapping, then she gives me the total, and I swing around to press my back against the counter. Raphael's gaze trails down the opening of my wet jacket, before snapping back up to my sweet smile.

"Yes?"

"Cough up, sugar daddy."

Biting back amusement, he tugs out his wallet. His arm brushes mine as he tosses bills onto the counter.

"Plus VAT."

"Oh, no sir. It already includes VAT—"

"Plus VAT," I repeat, not taking my eyes off Raphael.

With a slow shake of his head, he slams another twenty on the counter.

"Plus tip."

"But that's already much more than—"

"Don't worry about it, Libby," I say breezily. "Mr. Visconti is *filthy, stinking, rich.*"

Satisfaction pools in my stomach, partly because I enjoy even the tiniest triumph against Raphael, but partly because the laugh that slips from his lips and floats over the counter is deep and genuine.

Our food arrives in a grease-stained paper sack, and Raphael holds it like it's a poop bag from a dog he doesn't own.

Just as the doorbell chimes above our heads, an abrupt "Wait!" shoots through the diner and turns my head.

A server hot-foots it toward me. She sets down her coffee pitcher and lays a soft hand on my arm. "Are you okay, lovely?"

I blink. "What? Oh, right. He hasn't kidnapped me, don't—"

Her nervous laugh and wary glance up to Raphael cut me off. "No, sweetie. You were in here a few nights ago and you left so suddenly. You looked like you were about to be sick." She looks over her shoulder and lowers her voice. "We didn't make you sick, did we?"

Realization hits me. She means Thursday, the night with the drunk girls and the news report and the realization that my vengeful wave of a lighter over a vodka bottle was the worst mistake of my life.

The server's sympathetic smile stays in focus, but behind her, red booths and checkered tiles spin. I've always done this. I take the bad things that happen in my life, like worries and fear and trauma, stomp them down to a neat, compact package, then store them somewhere so deep inside me I forget they exist. Then they rear their ugly head when I watch the news, or I'm left along with my thoughts too long.

A strong hand grips my waist, and a dark, silky voice touches my ear. "You okay, Penny?"

Penny. I'd obsess over the fact Raphael called me anything but Penelope in that condescending drawl if panic wasn't rock-climbing up my throat.

I force it down, force a smile, and force a lie. "I was just a little under the weather, that's all."

Raphael's narrowed gaze scorches my cheek as he holds the door open for me. My heart thrums with the threat of interrogation in an aftershave-soaked car, but he simply slides into the driver's seat with a disinterested air and drops the sack of food on my lap.

"Hey, watch my book!"

He regards the canary-yellow spine and kicks the car into gear. "HTML *for Dummies,*" he drawls. "Heard it's one of Shakespeare's finest works."

I bite back a retort and glare out the misted window, watching as the safety of Main Street melts away. The Rusty Anchor's broken sign flashes to the left, and then we're back on the road where Raphael found me, climbing up into the abyss.

A hot prickle shifts under my skin. "Where are we going?"

His gaze cuts to me, a hint of amusement playing within it. "Somewhere no one can hear you scream."

Oh. Even knowing—okay, assuming—it's little more than a morbid joke, my throat still constricts. We sit in tense silence for a few minutes. The scent of deep-fried goodness rises from the bag in my lap. The radio hums with one of those festive songs that always get stuck in your head around this time of year, and Raphael's thick fingers strum against his thigh in time with it.

Eventually, we roll to a stop opposite the old church on the cliff. It's raining heavier now, and nothing beyond the dash is visible. Raphael kills the engine, and the sudden silence rings in my ears.

I clear my throat. Slide across the wide seat closer to the door. With a quick glance at my legs, Raphael shrugs off his jacket, lifts the paper sack off my lap, and drapes it over me. His warm hands brushing my thighs feel like static electricity and make my next breath shallow.

"Take your jacket off, it's wet."

I do as I'm told. He tosses it back on the seat, before turning on the engine and cranking up the heater. Clearly, he mistakes my discomfort at being trapped in a car with him for being cold. Truth is, I'm anything but. Despite being soaked through to my panties, I'm *burning.* My blood only grows hotter when Raphael unclicks his seat belt and shifts his body, subjecting me to all of his attention.

The burden of his gaze is heavy on my cheek. In an attempt to avoid the brunt of it, I unwrap my burger and take a bite. A river of ketchup runs down my chin and lands with a *plop* in the carton.

Raphael lets out a soft chuckle. "You've got it all over your face." He lifts his arm and for a breathless—and utterly ridiculous—moment, I think he's going to lean over and wipe it off my chin.

But of course he doesn't. Christ, why would he? He simply leans his elbow against the armrest and runs two fingers over his lips.

Although it was stupid to assume he'd touch me, the fact that he didn't sends a violent shiver of disappointment down my spine. I deal with it the only way I know how: being a dick.

I fumble with his jacket on my lap and whip the silk square out of the top pocket and wipe it across my mouth. "Thanks."

The hard sneer that settles on his lips puts the world to rights again.

"You not hungry?"

He regards me like I asked him to dance out in the rain, naked. "Do I look like I eat that shit?"

Instinctively, I glance down at the tight stomach under his semi-see-through shirt and push all intrusive thoughts out of my brain with an extra-big bite of my burger. *Not in a million years.*

"What do you eat then? The blood of forty virgins for breakfast or something?"

He grins. "Or something."

"I always had my suspicions you were a vampire."

Sweeping an expressionless eye over my legs again, he adds something that makes my heart still. "I have a question for you."

I stop chewing. Glance down at the door handle, but with a *click*, it locks shut, as if Raphael can see into my thoughts. He turns his attention to the windshield, leans back and runs a palm down his throat. "Why don't you sleep at night?"

My burger drops to my lap with a sorry thud. "Maybe I'm a vampire too."

"Penelope."

His voice wraps around my name like a hug, making my lids flutter shut. It's loaded with the perfect storm of impatience and softness, and I guess that's why the truth slips from my lips.

"Bad things happen at night," I whisper.

His jaw tenses, but he still doesn't look at me. "Like?"

Like grown men dragging me out into an alley and lifting up my dress. I settle for another example, though. One that doesn't hurt as much. "My parents were killed at night." I glance at the clock on the dash. "Three-forty a.m., to be exact. It's a time to be awake and alert, not asleep."

He nods slowly. I can't read the expression cut into his face, even when I squint, but he's definitely not surprised. I guess he probably did his research before giving me a job, and besides, men like him treat death like part of the furniture: always there and easy to gloss over. "Can't you be awake and alert in your apartment?"

"No."

His gaze sparks with irritation. "You're not immune to getting bundled into a trunk, Penelope."

We're back to saying my name like *that*, then.

Happy to have moved on from the topic of my parents, I slurp on my milkshake and shrug. "I'm lucky, remember? Proved it in the phone booth."

"You're not lucky," he snaps.

Instead of biting back, I fish around in the pockets of his jacket and find a loose coin. I hold it between us, a slow grin sliding across my face. "Heads or tails?"

He sighs, leans against the armrest, and hides his interest behind his knuckles. "All right. What's the wager?"

"You win, and you get your watch back," I wave my wrist in his face, his watch sliding up and down it. "I win; you eat the burger."

"Heads."

With a flick of my thumb, the quarter spins through the air and clatters on the central console. I peer over and laugh. Toss the greasy bag in his lap. "*Bon appetit.*"

He scowls. Unwraps the burger with the tips of his fingers. But then the jokes on me, because when he fists the burger with both hands and stares into my fucking soul as he takes a ridiculously big bite, hot, needling lust sinks to the pit of my stomach and sizzles against my clit.

Christ. It's just a burger. But there's something about how small it looks in his hands; something about the way his inked forearms flex and the primal way his teeth sink into the bun. It makes me think of other things he eats like that.

Head swimming, I inch open the window, subtly turn my head, and suck in a lungful of damn air. I'm about to steal another one, when a hot hand slides under the jacket and over my thigh, tightening my lungs.

What the—

My gaze drops to my book sliding across the center console. Raphael flips it open, tears out a page, and wipes it over his mouth.

I gape at the jagged edge.

"I—"

"Yes?"

"That's a *book.*"

"Aware, Penelope." He crumples the page in his fist and drops it in the food bag. When my jaw doesn't bounce back from the floor, he offers a nonchalant shrug and slides a French fry into his mouth, *whole.*

"Not like you're going to return it, anyway."

My eyes slant. "How'd you know that?"

"It says *Property of Atlantic City Public Library* on the spine."

Oh, right.

"Why are you reading that shit, anyway? Want a job in IT?"

"Don't think so."

"Don't *think* so?"

I don't know why I choose the truth over a sarcastic retort, because Neanderthals who treat books like that don't deserve honesty. "I play this...game."

His laugh is gruff. "Of course you do."

"I go into the library, close my eyes, and pick a random *For Dummies* book," I continue, ignoring him. "Whatever I choose, I tell myself I have to read."

"Why?"

"Because, like I told you, I'm trying to go *straight*," I say, exasperation shading my tone. Under the heat of his curious stare, I smooth down my top and take a deep breath. "I'm trying to find something I'm interested in. Something I can make a career out of." I glance sideways at him. "Don't want to work for you for the rest of my life, do I?"

Amusement brews under his tongue; he presses his lips together in an attempt to squash it. When he takes another bite of his burger. I get another hot flush.

"What makes you think you'll find your career in a *For Dummies* book?"

"It's wishful thinking, mostly," I admit. "I've tried other jobs, but nothing seems to stick."

"Like?"

"Well, I worked at a drive-thru, as a store clerk at the mall, a stripper, a receptionist..."

My words trail off when Raphael's forearm tenses against mine.

"Stripper."

His tone is calm. Too calm for comfort. Just one word, two syllables, but it soaks through my skin and crystallizes my blood. It's near-impossible to feign indifference as I drag my gaze up to meet his, but it doesn't stop me from trying.

"Yes."

The darkness that licks the walls of his irises is unnerving. "You were a stripper."

This time, I can only manage a nod.

A tiny flicker of something nerve-racking passes through his gaze. He scrapes his teeth across his bottom lip as he flicks a glance up to the roof of his car.

When his eyes fall down to mine, they're blacker than an oil spill and just as dangerous.

"Were you any good at it?" he asks tensely.

I jut my jaw in defiance. "Yes."

He lets out a dark huff of breath. Leaning back in his oversized seat, he strokes his chin and runs a slow, all-seeing eye up my thighs and over my chest. By the time it rests on my face, all of my nerve-endings are on fire, my lungs unable to keep up with tense breaths.

"So show me."

CHAPTER
Twenty-Two

Penny

I BLINK. "WHAT?"

"SO, SHOW me," he repeats, expressionless.

A chill drifts through me. Despite the planes of his face being completely devoid of humor, he can't be serious. He wants me to *strip* for him?

Another game. Just like the one where he boxed me into the phone booth with his eclipse-like silhouette and silk-clad threats, this game is designed to make me squirm. Swallowing the lump in my throat, I straighten my spine and pin him with my best look of indifference.

"You're eating."

He inches down the window and frisbees the burger into the night.

I swallow. "Here?" He nods. "There's no room."

Wordlessly, he reaches down beside his seat and it whirs all the way back, creating a large space between his knees and the steering wheel. Large enough for me to shake my ass in. I let out a ragged breath, butterflies erupting in my stomach. Fuck, I wish made men drove Smart Cars or Mini Coopers.

"It'll cost you."

Again, he does nothing but stare at me. His hand slides in the pocket of his door, and then a brick of notes falls among my French fries with a dull thud. I stare down at the wedge of hundred-dollar bills, bundled together by an elastic band. Christ, there's at least a grand there, much more than I've ever dreamt of earning in a night, let alone for one dance.

But this wouldn't be just any dance, for any man.

Grinding my jaw, I roll back my shoulders and meet his gaze. "You're serious?"

"Deadly."

The heater whirs. *Wham!* croons something about last Christmas on the radio. I slide my sweaty palms over the back of Raphael's jacket and try not to pass the fuck out.

The rain hammers against the glass heavier than ever, but I'm sure my heartbeat is louder. Each thump inside my rib cage ripples like a sonic boom through my nervous system and creates a pulse in my clit.

I'd rather carve my eyes out than lose a game to Raphael Visconti, so I guess I have no choice but to call his bluff.

"Fine." My admission slides from my mouth and blooms in the air between us. The *click* of my seat belt releasing reminds me there's no going back now, unless Raphael admits he was joking. But something about the tension cracking off his body tells me that's not going to happen. "No touching."

As I dump my food and his jacket on the back seat and rise, I catch sight of his large hands curling into fists on his thighs. "I know how lap dances work, Penelope."

Of course he does. This isn't going to be his first lap dance, but that doesn't stop hot jealousy from braiding with the knots in my stomach. Doesn't stop me from accidentally stomping on his toe as I slide into the gap in front of him, either.

He lets out a hiss, and I feel it crackle up the length of my spine. Even drunk on the idea of peeling my damp clothes off for Raphael in such close proximity, I have the good sense to face the windshield. If I had to watch his gaze roam my body up close, I'm not sure I'd survive it.

Gripping the steering wheel with one hand, I turn the dial of the radio up with the other. "Gotta have something to dance to," I mutter. As music fills the air, Raphael lets out a breath of amusement. I know why; *Driving Home for Christmas* isn't exactly a hit at strip clubs.

Knowing I can't delay it any longer, I focus on the steam misting up the windshield, and I slowly lower my body until the backs of my thighs rest on Raphael's lap. Denim crackles against expensive wool as I shift my ass forward, to his knees, and arch my back.

Despite my trembling hands, my top slides over my head like melted butter. The thighs underneath mine tense, and the soft hiss that comes from Raphael's direction makes my nipples tighten beneath my bra.

Spurred on by the heat of an impatient gaze on my back, I lift my ass off Raphael's lap in a slow, sensual roll. Any reservation I had about looking at him gets swept away by a heady cocktail of lust and adrenaline, and suddenly, I *need* to see the expression cut onto his face.

I peer over my shoulder and when my gaze clashes with his, I forget to take my next breath. His jaw is tight and his body is rigid, like he doesn't trust himself to move a muscle. The danger dancing in his eyes both thrills me and scares me at the same time; not a single trace of gentlemanly disposition exists within those irises. Not anymore.

Drawing a steadying breath, I don't take my eyes off him as I slide my damp jeans over the curve of my hip. His gaze tracks my movements, all the way down to my ankles, and then climbs up the back of my thighs, trailing the strip of my black thong.

I kick my sneakers and pants among the pedals and lower myself back to his lap. Now, the front of his thighs graze against my bare skin, and the feeling of warm, soft fabric brushing over my most sensitive areas makes my mouth water and my lower belly shiver.

Holding onto the steering wheel, I arch my back and roll my ass into the direction of Raphael's groin. The guttural tone of his grunt sends a shock of pleasure up to my clit. It's so animalistic, so *ungentlemanly*, that I'm desperate to hear it again. So, I slide back even further, until the tip of his swollen dick brushes between the cheeks of my ass.

Fuck. He's hard. Really fucking hard. The realization sends an electric thrill through my core and a warm, wet heat into the gusset of my panties. *I'm going out of my mind.* Heart picking up pace, I slide back and forward again, sliding higher up Raphael's erection with every roll of my hip. I could drown in the sound of his ragged breathing; curl up against the hardness of his muscles.

A rough finger slides beneath my thong. The snap and sting of elastic meeting skin elicit a moan of my own.

"I knew your panties would be ridiculous," he grunts.

Gasping, I tilt my head to the roof and let my lids flutter shut. "I thought you'd had lap dances before? You should know you get fined for touching."

A cool breeze whistles past my ear, and when I snap my eyes open, I see another brick of bills bounce off the windshield and skid across the dashboard.

Muscles shift underneath me, then a hot, ragged breath grazes my throat. "Turn around, Penelope."

Too breathless to think of a witty comeback, I rise on shaky legs and turn to face him. This time, I'm not prepared for the way he's looking at me. His stare is so intense it's borderline violent. It burns as it trails up the seam of my thigh and over my lower stomach.

"Beautiful," he mutters. It's more to himself than me, but still, I shudder underneath the weight of it.

Raphael Visconti thinks I'm beautiful. Dizzy with a new wave of confidence, I grip the back of his headrest and slowly lower myself onto his lap. It doesn't go to plan though; my foot rolls over my wayward sneaker and I fall backward against the steering wheel. I let out a little yelp when the horn sounds, but Raphael leans forward, catching me before I fall again.

Large hands with a hot, greedy touch slide behind my back to steady me. Black hair tickles my throat, and a chuckle works its way down my cleavage, making my nipples ache. Raphael's dry joke vibrates against my collarbone, lighting every nerve ending in my body on fire. "I'm beginning to think I overpaid."

"No refunds," I whisper back, a smile twitching my lips as I roll my clit against his throbbing cock. Christ, he's so warm and hard that I know I could get myself off with a lot less.

The dirtiest part of my brain races with possibilities, but the fingers sliding underneath the back band of my bra bring me back to earth.

Raphael looks up at me through dark lashes. "Take it off."

"Costs extra."

The *snap* as he drags his thumb out from underneath the band makes my back arch in pleasure. Jaw tight, his eyes run down the length of my throat and back up to my parted lips. "I'll take it off."

"That costs even more."

There's that animalistic groan again; my pussy clenches around it, and *fuck*, how I wish it was tangible. My fingers dig into the headrest, and raspy breaths tickle the planes of my chest. I shoot a half-lidded glare at the roof and feel a sudden weight in my lap.

I rake my teeth over my bottom lip to suppress a smile, familiar with the weight of his money now. "Not gonna cut it."

Another thud, this one harder, lands on my stomach. I shake my head. "Not even close—"

My sass morphs into a gasp as Raphael's thick fingers find purchase in the base of my hair and yank my head back. I open my mouth to protest, then something cold and smooth slides into it.

At first, I think it's another playing card, but when I pull it out, I realize it's a Black Amex.

My eyes clash with Raphael's.

"Pin is four, eight, four, two," he says quietly. He locks his fingers behind his head and leans back against the headrest. His gaze flashes like a warning sign. "Now, *take it off.*"

A numbness creeps over my body. I stand just enough to toss his card onto the passenger seat—like *hell* am I forgetting that pin number—and drop back onto his lap.

He stares at me expectantly. Three stuttered heartbeats pass before I muster up the courage to slide my bra off.

I throw it in his face, and when a lace cup slides off his chin, slow breath escapes his parted lips. Tension tightens the line of his shoulders as he rakes hungry eyes over my breasts. They grow heavier with every inch he covers; more sensitive with every flutter of his hot breath.

He cocks his head. Flexes his biceps as he readjusts his hands behind his head.

He nods. "Carry on."

Pussy throbbing with awareness, I lean back and grip his knees as I rock my hips forward again, lighting a path of ecstasy along the hard plane of his thigh. Of course, I'd never *grinded* on a patron like this at the strip club. I'd rather have caught the plague than saunter into one of the VIP rooms and indulge in any of the...off-menu activities.

But Raphael isn't a regular patron, and I'm no longer a stripper. Whatever this is, there's no denying we have a thing. A highly flammable thing, and it'll explode if we light a match to it.

Another hip roll brings out another moan from deep within me. Raphael's eyes narrow, his jaw ticking in realization. "Are you wet, Penelope?"

Flustered, I nod.

His gaze slides down to where my thong meets his slacks. "Pull your panties to the side. Leave me with something to remember this by."

I'm too high off the friction to argue. To flushed from the wet and the wanting. I slide my panties to the side and bask under the heat of his fascinated stare as I grind against his leg.

The pressure between my thighs builds and builds with every friction-filled glide, and with every brush of Raphael's bulge against the top of my clit.

"Fuck," he whispers in my ear as I slide my hands between his bent elbows and lock my fingers behind his headrest in order to get a better position. "You're really going to come on me?"

What type of fucking question is that? Maybe I'd be able to decipher the tone of it, if my pulse wasn't thumping so loud in my ears; if my body wasn't screaming with the need for release.

I'm hot, desperate, full of steam and depraved thoughts. In no fit state to answer his question, that's for sure. But he gets his answer and all it takes is a flex of his thigh. Buckling under the unexpected movement beneath my clit, I sink my teeth into Raphael's bicep to ride the orgasm that licks through my body like a forest fire.

After a few, star-filled moments, my high settles around me like dust. I melt into his chest—a storm to his calm, fire to his ice—to catch my breath back.

Only when my semblance comes crawling back to me, do I realize he hasn't moved. Hasn't fucking breathed. With unease and the embers of embarrassment crawling up my throat, I push off him and warily meet his gaze.

It's expressionless. The colors in it don't shift, even as he hands me my bra. Even as he drops my top on my lap. I tug it on, heart pounding for a completely different reason now.

Nerves pinching my skin, I slip off him and drop into the passenger seat, awkwardly tugging on my jeans and sneakers.

He stares at me.

"What?" I whisper. I wish my question didn't make me sound so vulnerable.

Wordlessly, he slips his blazer back over my thighs and turns his attention back to the sheet of rain on the windshield. The car comes to life, headlights casting a yellow glow beyond fragmented water, and a new, cheery Christmas song fills the car.

Throat growing thick, I stare at the glove box, unable to ignore how dread tugs at my heart like an anchor. I've been in a similar situation before—twice, actually. I've only slept with two men, and both managed to fool me. They laughed when I insulted them, leaned over dining tables and feigned interest when a few glasses of wine loosened my tongue and softened my defenses. Both times, I let them fuck me rough in the backs of their cars, and then never heard from either again.

And now here I am, sitting in silence, squirming in the passenger seat. It feels all too familiar.

But then a firm, hot hand slides under the blazer and rests on my thigh. I glance up at Raphael, but he's focusing on the gap between the whooshing wipers, steering the car with the palm of his other hand.

"Strip for another man again, and he'll die crossing the road."

Warmth grazes one side of my face, and when I roll my head to chase the darkness, the scent of leather and man assaults my nostrils.

Ice and instinct course through my veins and I bolt upright. Through bleary eyes, I blink at the low sun through the windshield. We're parked outside my apartment. It's early; I can tell by the frost cloaking the Santas and the shop owners shivering as they wait for their automatic shutters to open.

I slept in Raphael's car? Shit. I twist my aching head to find him sitting in the driver's seat, replying to an email on his phone. He's still wearing the same clothes as last night—slacks and shirtsleeves. In the cold light of day, the ink shrouding his arms looks all too real. *Sinister.*

"Why didn't you wake me?" I whisper, smoothing a hand over my hair.

He doesn't look up from his phone. "Wish I did, 'cause you snore like a donkey."

"No I don't."

He laughs easily, drops his phone in the cup holder, and pins me with a smooth smile. "You go that red over everything?" Before I can reply, he reaches out and runs a thumb down the indentation of my chin. "Relax. You fell asleep, and I thought if you got a good night's rest, you might not be so shit at your job."

He holds my gaze for a moment, before lunging over me and shoving open my door.

"Now, get out before I remove your adenoids with my bare hands."

CHAPTER
Twenty-Three

Rafe

N O MATTER HOW MANY contracts I glare at or how many whiskeys I sink, I can't get rid of the rock-hard erection straining against my slacks. Can't get rid of *her*.

I didn't think she'd call my bluff, not when it required stripping for me.

And now she's everywhere, yet, nowhere at all. The shape of her body burned into the backs of my eyelids; the wet heat of her pussy branded on my thigh. Don't even get me started on that mischievous glint in her eye—it's got my dick in a choke hold.

Her scent, smile, *sass*. They swirl like an incoming storm, and the door of my office can't shelter me from it. It's pathetic, but I'm relieved she's not on shift tonight.

Kind of.

I let out a bitter laugh and lean back against my chair. I'd find humor in the ridiculousness of it all, except there's nothing funny about it. Every time Penelope has dug under my skin, it's been my own fault. I pushed open the locker room door for the second time, despite learning the first time that what lay in wait for me was something I couldn't handle. I'd pushed back the driver's seat knowing if I found out what shade of pink her nipples were, there was no going back.

Now I'm paying the price for my impulsiveness: having to take all my meetings for the day over the phone because my body reacts like a twelve-year-old-boy seeing tits on T.V. every time I think of her.

I should...deal with it. Hate-fuck my fist in the ensuite behind me. But then, whether she knew it or not, Penelope would win again, and, despite my odd obsession with her, I'd rather stab myself in the eye with a rusty penknife than let her win.

Despite it being ten a.m., I pour another whiskey. Rattle my dice in the crook of my palm. My office is cold and silent, save for the thrum of the motors and the hum of a vacuum cleaner underneath my wingtips.

I could always just fuck her, but I know there's a major issue with that. By my own rule, if I wanted to use Penelope's thick thighs as earmuffs, I'd have to take her on a date.

Never going to happen. I couldn't muster up enough charm in the world to convince her to go for dinner with me, and besides, what would we talk about? She's feral, for Christ's sake. I've seen the way she eats, and no doubt I'll leave the restaurant a Rolex and two cars lighter. I've already paid for the most expensive lap dance of my fucking life.

I huff a sardonic laugh into my whiskey, before slamming it back and flicking the glass across my desk.

The only plus is that she believes love is a trap. I wouldn't have to worry about her hoping it'd go farther than one sordid night.

No. If I was to fuck Penelope, it'd have to be without all the airs and graces. I've never treated a woman like that, but then again, I've never threatened to clump one around the head with a hammer, either. She seems to have a habit of reaching through my charm offense and bringing out the darkness in me.

Suddenly, the door to my office flies open with such force, I can only assume somebody's kicked it in. My hand goes to the Glock next to my MacBook, but as I glance up, I drop it back on the desk with a sigh.

Well, that's one way to short-circuit a boner.

Gabe. He darkens the doorway like a sleep demon. Behind him, a pair of suit-clad legs lie on the floor at an awkward angle.

"Your men couldn't protect a password," he grunts.

I mutter something dark under my breath, but I have to admit, he's got a point. Twenty-three ex-special-ops guardians and none of them could stop one man getting to me. Sure, that man is Gabriel Visconti and I don't think a ten-foot-thick wall of iron would have stopped him getting through that door, but still.

He strolls in. Sneers at the photo frames on my shelf of me cutting red ribbons and holding oversized checks, and snatches up the whiskey bottle.

"Want a protein shake with that?"

"Already had three today." He fists a tumbler and narrows his gaze on me. "Where were you last night? You're usually belle of the ball."

Answering emails on my cell to the sound of Penelope snoring.

I feign boredom. "I see you idiots all the time now. Besides, Benny only has so many fingers, and I'm growing tired of watching you break them."

"I wish I could say the same for my wife." I look over Gabe's shoulder to Angelo in the hall. With a mild look of disgust, he steps over the legs of my fallen man and kicks the door shut with his heel. "Gabe has turned her into a sadist."

"That girl has always been a sadist," Gabe says, gulping back his drink.

Angelo glares at him, and I wipe away my smirk with the back of my hand. "To what do I owe the pleasure, brothers?"

Angelo hitches up his slacks and sinks into the armchair opposite. His gaze comes to mine, sparking with annoyance. "You forgot we had a meeting today."

And so I did. I suppose I was too distracted by the memory of Penelope sinking her teeth into my bicep as she came against my leg.

Shit. I've been so focused on everything Penelope that I'm embarrassed to admit the war with the Cove clan has barely crossed my mind. If I'm honest, I forgot Dante existed for a minute. The last I heard, Angelo and Cas arranged a meeting with Dante in Hollow a few days after the explosion. He'd rocked up to Cas's house with a ring of security and sat at the end of the dining table as meek as a bird. A real, hot-blooded don would have owned up to the attack, but not Dante.

Fucking idiot. A well-dressed bed is more of a made man than him.

"Me? Never," I drawl, leaning back in my chair with a lazy smirk. I turn to Gabe. "How's the chess game coming along?"

His glare tells me everything I need to know. It's dark and dangerous and I wonder how many men have been the subject of it and pissed their pants. He tugs a lighter from his pocket and, with a flick of his wrist, brings the flame to life.

"Needles in the neck. Heart attacks. Cut brakes."

I nod slowly, raking a cautious eye over that flame as it dances under his chin and shifts shadows over the hard planes of his face. Wouldn't put it past my brother to set my office ablaze, just for shits and giggles. "Sounds productive."

The flame snuffs out, plunging his molten gaze back into darkness. His palms slam against my desk with such force that half of my whiskey sloshes out of its glass. "It's child's play. I'm restless. Losing my fucking mind. I need more, I need something…" He huffs out a dark breath. "Something to silence it all."

What?

Slightly stunned at his outburst, I toss a look at Angelo, but he just rolls his eyes, a bored expression carved into his face. I have a feeling he's heard this already.

Somehow, I think it's safer to change the subject. "Well, I still haven't heard from Tor."

Now, Angelo's eyes come back to mine, flashing dark. "Yeah. Dante hasn't either."

My spine straightens on its own accord. "What do you mean?"

"What I said. He never went back to Cove after the explosion. I called Donatello, and he hasn't heard from him either."

Fuck. His words settle on my chest and push me back in my chair. I'd have bet both my yachts Tor wouldn't have chosen Dante over us. But disappearing entirely? This…I don't know. It seems worse.

Three heavy knocks on the door cut through my thoughts. Gabe's gun comes flying out of his waistband, and the noise is so loud that even Angelo twitches toward his weapon.

"Relax," I sigh. "In case you haven't noticed, we're on a yacht in the middle of the Pacific. The only threat onboard is food poisoning." I jerk my chin toward the door. "Come in."

Griffin bursts into my office and his stride screams trouble. He's old and bald and has seen enough sick shit in this world that almost *nothing* makes him walk fast. The sight pinches the back of my neck, and I find myself rising to my feet and picking up my gun, too.

He comes to a stop behind Angelo. "We've got an emergency."

Gabe's safety catch releases. "Mine."

Griffin's gaze slides sideways, tinted with disgust. "Not an emergency concerning you or your thugs." Shifting his attention back to me, he adds, "Lucky Cat's been hit."

My heart jolts at the mention of my Vegas casino. I suck in a whiskey-fueled breath, lean my palms against my desk and grind out, "I'm going to need more intel than that."

"Hit and run. Armed van crashed into the lobby and shook out all the ATMs in under two minutes. Took just over six mil in cash, by the looks of it."

"Yeah? And where were your men?" Gabe growls.

Angelo lets out a low whistle. "Who'd be that fucking dumb?"

Griffin chooses to ignore my more insolent brother. "Nobody on the West Coast. Has to be an outside job from a gang that didn't know better."

"Mine," Gabe repeats quietly, taking a step toward Griffin and cracking his knuckles.

"No way," Griffin growls back. "You and your thugs run rampage up and down the Coast, and that's fine. But Raphael's a prolific businessman, and part of my job is to uphold that reputation. We'll sort it, and we'll sort it *quietly*." He stabs a finger toward him and Gabe looks down at it like he's considering tearing it off with his teeth. "By the way, I saw what you did to Clive." He turns to say to me, "He left his head in the trunk of my Sedan with a cocktail umbrella in his mouth."

I bite out a laugh.

Griffin shakes his head, jaw ticking in annoyance. "I thought you were more *sophisticated* than that, boss."

I am. Usually. Griffin's *elimination* style has always worked perfectly for my agenda. It's quiet, elegant, and no bodies mean no leads back to me. But a cocktail umbrella? Come on. I'm not immune to the charm of irony, even on my darkest days.

As silence cloaks the office, Griffin's revelation settles on my shoulders, thick and lava-like. I'm burning up, so I turn toward the French doors and crack one open. Beyond them, the icy sky melts into dark waters, and through the small gap, the sound of waves lapping against the hull float in with the wind.

Ignoring the three pairs of eyes on my neck, I slip my hands in my pockets and rest my head against the glass.

Lucky Cat. *Bastards.* Out of the forty-eight casinos I own, they had to hit the one that started it all. Ten years ago, it was barely a box with four borrowed roulette wheels, and I couldn't get customers through that door even if I begged. I paid my staff with the bills fed into the slot machine in the corner. It was a *dive*, but I loved it—still do. It was the only one of my casinos my mama got to step foot in. She was used to the life of luxury but damn, did she sit at that bar in her Sunday best and sip her lemon drop martini like she was at the Ritz.

Emotion curls its hand around my throat and I flex against it. My breath misting against the glass is the last thing I see before I squeeze my eyes shut.

"Gabe."

Heavy footsteps lead out of my office.

When I turn around, two pairs of eyes touch me, both conveying different expressions. Griffin's gaze burns with fury while Angelo's is tinged with thinly-veiled amusement.

I stroll back to my desk. Rest my knuckles against it. "Griff?"

He glares at me in response.

I nod to the pair of legs in the hall. "Chuck him overboard before he wakes up."

My brother cocks a brow but doesn't say anything. Griffin's shock disappears behind the faceted wall of crystal as I slam my whiskey in one. Its contents carve a hot trail down my throat and stoke the flames in my chest. When it clatters against the desk, Griffin's gone and Angelo is holding a photo frame of our mother.

His eyes soften at the corners. Without looking up, he muses, "If mama was here, she'd say you were having an unlucky streak."

His words prickle against my skin sharper than he knows. "Yes, and mama was a sucker for bullshit."

If I ever got my hands dirty and he wasn't my brother, I'd sweep that smirk off his lips with a swift right hook. Instead, I drop to my armchair and regard him with a mild-mannered stare.

"Anything else? I've got shit to do."

He rubs his chin in thought. "Forty G's lost last Monday. You've lost Miller and Young, and your best bud has disappeared off the face of the planet under suspicious circumstances. Hmm."

"What?" I snap, growing hot under the insinuation in his tone. Red hair and playing cards flash behind my eyelids.

"I think I'd have to agree with mama on this one."

You could have all the success in the world, but the Queen of Hearts will bring you to your knees.

In case Penelope is the Queen of Hearts, I probably shouldn't have let her grind on me.

I scratch my jaw. Shrug. "Shit happens."

"Uh-huh."

"Fuck off now, please."

With a dark chuckle, he rises to his feet and casts a shadow over my desk. "Look on the bright side, brother. It's your favorite time of the month."

I frown. "Is it?"

"You shitting me?"

In the beat of silence, the realization hits me. *Of course it is.* Usually, we choose our Sinners Anonymous candidates on the last Sunday of every month, but that'll be Christmas Day this year, so we're doing this Sunday instead.

I can't believe I forgot. The Sinners Anonymous hotline is my baby, a love letter to the sadist that lives deep within the hollow of my chest. It's the ultimate game, and just once a month, my brothers and I come together to relive the better parts of our childhood. The simpler times, you know, before our father killed our mother and Angelo killed him in retaliation.

"I'm on it," I say, smoothing my collar pin. I jerk my chin up when I remember what I had to ask him. "Are you around tomorrow?"

"Depends."

"I've got a meeting with Kelly, and I'd like you to sit in."

Immediately, Angelo's expression sours. "You know I hate you working with the Irish."

"You hate me working with anyone who doesn't have a *nonna* with a secret alfredo sauce recipe."

When it comes to business partners, I don't discriminate. If they're smart and can front cash and connections, I'll look past their family ties. Kelly might be an O'Hare, but he's all right in my books. We've got three joint ventures in Vegas together—a casino, a bar, and a boutique hotel—and our partnership has worked seamlessly for the last eight years.

"What does he want, and why do I have to be there?" Angelo grunts.

"He...has a habit of wanting things that aren't his," I say with a tight smile. "Just need him to know Dip isn't unclaimed territory."

He nods. "All right. But I don't want you whining at me if he gets a bullet in his head."

I roll my eyes. "No whining."

Angelo leaves me in my office with a near-empty liquor bottle and violent thoughts.

In dire need of something stronger to distract myself, I decide I probably should choose my top three sins of the month for when my brothers and I meet in the church on Sunday.

I open my laptop, pull up the Sinners Anonymous voicemail box, and click *autoplay*.

One by one, the sound of sin fills the room.

There's always the usual shit when I listen. Shaky confessions of road collisions from the side of a highway. Drunken, unintelligible slurs from people whose demons only come out at three a.m. But occasionally, there's a sin that brings a perverted smirk to my lips and sweeps a thrill under my skin.

Today though, they aren't scratching the itch as well as they usually do. So, I reach over and open the sub-folder of calls I've removed from the shared network.

I slip a cigarette out of its carton and tuck it into the crook of my mouth. Swipe the flame of a Zippo underneath it.

Then I lean back, close my eyes, and let Penelope's silly ramblings soak into my skin like an ointment.

If I'm sinking to the bottom, at least her voice will keep me company on the way down.

CHAPTER
Twenty-Four

Penny

"THERE'S LOADS OF THINGS I miss about Atlantic City." I set my cell on the bathroom counter and drag a brush through my hair with a shaky hand. "But nothing...big, you know? The salmon and cream cheese bagel from that little cafe on the pier. The passion fruit martinis at Ronnie's bar. Um...what else..."

I pick up my phone and carry it into the bedroom, holding it up to my mouth while I rifle through my closet. I pick out a pair of jeans and a sweater, then drop my cell on the bed to change. As it bounces off the mattress, I get a glimpse at the call time and balk. *Jesus.* I've been on the line to Sinners Anonymous for forty-five minutes. Talking utter shit, simply to fill my empty apartment with something other than my own nervous energy.

Every bone in my body hums from the aftermath of last night. The ghost of textured wool still caresses the space between my thighs. Soft commands in strangled tones still nip at the shells of my ears. And every time I look at one of my stark white walls, the image of Raphael's inked skin flashes against them.

My nerves are tinged with something...odd. Something that toes the line between unease and defeat. I called Raphael's bluff and gave him a lap dance, so why don't I feel like I beat him at his own game?

Bringing myself to orgasm like a fucking rabid animal against the front fold of his slacks might have something to do with it. Or, you know, the fact that I *fell asleep* in his passenger seat.

My cheeks heat for the millionth time today. Why can't I repress last night like I can with all my other problems? The fear of being caught by Martin O'Hare barely rears its ugly head. Raphael Visconti, from his sharp suit to his hidden ink to his stupid collar pin: he fills every cubic square meter of my conscience, to the point I might burst at the seams.

Biting out a noise of frustration, I cross the room and peer out the window, taking in the empty street below.

"Doing nothing all day was torture. I'm also not working tonight and I have no plans," I tell the hotline. "Matt's coaching his hockey team, Rory's got a flying lesson, Tayce is working, and so is Wren. Well, I suppose I could go down and see Wren at the Rusty Anchor..."

Earlier, I almost told the hotline about Raphael, but something stopped me. I guess growing up with the line makes the robotic woman on the other end of it feel more like a childhood friend. I don't want to pollute her with sordid tales of lap dances and dry-humping. So, I keep it superficial.

Beep beep. Beep beep.

I frown, squint at my cell, and realize I've got an incoming call from Laurie.

Shit. Heart skipping a beat, I stab the 'switch lines' button. "Yeah?"

An easy chuckle floats down the line. "Relax, hun. I'm not firing you quite yet. Actually, I was calling to see if you can come in today? I know it's late notice but there's a super intimate meeting onboard and—"

"Yes! Yes, I'm free."

"Jeez, that was easy. Usually, I have to bribe people with double pay before I can get them to agree to come in on their days off."

Dammit. I'm about to backpedal when my gaze flicks to the mountain of money on my dresser. It's more than I've seen in my life.

She tells me the staff shuttle craft will be waiting for me in an hour and hangs up.

An hour later, I'm being hoisted off the small boat by a heavy-handed Blake. By the wink he flashes me as his grip slides off my hip, he hasn't realized I stole his wallet yet, or that it's a very real possibility I'll shove him overboard if he continues to wolf whistle every time I walk away from him.

I make a stop at the locker room to get rid of my shoes and coat, then follow Laurie's earlier instructions to head to the bar on the sky deck. It's only me and one other bartender today, so either barely anyone at this meeting drinks, or they're super low maintenance. Somehow, I highly doubt either is true.

As I reach the top of the stairs, I can't stop myself from rolling my eyes at the sight of Blake. *Again.* Christ, all of Raphael's men are idiots in one shape or form, but this one really is the biggest dunce of them all. Why is he *everywhere*? He's guarding the sky lounge along with a bald-headed lackey who doesn't talk much, and when I shove past without so much as a smile, I'm treated to another wolf-whistle.

It stiffens my back and makes white heat spark in my fist. "I'm not a fucking dog," I hiss.

"Bet you fuck like one, though," he mutters back.

Baldy snorts.

Glaring at the gold doorknob, I suck in a lungful of air and wait for the red mist to fade. *Gone straight. Gone straight. Gone straight.*

Fury cooling to a simmer, I roll my shoulders back and shove into the lounge.

The door is lighter than I think, so it crashes against the back wall and I wince. When I pop my eyes open, I slow to a stop.

Oh, shit.

I didn't realize it was happening in here; it's a smaller room off the sky lounge. But it makes sense, because it only consists of three people, a deck of cards, and a box of Cuba's finest.

And a *very* loud Irish accent. It belongs to a cherub-looking man with a gray buzz-cut and piercing blue eyes. But there's nothing angelic about his voice: he's obnoxious, and every other word that slides through his mouth is a curse. All three pairs of eyes come to me, but I train my gaze on my toes and scurry along the wall until I reach the safety of the bar behind another set of doors. I open this one a lot more gently, and turn to catch it before it slams shut behind me.

In the narrowing gap, I meet Raphael's amused gaze.

I smile sheepishly.

He *winks*.

Christ. Spinning off-kilter, I shut the door and drop my head against it, waiting for my blood to simmer down to a more appropriate temperature. I was so eager to get out of the apartment that I opted to do overtime without thinking of the consequences: seeing Raphael after *that*.

"Surprise!" A feminine trill makes my eyes pop open. Rory is sitting on a bar stool grinning at me. She's wearing a khaki fly suit unzipped to her waist and a white T-shirt underneath.

I break into a smile. "What are you doing here?"

"Angelo's got a meeting with Rafe and some old dude. Found out you were working so I decided to cut my flying lesson short and keep you company." She cranes her neck to peer into the storage room, then whispers theatrically as she taps the deck of cards on the bar. Waves her notepad around. "I've been practicing!"

I didn't even realize Angelo was here, I was so distracted by a loud Irish accent and the heat of Raphael's wink. I bite out a laugh, slipping behind the bar. "I hope you've been practicing in private."

"Oh, of course. Angelo thinks I've got a sudden obsession with gardening because I've been hiding in the shed." She snaps the deck with a roll of her eyes. "What grows in winter, seriously? Oh, by the way, what are you doing Saturday night? There's a game night in Hollow; you should come and watch me beat Rafe."

Before I can respond, a man breezes out of the storage room, face hidden behind the crate of beer in his arms. He sets it on the floor, returns to his full height, and does a double-take at me.

"Jesus. Am I seeing a ghost?"

It takes me a few seconds to realize who it is: Dan.

As in, *Dan, pass me the hammer.*

"I'm very much alive," I say dryly. "What are you doing here?"

"Well, I usually work at the Rusty Anchor, but I moonlight as Rafe's personal bartender." He hitches a shoulder and grins. "He calls, I come."

I have to grit my teeth to prevent an eye roll. Having a personal bartender only solidifies his status as the most pretentious asshole of the year.

Dan starts unloading beers into the fridge, chuckling to himself. "Can't believe Rafe chased you with a hammer."

Rory's gasp feels hot against the shells of my ears.

"Yeah, and can't I believe you handed it to him."

"Hey, what the boss wants, the boss gets."

"Okay, someone's gotta fill me in," Rory says, a breathless excitement to her tone. "What are you going on about?"

"She swindled Rafe out of his watch at the *Blue's Den* in Devil's Cove. It was *wild*."

Rory's eyes slide to mine then down the watch on my wrist. To be honest, it looks ridiculous on me. It's far too big and even on the tightest notch, the face constantly slides around to my pulse. I don't know why I keep swiping it off my dresser and putting it on every morning. I pull my arm off the bar and put it behind me, feeling defensive.

"What do you mean, swindled?" she whispers.

"Not *swindled*. We played a game, and I won his watch."

"You won his watch," she repeats, all-knowing mischief filling her gaze. "And now you're wearing it."

"And now I'm wearing it." I scowl back.

She opens her mouth, then closes it just as quick. She goes back to scribbling on her notepad, a smirk lifting her lips.

Click.

The sound of the door opening travels down my spine. Rory's head snaps up, and in a panic, she scoops the playing cards and the notepad to her chest and slides off the stool. "Gotta make a phone call," she mutters, before diving out the terrace doors.

Raphael's bemused gaze follows her, before coming to me. I smooth down my dress and give my best attempt at not looking flustered. Dan, on the other hand, is as easy as a Sunday morning. "What's up, boss? What can I get you?"

Raphael continues to stare at me for another beat, before sliding up to the bar and giving Dan his full attention. "Two whiskeys and a water that looks like whiskey." He runs a hand over his ticking jaw. "Think Kelly's been mixing his liquor with Benzo's again."

"On it, boss."

Dan disappears into the storage room, leaving me to bear the brunt of Raphael's attention all on my own. It's crazy that in the darkness of his car, high off his heat, I craved his gaze, yet in the sober light of day, it makes me want to crawl under a rock.

He looks down at my chest with a hint of disapproval. "No new uniform yet?"

"Laurie said it's coming in tomorrow."

He gives a tight nod and glances at a message that pops up on his cell screen.

Silence swirls us like a storm, me coming on his thigh and then falling asleep in his car for *over six hours* at the eye of it. I grab a rag and busy myself with wiping up imaginary spillages on the oak-clad bar, trying to ignore the sudden disappointment closing in on me.

I don't know... In the cold sunlight streaming through the windows, Raphael oozes corporate perfection. Fresh shave, pinstripe suit, shoes so shiny they reflect my glum expression.

Last night, he was a whole different man. Soaked in rainwater, his ink shone through his shirt as if they were his true colors. Being around *that* man gave me a different kind of thrill. It felt like he'd let me in on his dirty little secret. But *this* man is what he broadcasts to everyone else in the world. And for some reason, I don't like being lumped with everyone else.

His cell locks shut and he looks up at me through a half-lidded gaze.

"Did you sleep well last night?"

A simple question, but a wave of relief coasts through me so fast, I feel a little dizzy. At least I know it wasn't a fever dream.

Of course, I don't let it show on my face.

"Eh. Could have been better."

His lips tilt. "Yeah? How come?"

"No pillow, and the blanket was only a blazer. If your car was an Airbnb, I'd give it a four-star rating." I tap my lip in thought. "No—three and a half."

"Why'd you knock off the half-star?"

"There was also this creepy man staring at me all night."

He laughs a beautiful, raw laugh, and a rush sweeps through me knowing I'm the reason for it.

When the lines of his face settle back to neutral, I search it unashamedly. His eyes are bloodshot, and dark circles shade the undersides of them.

"Big meeting?"

"Mm."

"You look tired. Didn't sleep?"

He leans over the bar, warming me with his body heat. My breathing shallows. "Yeah," he says softly. "Seems I was too busy being a creepy man and staring at a beautiful girl all night."

My embarrassment is written all over my face in different shades of red. He huffs out a laugh and throws me another wink.

Christ, he's charming when he wants to be. Even though I know what's underneath, I could see myself being a little fooled.

Dan comes out with a tray of whiskeys and sets one slightly aside from the rest. Raphael raps his knuckle against the bar and returns to his full height. "Penelope, bring them in for me."

And with that, he breezes through the door, leaving the absence of *please* in his wake.

Dan doesn't say anything, just watches me with pursed lips as I clumsily take the tray through to the lounge.

Inside, the air is thicker than it was when I first walked through, partly due to cigar smoke hanging above the coffee table, and partly because of the cards splayed out on its surface.

Immediately, I recognize the layout to be this Visconti Blackjack they all play here, and a conditioned zap of adrenaline crackles through my core. *Past life, Penelope. Past life.*

My present life involves serving those at the table instead of sitting around it. I set a glass next to Angelo. His gaze slides to the watch on my wrist then up to me, something unreadable flickering in its depths. My heart lurches but he doesn't say anything.

I move to Raphael's side of the table. He doesn't acknowledge me, but still, my arm crackles as it brushes against the sleeve of his suit. Then, without a break in his stoic expression, his hand glides up the back of my thigh and comes to the hem of my skirt.

He *pulls* downward.

I stifle a gasp. Angelo snaps out a card from the shoe and tosses it on the pile.

Queen of Hearts.

Raphael folds.

He huffs out a breath and settles back into his armchair.

Shaky from the unexpected skirt grab, I set down the Irish man's drink a little too hard. He winces then turns to me with wild eyes. Something warm floods through them, and he shifts in his seat to get closer.

"Hit or stand, Princess?"

My jaw ticks at the nickname, but I can't stop my eyes from gliding to the table anyway. Only a quick sweep at the dealt cards tells me he should stand—there are too many low-value cards already played—but I clamp my mouth shut and plaster on a smile. "How would I know? I'm just a silly little Princess."

His laugh melts into a thick silence. Even with unfocused eyes and a reckless sway to his movements, there's something in his gaze that makes unease trickle down my spine like syrup. I move to get away from him, but he's quicker than he looks. His hand shoots out and grips my wrist.

Three pairs of eyes, including my own, glare down at it. In my peripheral vision, Raphael leans forward, resting his forearms on his knees.

"What's your name, sweetheart?"

Tips. Think of the tips. "Penny."

Again, another laugh. One too loud for a three-person meeting. "That's a very lucky name. What's that expression again? Find a Penny, pick it up, all day long you'll have good luck? Although, red-heads aren't very lucky on boats, are they?"

"Uh-huh," I say dryly, silently recoiling at the old adage that haunted my childhood. I tear my arm away, but his hand reaches for my necklace. He strokes the four-leaf clover pendant, expression curious.

"Kelly," Rafe says, too calm for comfort.

"You've got the luck of the Irish," Kelly murmurs, ignoring the way Raphael delivers his name in a silk-clad warning. "You got any Irish in you, sweetheart?"

"Nope."

"Would you *like* to have Irish in you?"

Raphael's on his feet, but I'm quicker, leaning in and hissing in Kelly's face. "If you don't remove your hand from me right now, I'll bite it."

He stares at me for long, awkward seconds. Somewhere in the room, a clock ticks. Raphael's gaze scalds my cheek. Angelo clears his throat.

Eventually, with a shit-eating smile creeping onto his thin lips, he releases me.

But not without a parting word. One I know is meant for my ears only.

"I knew it was you."

I blink, and then the dread hits. It's lazy, seeping into my veins hot and sticky, deadening my limbs. It pools in my chest and slows my heart rate; fills my lungs.

Knew it was you.

Numb, I stand to my full height and glance at Raphael. He's poised but his eyes are on me, simmering with unadulterated rage. Still reclining in his armchair, Angelo says something in clipped Italian, and with a slow roll of his head, Raphael begrudgingly sinks back to his seat.

I wade toward the bar, swimming through words filled with arrogance and amusement. "I was kidding," I hear behind me. "But how about we up these stakes a little..."

I slam the door shut with the heel of my foot and press my back against it. Rory's nowhere to be seen, but on the other side of the bar, Dan stops twisting a rag in a glass and cocks a brow at me. "Kelly really that bad?"

When I shake my head, the words I *knew it was you* rattle around in it. I don't recognize him, but even in his fucked-up state, it seemed like he recognized me.

Unless I imagined it? He said it so quietly, so *slurred*, that he could have said anything. But there's one niggling observation that makes his words impossible to dismiss.

He's Irish.

Martin O'Hare's Irish.

No. That'd be *terribly* unlucky of me. Wouldn't it?

With nerves racking through my body like a freight train, I nod and agree in all the right places as Dan takes me through the signature cocktail of the week—passion fruit martini—and rambles on about the snacks in the crew mess: salmon and cream cheese bagels.

I couldn't give a flying fuck about cocktails or food, and my cheeks ache from holding up a plastic smile.

When the phone rings behind the bar, I jump out of my skin.

"Yes?" I breathe down the line.

Raphael's voice comes smooth and somber. "Tell Dan to bring a water, no ice." He pauses. "Penelope?" I clutch the receiver tighter, my shoulders bracing for impact. "Dan. Not you."

He hangs up.

"Was that the boss?" Dan asks, tone too chipper for my frazzled state.

I nod, scrambling for a glass and filling it up with water. Why Dan? Why not me? Christ, my mouth is watering in suspense.

Maybe I do recognize him, and I just wasn't looking at him properly.

There's only one way to find out.

I slide the water on a tray and stomp into the sky lounge. Now, the air is thick from something other than cigar smoke and lighthearted competition. My gaze sweeps over the back of Kelly's head to Angelo's stony expression, then locks on Raphael. His eyes simmer with a cool green fury that suggests I'm in deep shit for disobeying his request, but right now, I don't fucking care. I drop the glass on Kelly's side of the table and glare at his profile.

No, I definitely don't recognize him.

He rolls his head on his neck to give me a smarmy smile. "Would you deal, Princess?"

I blink. Shift my gaze to the cards in front of him. He's playing the last hand of the game; there's a pile of discarded cards on the table, and only one card left in the shoe.

I don't know why it slides out of my mouth. Maybe it's because I want to keep him looking at me for longer, so I can truly study his face and see if I recognize him. Or maybe, it's because I'm a fucking idiot.

"Depends if you're playing the ace as a high or low value card," I whisper.

A second passes like the beat of a drum.

Raphael rubs the bridge of his nose. Angelo lets out a slow breath. And Kelly's resounding chuckle reverberates in the hollow of my chest. "Deal."

Raking a cautious eye over Raphael, Angelo plucks the last card from the shoe and flicks it on the table.

Ace of spades.

It's so quiet I can hear the tick of Raphael's Breitling on my wrist. The whir of the blender going on the other side of the door. How can Dan make passion fruit martinis at a time like this?

I look to Raphael for an answer, which is stupid, because I don't even know the question. Head dipped between his shoulder blades, he slowly drags his gaze up to me, and I don't like what I see in it.

It's soft. At odds with the suffocating tension pressing against the four walls of the room. When it drops to the pendant around my neck, it hardens with resolve.

"Penelope."

"Yes?" I whisper back.

"Tell me what the weather is like today."

I blink. I couldn't cut the air in here even if I had an obsidian knife, and he's worried about the weather? "What?"

As if trying to convey something calming with his eyes, he nods to the French doors behind me. "Look out the window, and tell me what the weather is like."

After a breathless second, I do as I'm told. My gait is clumsy as I make my way to the glass and press a sweaty hand against its cold surface.

I swallow. "Well, uh. It's cloudy, but I don't think it'll r—"

My forecast is sliced in half by a sound I'd know anywhere. It's a sound I've heard before, *twice*, as it took the lives of both my dead-beat parents.

Bang.

The gunshot reverberates off the walls and rings in my ears. Everything stops—my words, the time, my pulse.

"Penelope?" I latch on to the tranquility in Raphael's voice like a life-line. "Don't turn around. Just open the door and take a walk."

I follow the calm voice. Slide the door open with trembling fingers and step outside.

I suck in a lungful of icy wind and tilt my head to the sky.

You know, maybe it'll rain today after all.

CHAPTER
Twenty-Five

Penny

T HE WIND IS AS cruel as it is cold, carrying my most painful memories from the coastline, over the Pacific, and slapping me in the face with them.

The nastiest memories are always the ones that are the most visceral. The ones you don't just see, but feel, too. The crash of whiskey bottles smashing and the noxious stench of liquor rising up from the grubby kitchen tiles. My mother's blood, crimson and searing hot, coating the backs of my thighs. My father's cries, so fucking *guttural*, as he called out to a God that turned a blind eye. The hiss of a gun chamber spinning, steel against my temple, and the absence of the third *bang* that never came.

When I left the sky lounge, panic chased me down the side deck and my walk morphed into a run. I ran until the deck tapered off to water. Now, with nowhere else to go, I'm gripping the handrail of the swim platform, wondering if the current is as dangerous as it looks. My lungs tighten with every breath I can't catch, and the black spots in my vision dance underneath the gray clouds like low-soaring birds.

Warmth brushes my back, and hands land on either side of mine, caging me in.

"Breathe."

My stare falls from the sky to the hands. I look from left to right, right to left, wondering which one of them pulled the trigger.

"I—"

Soft lips on the nape of my neck cut me off. "That's talking, not breathing."

I inhale ice-cold air through my nose, wincing as it burns against the walls of my lungs. When I release it, it smears the gloomy sky like a shaky stroke of a paintbrush.

"Good girl," Raphael says gently. "Again."

The calmness in his voice is unnerving. A stark contrast to the heat of his chest, and to the act of violence he committed less than three minutes ago. A body lies dead on the deck above, and all he can do is tell me to breathe?

As I choke on my next breath, his hand slips off the railing and lies flat against my stomach. It's warm and stupidly reassuring, and when he swipes his thumb up and down, caressing the same inch of fabric over and over, I breathe in and out to the same rhythm.

"You told me your gun was fake," I rasp bitterly.

"I lied."

"I thought you were a gentleman. Lie about that, too?"

He moves closer, taking my body with his, until my bottom rib presses against the railing. Without a word, he scoops up all of my hair flailing about in the wind, and winds it into a bun at the base of my neck. He uses it like a joystick, gently tugging on it until my head rests against his chest.

"Just because I'm a gentleman, Penelope, doesn't always mean I'm a gentle man."

My grip tightens on the railing, my heart stuttering to an off-kilter beat. "Was that the first time you've..."

His stomach flexes against my spine. "No."

"And will you..."

"I'd assume so, yes."

I can't keep a strangled gasp from escaping. "You're a psychopath; you know that?"

His humorless laugh touches the pulse in my throat. "What makes you think that?"

I close my eyes, honing in on the sound of his heartbeat. "Your heart isn't even beating fast."

"I'm a made man, Penelope. We're just built this way." His hand comes off the railing and wraps around me, drawing me deeper into his warmth. I must really be traumatized to not push him away. "It's always horrible the first time you hear a gunshot."

My sardonic breath is bitter and tinged with disbelief. "Yeah, but it's not the first time. Not even the second."

"Paintballing in your teens doesn't count."

I know he's trying to distract me from the ringing in my ears, but his patronizing tone stokes a spark of annoyance. Maybe that's why I let him into my memories, or maybe the panic blurring my vision also blurs my judgment, too.

I glare at my knuckles on the railing, blue from the cold and white from the strength of my grip. I take a deep breath and let the wind carry my story.

"I was there when my parents were killed." I say it in a rushed, mumbled voice. "Two men in balaclavas. They could have been anyone. My parents were alcoholics and alcoholics have a tendency of pissing people off. They slid through the open window in the living room and shot both of them dead. Mom got off lightly. She was already asleep, passed out on the kitchen table after a long night of sobbing to Whitney Houston power ballads, so I doubt she felt a thing. But my father; he met a nasty end. Woke up from his whiskey-induced coma just long enough to see the barrel of a gun and make a run for it out the garden door."

I swallow the thick knot in my throat and slide my eyes up to the sky. "I'd heard the gunshot that killed my mother but I thought it was part of a dream. I didn't wake up properly until I heard my father's cries floating up the stairs." A sour laugh escapes my lips. "Wish I'd stayed in my room, because the men in balaclavas didn't even know I existed until I appeared in the kitchen doorway and started screaming. One dragged my father out into the garden and shot him like a rabid dog, and the other pinned me between the refrigerator and the washing machine and told me they'd been instructed not to leave any witnesses behind."

A lone tear carves a hot trail down my cheek. I don't move to wipe it away, because then Raphael would realize it was there. Instead, I blink, *hard*, and pray another doesn't fall. "He put his gun to my temple and told me to close my eyes and count down from ten. When I was younger, I had a doctor that'd use the same trick to administer vaccines, so I knew what his plan was. He'd probably let me get to, like, four or five, and pull the trigger so I wouldn't see it coming." My fingers slide to my necklace, and I run it up and down the chain, just like I did that night, too. "He only let me get to eight." I squeeze my eyes shut, remembering the *click* that followed the number leaving my lips. "The gun jammed. And you know what he told me? That I didn't know how lucky I was, that I was—"

"One in a million," Raphael murmurs into my hair, body growing stiff behind me. "That's why you don't like lightning, because getting struck is another one-in-a-million possibility."

I run my tongue over my teeth, giving a small shake of my head. "I know it's irrational and self-absorbed, but if it can happen once, it can happen again."

Despite the silence swirling with the wind, my breath comes out steady for the first time since I heard the shot. I guess talking about things really does help. Even if you're talking to a velvet-clad murderer. The feeling of his warm chest expanding and contracting against my back lures mine into a false sense of security: I'm not expecting it when his hand slides up from my stomach, over my breasts, and touches my necklace. "That's why you think you're so lucky."

My heart does a double-thump under his touch. "One of the reasons," I whisper back.

"Tell me the others."

I open my mouth but clamp it shut just as quickly. While the ghost of hands pulling up my dress grab me, I decide to stay silent. Instead, I attempt to wriggle out of his grasp and opt for a reply that'll put the world to rights again.

"Well, I beat you at absolutely every game, for one."

His hand slides off my necklace first, then his other hand gently unwinds my hair. Feeling it cascade down my back, I swallow and dare myself to turn and look up at him. His gaze searches mine, flickering with dry amusement. Relief tinges my skin; if I'd turned around and seen sympathy in his gaze, I might have had to claw my eyes out.

He stares at me for a beat too long, before the growl of an engine turns our attention out to the Pacific. Underneath pregnant clouds, a sleek black speedboat slices through the water at a ridiculous pace. There's a lone sharp figure behind the wheel, all broad lines, big muscles, and mirrored sunglasses. Just before the bow touches the swim platform, he steers sharply, pulling the craft up beside the yacht at the last second.

Raphael scowls. "Watch the paintwork, dickhead."

Gabriel Visconti pulls off his sunglasses, revealing a stony glare and a scar so angry it makes my throat tighten.

He tethers the rope to the platform post in heavy silence. My gaze falls down to his fitted black T-shirt—*in December*—and all of the ink that seeps out from underneath it.

He hops onto the platform and comes to a stop next to his brother. He turns to stare at me, then glares at my necklace for what feels so long my fingers twitch to rip it off and hand it to him.

"Paintwork is the least of your worries, my brother."

The yacht rocks more than usual as he takes the stairs two at a time and disappears from view. A shiver plays down my spine. If Angelo is the rough outline and Raphael is the clean, final portrait, Gabriel is the demon that lives in the artist's nightmares.

Letting out a huff, Raphael turns his attention back to me. His eyes soften to something warmer as they search my features. I shake off a shiver for a different reason when his hand cups my jaw, and his thumb trails the curve of my cheekbone.

"No crying."

My next breath grazes the back of his hand, shallower than the last. This is the same hand that just pulled a trigger and ended a life. So why does it feel so good against my skin?

My jaw flexes against his palm in an attempt to regain some footing. "Why do you care if I cry?"

He tracks his thumb as it trails further down, across my bottom lip and along my chin. He grips me there for a moment, regret coating his features.

"Because last night, I saw you laugh."

CHAPTER
Twenty-Six

Penny

THE SOUND OF A gunshot clings to my body like a nervous aura as I watch Matt thump the top of my ancient television set with his fist. *Again.* Seems like third time's a charm, though, because the grainy picture comes into focus, and the musical opener to *Pitch Perfect* crackles through the speakers.

He plonks beside me on the sofa and glares at my profile. I cram a fistful of popcorn into my mouth to muffle my sigh. *Here it comes.*

"How many bathrooms do they have?"

"I don't know, Matt. I only peed in one."

"Yeah, but if you had to hazard a guess?"

My eyes roll over the cracks in my ceiling as Matt starts tallying the potential powder rooms, ensuites, and shower rooms that'd come with a ten-bedroom home. He's talking about Angelo and Rory's mansion, of course. Hasn't stopped asking about it since I told him I spent the evening there, playing blackjack, eating candy, and watching *Romy and Michelle* with Rory. At least bathrooms are a safer topic of conversation than the reason I was there in the first place: because I'd just heard a man hit the ground like a sack of potatoes after being shot, and I was in no fit state to finish my shift.

Matt is like a Golden Retriever, all shaggy blond hair and happy smiles. I don't want to dull his wagging tail with negative talking points, like murders and the fact Anna doesn't even remember his name, let alone want to date him.

Did you see any of the cars in the garage?

Do they have one of those fancy hot water taps?

What about a panic room? They must have a panic room.

Matt's questions grow fewer and farther in between, until I steal a glance at him and realize he's fast asleep, the bowl of popcorn balancing precariously on his lap.

With a restless buzz in my blood, I watch the bright lights flicker from the television and illuminate the walls of the dark room until the credits roll.

It's nearing one a.m. when I switch the television off, and, despite the rock music vibrating the wall behind me, it's eerily quiet. Too quiet for a manic mind.

Knew it was you.

Bang.

Knew it was you.

Bang.

The afternoon's events play on repeat in my brain, and each time the gunshot rattles my insides, I grow more and more tense. That man knew who I was, and although he's now in a body bag somewhere, I have an awful feeling my secret didn't die with him.

Martin O'Hare could be on the way to the Coast *right now*.

Glaring at the wall, I run the four-leaf clover pendant up and down its chain, but it does little to calm my nerves. I can't tell if I'm suddenly the unluckiest girl in the world, because my past caught up with me in the third quietest town in the United States, or the luckiest, because Raphael shot Martin's brother dead for an unrelated reason.

Regardless, I should run. Grab all the money sitting in the top drawer of my dresser and cross the border into Canada. I came back to the Coast to escape my sins, but I'm starting to think all I've done is demote myself to a lower circle of hell.

As I close my eyes, the ghost of Raphael's soothing words against my ear and his hot hand against my stomach sweep a chill through me.

The worst part? I think I like it down here.

Orange light illuminates behind my eyelids, and I pop them open in confusion. A few seconds pass before the living room lights up again with two flashes in quick succession.

What the fuck?

Holding my breath, I slip off the sofa and peek out the window. A familiar G-Wagon is haphazardly parked on the other side of the street, its headlights pointing at my window. The moment I pull back the curtain, they flash again.

Oh, hell no. What is Raphael doing here?

My heart is beating faster as I step back from the window. There's no way I'm getting in that man's car, despite the deep, dark urge to feel his hands on my body again. He just killed a man over losing a blackjack game. Driving off with him into the night would be in the top three dumbest things I've ever done. And I've done *a lot* of dumb things.

My cell phone buzzes on the coffee table, making me jump. It's a message from an unknown number.

Ten.

I stare down at the text in disbelief. Another comes through.

Nine.

And then another.

Eight.

I'm not a patient man, Penelope.

The vibrations rattle the glass, and I stare, helpless, as the text messages count down like a ticking time bomb.

One.

I squeeze my eyes shut.

Silence.

And then the loudest horn I've ever heard pierces through the glass and fills my living room.

"Fuck," I yelp, slamming my hands to my ears.

Matt bolts upright, scattering popcorn across my floor. "What the fuck is that?"

An asshole with delusions of grandeur. The noise is unrelenting, and I know Raphael is petty enough to keep blowing his horn until I go downstairs. Muttering something about being right back, I race through the hall, snatching up my keys and stuffing my feet into sneakers as I go. Downstairs, I burst out onto the icy street, fling open the driver's side door, and scream at the darkness inside the car.

"Stop! Jesus Christ, stop!"

Raphael is the dictionary definition of unfazed. He lays on the horn with one hand, sleeve rolled to his elbow, and scrolls through emails on his cell with the other. His eyes lift from his screen and pin me with a look of indifference.

"Say please."

"Over my dead—"

"That doesn't sound like please."

Spurred on by a cocktail of frustration and stubbornness, I step up into the car and wrestle with his inked forearm. "For the love of god, I have neighbors—"

My rant is sliced in half when he tosses his cell onto the passenger seat, slips his arm around the backs of my thighs, and drags me onto his lap in one swift motion. Wearing only shorts, my skin crackles in anticipation as they slide against the soft wool fabric of his slacks.

His arm fastens around my waist like a seatbelt and the scream of the horn dulls, as if I'm now hearing it underwater. I'm too distracted by the hard, hot weight of his chest against my back, and the warm, masculine scent engulfing me. It's a dangerous combination that makes the streetlights through the windshield grow hazy.

His breath skitters over the nape of my neck. "Say please, Penelope."

"Please," I whisper.

"I can't hear you."

Irritation snaps me back to reality. I spin around and hook my fingers over the chain of his collar pin.

"*Please*," I growl.

Our gazes clash. As his hand slides off the horn and grazes the side of my thigh, the amusement dancing in his eyes simmers to something hotter.

His smirk melts off his face, and suddenly, the silence I was begging for is too loud.

"See," he says softly. "Wasn't so hard, was it?"

Heart hammering in tune with the newly awakened pulse in my clit, I scramble to get off his lap and into the passenger seat.

"God, that sound was annoying," I grumble, looking up at my neighbors emerging from their doors and craning their necks down the street.

"Funny—I think the same thing every time you open your mouth."

"You drag me out here just to piss me off?"

The engine shifts into gear, and with a full turn of the steering wheel, we're driving the opposite way down Main Street.

"No," he says breezily. "According to my lawyers, as your boss I've got a duty of care to make sure you're not displaying symptoms of shock or trauma."

"Horseshit."

"It's true."

"And those symptoms are?"

The corner of his lips tilt. "Irritability. Loss of appetite."

"I'm irritated, that's for sure."

He reaches onto the seat behind him. Dumps a fast-food bag onto my lap. "And your appetite?"

I stare down at the bag for a few seconds, my fists clenched by my sides. When I finally peel it open and see my regular order from the diner, something warm and unwanted pools in the pit of my stomach.

He remembered.

I clear my throat, growing hot. "Are you really checking for symptoms, or is this just an excuse to hang out with me?"

"It's me trying to avoid a lawsuit, sweetheart."

My gaze finds him. He's staring straight ahead, distracted. For a moment, I'm not so certain that he's lying.

"Well, I'd be open to settling out of court for cash compensation."

His laugh blooms in my chest, and as he glances down at the watch on my wrist, something soft passes over his features. "I bet you would."

We drive in restless silence until we reach the top of the cliff. Raphael parks up in the shadows of the old church and cranks the heater up. My nerves only tighten when four sets of headlights sweep through the rear window.

"We're being followed," I choke out, twisting to peer between the headrests at the cars behind us.

A hot hand slides over my bare thighs, and all coherent thoughts dissolve. Christ, why didn't I have the good sense to put on some clothes before I went flying out of the apartment? "Relax, it's just my men."

His grip is unwavering. Turning back around, I focus on what's happening on the other side of the windshield. Tree branches shivering in the wind. Thin clouds sliding in front of the moon.

Anything to distract myself from the pinky finger sitting too close to the inside seam of my shorts.

"They weren't following you the last time you dragged me into the car."

Silence swells between us, then Raphael's fingers graze over the curve of my leg and come to rest in the center console. When he speaks, his voice is toneless. Almost harsh. "Eat your food, Penelope."

My head is spinning too fast to do anything but listen. Under intense scrutiny, I unwrap the burger and take a bite. The car fills with the sound of my chewing and the nervous energy buzzing in my ears. As I go to take another bite, a large hand clamps around my wrist and stops me.

My eyes lift up to Raphael's. Without breaking my gaze, he lowers his head and takes a large, slow bite of my burger. *Christ.* My toes curl in my sneakers and my blood burns a few degrees hotter.

A little hiss of air escapes my lips, along with a question I didn't know I needed the answer to.

"What did you wager?"

He licks salt off his bottom lip, eyes darkening with something that tugs on my nerves. "Something I didn't want to give up."

My breathing shallows as he lifts my milkshake from the center console cup holder. He takes a sip, then his arm grazes mine as he tilts the drink to me. Swallowing hard, I edge closer, closing the gap between us, and put my lips where his just were.

His next breath grazes the tip of my nose, and Christ, chocolate milkshake has never tasted so sweet.

"Why did you bet it then?" I whisper. My voice is so quiet, so tense, that if my forehead wasn't almost touching his, I doubt he'd hear it over the pounding of my heart.

Bitter amusement passes through his features. "Because I was hoping I wouldn't be so...*sentimental* about it."

His stare has claws and they dig into my skin. It's too intense, too pensive, and the way it makes my lungs constrict is at odds with everything I believe about men.

As I lean back to draw in air that isn't contaminated by him, there's a flash of green and a strong hand grips the nape of my neck, keeping me in place.

"What—?"

"You're nervous."

I search his stoic expression in shock. "N-no, I'm not."

"You're a bad liar, Penelope."

I let out a shaky breath, scooping up all the composure I can hold. I attempt to keep it light. "And you're a bad blackjack player."

His gaze sparks black. Seconds drip pass, but they feel like minutes. Eventually, his fingers slide off my neck and he puts distance between us. Slipping a poker chip from his pocket, he flips it between his thumb and forefinger as he stares out the windshield.

"Seems like I'm bad at everything these days."

The air has shifted within the four walls of this car so fast it's given me whiplash. We've gone from sexual tension and sharing food to something that makes the hairs on my arms stand straight.

When Raphael's silky voice slices through the tension, my shoulders snap into a tight line.

"Kelly seemed to know who you were. Have you met before?"

I feel sick. "No."

"Odd, because his brother Martin owns the Hurricane bar and casino you used to work at."

Shit. Shit, shit, shit.

The words *I knew it was you* flash against the dash, and it feels like someone's tightened a belt around my lungs. It takes every ounce of discipline to stop my face from showing my panic.

"What a coincidence."

"Want to know what else is a coincidence?"

"No," I breathe.

He tells me anyway.

"That casino burned down on Wednesday, and you turned up on the Coast with a suitcase on Thursday."

I knew it was coming, but I still recoil from the blow. Blood thumps in my temples and my vision dims around the edges; it's becoming near impossible to keep my poker face.

"Look at me, Penelope." Stupidly, I do. I immediately wish I hadn't, because there's not an ounce of gentleman softening his features. Nor does it touch his tone when he grinds out his next question. "What. Did. You. Do?"

My eyes have a way of revealing my next move, so this time, I don't glance down at the door handle before I tug on it, lurch out, and break into a run.

Slippery pavement morphs into frosted leaves and the wind roars in my ears. I'm running into darkness and I don't know where it leads. That seems to be what I do when faced with the consequences of my impulsive actions.

I run away without a plan.

The moon disappears behind branches above, and when the silence between the tree trunks echoes louder than my thumping heart, I slow to a stop. As I turn a full circle in a tight clearing, the weight of another dumb decision presses down on my shoulders.

Fuck. Why did I run into the Devil's Preserve?

It's cold. Now that I've stopped running, the December chill nips at my legs and arms and racks my bones with a shiver. I step toward the direction I think I came from and my foot catches on a root, rolling my ankle underneath me.

"Fuck," I hiss out into the darkness. As I bend down to rub it, the silence is broken by something that makes the hairs on the back of my neck stand to attention.

The *crack* of a twig underfoot.

Raphael's presence crawls up my spine before he even utters a word. Before he grips my waist and shoves me against a tree.

He takes a step forward, blocking me in. "Did you burn down Martin O'Hare's casino, Penelope?"

My heartbeat flickers like a flame; part of me is grateful for his warmth, and the other part of me knows it'll be the last time I'll feel it.

I don't want to tell him the truth, and not just because I'm scared of the look in his eye. He already knows too much; I cracked like a fucking egg on the swim platform today, my childhood trauma running out of me like yolk. It feels like every piece of myself I give to him is another piece I can't get back. A piece I can't hide behind. What am I going to do: stand here, raw and vulnerable and fucking *soppy* in front of a man? A man I don't even like? Who doesn't like me?

My answer doesn't come quick enough, because his hand shoots out and wraps around my throat, shoving me backward until my shoulders scrape the rough bark behind me. I bite down a hiss and clench my frozen fists at my side.

"Going to need an answer, Penelope," he says, sounding bored.

The broad planes of his silhouette blur into the darkness behind him, making him appear larger—scarier. I shouldn't be alone with a man like him, and the black void that exists behind his irises tells me he agrees.

With an impatient breath, his thumb presses harder against my pulse. "Did you set fire to his casino?" The very real possibility of dying flashes behind my eyelids and forces me to nod.

His stomach tenses against mine. "Why?"

Here I go, cracking like that egg again. Flexing my throat in his tight grip, I tell him.

"When a new casino opened in town, I had no idea it was run by the fucking Irish *mob*," I croak. "I didn't even know who Martin O'Hare was; all I was thinking about were all the fresh marks. Well, one night, he caught me..."

My words trail off. "Swindling," Raphael finishes for me, gaze flashing black.

Card counting, actually. But I have a feeling telling Vegas's most prolific casino owner that I card count, while alone in the woods with him, would be a very stupid idea. Instead, I nod. "He told me to leave town and never come back."

His gaze narrows. "But why the fire? Why didn't you just leave?"

We stare at each other. "Because when Martin O'Hare cornered me in the alleyway outside the casino, he did the same thing as you're doing to me right now."

When O'Hare had his hands around my throat, it had reminded me of being ten, standing in the alley of another casino, with another man with a strong grip. Although it didn't have the same horrific ending, I was *bitter*. So bitter, I made the impulsive decision to light a vodka bottle outside his casino as I waited for the bus out of town on the other side of the road.

Three stuttered heartbeats pass. In that time, confusion sweeps like a shadow across Raphael's expression, then his gaze drops to his hand around my throat.

It slips down to my collarbone, and balls into a fist by his side.

"You're a dead girl walking, Penelope,"

I let out a shaky breath, a whisper of defiance rolling through me. Not because I believe I'm lucky enough to evade death twice in one lifetime—hell, I'm not sure if I'm lucky at all anymore—but because the image of my father curling up into a fetal position before he was killed has been burned into my retinas for the last seven years.

What an embarrassing way to go. Ever since, I made a vow that when death found me, I'd greet it with a straight spine and a staring match.

I tilt my chin up. "I don't want to play a game tonight. If you're going to kill me, just do it."

My teeth chatter. Branches whip in the wind above our heads. Eventually, Raphael runs a thumb over his lip and drags his gaze to the blackened sky.

"Now, where would be the fun in that?"

What?

Before I can reply, he stoops and wraps an arm around my waist. My feet leave the ground as he hurls me over his shoulder. Blood rushes to my head and my thighs tingle in perverse expectation under the heat of his palm just below the curve of my ass. I couldn't have run very far, because less than a minute passes before the moonlight cuts across the muddy ground and the car is in sight.

He drops me at the passenger door and flings it open. "Get in."

My mouth opens and closes again. I catch the eye of one of his lackeys smoking against a sedan across the road. He blows smoke against the black sky and shrugs.

"Where are we—"

"Get in before I change my mind about killing you, Penelope."

I don't have to be asked twice.

Heat blasts from the dash and scalds my limbs as I slide into the passenger seat. Raphael's door slams with more force than necessary, and we're peeling off over frosted pavement before I can even get my seatbelt on.

I'm confused, crawling with awkwardness and stupefied to my core. I keep glancing at Raphael, but the expression carved into his face is so unreadable that I can't tell if it'd be best to apologize or to crack a joke.

I settle for drowning in the silence.

I fidget with the radio.

Dig for discarded fries down the side of the seat.

As I start doodling on the condensation on the passenger side window, the car comes to an abrupt stop. My heart lurches forward with my body, and as I turn to face Raphael, he grabs me by the scruff of my neck and lifts my back up off the seat. When he drops me again, there's something soft under my head.

A pillow.

Expressionless, he reaches into the back seat again and produces a blanket. He throws it over my head and the engine whirs to life again.

"Go to sleep."

"But—"

"But nothing, Penelope. Forget about Martin O'Hare; he's my problem now."

CHAPTER
Twenty-Seven

Rafe

W HISKEY UNDER THE ROCKS, Devil's Hollow.

My monthly poker game is in full swing. On the surface, the cave bar hums with a good time, and the excitement of Christmas being just around the corner adds an electric edge to the night. Between the Christmas trees spilling out from every alcove, drinks flow over bars and dice roll over tables. Underneath, tension broils like a dangerous undercurrent.

After a few phone calls, my VIP clients were back on board with the night, but Tor hasn't shown up. I knew he wouldn't, but throwing one of these nights without him feels like a bullet-sized hole in my chest. And then there's the irritating issue of Angelo shooting eye daggers from the roulette table. He doesn't even play roulette, but he's still pissed at me for popping a cap in Kelly O'Hare's head yesterday. Not even because he doesn't want his sadist wife to be exposed to any more violence, but because now I've given Gabe an excuse to focus on something more exciting than lacing Dante's associates' cigarettes with cyanide: starting a war with the Irish.

"Um, okay. Hit, I think? Yeah, definitely hit."

Speaking of Angelo's sadist wife, Rory sits on the other side of Gabe, muttering under her breath. We're playing Visconti Blackjack. I usually refuse to play with her, and not just because beating her has become boring, but because I'm pretty sure she does something weird every time she loses.

Like spit in my drink.

But if my brother wants to ignore me, I'll happily take more of his money. Besides, Rory is the only family member who's not been giving me shit all night.

My jaw ticks as a bandaged hand comes down on my shoulder.

"Are the rumors true, *cugino*? You really shot from your own gun? *Dio mio*, what are your minions for, then?"

Keeping my smile tight and pleasant, I stare at the space above Rory's curls and ignore Benny. Unfortunately for him, he keeps going. "How was your aim? It must have been rusty after all these years."

I take a lazy sip of whiskey, set the tumbler down on the table, then draw my elbow back to connect with his groin.

"My aim is just fine, Benny."

He grinds out some profanity in Italian and hobbles off.

Despite the smirk lifting my lips, I get why my recent outburst is the talk of the family. I haven't pulled a trigger outside our Sinners Anonymous game in years. Griff's fuming. Gabe's amused. Everyone thinks I've lost my mind, and maybe I have, because why else would I be impulsive enough to put a bullet between Kelly O'Hare's eyes? He's been an excellent business partner for years.

It started how it always does: with me unable to say no to a bet. Only this time, I wasn't ready to lose what he'd asked me for.

Penelope.

Christ, I'd never bartered with one of my girls before. It's barbaric, something the Russians would do. But the way he kept looking at her, *touching her*, clawed under my skin and skewed my rationale.

Before I'd connected the dots between my newest employee and his brother's casino fire, the most bitter part of me hoped he'd take her off my hands. My favorite watch, the port explosion. Losing Miller and Young and the hit-and-run at Lucky Cat. Doom card or not, there's no denying my empire started to fall apart like a cheap suit the moment she stomped down the stairs at the Blues Den in those muddy boots.

So, I slid her across the coffee table like a poker chip, offering my morals with her. I didn't think Kelly would actually win—he was off his nut on whiskey and benzos, for fuck's sake.

Even before the ace of spades hit the table, I knew handing her over was never an option. There were only two: cheat, or shoot him.

And the day I cheat is the day my mother rolls over in her grave.

Ah, well. At least my hands are still clean. The day I have busted knuckles is the day I know what the bottom feels like.

Sucking in a lungful of festive air, I lean back in my seat and glance at the card Gabe, who's acting as dealer, just tossed on the table. Nine of diamonds. "Hit."

Gabe turns over the four of clubs.

My eyes move up to Rory. She's frowning, strumming her fingers against the table.

"All right, I need a minute."

I turn my attention back out to the crowd, but my mind is still on Penelope.

It's crazy. I've just lost millions of dollars and put a price on my head, all with the squeeze of a trigger, and my first instinct was to check on the girl I suspected started this mess. And then when I confirmed it—in the woods with no witnesses, of all places—I didn't squeeze my trigger again. No, I told her I'd handle it for her.

I'll have to kill Martin before he kills me now, but I have a niggling suspicion that, even if that wasn't the case, I'd hunt him down regardless.

As I lift my whiskey to my lips, the faceted tumbler refracts something red on the other side of it. I slide my gaze over the rim and see the devil herself floating through the door.

My chest tightens at the sight of her. Not only because her appearance is unexpected, but because she's a vision in satin and lace. Christ, the way her body is poured into that red dress; it can't be real. I don't want it to be—she's just walked in and already half the men in the room are looking up at her.

"Rory. Did you invite Penelope?"

"Yes, but her name's *Penny*. And Wren and Tayce."

Ah, yes. I didn't even see them behind her, and neither is the type of girl you miss.

"Why?"

"Uh, because she's my friend?"

I pretend I don't see Gabe smirk into his whiskey glass.

My eyes track Penelope's movements as she carves a path through the crowd, Wren and Tayce by her side. Sensing I'm watching her, she looks up at me and falters, as if she's as surprised to see me as much as I am her. As if I don't own thirty-three percent of the ground those ridiculous heels are sauntering over.

I slide my hand under the table and curl it around a poker chip. I'm trying—failing—to ignore the swell in my groin. The unease in my blood. Every part of my body is at odds with another, because tonight, she doesn't look like a delinquent that starts fires in casinos.

She looks like the Queen of Hearts. I look away.

"Looking as beautiful as ever ladies," I say to Tayce and Wren. I stand to pull out their seats on either side of me, while Penny sits beside Rory. Wren flashes me a nervous smile and glances at Gabe. Tayce plants a kiss on my cheek.

"Flattery will get you everywhere, Rafe."

"Apart from the top of your waiting list."

Tayce laughs. "God himself couldn't get to the top of my waiting list."

Feigning an eye roll, I sit down beside her. I don't just keep Tayce sweet because she's the best tattoo artist on the planet, although it's definitely part of the reason. But she's also laid back, witty, and I always enjoy her company, whether she's sitting in one of my chairs or I'm sitting in hers.

As I rest my arm over the back of her seat, she leans over and slips off my collar pin and unbuttons the first few buttons of my shirt.

"You know; I think you're meant to take me out for dinner first."

She ignores me in favor of peering down my open collar. "How's the serpent healing?"

"Beautifully."

Feeling a stare heat my cheek, I slide my eyes over to Penelope. Rory is whispering in her ear, but she's not listening. She's too busy glaring at Tayce's hand on my chest. A spark of satisfaction ignites inside my rib cage, because clearly, she makes me want to be as petty as a fourteen-year-old school girl.

I shift my attention back to Tayce. Pin her with a charming smile. "Tayce, have you seen Tor?"

She rolls her eyes. "No, the idiot didn't turn up for his appointment last week."

Unease stirs inside me. Tor would walk over burning coal in order to make an appointment with Tayce.

"Blackjack!"

Rory's excited squeal cuts over the table and catches me by surprise. Frowning, my eyes fall to the cards in front of her, and sure enough, they total twenty-one.

"I must be living in an alternative universe," I say dryly, raising my drink to her. "At least you can cross beating me at Blackjack off your bucket list."

Her gaze sparkles. "Let's play again."

"Feeling lucky?"

She grins. "You have no idea."

My eyes slide over to the four-leaf clover around Penelope's neck. Clearly her misplaced optimism is rubbing off on my sister-in-law.

"Very well. Let's order these ladies some drinks, first."

I beckon a server and he takes orders from the other end of the table. While Penelope is distracted by the menu, I take the opportunity to drink her in.

Who the fuck are you, girl? I wish she'd just use the Sinners Anonymous hotline for its intended purpose, instead of a sounding board for every vapid thought that crosses her brain, because now, I know shit about her I wish I didn't. Like what she prefers in her bagel, and the color she's going to paint her toes next Friday. Her ramblings haven't given me answers, just more questions.

I want to know why she can sleep in my car, but not in her bed. Why she's still wearing my watch, instead of selling it. What she puts in my whiskey to make me want to protect her, when I should be putting a bullet in her head.

My watch slides up her elbow as she hands the menu back to the server. Although I'm sure she's wearing it in the hope it'll piss me off, I can't ignore the sick thrill that sweeps through me. I suppose it's similar to how men get a kick out of seeing women wearing their shirts. Not me, though. They always get lipstick on the collar and embed the stench of their perfume in the fabric.

"I'll have a lemonade, please."

Wren has been so unusually quiet that I've forgotten she was here until the server asks for her order.

"Just a lemonade?"

She stares at the table, hands clutching the purse in her lap. "Yes, please."

"I can't tempt you with something stronger?"

She shakes her head, offering him a polite smile. "I don't drink."

"Aw, come on, it's almost nearly Christmas—"

The combination of Gabe's chair scraping back and the *crack* of his fist connecting with the table sweeps a deafening silence through the cave. Out of the corner of my eye, I see Angelo rise to his feet.

"She *said*, she'll have a lemonade," Gabe growls.

The server fumbles with the menu and scurries off. Wren turns red and mumbles something about using the restroom, and with a dark mutter under her breath, Tayce follows her through the crowd.

Bemused, my gaze heats the side of my brother's face. He doesn't look up from shuffling the deck in his inked paws.

"Fire him," he says, just loud enough for me to hear. "Or I'll carve his eyeballs out with my rustiest pen knife."

I groan into my whiskey. With all the problems clamping down on my shoulders, this is the last thing I need.

"Right, let's begin."

Rory is visibly relieved at my suggestion, clearly wanting to break the tension as much as I do. Gabe slams down both our cards with more force than necessary, and Rory stares at hers for a stupid amount of time.

Boredom biting at my edges, I nod to the two of hearts she's been dealt. "I'll give you a clue—two is pretty far away from twenty-one."

"Shh," she hisses, putting her fingers to her temples. "I'm *thinking*." A moment passes. "All right, hit."

I hit too, adding a seven of spades to my four of diamonds.

As the dealt cards grow and the deck in Gabe's hand thins, an uneasy awareness climbs up my spine and squeezes the nape of my neck.

Maybe I wouldn't have noticed if I wasn't so hyper-aware of every movement Penelope makes. If I wasn't already staring at her plump lips when she whispered, *low value*, or if I wasn't admiring my watch around her wrist when she squeezed Rory's arm.

I shift my attention to Rory and start honing in on other things I chalked up to her quirkiness. And then I realize: the strumming of her fingers against the table isn't a nervous habit; she's fucking *counting*.

"Blackjack!" she squeals again.

This time, I don't congratulate her. Instead, I drag my eyes up to meet Penelope's and raise my brows.

Something in my expression wipes the grin off her face.

"Penelope."

Her shoulders stiffen.

"I'll give you a ten-second head start."

But by the time the warning slides from my mouth, the little brat is already on her feet.

CHAPTER
Twenty-Eight

Penny

I MIGHT BE A liar and a cheat but so is Raphael. He definitely didn't count to ten before he rose to his feet and sliced through the crowd toward me.

Panic buzzing in my veins, I bolt through an unmarked door with no sense of direction. When it slams behind me, the thrum of the party fades, and the smell of damp earth assaults me. Another cave—great. Away from curious eyes, my brisk walk breaks into a clumsy run as I travel deeper into the darkness. This cave turns off into another, and then another, and then when I turn again and there's no light in sight, I realize I'm a fucking idiot. *Why do I keep running into places without knowing where they lead?*

I guess because the unknown ahead of me is still less frightening than the known behind me.

Biting down the dread rock-climbing up my throat, I keep moving, distracting myself by mentally brushing up on my monologue.

Card counting without any outside aid isn't illegal. There is no law stating that a player can't assign each card a high or low value to estimate the values of cards not yet drawn.

I've had this speech locked in one of those *break in case of emergency* boxes in my head for years, but I've never had to use it.

Tried to with Martin O'Hare, but his hand found my throat before I could get it out.

I wonder where Raphael's hands will go when he catches me.

On Thursday night, his hand flew to my throat, too. What I didn't expect was for them to slip off me when I confessed my worst sin, and then for him to tuck me up in his car and tell me he'll handle it. What does that even mean? Should I be worried or relieved?

A chill travels up my spine, and not just because it's freezing in here. It's even darker now, and I can't even see my ragged puffs of condensation painting the blackness.

My fingers graze the craggy wall, following the curve into *another* fucking tunnel, where I crash into something stone-like. Something with hot hands, a violent heartbeat, and no regard for my safety as it slams me against the wall.

If a million enemies had followed me into the cave network, I'd still know it was Raphael who'd found me. Because Christ, no other scent could light a fire between my thighs like the warm cocktail of cologne, mint, and danger that seeps out of this man's pores. Even the bitter breeze of whiskey leaving his lips and grazing my throat doesn't bother me; I'm too high off the weight of his body caging me in.

Gentleman. That word doesn't exist under the cloak of this darkness, and when his hands start to roam, I know I don't want it to. They fist the skirt of my dress and drag it up my thighs. If the urgency in his movements hadn't made me so dizzy, I'd tell him to be careful, because I'd left the tag on this dress in the hopes of taking it back tomorrow.

"Nice dress," he hisses, all silk-clad venom against the flickering pulse in my throat. "You steal it?"

His hands make contact with my bare hips, the fabric of my dress now draped around his forearms. Every inch of my body sings with anticipation, the icy chill whistling in the small gap between us reminding me that I shouldn't feel this fucking hot in December.

"Not this one," I grind out, my lips against his chest. "Bought it with my stripper money—"

A hard, hot slap connects with my ass cheek, and my yelp of surprise soaks into the expensive fabric of his shirt. "What did I say about stripping for other men, Penelope?" he says, his rough tone at odds with the slow, soothing circles his palm now makes on my stinging ass.

"I don't need to strip for other men. I've got this one client who overpays for lap dances in his car."

Another slap. This one so loud the impact echoes off the dripping ceiling. My moan rises up after it, like steam in a hot sauna. Before I can suck in another breath, his hips push me further into the wall, something hard and throbbing in the middle of them.

Fucking hell. A void opens up in my lower stomach and begs to be filled with friction. I don't have to give him the satisfaction of grinding myself against him like I did in his car, because both his hands slide round to my ass and cup my cheeks as he pulls me against his erection.

It nestles perfectly between my thighs, and I'm too delirious from the weight of it to come up with another sarcastic retort.

His lips brush the crown of my head. "You said you were going straight. Martin not teach you anything?"

"I am. I mean, I have—"

Another slap on my ass. This one is so violent that it lurches me forward, so my clit tingles on his bulge.

I'm going out of my mind. All I can hear is buzzing in my ears when he speaks again. "There's only one little brat on this Coast who'd teach Rory to card count."

Sparks run from the warmth of his fingertips down to my pussy as they trail along the thin band of my thong. When they connect under my navel, I stop breathing.

If he dipped those thick fingers lower, he'd realize my body doesn't hate him as much as my brain does.

But he doesn't. He only snaps the band with an irritated hiss and grabs my wrist. He tugs me into the darkness, and when I pull back, he tightens his hold on me.

"You won't make it out of here on your own, Penelope."

Yeah, not a chance. Ass stinging and heart thundering, I follow him blindly through the tunnels. *How the fuck does he know where he's going?*

His heavy footsteps echo against the thick walls, and as the sound of the party grows louder, my body grows lighter with relief. That was a surprisingly easy punishment for the crime committed. Just like yesterday when he chased me into the forest and I confessed the reason I was really on the Coast, he let me off easy.

We burst through a door and it's like we never left the club. Cheers rise up from the roulette table, drunken conversations float over cocktails at the bar. We've re-entered from a different door, and I can see the back of Rory's curly hair on the other side of the room. I take one step toward her, but a tug on my wrist pulls me into a booth in the shadows.

I sigh. Clearly, Raphael hasn't finished torturing me yet.

"Don't move."

He disappears, emerging shortly from the direction of the bar with two drinks in his hands. He holds the whiskey glass with the tips of his fingers and slams a passion fruit martini down in front of me.

I stare at it.

How did he know it's my favorite drink?

But there's no time to dwell on it, not when his heavy hand brushes back the hem of my dress and clamps down on my knee. Despite every feminist bone in my body, I can't help but squirm under the possessiveness behind his palm.

He pulls a deck of cards out his pocket. Turns over the top card. "Higher or lower."

My gaze slides to his profile. He's staring straight ahead, his expression neutral, save for the telling tick of his jaw.

"I—"

He squeezes my knee. "Not in the mood, Penelope."

I suck in a steadying breath. I know exactly what he's doing, because Nico did it with me, and I did it with Rory. It's how you practice card counting as a beginner. You go through the deck, guessing whether the next card will be a high or low value number. By keeping a running count of what's been dealt, the odds of guessing correctly grow significantly higher the closer you get to the bottom of the deck.

I'm the best at this game, but by the way Raphael is gripping my thigh, maybe I don't want to be.

I glare down at the three of clubs. Statistically speaking, the answer is obvious. "Higher."

The walls of my stomach tense as his hand slides a few inches up my thigh. Okay, I haven't played *this* version before. I look up at him, but still, his expression conveys he could be waiting for a bus.

The *thawp* of another card hitting the table. Four of spades.

I sigh. Flick my gaze to the rocky ceiling. "Higher," I whisper.

Jack of spades.

My fingers curl over the edge of the booth as the cold buckle of his watch glides up the outside of my thigh, and the soft pad of his thumb trails the inside.

Heart stuttering, I look around the room desperately. The festive glow of the party doesn't touch our corner of the cave, and I have no doubt party-goers don't even know we're here, let alone how close Raphael's thumb is to the gusset of my thong.

Jack of spades, okay. Fuck. Logically, I should say lower, but the ache of anticipation in my clit has other ideas.

"Higher."

Raphael's eyes slide sideways, lighting with something uncouth, and he turns over another card.

Queen of hearts.

He lets out a sardonic breath. "You have got to be shitting me."

As he hooks his thumb over the gusset of my panties, our gazes clash. By the darkness that clouds his irises, I know he can feel what's been brewing between my thighs since his hands lifted the hemline of my dress in the cave.

His knuckle presses into my slickness, then, gripping my inner thigh, he extends his thumb so it slides under the lace and carves a maddeningly slow path between my folds.

He stops dangerously close to my clit.

We stare at each other. I couldn't breathe even if I wanted to. The noise of the party fades as my eyes convey the desperation I can't conceal any longer. His soften with something that raises the goosebumps along my arms.

A flash of green and citrine and then I gasp as his thumb presses against my clit, and his free hand finds purchase in the base of my hair. He yanks my head back, presses his lips to my neck, and growls his next question against my throat.

"How did you learn to card count?"

"I didn't. You already know this, I'm lucky—"

My protest is cut off by a blaze of pleasure igniting in my core. *Sweet friction. Holy touch.* Raphael's thumb moves in fast, unrelenting circles, and white spots dance behind my eyelids.

"You're not lucky, Penelope. Not to me. Ever since you turned up on this Coast, I've been the unluckiest person in the world. I'm losing everything I've worked for, and it's all because of you."

Shock overriding my lust, I grip his hair and yank his head back, until his lips brush against mine. I grin against his mouth. "So you *do* believe in luck. Is that why you hate me?"

He laughs bitterly, and I drink every inch of hot breath like it's a lifeline. "I'm as superstitious as the day is long, Penelope. Didn't used to be. Don't want to be, either. Because nobody trusts a CEO or an underboss who avoids walking under ladders, or raps their knuckles against the nearest wooden surface when any ill-intended thought slips from their mouth. It's ironic, really. I've built my entire fortune on games of chance and statistical probability. I've never made a decision based on emotion, and then you fucking come along, and I'm suddenly killing business partners because they look at you wrong. You know, I'm starting to think that fucking fortune teller was right."

"What fortune teller—?"

A hot, thick finger slides into my entrance and all thoughts, including those of superstitions and fortune tellers, leave my head. Christ. He pushes deeper, in and out, in and out, like he's committing the walls of my pussy to memory. My forehead presses against his, our breath intertwining. His gaze drops to my lips and he groans.

"What, you wanna kiss me or something?" I say, my sarcasm tinged with hope.

"Or something," he mutters back, flicking my clit for my insolence.

My spine buckles under the electric shock, and I hook my finger over his collar pin to keep me close to him.

"Then why don't you?"

He laughs. "I'd never give you the satisfaction, Penelope."

Pride flares up in my chest like a nasty rash. "Yeah, well I wouldn't kiss you either."

"No?"

"Nah. I don't like the taste of whiskey."

He releases my hair, slides his hand down my back, and pulls me toward him by my ass, so his fingers can reach deeper inside of me. I cry out, squirming at the building pressure. Fuck, is this what foreplay is? Because if it is, how does any girl last until penetration?

"Bet you you'll kiss me first."

I laugh, delirium blurring my vision. "Bet you a million dollars my lips would *never* touch yours first."

Another flick on my clit. Another step closer to the edge. When he plunges back into my entrance, it's with two fingers this time. My tunnel burns with my dark satisfaction as it stretches to accommodate him. *I'm too close.*

"You don't have a million dollars," he says, sounding bored.

"Doesn't matter, because I'm not going to lose."

His laugh is so soft against my mouth that in my mindless state, I'm tempted to take out a bank loan then and there. Instead, I throw my head back out of the way of temptation and ride his fingers.

Sparks crackle and pop in my lower core, dimming my vision and spreading a heady lust throughout my veins. When Raphael speaks, I barely hear him over the ringing in my ears.

"You're a bad girl, Penelope."

"Yes," I gasp.

"And you know what happens to bad girls?"

I'm so close to an orgasm I can fucking taste it.

But then Raphael snatches it away, his fingers leaving my panties with a light *snap* of elastic.

Bewildered, my gaze falls from the ceiling to his, just as his damp hand comes to my jaw. He tracks his movement in dark fascination as he spreads my juices over my bottom lip.

"They don't get to come."

And then as if we'd sat down for a business meeting, he rises to his feet. Smooths down his slacks and swipes a thumb over his collar pin before strolling into the crowd. He leaves me with a thumping clit, a frustrated heart, and a new hatred for men with large hands and silky voices.

CHAPTER
Twenty-Nine

Rafe

T HE SUN HANGS LOW above the horizon, the last of its rays stretching over the Pacific and basking St Pius Church with an angelic aura.

It's an ironic sight, because this joint has seen sins better suited to the fiery pits of hell.

I park and bite back a smirk at the sight of both Angelo's Bugatti and Gabe's Harley already lining the side of the road. They're both earlier than me. I suppose there's a first for everything.

I turn up my collar and step out onto frosted gravel. The air crackles with festive anticipation, icy wind, and earthy bonfires as I cut through the graveyard toward the church. I told myself I wasn't going to stop, but my self-control isn't what it used to be, and I slow in front of our parents' joint headstone.

In loving memory of Deacon Alonso Visconti and his devoted wife, Maria.

A bitter laugh leaves my lips in a puff of condensation. Nine years ago, I stood in this exact same spot and believed true love had died with my parents. Only a few months later when I started Sinners Anonymous and Angelo called the hotline with a confession of his own did I find out it had never existed in the first place.

Our father had been fucking someone else all along, then had our mama killed to get her out of the picture. Listening to Angelo's voicemail fill my penthouse suite was the first time I was certain I'd made the right decision by choosing the King of Diamonds instead of the King of Hearts.

Tightening my cufflinks, I spit on the grave and continue into the church.

Mama's buried at the bottom of Angelo's garden, anyway.

Strolling through these rotted oak doors always feels like stepping back in time. Childhood memories chase me down the aisle. At the top of it, Gabe sits on the front pew, and Angelo stands in front of the altar. He looks up from his cell and pins me with a bored expression. "You're never late."

Ah, so he's still pissed about the Kelly thing.

"I was washing my hair," I drawl back, voice as dry as a bone.

Not entirely a lie. I'm sure my hair got plenty washed as I stayed in the shower for longer than usual to fuck my fist. The memory of Penelope's breathless moans against my mouth and her warm, wet pussy around my fingers had been taunting me all day. If I didn't give into the release, I'd have lost my mind.

In an attempt to avoid getting a boner in church—I'm sure there's a tenth circle of hell for that—I dive straight into business.

"Gentleman, before we start, I have a favor to ask you both. Whatever Sinner we choose tonight, I want them to myself."

Gabe remains expressionless as always. "I get Martin O'Hare, then."

"You don't get anything, brother."

I'm met with stony stares and simmering silence.

"Christ," Angelo grunts, raking a hand through his hair. "You're letting your golden retriever loose on Martin, instead of Gabe?"

He means Griff, but I don't rise to the insult. "No, I'll handle Martin myself."

More silence. I let out a sigh. "It's been a chaotic month, all right? Just need some release."

I'm sure my brothers think I want Martin dead so he doesn't get the chance to avenge his brother, which is obviously in part true. But if that was all, I'd have my men take care of him. Truth is, I'm still bitter about what Penelope had said to me in the Preserve while my hand was wrapped around her throat.

He did the same thing to me as you're doing now.

Her words snuffed out my anger like a hard blow to a candle.

In the spirit of not being able to think straight, the thought of another man putting his hands on her, warranted or not, sent a violent impulse through me. Now, I have four men taking shifts outside her apartment while I find the time to get to Martin and do away with him like I did his brother.

"That's a lot of deaths in one month, pretty boy," Gabe murmurs, staring at the wrought-iron grates underneath his boots. His eyes slide up to mine, quiet amusement dancing in them. "You planning on getting those hands dirty?"

I hold my hands out in front of him, turning them from front to back and back again. Then I look down at his busted knuckles. "When I turn into an animal, I'll let you know. Maybe you'll find room for me in your cage."

Angelo lets out a wry breath of amusement. "The day Rafe throws a punch will be the day a baby looks at you and doesn't cry, Gabe." He flicks an impatient glance to his watch and picks up his iPad from the pew. "Let's get this done and over with—got shit to do."

"Rory got you decorating the tree tonight, or something?"

Angelo's eyes me with annoyance. "Tree's been up for weeks. She wants to go to the adoption shelter, just to *say hello* to the strays."

"You're going to be running a zoo by morning, brother."

He sighs. "No shit." He turns the iPad so Gabe and I can see the spreadsheet on the screen. "You know the drill. We've each chosen four callers, and each has been assigned a random number between one and twelve." He nods to me, and I pull the dice from my pocket.

Adrenaline zaps down my spine like a lightning bolt. It's my favorite time of the month, made even better because all the best sins come in around Christmas. It's like people don't want to bring their dirty laundry into the New Year.

With my recent luck, I know it's highly unlikely the dice land on any of my callers, but I have faith that my brothers have chosen wisely.

With a flick of my wrist, I release the die, letting them scatter and bounce over the wooden floorboards and iron grates.

Silence. Then Angelo peers down to inspect them. "Four." He glances at the iPad and scowls. "Fuck's sake."

"What?" I snap, an uneasy feeling trickling into my bloodstream. "What is it?"

He runs a hand over the back of his neck, an expression I've never seen him convey cut into his face. He's...sheepish.

"It's some dude in Tacoma. Killed a cat with a pellet gun."

Gabe slides a wary eye up to him. "And then?"

"And then nothing. That's his sin." We both stare at him like he's lost the fucking plot. He rubs the bridge of his nose and gives a slight shake of his head. "I let Rory choose a sin this month, all right? Jesus," he curses. "What are the odds we'd end up with it?"

I let out a sardonic breath. "One in twelve, idiot. Pretty basic math."

My chest swells with the irony of it all, and I bite out a laugh of disbelief. Of course, the month I really needed to get sadistic would be the month a pathetic victim was chosen. Killing cats is bad, but we're used to dealing with serial killers and rapists. Sure, he could do with getting a bullet in his head, but what I had planned for him feels like overkill now.

Outside, darkness has swept over the cliff, bringing icy sideways rain with it. I tuck my chin into my collar and join my brothers under the weeping willow tree.

Angelo lights up a cigarette and blows out smoke into the quivering branches above us, before passing it to Gabe.

"How many men until we get to Dante?"

Gabe inhales, the cherry of the cigarette glowing an angry red. "Too many. At this rate, he'll get to ring in the New Year." As he passes the cigarette to me, his glare bores into my soul. "Next time, rocket warhead."

I huff out a dry laugh, before filling my lungs with chemicals. Sitting at Cas's desk in Whiskey Under the Rocks and swiping all the pieces off his chessboard feels like a lifetime ago. Man, I was so patient back then.

I pass the cigarette back to Angelo and turn to Gabe. "Any update on the cunts who hit Lucky Cat?"

"Dealt with it. As much as I hate to admit it, your lackey was right. It was a random attack." He cracks his knuckles. "Wanna know how they chose your casino?"

"No," I say dryly.

But he tells me anyway. "Pinned a map of Vegas to the wall and chucked a dart at it."

Through a haze of smoke, Angelo's amused gaze heats my cheek. "How terribly unlucky."

I run a palm over my jaw, my shoulders going rigid. Sucking in a slow, damp breath, I amp up the indifference in my tone. "I own most of the casinos in Vegas; the odds were always going to be stacked against me."

But I don't believe a single syllable coming out of my mouth, and I don't even know why I'm trying to kid myself anymore, either.

As Gabe takes the cigarette from Angelo, he stills. His eyes slide over my shoulder, and something lava-like sweeps through his expression.

"She's always there. Waiting."

What?

I glance behind me and see Wren standing under the bus shelter. She's wrapped up in a big puffer jacket, four plastic bags slumped at her feet.

"She never accepts a ride."

My jaw ticks as I remember the sound of Gabe's fist hitting the table last night. His quiet threat about rusty pen knives. "Were you trying to get her into the passenger seat or the trunk?"

"Wren doesn't accept lifts," Angelo says sharply. "She doesn't get into cars. And you"—he grinds the cigarette under the heel of his wingtip—"are going to leave the girl alone."

Gabe presses his lips together and glares at Wren for a few more seconds, before turning his back to us and storming over to his Harley without another word. The engine roars to life, headlights sweep over headstones in the graveyard, and he's gone.

Angelo mutters something under his breath. "I think I'll wait around for a while."

The insinuation drips from the end of his sentence. *Until Wren gets on the bus.*

I nod tightly, before fishing my car keys out of my pocket. "Tell your wife Chef Marco is making her favorite chocolate lava cake tonight, so if she gets bored of petting abandoned ferrets, you guys should swing by—"

Angelo slices me off with a hand on my arm. My gaze drops to his grip, then up to his softened expression. He holds his other hand out in front of him, and I feel a knot form in the base of my throat.

I swallow it. Hold my brother's eye as I put my hand out beside his. It's still. *Convincing.* Seemingly satisfied, Angelo nods and turns his attention back to Wren.

"We'll be onboard tonight. Rory and Tayce want to hang out with Penny, anyway."

As I head back to my car, my eyes find the twinkling lights of *Signora Fortuna* over the water. A dark glee shivers down my spine and into my groin.

If I have to wait to take my frustrations out on a man, I'll pass the time by playing with a certain red-head, instead.

CHAPTER
Thirty

Rafe

A S THE SHUTTLE BOAT bumps against the yacht's fenders, I can just about make out Laurie's shadowy silhouette standing on the swim platform. She holds an umbrella over her head and a folder clutched to her chest.

"Well, isn't this a five-star greeting," I drawl, taking the umbrella handle from her and holding it above our heads. "You shooting for a raise, or something?"

She grins up at me. "I mean, I wouldn't say *no* to a raise."

I laugh and fall into step with her as we head down the side deck. "How's the sea sickness?"

"I've got it down to one cookie-tossing per shift, so there's that."

"Perfect. Not looking to go back to Vegas, are you?"

Her gaze skims up to the underside of the umbrella. "And miss this beautiful weather? Here." She holds the folder out. "I need you to sign off on the budget for the staff Christmas party."

"You know the rule, Laurie. There's no budget for staff parties."

"Good, because I just bought myself a new Audi as a Christmas present and stuck it on the company card."

"Dammit. I better take the one I bought you back to the show-room, then."

She opens her mouth and closes it again, settling for a sideways glare instead of a witty response. While she's joking about the

Audi, she's not sure if I am. A valid thought, considering last year I flew her to New York and let her choose whatever she wanted from Tiffany's.

Amused, I snap the umbrella shut and hold open the door to the casino for her. "Anything else?"

She glances around the casino to the servers wiping down tables and restocking the bar. "Uh, yeah. There's a...brown stain on the carpet in the sky lounge. The cleaners can't lift it with domestic products. Need me to call a specialist in?"

My attention is diverted over her shoulder, where Penelope dries champagne flutes behind the bar. She's glaring at the rag like her life depends on it, but I don't miss the shells of her ears turning red.

Fucking Gabe. Clearly he's not a pro with the scouring brush. I pin Laurie with a polite smile and tell her, "I'll handle it."

She nods, crosses through to the double doors, and jabs a finger at me. "White leather trim, heated seats. Got it?"

I wink at her and watch her disappear. This is why Laurie gets shopping trips at Tiffany's and premium cars. She doesn't ask questions.

"Boss?" I shift my gaze to find Anna. She drops a box of Christmas decorations and saunters over. "New uniforms are in. What do you think?" She punctuates her question with a twirl.

My eyes fall absent-mindedly down her body and then over to Penelope. She's got her back to me now, bending over to restock the mini fridge. My jaw tightens at the sight of her thong outline in those tight pants. Christ. How does this girl make pants and a shirt look sexy? Maybe I'll get Laurie to order branded trash can liners and make the staff wear them instead.

She called Sinners Anonymous at four a.m. last night. Twice. Both times, her breathy silence crackled down the line, through my MacBook speakers, and tugged on my dick. I'd had too much liquor to drive over to her place and flash my headlights against her window, so I settled for sitting behind my desk in wait, fists clenched on either side of my whiskey glass. I was sure she'd call to moan about me bringing her to the crest of orgasm then snatching it away at the last minute, but no dice. Then again, she's never actually called the hotline to moan about anything of importance, anyway. Only trivial things, like her running out of conditioner or how her neighbor farted in her living room but it's too cold to open the windows.

I make half-hearted pleasantries with Anna, then stroll past the bar just as Penelope spins around with an empty crate. She drops it on the bar, meets my eye, and smirks.

Well, that wasn't the reaction I was expecting. Not after I caught her red-handed helping Rory card count, and subsequently wiped her pussy juices along her mouth. She licks her bottom lip, as if looking at me makes the memory resurface.

Fuck. I'm going to have to double-lock the door when I get into my office.

Aware of Anna and Claudia's eyes on my back, I swipe a steadying finger over my collar pin and flash her a pleasant smile.

"Hello, Penelope."

"Hello, *boss*," she replies, matching my plastic tone.

My attention drops to her hand, which is now sliding across the bar. When it reaches the salt shaker, she gives it a hard tap. It falls over, salt granules scattering over the surface. "*Oops.*"

On instinct, the line of my shoulders snaps taught. I run a palm over my jaw to conceal my initial annoyance, then force a mask of indifference.

How did I forget so easily? Last night, I told her my biggest secret—I'm superstitious. I suppose the girl could have gotten anything out of me when I was knuckle-deep in her pussy, and now I'm going to make her pay for it.

Our eyes clash. The simmer of irritation bubbles into something more electric. I haven't felt this alive all day.

"I'll have a Smuggler's Club brought down to your office right away, boss," Dan says, emerging from the stock room and slinging a rag over his shoulder.

My eyes never leave Penelope's.

"Make it a vodka."

CHAPTER
Thirty-One

Penny

"YOU TOLD ME YOU were going straight, Little P."

Nico's voice touches my back from the other side of the bar and I sigh into the cocktail shaker. Last night, as I scurried through the cave bar trying to make the most of Raphael's phony ten-second head start, I caught Nico's eye from the poker table. He looked at me, then to his cousin and back again, and by the spark of annoyance in his gaze, I knew this conversation was imminent.

"I'm as straight as a ruler these days."

"There's nothing straight about teaching Rory how to card count."

I brave looking at his reflection in the mirror behind the bar, hoping my angelic smile will soften his edges.

It doesn't.

"And you better have kept my name out of it."

Now *that's* a promise I won't break. "C'mon, Nico. That's a given."

Ignoring the heat of his eyes on me, I pour rum, sugar syrup, and mint over ice, glancing at the recipe I've written on the inside of my wrist to make sure I don't fuck it up. Turning around with the cocktail shaker in hand, I try my angelic smile on Nico again.

You know; just in case he didn't see it the first time. "Fancy being a guinea pig for my first-ever mojito? It's on the house."

He stares at me. "I'm a Visconti. Everything's on the house."

"Christ, how this yacht makes any money I'll never—"

"Listen." Nico cuts me off, leaning his forearms on the bar to close the gap between us. "Rafe gave you this job as a favor to me, and after last night's stunt, you're lucky to still be employed today. I know all you girls think Rafe is this..."

He strums his inked fingers on the bar, summoning the word.

If he says gentleman, I swear I'll—

"Gentleman."

Sigh.

"But just because he's nice and smiles a lot, don't be fooled. He's still..." More strumming. "He's still Raphael Visconti."

I haven't been entirely untruthful. For the most part, I have gone straight. Lifting Blake's wallet aside, the only man I've played games with since returning to the Coast has been Raphael. Hell, every interaction we have is a game. Every time he's near me, I feel like I'm standing beside a roulette wheel, eyes closed, about to bet my entire soul on black.

My eyes dart toward the door of the casino, like they have done every two minutes for the past hour. I woke up this afternoon in a state of delirium, high off having Raphael's hands in my panties and his damning confession in my ear.

Fuck Martin O'Hare and his disgusting brother; Raphael admitting he's superstitious has been all I can think about. And not only is he superstitious, he thinks I'm bad luck. *Me.* The girl with the necklace and a history of making it out of sure-fire deaths alive.

And fuck, if I'm not going to use that to my advantage in all games going forward.

Well, that was my plan, until Raphael strolled through the casino door, took one look at my shit-eating grin, and ordered a vodka. Now, I'm not feeling so smug.

A slimy drawl pulls my attention away from liquor-fueled kisses and million-dollar bets. "If Rafe fires you, you can always come and work for me, baby."

Benny. He slides up to Nico's side and delivers his sleazy line to my chest.

I slam down the cocktail shaker and glare at him. "What tit are you offering a job to, Benny? Left or right?"

His gaze skims up to mine, mischief accompanied by a lop-sided grin. "Two for the price of one. What'd you say?"

Nico mutters something under his breath and turns to his cellphone.

"You know every drink you order off me tonight will be spat in, don't you?" I snap back.

He licks his lips. Winks. "Adds to the flavor."

Jesus.

I've never liked Benny. Even when we were kids, he was always just Nico's asshole older brother. Always fighting, always disappearing into rooms at the Visconti Grand with various girls. I doubt he's got more than three brain cells rattling around in that head. It's probably too full of boobs, brawls, and bets.

Just before he opens his mouth to add another layer of sleaze to the conversation, a hand smacks him upside the head. Laurie materializes behind him, an annoyed expression on her face. "Stop harassing my staff, Benedicto."

"Fuck me again and I'll think about it." His eyes trail her ass as she moves toward the stockroom.

"Last time I fucked you, I had to change my number because you wouldn't stop blowing up my phone," she throws over her shoulder.

I burst out laughing and Benny's hard gaze comes to me. "That's not true," he grunts, sliding off the bar stool. "*Cazzo...*"

He storms off after Laurie and I turn my attention back to Nico. "Your brother is a dick."

"He has his moments." He produces a wallet from his pocket. Immediately, I know it's not his, because the initials BV glint in gold under the recessed lights. "Here." He flips it open and tugs out a sheaf of bills. "Call it compensation."

I tut, but slide the money into my bra regardless. "You're a bad influence, Nico."

"Do as I say, not as I do, Little P," he retorts, a twinkle in his storm-gray eyes. "Seriously, though. I know you said you didn't want to work in Hollow, but if you do get fired, I've got the perfect job for you."

"I won't bullshit you. I'm *very* bad at bar work." I flash him the recipe scrawled on my wrist in smudged ink. "See?"

"I can tell by the color of that mojito. They aren't meant to be brown; you know?" He slips off the stool and raps a knuckle against the bar. "It's something I think you'll find a lot more interesting than hospitality." He glances at his cell in his hand. "I'll see you at the staff Christmas party all right? We can discuss it more then."

With a lazy wave over his shoulder, he puts his phone to his ear and disappears into the next room.

I chew over his words. What the hell could I possibly do in Hollow that isn't hospitality? The whole town is one big cave full of poker games and parties. The posh academy is there too, obviously, but I didn't even finish school myself, so I doubt I could work in one.

Before I can put too much weight to it, the bar phone rings. Absent-mindedly, I lift the receiver and tuck it between my ear and shoulder.

"Yes?"

Raphael's velvet drawl trickles down the line and caresses my cheek. "Ah, just the little arsonist I was looking for."

My heart forgoes its next beat, and I clutch the receiver in an attempt to remain nonchalant. "Another vodka to your office, boss?" I say sweetly. "Or some sage to ward away the bad spirits?"

A huff of amusement crackles down the line. "No, Penelope. Just yourself."

Click.

Stomach clenching, I stare at the mouthpiece, before putting it back on the hook with a defeated sigh.

Raphael wants to see me in his office? This can't be good.

The unrelenting storm rocks the cream hallways and rain taps on the portholes like fingers desperate for my attention. Each room I cut through grows quieter in sound and louder with nervous expectation.

Outside Raphael's office door, I take a steadying breath and knock. No answer. I knock again with a little more flair, but the silence is unwavering.

Growing irritated, I shove my shoulder against the door and immediately regret my haste. The air feels different in here. Too cool for comfort; too silent for peace. From his leather chair behind his desk, Raphael's presence seeps from his perfect pores and winds around my neck and wrists like silk-clad chains.

Self-preservation makes me grip the door.

The imaginary *hiss* of a roulette table and the *click-clack* of dice make me kick it shut with the heel of my bare foot.

"You wanted to see me, boss?"

Lit only by the fragmented moonlight fighting its way through the rain-stained glass, the hard lines of Raphael's silhouette are motionless. Only his gaze moves as it slides up from the golden poker chip in his hand to my face. It's ink black. Immoral. Suddenly, the silence has a heat to it, eating through the frosty air and blistering my skin.

I curl my toes into the plush carpet to keep myself from folding.

"Would you like to play a game with me, Penelope?"

A *game*?

"What game?"

"Heads or tails. The classics are always the best, aren't they?"

His eyes flash with wicked amusement, while mine fight to convey indifference.

I move one step forward, closing the gap between me and danger. "And the wager?"

My gaze tracks his hand as it reaches for the crystal tumbler on the desk. Both the clear liquid and the face of his wristwatch glint as he takes a sip. "You win, I kiss you. I win, you kiss me."

My mind dislikes the idea with a passion. With a one-in-two odds and a million dollars of non-existent money on the line, I'd be an idiot to agree, no matter how hot the pendant around my neck sizzles.

My body, on the other hand...

The space between my thighs beats with the idea of having his lips against mine. My mouth waters with the thrill of taking such a risky gamble.

With a reckless haze sweeping through my bones and spurring me on, I place my hands on his desk and lean over it.

"What's the catch?"

His stare is hot and unapologetic as it tracks the curve of my throat and settles on my necklace. "No catch."

"Then tails never fails, baby."

It's out my mouth and wading through the thick air between us before I can stop it.

He continues to stare at my necklace, a slow, devilish smirk stretching across his lips. Those dimples deepen with mischief and something uncouth.

My heart beats on the double as he pulls a penny from his slacks. Blood *swooshes* in my ears as he balances it on the back of his thumb.

He looks at me quickly, and when he *flicks*, I feel it against my clit.

Everything slows except my pulse. *One revolution. Two revolutions. Three.* I can count every spin of the coin as it falls to the desk.

The clattering of copper against wood is deafening.

It lands between the glass tumbler and a paperweight. Holding my breath, I lean over and look at it. Raphael doesn't bother, he only leans back in his chair, runs two fingers over his lips, and studies me for my reaction.

Tails.

The cocktail of excitement and relief floods through me so violently it buckles my knees and buzzes in my fingertips.

Laughing maniacally, I push off the desk and stroll around the office like I own it. I don't know what I'm high off of; the thought of becoming a mushroom millionaire, or discovering what Raphael's tongue tastes like.

Hell, who am I kidding?

"A *million dollars*. Whew. Maybe I'll buy a yacht of my own, anchor it right over there—" I gesture to the pitch-black ocean beyond the window "—and point a laser beam into your office every time you're trying to work." My hand glides down the silky curtain. "Or I'll buy up every collar pin in the world, so you have to go back to wearing boring old ties."

I turn around and meet Raphael's gaze. He's watching me with a hint of amusement, turning his chair to follow me as I prance around his dimly lit office.

"Where do you want to kiss me, then? I suppose we could do it upstairs in the casino so everyone knows you're a massive loser. Or..." I turn back to the French doors and press my hand up against the rain-streaked glass. Let out a dramatic sigh. "We could do it out in the rain. You know, like the scene in *The Notebook*?"

"Never seen it."

"Christ, then you've never lived." I turn around again, expectancy written over my face. "Well?"

He digs his heel into the carpet and rolls his chair a few feet away from his desk. His hand thumps the edge of it twice. "Up here."

"What?"

He cocks his head, the punchline to his joke burning bright behind his eyes. "Do I look like the type of man that gets on his knees, Penelope?"

"I-I don't understand."

He regards me for a few beats, as if drinking in my confusion to quench his own enjoyment. Then he feigns a look of surprise.

"You didn't think I was going to kiss you on your *lips*, did you?" He shakes his head while he unbuttons his cuffs. "Why, that'd mean I owed you a million dollars."

My ears ring, then the realization settles like dust on my skin, cooling the fire beneath it. My limbs grow heavy, and my brain fogs.

"You said you'd kiss me," I whisper, too numb to care how whiny my tone is.

"And I will."

"B-but, you said there was no catch."

He frowns. "There isn't a catch. I said, if you win, I kiss you, and if I win, you kiss me." A sinful glint heats his eyes. "I didn't say *where*."

Heart palpitating, I step back and press my shoulder blades against the glass. The condensation does little to cool my blood or bring a rational argument to my brain. Surely, he doesn't mean...*down there?* My gaze slides up and clashes with Raphael's, and we enter a new battle—one of wills.

I stare at him.

He stares at me.

Since I stepped on this Coast and stomped down those stairs, Raphael and I have been playing a game of chess. Both of us play dirty, and neither of us likes to lose. Now, I've found myself alone on the board without so much as a fucking pawn to protect me.

What options do I have? I either walk over to his desk or I walk out the door. And if I choose the latter, not only will the defeat eat me up from the inside out, but this arrogant asshole wins twice over.

So, I take the six steps over to Raphael's desk. His eyes darken to something more sinister as they track my movements. I wonder if he thought I'd choose the door instead of calling his bluff?

As my ass slides over the edge of his desk, a rush of nerves scrapes through me, settling into a wet heat between my thighs. My breaths are louder than the storm beating on the windows, and with every tense second that drips by, they grow more ragged.

Raphael, on the other hand, is the dictionary definition of cool. He leans back, brings his vodka glass to his lips, and clinically assesses the sight in front of him over its rim. Finally, he sets the drink next to my right thigh, the cold glass singeing me through my work pants.

He licks his lips. Meets my defiant stare. Then, with a sigh that suggests following through with this bet is as exciting as filing his taxes, he leans forward.

My vision dims as he runs his flat palms up the fronts of my thighs and comes to a stop at my hips. He hooks two index fingers into my waistband, pinching my pants and the band of my thong together. He paints on a charity fundraiser-worthy smile that's at odds with the sinner that lives behind his eyes.

"May I?"

It's not a question. Not really. If it were, he would have waited for a response before roughly tugging off my bottoms. They slide down my legs like butter, but only because the shock of it made me throw my palms behind me and arch my back.

Raphael takes his time sliding my pants over my feet. He's still and expressionless as he untangles my thong from the fabric and holds it between his thumb and forefinger in the space between us. My pulse flickers at the sight of him *holding* the scrap of lace. Like he's just had the inconvenience of finding it in his dry cleaning.

He rakes an eye over the thong. Swallows. "This is highly inappropriate for work, Penelope."

The tautness in his tone only makes my skin burn hotter.

In silence, he straightens my pants. Folds them in half on his lap and half again, then drapes them over the edge of the desk beside me. Then, he starts to do the same with my thong. Every slow, silky movement he makes is another second of torture endured. It's as if he's avoiding the inevitable, either as a punishment to me or to himself.

The anticipation is making me dizzy, and I can't stand another second of it.

Dropping back to my elbows, I part my thighs. Through a half-lidded gaze, I watch as Raphael stills. He doesn't look up from my work pants, and the delicate fabric of my thong disappears inside his fist.

Eventually, without moving his head, he slides his gaze between my legs. His eyes darken and he runs a hand down his throat.

"You're…" his jaw ticks. "Natural."

Despite the maddening lust crackling in my lower core, annoyance fills me. I keep it *well maintained* down there, but there's definitely no baldness going on. I don't know how he didn't realize when he was fingering me in the shadows of Whiskey Under the Rocks.

"Not quite. Problem?"

He lets out a soft, bitter laugh, like he thinks I'm a fucking idiot.

"I'm not one of the little boys you're used to fucking, Penelope."

Well, I've only fucked two boys, neither of which did *this*. The reminder of how much older he is than me is intimidating, and my thighs twitch to clamp shut.

He clears his throat and rolls his chair so he's between my legs. The sleeves of his suit jacket graze against my inside seams, making the walls of my stomach tighten.

I'm burning up. Squirming under the intensity of his gaze, under the burden of the silence. I turn my attention to the ceiling in an attempt to slow my breathing.

When Raphael speaks, his hot breath tickling my clit makes my eyes damn near roll to the back of my head. *He's so fucking close.*

"You're wet already," he says, tone void of emotion.

Jesus, what's with all these observational statements? Is this another method of torture I haven't heard about?

I grind my molars together and feign boredom. "I'm twenty-one; I'm always wet."

A vodka-tinged hiss crackles against my clit. *Christ.* "Wet, for *who*, Penelope?"

I lap up the annoyance in his tone. After the dirty tactic he used to get me into this position, he should feel at least a fraction of my discomfort. "Any hot man that steps onto the boat."

He mutters something in Italian under his breath, then grabs both my ankles and forces my feet up onto the desk, so my heels press into the backs of my thighs. The movement stuns me, slides my back half a foot up the wooden surface, and sends papers cascading to the floor.

I hope they were important.

Balling my fists against my sides, I squeeze my shoulder blades together and attempt to ride out the warm flush spreading across every inch of my skin. Down south, a cool breeze combined with hot breaths reminds me how exposed I am.

Without warning, his mouth clamps down on my clit, his tongue flattens over the bundle of nerves there, and he *sucks*.

Slowly. Sloppily. It's a move so at odds with his silky image that it makes it ten times hotter. My blood burns so hot it turns to steam, sizzling through my body and contorting it in a way only lust can. My spine bends and my hips tilt. My throat opens to let out a strangled gasp.

And then he pulls away.

It's instinct that fuels me to bolt upright and grab his hair to hold him in place. He tilts his chin, my juices glistening in the cleft of it, and meets my gaze with a crazed one of his own.

He licks his lips. "Yes?"

I glare at him, barely able to think over the thumping in my pussy. His breathing slows with every silent second and his eyes grow hotter with a challenge.

"Something you want to say, Penelope?" he rasps.

Yeah. I want to beg him not to stop. I want to beg him to toss that coin again and hope I win another round. But none of that will leave my lips without a gun pressed to my head. Because all of that requires *begging*. He's already winning; I'm naked from the waist down on his desk, for Christ's sake.

I need to level the playing field.

Maybe it's the lust driving me insane, or maybe I'm bitter about him stealing two orgasms from me within the span of twenty-four hours, so I do what he did to me.

His gaze tracks my hand as I unwind it from his hair and slide it over my pubic bone. I cup my pussy. Realization slowly sweeps over his face, snuffing all the triumph out from behind his eyes. When I curl two fingers inside of myself, an embarrassing *squelching* sound bringing attention to my wetness, he grips the inside of my thigh and watches with fascination.

"Penelope..."

"You're a bad man, Raphael," I say, deepening my fingers in my entrance. "And you know what happens to bad men?"

His shoulders go rigid, and with a steadying breath, he reluctantly brings his eyes to mine. Recognizing his own words from last night, a demonic smirk creeps onto his lips.

He knows what's coming.

He doesn't push me away when I put my free hand on the base of his neck. Doesn't jerk his head when I pull my two fingers from my pussy and slowly rub my juices over his bottom lip.

His groan is guttural, cooling my knuckles as I coat his mouth with my wetness. Christ, I'll never be able to look in the mirror and attempt to convince myself I'm a lady ever again. It's so animalistic. So depraved. Something only maddening lust and spite could drive someone to do.

"They never win," I whisper.

With a flash of his citrine ring, he grabs my wrist, halting my movements as I trace his bottom lip again. He holds me there, then with a lazy, half-lidded stare, he watches me as he slides my fingers into his mouth, sucking all of my juices clean.

In my mindless state, I grind out a moan at the sight. He looks as depraved as I feel. Like the bespoke tailoring and the gold and the perfect haircut are no longer thick enough to hide the monster that lives within. Once he licks my fingers clean, he captures his bottom lip in his mouth and smooths down the front of his slacks.

"Go back to work, Penelope."

While his face is expressionless, his tone sounds almost defeated. I think I won that game. Didn't I?

Or maybe we're both just losers.

Regardless, I don't protest. If I don't get out from the darkness of this office now, I fear I may never see the light again. Heart and clit thrumming to an off-kilter beat, I slide off the desk and pick up my pants.

My gaze drops to Raphael's fist clenched against his thigh. The trim of my lace panties peeks out from the top of it.

"Can I...?"

His grip tightens. "No." I flick my gaze up to his. "They're mine now."

Intoxication swirls through me, sweeping all sarcastic retorts away. Instead, I pull on my pants, sans my thong, knowing the dampness between my thighs will stay with me for the rest of my shift.

I move to the door on unsteady legs, willing myself not to look back, because I'm not sure I'll be able to handle what I see sitting behind the desk.

Out in the light of the bridge, I let out a shaky exhale.

Behind me, the office door locks.

Twice.

CHAPTER
Thirty-Two

Rafe

MY CAR IS CLOAKED by that type of stillness that only exists after three-am. Outside, the first flakes of snow settle on the bonnet, and frost spreads like spider veins along the windshield. But inside, heat blooms from Penelope's sleeping body and fills the space with a drowsy warmth.

When I flashed my headlights against her living room window at one a.m., it was with a vengeance. I'd spent the entire evening with a throbbing cock, and all I could think about was what I'd started in my office, and if there was enough room to finish it on my back seat. Now I know what her pussy tastes like, the urge to taste it again was maddening. Her wet thong around my cock wasn't going to cut it, because that shit she said about always being wet just pissed me off. I'd planned on punishing her for making me dwell on it all night, but then she emerged from her apartment building holding two cups of hot cocoa, her pajamas peeking out from underneath her puffer jacket. She slid into my car, handed me a cup in silence, then drank hers while staring sleepily at the dash.

The ache moved from my groin to my chest and filled the black hole there. It was heavy with a perverse satisfaction, and for once, it didn't stem from winning a petty bet. She was comfortable here, in my car, beside me, her hair piled on top of her head and her face make-up free. It was with a sickening sweetness that I realized she sought out the warmth of my car to do the most vulnerable thing a human can do: sleep.

My satisfaction was tinged with unease, but still, I drove around Devil's Dip with the heater on full blast until she was snoring under the blanket I'd bought her. I went down to the port to check on reconstruction efforts, before driving over to Hollow to discuss New Year's Eve plans with Cas and Benny. Now, I'm parked in front of my father's old church, fighting fires over email. The brightness of my MacBook screen is turned down as far as it goes and I'm trying not to slam on the keys.

I'd laugh in disbelief if I was certain it wouldn't wake Penelope up. If my business partners could see me now, running my multi-billion-dollar company hunched over my steering wheel, they'd think I'd lost the plot.

I have.

My cell buzzes on the center console, disrupting the silence. With a cautious glance in Penelope's direction, I snatch it up to mute it, but freeze when I see the name on the screen.

Gabe.

My brother never calls me. He doesn't text me, either. Our iMessage history is all blue boxes and read receipts. I text, he turns up, and that's the way it's always been.

Despite my heart racing, I slow my movements to get out of the car. I shut the door behind myself with a soft *click*, and crunch over fresh snow to get to the edge of the cliff.

"What have you done?"

"Why are you whispering?"

I roll my eyes at the Pacific. "It's four a.m., brother. People whisper at this time of night. What's wrong with you?"

The line goes quiet for a moment. I turn around and, through the sleet, see Griffin slipping out of his armored Sedan. He creeps toward me and jerks his chin, silently asking if there's an issue. I dismiss him with a shake of my head.

"What do you need, Gabe? Medical attention? A lawyer? A shoulder to cry on?" I run my hand through my hair. "Fuck, please don't let it be a shoulder to cry on."

"Meet me where we strung up Old MacDonald."

The line goes dead.

I stare down at my cell until it locks itself due to inactivity. Is *he serious*? Growing up, Old MacDonald was our nickname for the creepy groundskeeper at Devil's Coast Academy. We always thought there was something off about him, but it was confirmed when, one Sunday, he slid into our father's confession box and admitted he'd touched up one of the school girls underneath the bleachers. Naturally, we chose him as our sinner of the month. We strung him up from an old oak tree in Hollow, but only after Angelo had snapped his neck.

He'd wanted to know what it felt like.

Glancing through Griffin's windshield, I jab a finger in the direction of Hollow. He nods, and his car engine comes to life.

I drive slowly, only taking my hand off Penelope's blanket-clad thigh when we reach Grim Reaper road. Little more than a strip of asphalt cut into the curve of the cliff, it's a bastard of a route in optimal conditions, let alone during the first snow of the season. I curse Gabe under my breath for making me descend it in the middle of the night with Penelope in the car. The road tapers off into rocky terrain and ravines, and as the oak tree comes into view, I kill the engine and let out a quiet hiss.

What the fuck are you playing at, Gabe? I'm just about to ask him via text when a shadow shifting between the thick brush lining the road catches my eye.

Gabe strolls into the beam of my headlights, shirtless and covered in blood.

Unease quickens my pulse, and I grab the Glock from my side door pocket and jump out the car.

"*Dio mio, cazzo. Cosa è successo?*" *What happened?*

His lazy gaze drops to my gun. "Not mine," is all he grunts, before disappearing back into the bushes.

My breath of annoyance comes out in a white puff and mingles with the falling snow. Keeping my eyes trained on Penelope sleeping on the other side of the windshield, I walk back to my car. I left the door open, because I knew if I shut it, I'd slam it. I drop to my haunches in the driver's seat and study her.

The red strands have escaped her hair tie and fan over the pillow like a copper halo. My gaze sweeps over her pale skin—the perfect pink from the warmth of her heater—and then drops to her plump pout, parted in sweet serenity.

Fuck's sake. A tug-of-war plays out inside my chest, a tussle between logic and superstition.

Logic tells me a million dollars is nothing.

Superstition tells me to kick her out to the curb and drive off.

I settle for wiping the hot cocoa stain off her chin with my thumb and tucking the blanket tighter around her.

Cranking up her heated seat another notch, I close the door quietly and move on to the car behind. Griff's unamused expression comes into view as he rolls down the glass.

"Are we filming the new *Blair Witch Project*?"

I ignore his smart-ass mouth and toss my keys into his lap. "Watch my car."

He stares at me for a few beats. It's the type of stare that conveys he's sick of my shit and wishes I'd move back to Vegas, where the only things he had to worry about were white-collared criminals and the occasional opportunistic idiot.

But it's the dick in the passenger seat that speaks first. "Watch your car, or your girl?"

My eyes slide up to meet Blake's shit-eating grin. You know what? The kid's been strumming on my last nerve far too long. I round the car, tug open the door and grab his collar. His gasp skitters over my sleeve, and I'd be lying if I said I didn't enjoy the fear in his eyes.

"Breathe near the girl and it'll be the last breath you take," I say calmly.

Griffin's bewildered stare burns into my back as I follow my wayward brother into the bushes.

He's waiting in a clearing, puffing on a cigarette. I shoot a look of disgust at his torso, with hard muscle and ink painted red. I take a step to the side, not wanting to get that shit on my new wool car coat. "Clothes just really don't appeal to you, huh?"

He doesn't reply. We walk under snowfall and heavy silence, the light from my phone and Gabe's occasional gruff warning, "Tree stump. Root. Ditch," guiding me. When the trees taper off on the lip of a steep ravine, my wingtips come to a slow stop.

"I'm not going down there."

"Worried you'll ruin your suit?"

"Yes, in fact."

Gabe's gaze flashes black. "You'll walk down it, or I'll sling you over my shoulder and carry you down like a little bitch."

"Remind me how we're related again?"

He grunts in amusement, and, probably knowing he'd get a swift punch to the nuts if he tried to fire-man carry me down the side of the bank, he starts his descent.

Italian tailoring be damned. My leather shoes sink into icy slush, and my coat pills as it catches on branches on the way down. At the bottom, we turn right, following the frozen ravine up-stream. Straight ahead of us, the mouth of a cave grows wider with every step until its black void engulfs us.

The darkness comes with a new damp chill. I turn the brightness up on my phone light and follow the sound of Gabe's heavy footsteps as he plows ahead of me. We duck under a low dip in the ceiling, and when I straighten up on the other side, heavy rock music floats through the darkness and touches the frozen shells of my ears.

"If you've decided to get into the quirky entertainment space without consulting me, I'm going to be pissed, brother."

A turn of a corner, then a warm glow washes away the darkness. There's a heat to it, and an ominous flicker as it dances against the walls of the cave. As we cross into a cavernous space, I realize it's coming from a bonfire.

Despite the heat, my blood runs cold.

"What the fuck, Gabe?"

Wordlessly, my brother strolls around the bonfire and drops down on a battered sofa pressed up against a craggy wall.

"It's technically Dip. The entrance is just in Hollow."

My lids fall shut. The man is out of his mind if he thinks I'm talking about territory lines and not the dude gagged and bound to a chair on the other side of the fire.

Unbuttoning my jacket, I sweep the surprise from my mind and flip into fix-it mode. I'm well-versed in damage control, especially when it comes to my idiot brothers. Only last month did I have to fly back from Vegas to sort out the mess Angelo made when he blew up Uncle Al's car.

Step one—assess the damage. I run a finger over my collar pin and rake an objective eye over the cave. The cracked leather sofa my brother is sitting on. The towering metal locker with a lock and chain securing its handles. The sweaty man withering in ropes.

His gaze meets mine, desperation tinging the fear within it. That's the thing about my nice suits and fresh shaves. They do exactly what they are meant to: fool people into believing I'm a gentleman.

I look away.

"It's too late to pay him off. Just put a bullet in his head; the bears will have his body by morning."

With a lazy smirk, Gabe leans back and lights up another cigarette. "Not done with him."

"What the fuck do you need me for, then?" We stare at each other, the rock music bouncing off the walls and pounding in my ears. "Turn that shit off," I snap. "Can't hear myself think."

Gabe kicks the subwoofer at his feet, and the din crackles to a stop. "That's your problem. You *think*."

I ignore his usual jibe about me sitting behind a desk for forty-percent of my day, and sweep a hand over the cave. "Why here?"

With a grunt, Gabe tucks the cigarette into the crook of his mouth and moves toward his captive. I don't know how long he's been at my brother's mercy, but judging by the limp hang of his head and the amount of blood on my brother's torso, it won't be much longer.

He flinches when Gabe's body casts a black shadow over his shoulders, but he doesn't have the energy to do much else. That changes when Gabe yanks his head back, pulls the cigarette from his lips, and sticks it into the man's eye. Suddenly, he musters up the energy to fill the cave with a deafening scream.

My brother's crazed gaze comes to mine. "I like the acoustics."

Christ.

I've never wondered where he gets his darkness from; it runs through all three of us like an extra strand of DNA. No, I've only wondered why it is that I conceal the sadism. Angelo tried to run from it, but Gabe decided a few years ago he'd dive head first into his, as if desperate to find out what's at the bottom.

"Who is he?"

"One of us."

I frown. "A made man?"

"A Visconti. One of our distant cousins from Sicily. Dante shipped over a boatload of them to help him out."

I run my tongue over my teeth, annoyance flaring inside of me. "You're not sticking to the plan, Gabe. We said *subtle*. This doesn't feel like a chess move."

His face is expressionless as he stares into the fire. "Chess bores me, and bad things happen when I'm bored."

I let out a sardonic huff. With my mind drifting out of the cave and up to Penelope in the car, I smooth a hand down my shirt and cut to the point. "I thought you needed help. Did you only bring me down here for a family reunion?"

"No, for some relief."

"What?"

He nods to the back of the man's head. "Your perfect life has gone to shit. Knock yourself out."

We look at each other over angry flames and a sweat-drenched forehead as realization fills me.

"You're serious."

He only stares back.

Amusement and disbelief tilt the corners of my lips; I wipe both off with my palm. "You're deranged, but you already knew that." When he doesn't reply, I hold up my hands, flaunting my unblemished knuckles; the only part of my facade I can't peel off at the end of the day. "Not really my thing, brother."

He nods. "I haven't forgotten, pretty boy." His footsteps echo off the craggy ceiling as he crosses over to the chest, yanks a key from the back pocket of his jeans, and cracks it open.

Torn between disgust and morbid fascination, I walk over and assess the rows of tools. At first glance, it appears to be a pretty standard torture kit, but when I pick things up to feel the weight of them in my palm, I notice...modifications.

Axes with three blades. Nunchucks wrapped in electrical wire. With a small shake of my head, I look up at my brother. "Really?"

He doesn't respond.

I run my finger over the blade of the meat cleaver. Its handle has been removed and replaced by the body of an electrical screwdriver. As my mind works to piece together the mechanics of it, something sour and venomous seeps out from underneath the disbelief, rising to the surface of my skin and settling there.

I can't lie; it'd be refreshing to feel a tortured scream in my ears. And throwing some weight around would release some of the tension knotting my back, I'm sure. Besides, our Sinners Anonymous game isn't going to be as satisfying this month, now that Angelo went and got his PETA-preaching wife involved.

Licking my lips, I replace the weird butcher's contraption and pick up something more timeless—a hammer. It's always been my weapon of choice. Not only does the handle fit comfortably in my palm, but the length of it has a nice way of detaching me from whatever is breaking underneath it.

I drop it on the worktop and snap off my collar pin. Unbutton my shirt and fold it neatly over the armrest of the sofa.

"Best we don't tell Vicious about this."

Gabe leans against the work bench and lights up another cigarette. "Best we don't."

Metal scrapes metal as I pick up the hammer and turn to the bonfire. Heat, sweat, and pre-emptive whimpers dance over the top of it. Its flames brush my bicep as I round it, and before those whimpers turn into screams, AC-DC fills the cave again.

Gabe's music taste may be obnoxious but it sure is fitting.

Daybreak is seeping into the mouth of the cave by the time we depart it. Cold light fights through the trees and birds chirp overhead. It's disorientating, and suddenly, I get why Gabe disappears for weeks at a time. Cracking bones and gurgled pleas seem to swallow hours whole.

The icy wind chills the sweat under my shirt. My eyes fall to my brother's naked torso beside me, the blood caking it now a rusty brown. His appearance looks even more obscene in the cold light of day, and it won't bode well for the family aesthetics if any locals driving their morning commute see him in all of his violent, naked glory.

"You look like the villain from a nineties slasher movie," I grumble, straightening my collar pin. "Don't follow me out to the road."

There's an easy saunter to his step, like he hikes through snow-coated ravines in his sleep. "Wouldn't want to ruin your reputation as a gentleman," he says dryly.

"One of us has to keep up the appearance."

"Mm. But anyone with half a brain would realize if you lie with dogs, you wake up with fleas."

I grind out a laugh. "Good thing no one on this Coast has half a brain, then."

He slows to a stop a few feet from the brush that lines the road and runs an indifferent eye down the buttons of my shirt and the sharp front pleat of my slacks.

"If it's any consolation, you don't look like you've just cracked open a man's brain with a hammer claw and then donkey-kicked him into a fire."

I bite back a smirk. "I think that might be the nicest thing you've ever said to me, brother. Maybe we're bonding."

"Maybe you have smoke inhalation." He watches me for a moment. "Feel better?"

Fuck yeah, I do. There's a buzz in my blood and a lightness in my chest. Despite the ache between my shoulder blades and the thin veil of sweat cloaking my skin, my suit fits a little better now. Like the monster underneath has lost some bulk and is easier to conceal.

Of course, Gabe gets a much simpler response. "Feel all right."

His gaze slides behind my head and darkens. "What's in your car?"

It's a simple question, but because I know the answer, it pulls my muscles taut.

Penelope.

I turn around and the buzz in my blood instantly falls stagnant.

Violence, impulsion. Poisonous traits that belong in my brothers' bones and not mine blinker my vision. I cut through the bushes toward Blake.

The cunt doesn't see me coming. He's too busy stooping at the passenger side window, his hands cupping his eyes against the glass.

Rage. Resolve. A swish of my coat and my fingertips are brushing over the grip of my gun, but they don't find purchase. Instead, they curl into my palm and form a fist that draws back and severs the last thread of my composure.

Pain. Satisfaction. My punch connects with his cheekbone and as he falls, he falls in slow motion, giving that small voice in the shadows of my brain time to whisper, *one punch is enough.* I can bounce back from one punch. It's just pebbles underfoot scattering over the edge of the cliff; no need to throw my body over it, too.

But tell that to my left fist. It meets his jaw on the way down, snapping his neck back and giving me a full view of the panic in his eyes.

Gratification. Delirium. The way his skull bounces off the icy road only spurs me on. I hold him up by the scruff of his polyester shirt. Another punch splits the skin on my knuckles, and, well, I know there's no point turning back now. The next blow causes a *crack* that sounds irreparable, and any man with an ounce of sportsmanship would leave it at that—it's not a fair fight. Never was. But under the serene dawn sky, I'm not a man. I'm an animal in a very nice suit, protecting what's his.

Blake's defense fell when he did, and it's not Griffin's roars of protests that stop me, or the chorus of my men muttering expletives, but my brother's strong grip on my shoulder.

"*Basta*," is all he says. *Enough.*

I let the lifeless body fall and stare down at my knuckles.

Irreversible. Remorseless.

My ragged breaths burn my lungs and I tilt my chin up to the pearl-gray sky. If mama could see me now, her silver-tongued son using his fists and not his words. And for what?

As my gaze falls, it lands on another.

Blue. Fathomless.

"Go," my brother says. "I'll finish this."

I don't take my eyes off Penelope. Can't. Not when I step over a puddle of fresh blood, nor when Griffin's hushed "what have you done?" touches my ears as I yank on the car door and slam it shut behind me.

Six pairs of eyes stare at me through the windshield. None of them are hers, so none of them matter. I slam the car into gear and don't bother looking over my shoulder as I reverse.

Her gaze stings my bloodied hands curled around the steering wheel. "What the fuck, Rafe?"

Rafe. It's the first time she's called me by my nickname. I like the way she says it, too. With shock marred by a breathless edge. It makes my lids shut for longer than safe when driving at eighty-miles an hour down a country road.

I don't reply. Instead, I stare through the road ahead and think about the moment I first thought the red-head in the stolen dress might be the Queen of Hearts. It was my brother's wedding night, and the explosion at the port had just lit night's sky orange. I'd wondered, albeit not seriously—if this was the start of my fall, what it'd be like at the bottom. Turns out, it's full of Penelope's heavy breathing, her citrus perfume, and the sound of Bing Crosby's *White Christmas.*

Tranquility. Acceptance. A calmness washes over me and I breathe out easy. It's comforting, I suppose, knowing I've fallen to the bottom and can fall no further.

Penelope's eyes trail the river of red trickling down the back of my hand until it disappears under the cuff of my shirt.

"Where are we going?" she murmurs.

My hand slides off the steering wheel and finds her knee.

"Home, Queenie."

Chapter 9

No prison has ever managed to hold me, but I resolved that this one would. At least until the Dark Lord Emperor made his decision.

The warden opened my cell and raised a key to my manacles.

"Don't you want to leave these on?" I asked.

The warden tapped a finger to the side of his nose. "Oh, I don't think that'll be necessary, young lord. This is our most impenetrable cell. You're quite secure in here, no one's ever escaped."

I shrugged and walked inside. The cell was a mix of masoned stonework and natural cave and looked to be meant to hold several prisoners. My only other company was a skeleton leaning against the wall, wrists still held in cuffs secured to an anchor in the stone. The warden tried to close the door behind me several times, but the latch didn't seem to want to cooperate. Eventually he tied it off with a bit of loose twine and leaned a rock against it to give the appearance of it being closed and locked.

"Now don't you make no attempt," said the warden, winking rather more than was necessary.

"I won't," I said, and sat on the bench.

"That's good," *wink*, "because I didn't catch much shut-eye last night." *Wink*, "And I've got a few pints here to help pass the time."

The warden moved the table over a few feet, then gauged the distance to my cell and moved it another foot closer. I think it was just far enough that I'd have to come up with some clever contrivance to reach him from between the bars. Once the warden was satisfied, he sat down with his ale and set to reading a copy of the Dark Empire's extensive binding laws and regulations.

I crossed my arms and waited. Sure enough, it wasn't but a few minutes until his head lolled back and his snores echoed up and down the hall. His keyring fell out of his pocket, thumping on the dusty floor just out of reach. Not that I needed it, since my cell had never been locked in the first place. I sighed, rubbed my temples, and pressed my back against the column to wait.

I didn't have to wait long. A wet cackling began to issue from one dark corner of the cell, and out shambled a grey-bearded hunchback. He had a walking stick almost as crooked as his spine but not nearly so crooked as his teeth, which seemed at a loss for any unified direction or color. I was quite sure that corner had been empty when I'd come in.

"Ah, my young friend. Fate has brought us together. I have a proposition for you."

I waited.

"You wish to topple the Dark Lord Emperor. I have the means; it lies within a secret temple."

"And for some reason you need me to get it for you."

"Just so, and the rewards will be beyond your wildest dreams," said the old man, and he tapped out a sequence on the stones with his stick.

The wall slid away, revealing a vast red desert of rolling dunes beneath the sun setting in a sky full of stars. I stared at the hole, and then back at the old man. "Are you kidding me?" I asked.

The geezer cackled again. "I assure you, the treasure is quite real."

"No, I meant *that*," I said, pointing to the desert. "The Capital is on a plateau in the middle of a forest. There's not even a desert within a hundred miles of here."

The old man shifted uncomfortably.

"Plus, I came at mid-morning," I said, pointing to the cell opposite us. "Look, there's a window over there. Not only is it not sunset, but it's completely overcast."

I crossed my arms. "Besides, your hump just adjusted itself. And your beard has hooks in it. I'm pretty sure you're the vizier in disguise. It's a well-known fact that all viziers eventually betray their masters."

"That's not necessarily true," the old man protested, but a tiny voice whispered from under his shirt, *"Rahim, he's on to us!"*

I turned my back on the pair. "I'm quite content to wait, thank you."

There was a quiet argument behind, then nothing. When I looked again I was alone in the cell once more. Annoyingly, the opening to wherever was still there. I leaned a loose board over the hole, so wouldn't have to think about it and tried to sleep. I must have been successful because the next thing I remembered was the warden shouting that I'd escaped.

It took almost a minute to get his attention as he looked for me everywhere *except* my cell. But once he saw me he calmed down. "The Dark Lord Emperor is calling for you," he said.

I undid the twine and pushed the door open, sliding the rock across the dirt. "About time."

He offered to walk me back up to the throne room, but he really did look tired, so I assured him I could find my own way. Once I navigated the twisting tunnels I found the throne room in much the same state that I'd left it, with the Dark Lord Emperor brooding in his throne.

"Arturus Kingson. I am conflicted. I have considered your suggestion, but I can't let you enter my service without first proving your worth. My advisors have counseled that I give you some quest or trial."

"Can I offer a suggestion?" I asked.

The Dark Lord Emperor shrugged. "That seems expedient."

I nodded. "How about I root out corruption in your ranks. If I expose a plot against you would that work?"

The Dark Lord Emperor climbed to his feet. "That would indeed be an adequate service to me."

I pointed to the vizier. "He's plotting to overthrow you," I said. Lightning and thunder crashed outside the fortress.

Chapter 10

"**P**reposterous, Rahim is my loyal servant," said my Dark Lord Dad.

"He's a vizier," I said.

"So?"

"So?!" I demanded. "Why do you even *have* a vizier? You're not a Sultan or a Caliph."

"I..." said the Dark Lord Emperor, and then stopped. He turned to Rahim. "Why *do* I have a vizier?" he asked.

"Because you are a *fool*," Rahim snarled, raising his and hand and pointing his index finger at my father. He began to chant a spell at the Dark Lord Emperor, but I was ready. I pulled the None Ring out of my pocket and flicked it in his general direction. For some reason the artifact is attracted to extended fingers. The thing just loves being worn, I suppose. It changed direction midair and shot directly onto Rahim's hand. Everyone in the throne room except him vanished. The vizier stopped, caught off guard, and looked at the now empty throne room. I had already covered most of the distance before he realized things were not going as he planned, and I sunk my fist so hard into his midsection that the None Ring popped off and dropped flat on the floor at his feet without even bouncing. He doubled over, eyes bulging as he wheezed. I grabbed the now-visible gyrfalcon from his shoulder.

"Fess up, or I'll brain your little bird noggin," I said, shaking the falcon.

The gyrfalcon squawked, flapping its wings to no avail. *"It's true Forgive me, Prince Arturus! I didn't want to, but he made me! I'll tell you everything!"*

"I think I've seen enough," said the Dark Lord Emperor, descending from his throne and approaching Rahim. "Take him down and see that he gets his reward."

Lightning streaked across the sky outside the window.

"His *eternal* reward."

262

Scott Warren

Epilogue

With the position of vizier vacant I offered my services. Having proven myself, my Dark Lord Dad accepted, and I even got a free bird out of the deal. It turned out that the Dark Lord Emperor wasn't terribly interested in the day-to-day running of the empire, so I was able to enact several policy changes to better the citizens and provide better healer services for the Imperial Army, as well as hire a decorator to redo the fortress interior.

Mara had suggested that I make overthrowing my father impossible, but the problem is that when it comes to prophecy nothing is impossible. What I had done instead by usurping Rahim was make it *inevitable*. After all, it's a well-known fact that all viziers eventually betray their masters. It seemed to have worked, as fate stopped pushing and pulling me toward magic swords, and mysterious figures could now enjoy a drink without the threat of violent death hanging over them. Princesses became less common as well, aside from the ones that visited the fortress. I felt no ill will toward the Dark Lord Emperor. He was as much a victim of these legends as I was. Still, after a few years of ruling by proxy I overthrew him right to a retirement village in the southern part of the country. He's still there. Dark Lord Dad spends his days riding horses, polishing his armor, and recruiting the local boys to harass the caretakers. It turns out he's happier without having to worry about me gallivanting around the countryside raising rabble and riots.

As for Mara, she stuck around for a while. I did owe her a new sword after all, after she lost the Sword of Half-Truth protecting me. And I happened to know of a blade lodged in a church yard nearby.

The End.

Made in the USA
Las Vegas, NV
14 October 2024

96859598R00152